The Whole Way Home

ALSO BY SARAH CREECH

Season of the Dragonflies

The Whole Way Home

SARAH CREECH

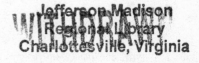

WILLIAM MORROW

An Imprint of HarperCollins*Publishers*

THE WHOLE WAY HOME. Copyright © 2017 by Sarah Creech. All rights reserved. Printed in the United States of America. No part of this book may be used or reproduced in any manner whatsoever without written permission except in the case of brief quotations embodied in critical articles and reviews. For information, address HarperCollins Publishers, 195 Broadway, New York, NY 10007.

HarperCollins books may be purchased for educational, business, or sales promotional use. For information, please email the Special Markets Department at SPsales@harpercollins.com.

FIRST EDITION

Designed by Bonni Leon-Berman

Library of Congress Cataloging-in-Publication Data has been applied for.

ISBN 978-0-06-240929-4

17 18 19 20 21 LSC 10 9 8 7 6 5 4 3 2 1

FOR MORRI

Of love and hate and death and dying, mama, apple pie, and the whole thing.
It covers a lot of territory, country music does.
—JOHNNY CASH

In memory everything seems to happen to music.
—TENNESSEE WILLIAMS

The course of true love never did run smooth.
—SHAKESPEARE

Where Thou art—that—is Home
—EMILY DICKINSON

The Whole Way Home

*G*ood morning, Nashville—best music listeners this world over, better than New York, better than LA—Nashville audiophiles, those of you listening to old Floyd Masters, know the best of the best when you hear it. Yes, ma'am, you do. And you like it early. Five AM is always a good time for real country music. I've got quite the playlist coming your way this morning. There's been all that hubbub about male country singers being the lettuce in the salad and female country singers being the tomatoes everybody eats around. That you can't play back-to-back songs by women on Top 40 country radio or else you'll lose your listeners. First of all, that's one dumb metaphor spoken from the mouth of one dumb radio disc jockey. Not me, for once. Hallelujah for that.

Someone failed to tell him that nobody in the South likes salads. Not really. Put some salt on those homegrown, straight-from-the-vine heirlooms and we'll choose tomatoes over lettuce any day. I'm pretty tired of the boys' club on the radio, folks, where every song's about trucks, drinking beer, parties on the weekends, girls in bikinis, more trucks. All that music's written by the same handful of songwriters, all of it's divorced from the rich tradition of country music. Good country music should make you feel something, should cover the entire territory of the heart.

Glad Jo Lover's speaking up about women being the unwanted tomatoes of Top 40 country radio. She had a real good interview on CMT and Good Morning America. Not that it'll make that hardheaded DJ believe any different. Men might dominate the radio playlist on Top 40 stations, but rest assured, my friends, I've got a full female playlist for you this morning and every morn-

ing for the next couple of days. Patsy will follow Dolly will follow Loretta will follow Tammy will follow Reba will follow Joanne will follow Mother Maybelle and back again. You'll see just how well these ladies follow one another.

I bet nobody will be calling in and saying, "Oh, Floyd, please, please, please play J. D. Gunn and the Empty Shells. Please give us some of that lettuce music!" No, I bet you won't. Even if you do, I don't have to listen because this here is independent radio. And if you're listening, Joanne Lover, which I know you're not, congratulations on your debut tonight as the newest Grand Ole Opry member. She's preserved the tradition in her songwriting, carried on the history in that voice of hers. Finest female vocalist this side of the Cumberland River. The next queen of country, I have no doubt.

And she broke my heart by saying yes to the brightest producer Nashville's seen in decades. He's a handsomer devil than old Floyd Masters, I'll give him that. Joanne Lover and Nick Sullivan will make some good-looking babies. All right, folks, I guess that's enough talk from the slickest voice in country radio. Here's "Your Cheatin' Heart" by Patsy Cline. Your first fix for the morning. There's more to come, so keep it tuned right here to 87.3 FM, Vanderbilt's WHYW morning broadcast.

CHAPTER 1

The Wrong Chord

JOANNE LOVER WAS ready to stand beneath the bright red lights of the Ryman Auditorium—under those lights she'd feel more herself than she did hiding here in the darkness. Her band members twisted their tuning pegs while stagehands shifted the electrical cords around like they were making calligraphy on the wooden floor. Jo rocked from heel to toe in her red cowgirl boots. Her earlobes turned pink before she walked out onstage; her upper lip could sweat more than her armpits, which amazed her; and the left side of her mouth twitched. Same thing happened to Elvis but he made it billion-dollar cool.

Jo searched for the king of seventies country music, Phil Doby, due onstage any minute now to invite her out where all of the greats—like Patsy Cline, Dolly Parton, and Loretta Lynn—had once held a microphone and filled the room with their sweet melodies. She'd been waiting her whole life to be standing out there as an Opry member, and she wished to do right by all that talent tonight. Jo crossed her arms and took a deep breath, and as she exhaled, her dress's spaghetti strap slipped off her right shoulder. She returned it to its proper place, then she began adjusting every part of her outfit: lifting her boobs up in the low-cut dress, a navy one with a pattern of tiny red apples; fluffing the bottom part of the dress; smoothing it back out; fluffing it again. She should've followed her instincts and worn her jeans, but her stylist had insisted on this classic outfit for the Opry induction. Her mama would've most certainly agreed. Jo could hear her now: *You're going to church, Joanne. You will not be shameful. You will look nice before God.*

Back in Gatesville, every Wednesday and Sunday of her childhood, her mama had made her dress up just like this, and just as soon as she could, Jo would tear off that suffocating dress and hike down to the creek behind their shotgun house. She'd stay down there for hours in the shade of the rhododendron and paint her face with the mud from the creek and pretend she was putting on makeup. If her mama ever saw her, she knew she'd accuse her of wearing the devil's mask. Sometimes she painted her feet and legs too and then washed them off in the cold water that stayed icy like that year-round. Jo patrolled up and down the creek with a wooden stick in hand. Little minnows nibbled at her feet as she passed. She stacked smooth stones from the creek to make towering sculptures in different places along the way to help mark her path. Robins and cardinals rested on her creations and kept her company. On one of these hikes Jo discovered her daddy's moonshine jugs anchored in the deepest part of the creek. She helped herself to a sip every now and then. Her mama never noticed.

Jo pretended to be queen of a river that had the power to deliver her from the life she was living. The little Cleopatra of Appalachia. As long as she could remember, she'd played that game. She'd wanted to be queen of something somewhere someday, and now country music's most important stage stood wide open before her. Jo hoped little girls would admire her and imagine standing up on that stage too, just like Jo did the nights her daddy turned on the Opry broadcast on the radio and her family gathered around it like it was a fire. She'd heard Dolly Parton sing there for the first time and Jo's entire body had warmed with a desire she'd never felt before. After that night, the little creek turned into Jo's stage, the birds her audience, and she would sing and sing and sing church hymns and ballads like "Barbara Allen" until her voice felt hoarse. She had one spot where the tree canopy opened to the sky and she sunned herself there, dreaming of the day she'd become a member of a different family.

Jo felt the audience's anticipation now, just like she always sensed a thunderstorm coming over the mountain—the air pressure dropped, the wind picked up, and the sun disappeared. Jo adjusted the silver turquoise rings on her sweaty fingers, which covered both of her hands like brass knuckles. Jo lifted her thick hair upward to cool her neck, and her dress strap fell off her shoulder again. Now a regular drumbeat was going onstage. The audience began to clap. Phil Doby walked out to the front of the Ryman Auditorium stage to thank her opening act, the Wayward Sisters. He had a mane of white hair, thick as kudzu, and he wore a silver and blue rhinestone suit so shiny he refracted himself all over the auditorium. He wore a white cowboy hat to match.

Phil said, "We're broadcasting the Grand Ole Opry live from the Ryman Auditorium tonight just like we used to for many, many years. It's so good to have y'all here with us at the mother church of country music tonight, whether you're at home listening or right out there in the audience. We've got albums on sale outside this auditorium." Phil adjusted his metal belt buckle.

Jo looked over at her assistant, Marie, who usually kept quiet when

Jo was nervous like this. The blue light from her cell phone illuminated her delicate face. Marie was twenty-two years old, with a blond pixie cut and bangs swept to the side, with a degree in business from Vanderbilt and a self-taught love of country music. She reminded Jo of a woodland fairy. "Everything okay?" Jo said.

Marie turned off her phone. She scratched her cheek with her manicured fingernails. "Just confirmed with *Vanity Fair* for tomorrow. You good for taking pictures with fans after tonight's show? And signing merchandise?"

"Happy to." Jo wiped away beads of sweat from her lip.

Phil reached out his shiny arm to the side of the stage. "Now I want to welcome the newest darling of the Grand Ole Opry to the stage. This is her first performance as a member of the family. Long overdue, if I say so myself. This fine Virginia lady's music is beloved by fans and critics alike. She has a voice like an angel and boots that stomp like the devil. Let's put our hands together for Ms. Joanne Lover."

The crowd called for her with whistles and clapping.

She secured the straps of her dress in place, stomped the heel of her boot onto the ground two times, slapped her thigh once, and then ran out and stood on the center staircase at the front of the stage. Jo paused to listen to the crowd clapping for her, their behinds up and out of those wooden pews. She held the fiddle slack in her hand. The sun had set on the streets of downtown Nashville, and the stained glass panels in the back of the auditorium no longer glistened. With the red barn behind her; the lights glowing from the ceiling; the pews situated to the left, to the right, and in the balcony; and the stage floor beneath her, Jo felt like an epicenter—the spirit of the revivalist preacher who first took this stage back in 1892 never had died away.

Her fans usually consisted of mothers and daughters or big groups of friends who chanted, "'Red Boots,' 'Red Boots,' 'Red Boots.'" Jo smiled. These women—nurses, bankers, teachers, mothers, executives, mechanics—worked so much and still had the energy to come out and support her. Maybe they listened to her album in those rare quiet moments driving home from work, before picking up the kids. She made music just for them, to make them feel like their experience as women was represented in country music, to give them a living heart in a song.

From deep in the audience someone raised a single red boot up high enough for Jo to see. She pointed at it with her bow, and then she tucked her fiddle beneath her chin before putting the horsehair to the strings. She turned around, left the staircase, and stepped onto the main stage of the Ryman, where her backup band began adding beat and rhythm to her sound. She circled around her microphone as she picked up the speed on her fiddle. The audience clapped faster.

Jo stopped playing but her band continued, just a little drums and some rhythm guitar behind her. She took the microphone in one hand. "How you doing, Nashville?"

Whistling and clapping answered her.

"We've been on the road these past few months. It's so good to be back. Ain't that right, boys?" She turned around to look at her band. They all nodded. Jo looked down into the center pews and spotted Nick sitting next to his father. She winked at him and he smiled back at her.

"My fiancé's here tonight—" The crowd erupted with hollering and applause. Jo laughed and wiped her brow with the back of her hand. "I'm still getting used to calling him that. Best producer in this business. He's one of the biggest reasons why I'm standing up here tonight. And I want to thank the Opry for inviting me to be part of this wonderful family. Growing up, I never expected to make it out of Gatesville, let alone make it this far. I'm on the greatest stage country music has ever known. A dream come true."

Women screamed in that way men never do.

"I intend to get a few of you ladies up here with me a little later on. We've got some stomping to do. But first I want to give a shout-out to the Battered Women's Shelter of Nashville. Half of all ticket sales tonight go to support them. It's a place that matters very much to me, so thank y'all for supporting it too."

Jo turned around to her band and tapped her foot to count them off, and the drums bore down hard, the bass and the rhythm guitar joining in before the banjo. Jo was last to enter the song, with her fiddle. Everybody in the two-thousand-seat auditorium would know the words to "Red Boots": her first big single from her debut album. This song changed her life. Put her on the charts for the first time. She and the band went from the intro to verse to chorus to bridge to verse again, like it was a well-worn hiking path. She'd know her way in this song for the rest of her life.

She sang the chorus with help from the audience: "*I'm thinking of him tonight / He's thinking of me none / Tell me, girls / Where have the good guys gone?*"

The audience cheered. Jo spun around on the heel of her boot, the bottom of her dress lifting up around her. The boys ended their part of the song and left the sound of her fiddle filling up the auditorium all by itself. She lessened her pressure on the top string, brought down the sound to the real close of the song. Jo rode the momentum of the applause into the next song, titled "Journey Woman," about a medicine woman out west and the child she bears alone. The lights above her shifted into an upside-down V, and the color changed from pearl to red. She and the band played that one straight. Jo paused after that song and put down her fiddle on the stand behind her before picking up her Gibson F-style mandolin, which she loved as much as anything else in this world. The fiddle and mandolin were cousins, same tuning and similar length of scales. She could transition easily between the two.

While she tuned the instrument, Jo said, "You know, when I was young and first starting out in Nashville, I was broke. Had no health insurance. Made sure I had insurance on my instruments though. If I got sick, my friends chipped in to pay the bills. We all did that for each other. The community here in Nashville's good that way."

The crowd clapped as Jo adjusted the microphone. She was sweating so much, less from nerves now. Jo quickly braided her hair and draped it over one shoulder. Someone in the crowd whistled and shouted, "Play 'Cowgirl Blues,'" and other people clapped in agreement.

"Hang on, hang on," she said. She started plucking her mandolin softly to make sure it was ready. "There's always been a lot of guessing about who I write my songs about. But I think what really matters is heartbreak. Anyone here ever experienced one of those?"

Multiple women shouted, "Hell yes," and others clapped.

Jo stopped playing the mandolin and nodded her head. "Anybody ever had something important taken from you?"

The Ryman was quiet, but then one woman raised her hand, and then another, and more still, until most of the audience had hands raised high in the air as if they held lighters aflame.

"Yeah," Jo said in a low voice. "Me too. That's what 'Cowgirl Blues' is about."

The crowd erupted into a sustained scream for this song, the most requested one off her recent album. "Cowgirl Blues" might've been about heartache, but from the sound of the music alone it would have been hard to tell. The rolling bass solo and the fast drum work, along with the addition of the steel guitar, made people dance from the start. That was something she'd learned to do—dance despite the heartbreaks. She was practiced at the art of putting trouble aside.

Jo put down her mandolin on the stand, but the boys kept playing. She scraped her boots on the stage to get good traction, and then Jo jumped in the air and landed, hands on her hips, slightly crouched. She danced a breakdown, flatfooting from one side of the stage to the other, knees as high as they could go, the heels of her boots leaving marks on the stage. Jo moved her arms out to the sides and above her head like a ballerina. She paused to take a breath and looked out at the seats, where arms were waving for her to come down.

Returning to the microphone, Jo said, "All right, ladies, I'm coming. Gotta show off those red boots."

Jo walked down the front steps and the crowd erupted with energy. Fans jumped up and down trying to get her attention. She liked standing among the pews, the stage towering above her. Jo walked through the aisles, smiled, and held the offered hands. One older woman with her silver hair in French braids had red cowgirl boots painted on her cheeks, so Jo chose her, and then Jo spotted a pair of red combat boots on a short, stocky teenage girl that went all the way up to the middle of her exposed thigh. Not really cowgirl boots but powerful nonetheless. "Go on up there," Jo said to her. She screamed, "Oh my God, thank you," and hugged Jo.

Jo canvassed the crowd, looking for the most enthusiastic of them all to join her onstage and close the first set. She walked a little further and hugged her fans as she went, said thanks for coming, that she hoped they were having a good time. Then, right before she turned around, Jo spotted him like a clay pigeon she was about to shoot. His bright smile flashed at her, his dimples visible, his skin glowing like he was a lantern lit from within. How did she miss that white Stetson in the audience? She stopped moving and just stared at him as if she'd been transfixed by a stranger she'd passed on the street. She lost her breath, lost her intensity, and forgot what she was supposed to be doing. The inside of her chest felt hollow. J. D. Gunn and his band were supposed to be on tour but here he was. J. D. kept his blue eyes locked on Jo's. His looking at her like that, right there, and so close, made her feel exposed more than that frilly dress ever could.

The crowd began chanting her name, reminding her that she was supposed to be performing. She turned away from J. D., walked slowly back to the stage and up the steps to her fans. Jo felt like she'd lost all her strength right when she needed it most. She encouraged the women to gather around her at the microphone, and Jo picked up her acoustic guitar and wiped the sweat from underneath her eyes. The women onstage wanted her to play a fun, fast song for their dance, and she would, but first she had a different song in mind: "Ms. Loretta Lynn wrote me a sweet note and apologized for not being able to make it here tonight. I want to play one of her hits for you now. 'The Pill' is one of her best-known songs and one so controversial that some radio stations refused to play it back in the seventies. I've always loved a rebel woman."

Jo could feel him. She'd always been able to feel him, right there in the center of her body like a hive of bees. The women she'd brought onstage started dancing as soon as the band began to play. She looked up once, and there was J. D.'s face, luminous as a full moon, as if his were the only face in the entire audience. The entire world. Her fingers held their position on the strings like they were stuck there, and she missed the A7 chord change, lost her pace with the band. Something so simple, and she missed it.

CHAPTER 2

Her Choice

J. D. GUNN STOOD up from his wooden pew in the Ryman and joined the entire audience as they clapped and whistled for Jo to return to the stage for an encore. It felt good being on this side of the stage for once, just another audience member looking up with awe at a stellar performer. Nashville's finest musicians, critics, and business folks had gathered in these pews to witness her performance, alongside some of the most devoted fans he'd ever seen. J. D.'s ears were ringing from all the screams unleashed for her.

He and the band had cut their Northeast tour short a day to come to the Ryman for Jo's induction into the Grand Ole Opry family. He and his band had been members for five years and he tried to make it to every new induction. Now he was second-guessing that decision. He figured enough time had passed between them that his presence here wouldn't bother her, that maybe she would've expected to see him and be happy about it. But there was something about the way she looked at him, like there was a glitch in her system. And Jo Lover, who was master of her instruments, one of the finest musicians he'd ever known, had messed up that easy Loretta number.

J. D. put his fingers in his mouth and let out a wolf whistle. His bass player, Rob, stood next to him and shouted Jo's name over and over. Rob wore the same black and white Willie and Waylon outlaw T-shirt he'd owned since middle school. J. D. was an only child and Rob was the closest thing to a brother that J. D. had. J. D. and Rob had snuck out of the house and hitched a ride away from Gatesville to attend that Willie and Waylon show together. Rob waited in line for almost an hour to have his shirt signed. When it was finally his turn and he had the chance to talk to Willie, he almost didn't speak, just stood there adjusting his thick glasses. J. D. shoved him and Rob finally said, "You guys are so cool," and Willie said, "So are you, kid." Rob had talked about it for months. Still brought it up when they got drunk. All they wanted back then was to be those guys. Swore they'd grow up to be outlaws and not ruin their bodies at the quarry like their fathers had. They swore they'd find something better to do with their hands.

Rob leaned over to him. "You think she'll come?"

"She likes the wait." J. D. looked around at the faces in the audience, all aglow from the soft yellow lights up above. They leaned forward for her, big smiles on their faces. That's what music did for people, made them happy to be alive and part of the community. That was why J. D. and Jo and Rob had started playing music in the first place all those years ago in Gatesville, to find a way to bring happiness to people. No matter how much they dreamed about the money and the fame that would surely someday come to them, it was always about this feeling of desire and gratitude that people felt for music. They used to wear their guitars strapped around their necks like a priest wears the cross, and they practiced for hours every day in the loft J. D.'s daddy built for him in the barn or played down by the fishing pond. All they wanted was to master their instruments so they could express what they were feeling through song, to cross that boundary with the listener and make them feel those emotions too.

It was a magic they devoted themselves to as children. It never had been about the cars, the million-dollar contracts, the houses, the boats, the vacations, the clothes, the groupies, the tours around the world. Those things were amazing. He'd visited Buddhist shrines in Japan, karaoke clubs in South Korea, snake charmers in India, and all of Europe more times than he could count, but it never would be about those things. They'd all made it here—not together like they said they would, but they'd made it. He wished he could go up there, sing with her, and not have her look at him like he was a ghost she didn't recognize.

"Come on, Joanne," Rob shouted.

And then there was a burst of applause as Jo entered from stage right. She carried her fiddle in one hand and waved at everybody with the other. At the microphone she bowed her head and smiled like she was bashful from all this desire for her. J. D. heard her breathe into the microphone—that was a sound he knew well, a sound he'd never forget. He used to stay up well past her falling asleep beside him and listen to her rhythmically breathing like a metronome. Her facial features softened while she dreamed, and there was no trace of the sorrow she'd carried around since they were kids. He loved when her face lit up like it did now, right before she performed.

He used to live for the hour when school ended and his farm chores were done so he could pick up Jo and Rob with his daddy's Gator and drive them all the way down to the pond with their fishing gear and instruments strapped to the back with bungee cords. After they'd set up their lines with bait and dropped them in the murky water, Jo sat on the grass in the long denim skirt and long-sleeved shirt her mama always made her wear even at the height of summer, and she'd roll up the sleeves, cross her legs, and place the guitar in her lap to play whatever new gospel song they were working out together. She dropped her head when she played and her long dark hair fell over her face like a mask. Jo was the sharpest, toughest girl he knew in Gatesville, but she sang as sweet as a canary. J. D. missed that girl. He hardly recognized this woman on the stage with her hair curled big and all that heavy makeup on, wearing that silly country dress and huge diamond ring catching the light every time her left hand moved up and down the neck of her instrument.

He wanted Jo to look at him now like she had before she sang that Loretta Lynn song, but she kept her stare fixed on somewhere just above the audience. She adjusted the microphone. "Thank y'all so much for such a great night. You've been an amazing audience. I'd like to sing one more song for you from the great Southern songbook. Feel free to sing along with me. I bet you'll recognize it."

And then she and the band opened with the G-C-G chords of "I'll Fly Away" before moving into the lyrics. Everybody remained standing while she played. J. D. closed his eyes to concentrate on her voice. She played it softer than he might've but it sounded beautiful. He opened his eyes, only to find hers closed as she played, the fiddle secured beneath her chin, her long elegant arm moving the bow up and down the strings.

Jo's fiancé stood a few rows ahead of J. D. in the center of the auditorium. Nick Sullivan could reach out and touch the stage if he wanted. He was the most sought-after producer in Nashville, maybe in the entire music industry—he could play bass, guitar, pedal steel, accordion, harp, mandolin, piano, percussion, horns. As a teenager Nick had performed as a studio instrumentalist for the biggest bands in the nation. Not just country. Rock bands too. And he collected signed instruments. Supposedly, Nick owned guitars signed by Elvis and Willie and Hank, all on display in a room at his father's estate in Williamson County. Not too far from J. D.'s house. Not too far.

Nick stood next to his father, Mr. Sullivan, CEO of Asphalt Records. Nick was music industry royalty. Born into it. J. D. would have disliked Nick more if the guy wasn't so talented. Never in a million years would J. D. have guessed that Jo would go for a man like Nick, a guy who'd known privilege his entire life. Nick was probably a decent person, and J. D. felt secure enough to acknowledge Nick's good looks, but he wasn't the one for Jo. There was no way Nick knew anything honest about her.

Jo finished out the song with her eyes closed. When it was over she opened them, smiled wide, and said, "Thanks again for coming, everybody. It's been such a good time." She waved once more, and then the lights faded and Jo exited the stage.

J. D. leaned over to Rob while he clapped. "Let's go backstage."

Rob pushed his glasses up the bridge of his nose. "Not tonight."

"She'll be happy to see you."

"I know she'll be happy to see me, J. D. Don't know about you."

People started filing out of the auditorium, and already a crowd was gathering at the end of J. D.'s pew. Young girls were waving at him, and so were their mothers. J. D. waved back at them. Rob said, "You'll be too busy anyway."

Nick Sullivan walked up the aisle without a passing glance like he was in a hurry to join Jo backstage. J. D. squeezed Rob's shoulder as they walked toward the aisle. "Go catch Mr. Sullivan for me. Tell him we want to give our regards. Real quick."

Rob glanced back at J. D. and gave him one of his scolding looks, but he knew Rob would do it because he was loyal that way. Rob and the rest of his bandmates filed out of the pew and left J. D. to the flock of Jo's fans who were waiting for him. They all held out their cell phones and asked for pictures and autographs. J. D. put his arms around groups of women, a permanent smile on his face. He signed his name on programs, purses, arms, then switched back to taking pictures, then he signed some more programs as he waited for Rob to return.

A young girl with her brunette hair in pigtails and red cowgirl boots painted on her cheeks tugged at his arm and said, "How come you're so tall?"

J. D. pulled one of her pigtails gently. "How come you're so short?"

She giggled.

J. D. said, "This is just how God made me I guess." He bent down so he could take a good picture with her. She kissed him on the cheek before he stood back up. J. D. put his hand there and acted surprised, and the girl's mother smiled at him and mouthed "thank you" before ushering her away.

J. D. looked to the back of the auditorium and saw Rob standing up there with the rest of his band with Mr. Sullivan. Rob raised his arm and waved J. D. forward like an airport ground controller. J. D. signed a few more programs before he said, "Y'all are way too good to me. I loved seeing every last one of you. But I've got to go now." He heard a few groans as he turned away from the crowd, and they held up their phones and recorded pictures of him even as he walked away.

CHAPTER 3

Backstage

J O FINALLY MADE her way back to the dressing room and her quads felt like logs. She needed to take off her boots, put comfrey balm on her feet, and rest. Tomorrow night someone else would be onstage singing better than she had tonight, and that someone else would be sitting on this couch afterward. Just like the planes she rode on and the hotels where she stayed, somebody else would take her place. She'd move on to the next gig—this was the gypsy life full of devil music her mother always talked about. Jo picked up her phone and called her mama. It took a few rings before she picked up. "Joanne?"

"Yeah, it's me, Mama."

"Heard you on the Opry. Sounded nice." Her mama's voice always sounded rough, like sandpaper. She couldn't carry a song in church no matter how hard she tried. Sounded like she'd smoked cigarettes her whole life, but those were too unclean for the temple of her mama's body. The first time she'd smelled cigarettes on Jo's fingers she whooped her so bad it was the last time too.

"I wore a pretty dress you would've liked." Jo placed the fallen strap back on her shoulder.

"I hope so."

"How's Daddy?"

"Fine."

"And Isabell?"

"Fine too."

"Did she listen?"

"Izzie's at her friend's house down the road."

Marie came into the room and arranged multiple bottles of water and a platter of strawberries and almonds on the coffee table. Her mama coughed loudly into the phone and Jo had to pull away. Then her mama said, "When's the wedding?"

"Not sure yet. I'll let you know. But, hey, I've got to go now, Mama. I love you. I'll call soon. Tell everybody hi for me."

"Will do," her mama said, and then she hung up.

"Should I go?" Marie said.

"Stay," Jo said. "Is it time for pictures?"

"I'll go check."

"Hey, Marie."

Marie paused at the door.

"Was it that bad?"

"You were fantastic, as always."

Jo ate a strawberry whole, leaned back on the brown leather couch, and stared at a black and white framed picture of Dolly Parton singing onstage at the Ryman in the 1970s. Dolly, with her Frederick's of Hollywood high heels and her cleavage piled up for men to ogle and that tiny waist for women to envy; Dolly, who seemed like an angel and a holy spitfire all at once; Dolly, who had a part-time husband, no kids, and tons of money and many businesses she controlled; Dolly, who was a poor Southern Appalachian good-values kind of woman, whose fans believed she was just like them—Dolly would not have been proud of Jo's performance tonight. Neither would Loretta. Those women controlled their presence onstage and their private lives and kept them separate. J. D. Gunn would've never caused them to miss a chord.

Jo guzzled a bottle of water. She removed her boots. The rose embroidery on the leather was so faded she could hardly make it out anymore. She'd bought them herself. Stolen her daddy's moonshine out of the creek and sold it to a drunk down by the general store. She was thirteen years old. That's when her feet stopped growing. Her daddy never figured out where that moonshine went. Jo kept her red Ariat boots hidden at school and switched them out as soon as she got there. The girl who sold them to her in the alley behind the general store gave Jo a fair price. At school, her peers talked about her—couldn't believe that Jo Lover, poor as she was, could afford that brand of boots. Now Jo was the spokeswoman for Ariat. She received handmade cowgirl boots from Heritage in Austin, and her closet was full of boots. But this pair on her feet was more than twenty years old and had been repaired too many times to count. They'd known the red clay dirt of Virginia and stomped the hallowed stage at the Grand Ole Opry.

There was a soft knock on the door and it began to open before she responded. She figured it was Marie again, but instead Nick walked in with two bags of ice in hand. "Medic delivery."

Jo stood up and walked over to him. She kissed him softly on the lips. "You're so sweet. That's exactly what I need. Plus a bourbon."

"I'm sure we could arrange that." Nick walked over with her to the couch and helped her set up the foot-icing station.

Jo sat down and watched as he placed two pillows on the table and gently lifted her feet to rest there. He laid a towel over her feet and adjusted the ice packs so they stayed put. Sometimes she thought that Nick's kindness, talent, and good looks were more than she ever deserved. He was tall but not lanky. Strong chest and arms. Strong calves. Skin so smooth it seemed made without pores. Nick let his sandy blond hair fall wherever it wanted. He had no tattoos, no long beard or shaded glasses like a lot of guys in Nashville these days. No cowboy hat or rhinestone boots like the old guard. He liked jeans and a collared shirt, sometimes even khaki pants. His style was a little preppy, which, it occurred to Jo now, was a little bit rebellious in this industry.

"Did your father say anything?"

Nick finished icing her feet and leaned back on the couch. He put an arm around her and drew her close. "It was a great show. I was wanting to be up there with you the whole time."

"I wish you had been."

"Next show," he said, and moved a loose hair off of Jo's cheek. "That stage belonged to you tonight."

Marie entered the room saying, "I can't figure out when—" and then she said, "Oh. I'm sorry. I'll give you two some privacy." And then she shut the door.

Nick reached out for Jo's hand. "Do your feet feel better?"

"Better." A bag of ice fell off Jo's foot. Nick reached forward and placed the bag back where it belonged. Sitting here and quieting the pain like this didn't make her feel like the next queen of country. The entire evening had made her feel a little bit broken. Jo rested her head on his shoulder. "I sucked tonight."

Nick ran his hand through her hair. "It's only a cover."

"No, the whole second set was off."

Nick stroked her hair. "How come?"

"See," she said, and lifted her head off his shoulder. "You did notice."

He laughed in a defensive way. "I was only asking."

"Uh-huh," Jo said, and put her head back on his shoulder. "*Music Row* will notice. Who knows what they'll write. And Floyd Masters was here too. You know he'll be mean about it."

Nick said, "You're Jo Lover."

"So?"

"Screw what everybody else thinks."

Jo looked up and kissed him. A tender kiss that turned deeper, and the ice bags fell off her feet. She pulled him close and combed her fingers through his silky hair.

"Right here?"

"Why not?" Jo said in his ear. She continued to kiss down his neck, and then she started to unbutton his collared shirt. Nick rubbed his hands up and down her back as he buried his face in her chest and pulled her to him. She had moved her hands down to unzip his pants when another knock came from the dressing room door. Jo paused and then laughed with her cheek against his.

Nick said, "Not even two minutes."

Jo frowned and then kissed him on the nose. "I'll make it up to you."

Nick adjusted his jeans. She answered the door and the Wayward Sisters, Jo's opening act, hustled through and surrounded Jo with a big hug.

"We're your biggest fans," Pauline, Gaylene, and Gwendoline Lucille all said in unison. Jo laughed and let them squeeze her. They were a band of sisters from Princeton, West Virginia, and they played a haunting style of folk music that sounded like a deep lament, like three young Gillian Welches all in one, but they knew how to turn up the tempo too. Jo and Nick had heard them play at a house party six months back and helped them secure a recording contract with Asphalt. She loved the Wayward Sisters, loved being around all these bright twentysomethings.

Jo was almost thirty-two now and every year older in Nashville was starting to feel exponential. She worried about the day the Wayward Sisters realized that no matter how talented they were, the business was still a boys' club for bands like J. D. Gunn and the Empty Shells. She wished she could tell them there were no limitations anymore. There was so much young talent in Nashville that promised a bright future for country music, but the business had a way of doing things the way they'd always been done before. Maybe this new generation of musicians would change all that.

Pauline said, "You coming out with us?"

Jo pointed at her feet. "Gotta give these girls a rest."

Gaylene said, "If you change your mind, text us. We're going to the Thirsty Baboon to hear a band."

"Have fun for me," Jo said, and hugged them good-bye.

Mr. Sullivan rapped on the door just as the Wayward Sisters were leaving. He moved to the side to let them pass. "I hope I'm not disturbing anything."

He walked in with all the good looks money could buy a tall man at sixty-five—handsome suits, fine cologne, physical trainer, high-end grooming products. His salt-and-pepper distinguished look had landed him four Mrs. Sullivans, each one younger and thinner than the one before. Mr. Sullivan was famous for discovering Will McCoy and Lucy Heart, the king and queen of nineties country, whose framed pictures seemed to be everywhere backstage at the Ryman. During their reign, they were the biggest artists in country music and they'd made Mr. Sullivan a very powerful, very wealthy man on Music Row.

"Great show, my dear." Mr. Sullivan kissed Jo on the cheek and handed her a bouquet of sunflowers. She placed the flowers on the coffee table and the yellow petals scattered to the floor.

He reached out and shook hands with Nick like they were business partners instead of father and son. "J. D. Gunn and the boys are outside."

Jo said, "I'm about to go take pictures with—"

"Should only take a moment," Mr. Sullivan said, and before Jo could protest, Mr. Sullivan went back to the door and called the guys in. Jo moved quickly to put on her boots, smooth down her hair, and pull it over one shoulder right before J. D. walked through her dressing room door. Tall as he was, he ducked a little to make it through without hitting his hat. He'd hit a growth spurt at thirteen and shot up like a sprout, and Jo remembered that ever since then he'd been mindful of doors. They hadn't stood this close together in almost five years.

J. D. offered his hand to Nick first. "Good to meet you. Big fan of yours."

"Likewise," Nick said, and shook hands with J. D. like they were two CEOs making a deal. Jo had never once heard Nick say anything complimentary about J. D.'s music. He always agreed with Jo that J. D.'s music represented everything that was wrong with Top 40 country music. Nick called it pop music with a twang.

J. D. turned his attention to Jo now. "Great show. And congratulations on your engagement," J. D. said, more to Nick than to her. "When's the date?"

"Probably this fall," Jo said. "After the summer tour ends."

"Makes sense." J. D.'s tone shifted and sounded much softer than before.

"Rob," Jo said, and stood on her tiptoes to see beyond J. D. "Get over here."

Rob broke through the other guys and wrapped Jo in a big hug, lifting her feet off the ground. "Joanne Lover. Grand Ole Opry royalty."

Jo laughed. He put her back down and Jo went to Chase B next. "You know I need a hug from you too." Chase B was as burly and scruffy as ever. And warm. He gave the best hugs. Jo accidentally knocked off his trucker hat when she wrapped her arms around his neck.

Chase B said, "Danny and Aster went back to the room. They pass along their congratulations."

"That's nice," she said.

"Feels like a reunion," Mr. Sullivan said.

"We go way back," Jo said. Before J. D. could cut in, she beat him to it. They were her stories too, even if they weren't all in a band together anymore. "Me, Rob, and J. D. grew up together. I discovered Chase B."

J. D. took off his hat and smoothed down his thick, curly black hair before securing his hat once more. He smiled. "She's always bragged about that."

Jo didn't look at him when she said, "I used to wait tables on Broadway. Full of tourists."

Nick said, "I didn't know that."

Sometimes Jo couldn't remember what Nick did and did not know about her past, but this seemed like a minor detail. "I was super broke."

Chase B said, "She was the best waitress there."

"Is that a compliment?" Rob said.

"Anyway," Jo said, "I saw Chase B play the pedal steel guitar with his band there. He made it look so easy but you know it's hard as hell, like flying a helicopter."

"You were homeless then, remember?" J. D. said, and put his hand on Chase B's shoulder.

"I was living out of my car down by the footbridge," Chase B said. "That's homeless?"

Nick put his arm around Jo. "You guys came a long way."

Mr. Sullivan turned to Nick. "This could be a great collaboration, don't you think, Nick? Jo with J. D. and the Empty Shells."

"I don't think so," Jo said, and walked away to pour herself a bourbon.

"Why not?" Mr. Sullivan said. "You played music together before."

Jo normally only poured one shot, but this time she made it a double. She dropped two ice cubes into the tumbler. Without turning around, she said, "That was many, many stages ago. A whole different life." She checked her cell phone on the vanity table to see if Marie had texted her to come take pictures, but she hadn't.

"Wasn't that long ago," J. D. said.

Jo turned around, drank her bourbon slow, and studied J. D. over the rim of her tumbler. He dressed like a walking Wrangler advertisement. He had to lift weights for hours every day to be that stout. Multiplatinum-selling country music megastar J. D. Gunn. King of the party anthem. She had no idea who he was anymore and she didn't care to know either. He'd divorced himself from everything that mattered to them growing up.

Mr. Sullivan said, "You could produce it, son. Make it magic."

Nick squeezed his father's shoulder. "He's always thinking about the next big thing."

J. D. nodded. "That's what I hear."

Mr. Sullivan said, "We'll keep talking about this. Maybe you could collaborate on one song on their next album, Jo. I've got a good eye for these things."

"I know what it is," J. D. said, and crossed his arms.

She disliked when he played these little leading games with her. It felt like teasing. He'd always done that growing up too.

"I've read the interviews. I know you hate my sellout music."

"*Our* sellout music," Rob said.

"I never called it that."

J. D. smiled. "But you think it."

"Lots of people love your music," Jo said. "They relate to it. It's not my style, that's all."

What more could she say without hurting his feelings? Songs about partying and picking up girls and living for the weekend—was that all he really cared about anymore? He used to write his own songs. Now he just performed songs written by other people, and they sold in the hundreds of thousands. The person who stood before her was not the boy she'd started playing bluegrass music with in the highlands of Virginia, not the boy who swam with her at the Devil's Bathtub, who sipped the same stolen moonshine she did, who listened to the Carter Family and Hank Williams. It's like they shared the same root system but fake platinum trees sprouted for J. D.

Mr. Sullivan put a hand on J. D.'s shoulder in a familiar way. He said, "Son, you're much too successful to be self-conscious about your music."

Jo wasn't sure how they'd come to know each other so well. She'd hardly ever seen Mr. Sullivan act at ease this way around Nick, and Nick was his own son.

J. D. tipped his hat at her like he could tell what she was think-

ing. He said, "We better get going. It was good to meet you finally."
J. D. and Nick shook hands once more. And then J. D. walked over to
Jo. She extended her hand out for him to shake but he stunned her
by wrapping her in a deep embrace. It had been so long since they'd
touched each other and Jo felt time fold into itself like an accordion.
J. D. smelled like red clay earth, like composting leaves on the forest
floor, like the honeysuckle vines and Confederate jasmine blooming in
early June, like wild irises growing on the side of the road and fresh
honey from the hive and barn straw and his daddy's cow pasture after a
spring rain, like the metallic air before a storm. He smelled like home.
His warm breath moved through her hair as he said, "So good to see
you, Jo. You were amazing tonight."

Jo let go, and without looking up at him she said, "Nice to see you
guys too."

They all followed J. D. out the door, but J. D. looked back once and
waved good-bye. She waved back, all the while feeling Nick's eyes
studying her face. Once they were gone, Jo shut the door.

Mr. Sullivan sat down on the couch and stretched his arms out to
the sides. "They're nice fellas."

Jo nodded.

He kicked up one leg onto his knee and formed a square of empty
space between his legs. "You two have a good time out at the estate
this weekend?"

"Great time," Nick said, and sat down in the plaid wing-back chair
across from his father. Jo struggled with this shift in conversation, as if
J. D. and the boys had never really been there.

"How are the horses?" Mr. Sullivan said.

"Healthy."

"Get any wedding planning done?"

"Some," Jo said, and sat on Nick's lap. He wrapped his arms around her waist.

"Are you free tomorrow for lunch? Talk logistics for the wedding."

Jo looked over her shoulder at Nick, who looked up to her for confirmation. "I have *Vanity Fair* in the morning."

"After that," Mr. Sullivan said. "Jack's?"

"I guess that could work," she said.

"Figured since you're both here I might as well tell you I'm signing J. D. Gunn and the Empty Shells to Asphalt. Announcing it tomorrow. We've kept it quiet but it's close enough now."

"So it's true?"

Jo stood up and said, "Wait. Say that again."

"Who told you?" said Mr. Sullivan.

"Overheard it in the studio today."

Jo gripped Nick's forearm. "Why didn't you say anything to me?"

"I haven't seen you all day," he said.

"I should've been told," Jo said, more to Mr. Sullivan than to Nick. Every musician in the business knew a story of some label who signed a huge band and funneled all of its resources and attention into that one group at the expense of all the other talent on the label. Jo's career was a bird in flight, and she didn't need J. D. Gunn signing to her label and blowing off course everything she'd worked so hard for in her career.

Mr. Sullivan said, "Come on, you two. Be nice. This is great news for Asphalt. For you too, Jo. For all the artists on the label. All boats are lifted with these boys on the ticket. I would've told you sooner. Lawyers' orders."

"He's in a contract with Solar," Nick said. "They know?"

"They'll know tomorrow. Less drama for my team up front." Mr. Sullivan stood and smoothed the lapels on his suit jacket.

Nick stood up too and sank his hands into his pockets.

"What, son?"

"Is there a buyout clause or not?"

"Tell me you're not worried about the well-being of one of the three major corporations left in this industry, held by an international conglomerate company with investments in film, real estate, chemical companies, telecommunications. If they have a free finger they'll stick it anywhere."

"I'm not," Nick said in a defensive tone. "I'm asking—"

"Look, Solar alienated a blockbuster artist." Mr. Sullivan crossed his arms and stood in a wide stance. "That's their error and Asphalt's gain. You both know the reality. Consumers download singles, stream music or steal it. And J. D. Gunn and those boys can still make albums that people are willing to pay for. They wanted the support and freedom of an independent label. They came to me. Releasing another greatest hits album doesn't qualify in the multialbum deal they signed. Solar violated their contract. Enough years have passed that they're legally allowed to leave that contract. I'm certain of it, as are my lawyers."

"Solar will sue you," Jo said.

"Likely," Mr. Sullivan said. He gripped Nick on the shoulder and put one hand on his face. This tender gesture was the first Jo had ever seen Mr. Sullivan extend toward Nick. "This is good news for the longevity of this label. Asphalt will be yours soon enough."

Nick nodded, but dropped his head down and pulled away from his father's embrace. Jo knew he didn't want Asphalt. Early on in their relationship, Nick had told her that he never wanted to be CEO of a label, but Mr. Sullivan kept treating him like the heir apparent. Jo walked away from them to the other side of the room and poured herself a shot of bourbon. Now her label would be tied up with J. D. Gunn and a litigation. What would be left over for Jo, let alone all the young, rising talent like the Wayward Sisters?

Mr. Sullivan said, "See you tomorrow."

Marie opened the door and poked her head into the room. "Jo, they're ready for you."

Jo finished her drink and left the empty tumbler on her vanity. Nick walked out of the room behind her, and she watched Mr. Sullivan disappear down the hallway. A sound technician passed by, raised his hand to her, and said, "Great show." The house lights were on and cast everything in a vivid light where empty coffee cups, misplaced pieces of paper, and discarded water bottles were on display. An old man walked around and picked up the trash. Guys dressed in all-black clothes with their headsets around their necks pushed equipment down the hall on rolling carts. People talked together in groups and moved slowly, unlike earlier, when people had sprinted back and forth to make sure the show started on time. The stage cast a spell and invited the audience into a fantasy that ended behind the curtains, where everything turned real.

CHAPTER 4

Hello, Darlin'

DENVER STOOD OUTSIDE the Thirsty Baboon during the set break, smoking cigarettes and talking to the regulars who streamed in and out of the front door with Tecate cans popped open. It was well past midnight. The late-night crowd had arrived. Denver drank a Lone Star to lubricate his sore vocal cords. He was worried he was coming down with something, laryngitis or strep. He was always the strange kid who avoided illness all winter only to get knocked down in the spring, but his bandmate Alan never got sick. He had the immune system of a breast-fed baby—he couldn't remember who came up with that line, some friend at some bonfire years ago. His life worked that way now. He was starting to understand that what felt so present and important and critical to his life right now became kindling for the burning process of memory. His father complained often about the important moments he'd forgotten. Denver always brushed it off as old-man troubles. Maybe Denver was becoming an old man in his twenties.

A red flash of a Harley motorcycle cruised to a stop in front of the bar. Denver snuffed out his newly lit cigarette. He shouldn't have been smoking them anyway. He walked over to Alan, who was talking to the only other black people at the bar. Alan was laughing with them and gave a guy one of his signature close hugs. When Denver had first met Alan at UT Knoxville, the hugs took some getting used to, but he'd come to expect them now.

"What's up, Denver?" Alan said, and slapped hands with him and brought him over for a shoulder-to-shoulder hug. "You remember me telling you about Mark and Dittle, right? We grew up together in Birmingham."

"Y'all live here now?"

"Sure do," Dittle said.

"Come by the house after the show tonight," Denver said.

The guys nodded. "Good idea," Alan said. Then he pulled Denver's neck down and gave him a noogie. "Denver's always thinking."

Denver pulled Alan aside. "Floyd Masters just showed up."

Alan was gifted at seeing without looking directly at the subject in question. This skill made him an irreplaceable asset when beautiful women were around.

Denver said, "Think he might mention us on his show?"

An older woman wearing a pink cowgirl hat, a leather fringe vest, and a leopard-print skirt two sizes too tight passed in between them. Alan tipped his cowboy hat to her, and then he said, "Don't think Floyd Masters likes black dudes fronting country bands."

Denver shook his head. "He championed Charley Pride."

"Yeah, I know," Alan said. "Despite him being a nigger. That's what he said, Denver. It's quoted. He called Charley Pride a nigger, man. Written down in the books."

"That was another era."

"You think an old dude like that would change his mind? That's magical thinking."

"But if he did mention us, that'd be huge. That's what we need, Alan."

Buster, one of the two brothers who owned the place, came outside carrying an overstuffed black trash bag. Denver could see the outlines of empty bottles and cans pushing through the plastic. Buster passed by them on his way to the Dumpster. He said, "Y'all about ready?"

"Sure," Alan said, beaming that big smile. His dad was a dentist. Denver's teeth were stained from cigarettes and coffee.

Alan went inside the Thirsty Baboon as Denver tossed his Lone Star can in the blue plastic trash can by the door. Before Denver made it inside the bar, he heard tires skid to a stop right out front, and he turned to see a Toyota truck jacked high off the ground with oversized tires. No one parked a truck in front of the bar. It was reserved for motorcycles only. Four doors opened and Denver heard an entire chorus singing Dolly Parton's "9 to 5" as the song blasted from the speakers. Girls filled the cab of that truck. Their long, lean legs with high heels were the first things Denver saw coming out of the doors like some kind of octopus-girl machine come to swallow everyone. These weren't just regular voices. These were professionals.

Someone close by said, "Who the hell is that?"

Alan poked his head back outside. "You coming?"

Denver stared at the truck. The heels connected to the ground. The doors slammed shut.

"What do we have here?" Alan said.

"Girls," was all Denver could say.

He couldn't stop staring. They were all beautiful, but the one who caught his attention was the shortest girl in the group. She wore Converse sneakers and had bright blond hair cut super short, with features as delicate as a bird's. She looked spunky. Denver needed to know her. He wasn't sure why he felt this way, he just felt it. Urgently, urgently felt it. Urgently. Floyd Masters walked over to the other three girls she came with, all of whom were very tall and familiar somehow. If Floyd knew them like that, they had to be something special.

Alan's electric steel guitar shouted at Denver from inside the Thirsty Baboon. He waited though, just a moment longer. He needed this girl to see him looking. She stood with the other women as they talked to Floyd. She laughed some. Her smile was as perfect as an orange slice. Who made her? Denver wanted to know everything about her. Girls distracted Denver pretty regularly, but he'd never felt anything like this before. She looked up and saw him staring at her. Denver was so struck by her ability to sense him that he laughed out loud even though he stood alone, but then she turned her attention to Floyd again. Denver went back inside, where people were seated on bar stools. He sat down at his drum kit but couldn't focus.

Floyd walked in with the girls following behind him. Now that they were up close Denver recognized the three tall ones. They were the Wayward Sisters, who were fast-rising stars in Americana music and opened for Jo Lover's tour. He was sure he'd never seen them at this dive before. His girl walked in after them, but he didn't recognize her. She might have been their manager, or someone important, anyway.

Alan said, "Howdy there, folks. Oh, what? What y'all staring at? Black dude can't be up front with the microphone, not in a country band? Surprise then. Here I am. My name's Alan Rockshaw, and that's Denver Colorado on the drum kit."

People laughed. Denver's girl tucked herself in close at the bar where he could hardly see her anymore because she was so short. But he could see her sneakers.

"I'm just joking with you," Alan said. "His name's Denver Boulder Colorado."

Denver added a drum roll, and then he shattered the cymbal.

"We're the Flyby Boys. So glad you could make it out here this evening. We've got CDs and pretty cool T-shirts for sale in the back on the pool tables. Be sure to tip your hardworking bartenders. And keep coming to the Thirsty Baboon. There aren't too many more places like this one left in Nashville. Damn if they won't try to tear it down too."

Somebody shouted, "Fucking A," from somewhere deep in the bar.

Denver added a kick drum beat.

Alan turned around to Denver and said, "Let's do Twitty."

"Got it."

"Here's a special one for all the pretty ladies who came out here tonight." Alan kicked off their cover of "Hello Darlin'."

One of the Wayward Sisters shouted "hello" at them. Denver's girl moved out from behind her friends to where he could see her and she smiled right at him. He smiled back at her and then she winked. Denver forced himself to look away, to focus on beating his instrument with the sticks in his hands. Her eyes were on him though. He didn't have to look at her to know. Her stare expanded his nerves into constellations, like a big bang explosion in his heart.

CHAPTER 5

Boys in Bands

WHAT'S WITH BOYS in bands? They're so obvious at first, then so distant when they finally have the chance to talk to you after a show. Marie stood at the bar waiting to close out her tab. She'd drunk one Corona, and that was plenty. The music kept her attention, especially during that second set, and she didn't need to drink more to have a good time. She loved what the Flyby Boys had going on. Minimal equipment. Big sound. Each of the guys was an extreme talent on his instrument. When Denver Boulder Colorado stood up and played the washboard while maintaining the kick drum, only to sit back down and rip a tremendous drum solo, Marie knew that he was something special. But so was Alan. That guy could sing like a troubadour but play guitar like an outlaw. His songs felt so true to country. She heard the blues in there too. Spirituals. Rockabilly too. Even some Western swing. She heard the entire Southern musical tradition in his artistic vision. How often were two musicians as talented as these guys in the same band? Marie felt like she was witnessing the moment before the rise. This must have been the feeling all those A & R guys felt when they discovered the next big thing. Marie would recommend them to Jo the first chance she had.

Marie glanced around the room to find her friends, but also to see where Mr. Denver Boulder Colorado stood. Same spot, with his band-mate Alan, surrounded by a gaggle of other girls in serious honky-tonk gear. Skintight animal-print dresses and bedazzled cowgirl boots with hats to match. Marie felt out of place in her cropped blazer and Converse sneakers. She wished he'd come over and talk to her, make her feel like she should stick around. He was cuter than any guy she'd met in Nashville since she moved here for school. It was something about his smile, something tender and innocent. Something kissable. He had nice blue eyes too, almost neon blue, flashing like a lighthouse from across the room. That haircut worked for him. Shaved on both sides, long on top, slicked back with gel. Marie had considered getting that haircut before she went for the pixie. Maybe she'd try it out soon. Maybe they'd be dating and have matching hairstyles.

Why did she always go there? Why did she always imagine a future with a guy she hadn't even spoken to yet? A bad habit. She should go home. Yes. She should go. Marie let her gaze linger just a moment longer, and it was long enough for him to check in with her, which he'd been doing every few minutes.

"Mariiiiieeeeeee." A pair of arms wrapped around her neck from behind. She turned to Gaylene with a big smile on her face. Sometimes she couldn't tell which sister was talking to her since they sounded so much alike.

Marie stood on her tiptoes and leaned into the bar to try to flag down the bartender who stood at the other end talking to Floyd.

"Gwennie's too drunk for public."

"Who's driving?"

"You are, I guess."

Marie rode a bike to work, unless Jo sent a car for her. Marie didn't know the first thing about driving a truck. Growing up in Austin, Texas, she'd seen plenty of them, but her parents were Prius people. "I can't operate tires that big."

"You're Marie. You can do anything." Gaylene sucked her whiskey and ginger dry. "Don't pay. They're taking too damn long."

"That's terrible."

"Send them a Christmas card," Gaylene said, and hooked Marie's arm. "Let's go." They had to pass Denver to get out the door. Gaylene stomped forward, leading Marie out.

Alan reached out and caught Gaylene by the arm. "What's the hurry?"

Gaylene smiled at him. "Great show. Truly. But this party's done."

Alan broke away from Denver and the others and turned all of his attention to Gaylene and Marie. "We're moving this party to our house. You should come. We can mess around on the guitar. I'm a big fan of yours. Of all the sisters. You can teach me some things."

"I don't know about that," Gaylene said. "You're pretty damn good yourself. Floyd Masters told us to check you out."

Denver nearly jumped over the flock of other girls to stand next to Alan.

"Hi," he said, and extended his hand to Marie. "I'm Denver."

"I know." Marie bit the inside of her cheek to keep from smiling too wide. "I'm Marie."

Alan turned to Denver. "You hear that? Floyd Masters told these ladies to come check out our show."

"You're kidding."

"He did," Gaylene said.

"We're having people over to our place. Y'all should come," Denver said.

Marie looked at Gaylene, who was still smiling at Alan.

"Y'all got food?" Gaylene said.

Alan rubbed his lips together. He broke into a big, warm smile that any girl would find intoxicating. Marie did. He could stop traffic with that smile and that was perfect for a front man. But Marie liked tall and stormy, tough but with a sense of tenderness underneath it all. A little like J. D. Gunn. Denver had that going on. Plus, he had great arms, like most drummers.

"I'll grill you some meat," Alan said.

"I'm vegetarian." Gaylene frowned.

Alan put a hand on her shoulder. "I'll grill you a zucchini."

"You've got zucchini?"

"I do."

"All right then. We'll come," Gaylene said.

Denver grabbed Alan's shoulder, and Marie knew that meant "thank you" in guy world. He was too cute.

"What's the address?" Marie said.

Alan gave it to her.

"See you there," Gaylene said.

As they were walking out of the Thirsty Baboon, Gaylene said, "Alan is so damn hot I can't hardly stand it."

"He likes you," Marie said.

"Not as much as that Denver boy likes you."

Gaylene stumbled on the gravel. Marie grabbed her arm to steady her. Gaylene said, "Can you drive the truck or what?"

Marie had no choice but to handle that truck if she wanted to see Denver again. The risk of getting in an accident seemed worth it, though, in order to find out what that boy was all about. She wanted to feel his eyes lock on her again, to feel the way her heart beat when they did. Marie said, "Sure, I'll drive."

Gaylene tossed her the keys, and Marie caught them with one hand.

CHAPTER 6

Late Night

I T WAS THIS experience Denver lived for, one of the biggest reasons he and Alan had ditched job searching and come to Nashville in the first place. For the community that popped up each night in different configurations, always after midnight, always at different houses. That's what he craved. He found it here in ways he'd never imagined. Denver, Marie, Gaylene, Alan, his friend Dittle, and a few of his neighbors from two houses down who played in a Mexican polka band were all sitting in a big circle around the fire pit and playing the blues. Some Muddy Waters here, some Howlin' Wolf and Bessie Smith there. A little DeFord Bailey–inspired harmonica too. Marie knew how to listen to music. She knew how to listen without thinking, how to listen like it was meditation. It was hard to find a person who could listen like that. He had always hoped to find a girl like Marie. She might not have been a musician but she understood music, and she liked shaking the tambourine.

Denver wanted to keep playing music with the group but somebody had to tend the fire. Alan had grilled and fed everybody so it was Denver's turn to work while Alan played. In between spreading the glowing coals and adding new logs to the fire, Denver paused to stare at Marie, who leaned back in the plastic Adirondack chair and closed her eyes. So that's what she looked like when she was sleeping. He wished he could wake up in the morning and see her next to him looking just like that. The fire crackled and Marie opened her eyes. Denver offered her one of the beers he'd brought outside but she shook her head. He added three logs to the fire, and then Denver sat on the wooden stump next to her chair.

She smiled at him. "So who is Denver Boulder Colorado anyway?"

"What do you want to know?" Denver used a long stick to turn a log and expose the glowing orange embers beneath it.

"Anything."

"I was born up in West Virginia."

"That might be a deal breaker." Marie smiled. She took Denver's beer off the armrest and took a sip.

"We moved to East Tennessee when I was three."

"That's not so bad."

"Glad you approve."

Marie offered his beer back to him, but Denver opened a new one. "All yours."

"Why'd your family move?"

"Daddy died in a coal mine."

Marie's face immediately lost all its joy. "Oh my goodness, Denver. I'm so sorry." She turned more sorrowful than he'd expected and he immediately regretted lying to her.

Denver said, "That was a bad joke, I'm sorry."

"So he's not dead?"

"No."

"You shouldn't joke about that, Denver."

"I know." Denver stood up and added another log to the fire. The flames reached high now, nearly up to his torso. "My father left when I was three."

"Oh," she said. "Is that true?"

"That's true."

He sat back down. She reached out her hand and he held it. Her skin was smooth against Denver's callused palms.

"I went to UT Knoxville, just like my daddy did. I guess I wanted to make him proud or something."

"What was your major?"

"I switched majors a bunch. Ended up with a degree in business, which has been very useful, as you can tell."

"Clearly." She laughed and squeezed his hand. "So how'd you meet Alan?"

"College. He had a full ride. And if he was listening right now he'd interrupt and say, 'For academics. Not sports.'"

Alan stopped playing the guitar and smiled at Denver, which signaled that somehow he had been playing music and eavesdropping on their conversation.

"What was your major, Alan?" Marie said.

"English lit. I loved the old stuff. Shakespeare, Milton, Spenser, Wordsworth. Made me want to write lyrics. And engineering. Parents made me double major."

"No kidding," Gaylene said. She drank her beer and then said, "Charming and smart. This guy's a winner."

Denver deepened his voice to sound like Alan's dad and said, "So if this music thing doesn't work out, you will be an engineer, correct, son?"

Alan shook his head. "Hell no."

Marie laughed. Denver flipped one of the big logs on the fire, exposing its bright orange underbelly. Gaylene and Alan agreed to another blues song and began strumming together. Denver remembered Alan strumming just like that on some stranger's acoustic guitar at the house party where they first met. In honor of the Volunteers winning a football game, the frat house had paid for one of the local bands to play. During the band's set break, they scattered to go do keg stands and left their equipment behind. Denver heard music from one room over, where he was playing beer pong in what should've been a dining room. A brass chandelier hung above him but the rest of the room was devoted to the Ping-Pong table. Denver quit his round and another guy took his place. He went to the sound of the blues guitar and found a guy standing there alone, shoulders slouched, his head hung over the pale yellow face of the Taylor guitar. He'd started messing around with the lead singer's guitar without permission, and that made Denver like him instantly. The blues sound he created made Denver want to play drums, which he hadn't done since he'd come to college a few months before. Denver jumped onstage and settled in at the drum kit without even introducing himself. They started improvising together and people started to gather. Even the guys from the local band came to listen to the music they were making on this borrowed equipment and invited them to keep playing. Denver couldn't remember how he ended up at that party, but he'd never forget meeting Alan that first time. After that night, he and Alan were inseparable. They synced their class times so they could schedule their band practice with ease. No night classes allowed. Alan and Denver started off playing Southern rock music so they could learn each other's styles, but soon after that Alan introduced Denver to old-school country and blues bands. It was the only real friendship Denver had made during college. It was the only friendship that mattered.

Denver finished moving the logs around the fire and the flame grew higher. He sat back down, and Marie said, "Fire master."

"That's me." Denver drank his beer. "So, your turn. Who's Marie?"

"Let me think."

"Take your time."

Immediately, she said, "Well, my favorite *Hee Haw* episode is the one when Dolly Parton first appeared. Major girl crush on Dolly. Major."

"That's respectable."

Marie squeezed his hand. "I know how to make passion flower tinctures to heal chronic headaches. Do you have headaches?"

"Sometimes."

"My mother owns a health food store in Austin. My dad blows glass. He's pretty famous, actually. His glass pipes are in high demand among all of Willie Nelson's friends."

"You're kidding."

"I'm serious. I grew up around musicians. My dad played bass in a Texas swing band."

"Like Bob Wills music?"

"Basically."

"What else?"

"Let's see." Marie hugged her knees to her chest and said, "One summer I interned on an organic farm in Virginia and the cabin I lived in had dead rats in the walls. Smelled so bad. I fell in love with old-time string music while I lived there. Then I went to Vanderbilt for college, but mostly to be in Nashville for the music scene."

"Smart way to choose a college."

"I thought so. Okay, now your turn. Did you always want to be a musician?"

"Once Alan and I started playing in college, yeah. Before that I just liked playing around on the drums for fun."

Marie moved to the edge of her chair. "I think you guys are incredible. Seriously."

"Thanks." Denver poked the fire and sparks rose above the flames, into the night air, where they turned to ash. "We play gigs almost every night. Can't seem to get beyond the dive bar circuit."

"Your break's coming," she said. "Y'all are too good for it not to."

"Hope so," Denver said. He still didn't know anything about why she was here in Nashville or how she knew the Wayward Sisters. What did she do all day long? He wanted to ask her out to lunch since he couldn't really afford to take her to dinner.

Denver was about to ask her to go to Jack's Bar-B-Que with him tomorrow when Marie stood up. "You okay?" he asked.

"Fine," she said. Her eyes were heavy with half-sleep.

"You need to go home?"

She grabbed Denver's hand, and he felt something like electricity move from inside her and into him. It overwhelmed him so much he almost pulled away, but she wouldn't let go. Marie led him away from the group. "I like you, Denver," she said softly.

He wasn't sure what to say back. There was nothing to say. All he could see was her lips in the faint glow of the firelight. Denver took her chin in his hand and kissed her, and then she leaned into him and kissed him harder. He let her be the one to pull away. Marie rested her head on his chest and he held her.

"May I spend the night?" she said.

"With me?"

He felt her laughter on his stomach.

"Yes with you."

Denver kissed her again, for a much longer time. The music stopped around the fire. Alan sang out, "Let's get it on," and matched the Marvin Gaye tune on his guitar. Denver and Marie stopped kissing and started laughing. Then the group began playing Muddy Waters.

"Let's go inside," Marie said, and took his hand in hers. Denver led her away from the fire, away from the voices rising all around them, united by the late-night blues.

CHAPTER 7

Insomnia

NICK SNORED IN the bed beside her. Jo couldn't sleep, so she got up and wrapped her white plush robe around her naked body. Her husky, Max, followed her to the formal dining room, where she kept a well-stocked bar with aged bourbons and whiskeys from small distilleries all across the South. Jo tossed Max's chewed-up rawhide bone down the dark hallway and he took off to fetch it, his nails on the hardwood floor the only sound in the house. He trotted back to her, his icy blue eyes eager for her to toss the bone again. She worried about waking Nick, so she said, "Sorry, boy, that's enough," and hugged him around the neck.

He settled down on the woven rug beneath the table and began to lick his leg. The clinking of his tags seemed to echo throughout this space, which, of late, had begun to feel as big and empty as the belly of a blue whale. She lit the white candlesticks on her table, opened her liquor cabinet, and selected a rare Kentucky bourbon one of her fans had given her after a show in Portland. Kimberly, that was her name. Jo remembered she installed windows for a living. She had long, sculpted arms and looked better in a tank top than anyone Jo had ever seen before. Jo had never met a woman who worked construction—all the asphalt highways stretching across the nation, and the bank buildings, the supermarkets and fast-food joints that lined the roads, the homes people came back to at the end of the day, almost all of it was built by men. Country music was still a man's world too.

Jo poured herself a glass of Kimberly's bourbon neat, leaned against the bar, and drank it down in full before pouring a second one. Jo sat down at the head of the table, hoping this nightcap would do its job and send her to sleep. She slid the leather-bound booklet from the center of the table toward her and then opened it. Designers from all over the country had sent her samples after the announcement. The wedding planner had sent this collection to her a week ago with photograph spreads from famous wedding dress designers—Vera Wang, Carolina Herrera, Jenny Packham, Michael Kors. Satin and tulle. Hand-stitched crystals and lace. Everything angel white, as her mama would say, and flawlessly constructed. Nick asked her yesterday if she'd found any dresses she liked, and she lied and said, "A few." Jo flipped from page to page in search of a simple dress, something off-white, champagne colored perhaps, but she found nothing she wanted there. Jo couldn't concentrate and shut the book.

As she drummed her nails on the cherrywood table and looked down at the nine other empty chairs with their intricate hand-carved backs, each one made to order for Jo, she tried to remember the last time she'd even used this room. There was that dinner party eight months ago for Nick's friends from LA, but since then? She and Nick always ate at the breakfast nook in the kitchen.

Jo had bought this run-down house in the West End a few years back so she could have a view of the massive Parthenon in the center of Centennial Park, where she liked to run in the fall and winter. The house was only minutes from downtown Nashville too, so that was a draw. She'd hired a team of people to renovate the Arts and Crafts bungalow into a six-bedroom, six-and-a-half-bathroom livable space, and soon afterward her PR team made sure the house was featured in *Architecture and Life, Better Homes and Gardens, Southern Living.* Jo never intended to buy a big new mansion out in Williamson County, how-ever much that verdant landscape reminded her of home. Jo loved that she'd rescued this house and preserved its history, and now it was on the Nashville tour of historic houses.

Years had passed and it still didn't feel like home, no matter how much she filled it with handcrafted items. Jo had ordered this table from Floyd County, Virginia. She bought hand-dipped candles, jewelry from the Appalachian women's cooperative, paintings and photographs of the Appalachian Mountains at sunset, in a morning fog, bare winter branches like a sketch against a gray sky, creeks flanked by bright moss and spring grass. She ordered her soaps from Virginia, and pottery for entertaining, and one-of-a-kind fiddles made by generations of families living in cabins way up in the highlands. She filled her freezer with venison hunted in the woods she'd grown up in. Her cellar housed many Virginia wines.

Home is made up of the people inside it, her mama always said. And don't get above your raising. She always said that too. On nights like these she felt like she was living on a lone ship in the middle of a dark sea and all she wished was that she was back at her white farmhouse outside of Gatesville with two hundred acres of privacy and thousands more of protected forest beyond that. It comforted her knowing there was a place where she belonged. Someday she'd retire there. Someday. Jo scrolled through the music on her phone and selected "Love Me Tender." The song linked to the wireless speakers in the dining room and filled the space with Elvis's earnest, trembling voice. Jo kept the volume down low.

Whenever all of her distractions were exhausted, her thoughts wandered to him. That was the way it was. The way it always had been. And she always forced herself to push thoughts of him away. Years ago when J. D. left her, she'd felt like she had the flu every day, like someone had packed wet laundry into the place where her heart used to be. She only felt that pain occasionally now, and never with so much intensity. But J. D.'s arms wrapped around her in that embrace tonight, feeling his warmth and smelling his skin—nothing else hurt like that. Nothing had hurt like that in a long time. She pulled up J. D.'s Instagram. There was a shot of J. D. with his arm around two girls on either side of him, taken right after Jo's show ended. One girl had red boots painted on her face. Jo couldn't help feeling a little bit betrayed by her fans. J. D. was the pillar between them, his smile charming and his face radiant.

Max stood up from the carpet suddenly, left the dining room, and trotted down the dark hallway. Jo hid her phone in her lap and waited to see if Nick would appear in the hallway. She sipped her whiskey. But Max returned alone with a rotten tennis ball in his mouth and settled down at her feet once more. Jo returned to her phone, to J. D.'s page. He had received over four thousand likes on that post and a long list of comments, mostly from women, mostly about his big blue eyes. Women posted about their jealousy that his arm wasn't around them. Choose me, J. D.! They begged for him. He made smiling look so easy. Jo drank her bourbon, a big, long pull, and vowed not to scroll through his other posts. Jo left his page behind and felt proud, like a reformed drug addict turning down a hit.

It was four AM. She'd start preparing for her *Vanity Fair* interview in just a few more hours. Hopefully the hair and makeup team had the power to erase any trace of this sleepless night. She switched the music over to a Bob Dylan playlist, and then she opened her Instagram to find the pictures Marie had posted from the Ryman performance. There were good shots of Jo down among the pews and up onstage dancing with her fans. Jo paused and stared at a picture of herself all alone on-stage. She held her fiddle high in the air, a big smile on her face.

That was the Jo people saw. Independent, confident. If her fans knew she still thought about the man who broke her heart, that she'd allowed him to disrupt the most important night in her career—what would they think of her then? There were two kinds of women in country music. Sweet as a caramel apple or spicy as Nashville hot chicken. If she were the apple type, maybe her fans would understand, but that was not who they needed her to be. Jo had stopped loving J. D. years ago. Of course she didn't love him—he was vain, selfish, shallow. No. How could she ever love the man he'd become?

*G*ood morning, good people of Nashville. It's that gravy-dipping, coffee-drinking, cigarette-smoking, fried-chicken-eating Floyd Masters coming to you from Vanderbilt's WHYW FM morning broadcast station. Eighty-seven point three. That's right, you're waking up with the best of Nashville audiophiles. All those people out there with bad taste in music are still rolling over in a warm bed this partly cloudy morning. It's May fifteenth, folks, if your head's so full of good music that you can't keep up with the days—that's what I'm here for. You can count on Floyd Masters to know the very best in country music and to keep up with the days of the week and the weather.

It's May but April forgot the rain. Where'd it go? Not downward, that's all I know. Limp flowers everywhere. Dying for a damn drink. Hey, flowers, I know all about it. Floyd Masters understands. Set to be another drought blight of a summer ahead for us. A hot touring season. There's a climate and it's changing. Yes, sir. Who can deny it? There's certainly no denying the bad performance going on at the Ryman Auditorium last night. I'll be opening the phone lines to get your opinions on the Jo Lover concert last night at our mother church of country music, a place that should not be defiled by such bad musicianship as I witnessed last night. It was her debut as an Opry family member, folks, and she looked spooked. Or checked out. I don't know.

It's a shame, too; as all you loyal listeners know, I was a great big champion for that little lady when her debut album came out. She demonstrated a knowledge about where her music was coming from, the rich history of our Southern culture, our music, and she was something different on the stage from all that *pop country that keeps getting aired. She was a spitfire too; I liked that—maybe it's fame, maybe it's money, maybe it's all the attention being a success-ful artist gets you, but something was mighty different last night. Maybe she can't transition anymore from an arena performance to a Ryman performance. That's a shame if so. Jo needs to get back to her roots, then. She can't forget where she started. She's been speaking out about how women in country music need better representation, but maybe she needs to focus on her music and what got her right where she is.*

Oh, boy, my phone lines are lighting up bright red. Seems like I've struck a chord with the listeners this morning. Now you're awake, folks. You're welcome. Okay, we've got Cherie Campbell on the line from right here in Nashville. Hello, Cherie, you're on the air. Hi, Floyd, good morning. *Good morning to you.* I listen to you every morning, and I'm an old gal so I was listen-ing to your music when I was a young thing, and I appreciate your music and this show. *Why, thank you, Cherie.* But I think you're real wrong about what you said about Ms. Jo Lover. I'm a Lover fan, and I was at her concert last night. I think it was wonderful. Just a good-time kind of show. As fun as always. She cares, you know. You might not think she does anymore. But I do. What else matters?

Well, Cherie, I appreciate your thoughts, but I think a whole hell of a lot extra matters. She messed up on some very simple chords on some very simple songs and she seemed like a deflated balloon onstage by the end. Cherie? You there, Cherie? I think we've lost Cherie. Next caller, hello. Erin from Davidson County. Hi, Floyd. I just want to say that I think you're a fool. I think Jo has to keep speaking out about all the bad songs about tailgate parties and girls in the passenger seat of jacked-up trucks that we hear on the radio over and over again. You yourself supported her speaking out about it. If I hear about a truck one more time in a song on the radio I think I might explode. *That's pretty dramatic, Erin.*

I mean it, Floyd. You made real country music in the sixties. Real music. This music is so bland and cliché. And for you to say she should stop speaking out about it is just as misogynistic as the lyrics. Isn't it, Floyd? Isn't it? Jo Lover, if you're listening for some reason, please keep on doing what you're doing. We love you. *All right, Erin, thanks for calling.*

Let's turn now to the biggest news in country music this morning. Let it be known you heard it here first. Asphalt's set to announce a deal with J. D. Gunn and the Empty Shells at the Country Music Hall of Fame this afternoon. They've managed to keep it under wraps until today. How they managed that is a secret of the gods. But now Floyd Masters knows and I'm sharing it with my devoted listeners. Mr. Sullivan, CEO of Asphalt Records, has now stacked the hottest bands in country music on his label. It's officially the best independent label in Nashville. Maybe the best label there is. I understand why J. D. Gunn and the Empty Shells want to be housed there. More artistic freedom and flexibility, but y'all watch out for some litigation around this deal. Mr. Sullivan thieved talent away from Solar. And why is Asphalt going around stealing talent from a label that has an active contract with an artist? I think he's got an eye on that Clear Channel streaming deal where only country music made twenty-five years ago or sooner will get played. Streaming deals are good for label profits but bad for artist rights. I'll keep looking into it, so y'all keep listening.

And keep supporting your local venues. I heard a real good band at the Thirsty Baboon last night called the Flyby Boys. Young guys, great songs. Big-time talents on their instruments. Check those boys out. Okay, enough about all that. Let's start with some oldies. By God, let's listen to some Kitty Wells to remember what real country music sounds like.

CHAPTER 8

Morning, Marie

D ENVER, WAKE UP!" Alan banged on the bedroom door. Denver
moaned. He rolled over and draped his arm over Marie. Sweet,
sweet Marie. Most mornings he clutched a pillow, but this was far supe-
rior. Marie squirmed beneath the weight of his arm. She rolled on her
side and placed one warm palm on Denver's cheek. He'd brought girls
home before, but none were ever gentle to him like this in the morning.

"Mmmmm." Marie stretched her arm out. The blue sheets were
caught between her bare, tucked legs. Denver pulled her closer. "Last
night was fun," she said. Her voice sounded heavy with sleep.

Denver had other words to describe what they did last night, and
all he knew was that he wanted to do it again and as soon as possible.
He kissed her long neck. Marie moaned. Denver guided his right hand
beneath the sheets and clutched her thigh. She had light brown hair
growing on her upper thighs. Denver liked that she didn't shave that
high up.

The doorknob jiggled.

"What's that?" Marie said.

"Don't do it, Alan."

"Too late," Alan said, and pushed the door open with a bang. "Morning, Marie."

Marie jumped away from Denver. She raised the sheet up to cover her shoulders, burying herself beneath the blankets.

Denver propped himself up by his elbows. "I don't barge in on you, dude."

Alan was showered and dressed for his job working the front desk at the African American Country Music Association. He looked way too put together after such a late night of drinking and hanging out. Alan held an oversized red coffee mug that said HI, NEIGHBOR in big white letters.

"Guess what Junior just texted me."

Marie leaned over the bed. "Where's my phone?" She searched the bedside table. "What time is it?"

Alan checked his phone. "It's nine fifteen."

Marie made a low, sustained noise. She launched out of the bed, taking the covers with her. Alan turned to the side and put his hand up to shield his eyes.

"Where's my phone?" Marie repeated over and over.

"I think I saw it on the coffee table," Alan said.

"Please help me find it."

Denver crawled out of bed in his boxers and put on a T-shirt. His head hurt from too much PBR. "Are you okay?"

"No." Marie pulled her jeans up lightning fast. She buttoned up her white-collared shirt, grabbed her blazer off the floor. She glanced into Denver's smudged mirror over his dresser and tousled her hair with her fingertips. Alan returned with her phone. She carried her sneakers in one hand and reached for her phone with the other. "It's so late." She looked up at Denver with big, worried eyes and then pressed the phone against her ear with her shoulder while she put on her Converse sneakers. Marie said, "Please send a car."

Alan raised his eyebrows at Denver and pointed his thumb at Marie. Having a car sent for you seemed sort of big-time, which suggested Marie was famous or super rich or both. Denver wanted to know who the hell he'd slept with last night.

Marie recited Denver's address, and it impressed him even more that she remembered it. She put her phone in her pocket before locking herself away in the bathroom.

Alan whispered, "A car, dude?"

And then Marie returned. "I have to go. Like right now. Thank you for your help, Alan."

"No problem."

Denver hustled over to give her a hug but what he wanted most was her phone number and to ask her who was sending that car. Marie kissed Denver hard on the mouth, and then she pushed by Alan before Denver could say anything in response. He watched her grab her oversized sack of a purse from the coffee table. She let the screen door slam behind her.

"A car, Denver."

"I know." Denver sat on his bed and pulled the covers from the floor onto his lap.

Alan sipped his coffee. "Maybe she's a secret agent."

Denver threw a pillow at Alan. For all he knew, that could be true. "I didn't even get her number."

"Good thing I got Gaylene's."

"She stayed the night?"

"Wasn't as lucky as you."

"That's a first," Denver said.

"Let's not dwell on the negatives. Point is, we can find Marie."

Denver wiped his face with his hands, scratched his hair. "I got to get ready for work."

"Internship, you mean."

"Work's work," Denver said. "Just because I don't get paid doesn't mean it isn't work. You got employment prejudice or something?"

Alan put a balled fist into his mouth and laughed at him. "Got to have it in this economy, brother."

Denver stretched. "I need to piss."

"Take a shower and wipe that girl's spit off you."

Denver grabbed a used bath towel from the floor. He followed Alan out of the room. Their apartment was so small that the bathroom opened up to the kitchen. Right before Denver closed the bathroom door, he said, "You woke me up for work?"

Alan poured coffee in his mug. "Now you want to know?"

"Know what?"

"What Junior texted me."

"You woke me up for Junior?" Junior was the most paranoid person Denver had ever met. He had a million theories about a million different conspiracies. He believed the president was a Muslim, a terrorist, a Christian scientist, a saint, all depending on the day. He smoked pot morning to night and rarely slept.

"Junior listened to Floyd's show this morning."

"Oh, Christ."

"You think I'd be standing here drinking coffee and telling you this shit all calm if he railed on us? No, man. He railed on Jo Lover's show at the Ryman. But he said good things about us."

Denver leaned against the door frame. "I can't tell if you're fucking with me."

"I'm serious."

"This is a big deal." He gripped the door frame above his head.

"Could be." Alan tossed the rest of his coffee into the sink, rinsed out the mug, and placed it on the drying rack. "Go to work, Denver. Don't sit here writing songs about your long-lost Marie."

"Yes, sir."

Alan put his leather satchel over his shoulder. "We'll find her."

CHAPTER 9

Suiting Up

THE SMELL OF grass stuck to J. D. like cheap cologne. His father always told him that when a man owned a plot of grass and refused to cut it himself, he lost an opportunity for dignity and humility. J. D. drove the John Deere up the hill toward his white brick Georgian-style mansion with large columns and black shutters, which reminded him of all those historic homes he'd visited on field trips back in Virginia. The sun rose beyond the house toward a noonday position. The skyline was no longer filled with the soft pinks and oranges of sunrise. He cut grass early in the morning just to see those colors. Every Sunday after church his daddy would take him to the general store on Main Street for a single scoop of sunrise sherbet, and if heaven were willing, he'd trade this fifty-acre estate for just one scoop of that cold sweetness.

It was gearing up to be another awful hot day in Williamson County. J. D. wiped the sweat from his face with a red handkerchief and rode past Rob's chicken coop and the tennis courts, past the swimming pool to see all those helicopter seeds gathered on the cover. Making those seeds fly had given him hours of entertainment and pleasure when he was a boy. The soft green grass in the low rolling hills dotted with bright yellow buttercups reminded J. D. of home, as did the fishing pond framed by old willow trees. Out here, just south of Nashville, J. D. felt like he had some privacy. He parked the rider at the back of the house so that Juan could clean it up and take it to the storage house for him. J. D. knocked his grass-stained boots against the stone fireplace on the patio. He almost went inside without taking his boots off, but then he remembered Rob's getting on him about tracking grass all through the house. Allergies.

J. D. entered the billiards and dart room at the east ground-floor entrance. After he'd hit multiplatinum, J. D. had bought this twelve-million-dollar estate with fourteen bedrooms, fifteen bathrooms, indoor and outdoor pools, a fishing pond that was well stocked year round, a recording studio, professionally landscaped grounds with a three-mile-long walking-trail loop, a greenhouse, and tennis courts— a sport for which he and the guys had no talent, so the courts remained unused. The subterranean spa with mineral waterfalls had convinced him this was the place to buy. With all its splendor, J. D. felt obligated to make sure the estate was well appointed, so he hired a woman who told him upon first introduction that she loved her job so much it featured prominently in her dreams at night—J. D. appreciated that kind of focus and opened up his wallet to her. She designed the house in a chic rustic style. She narrowed down selections of stone, tile, fixtures, fabric, and color chips, he made the final decisions, and at the end of it all he had a very nice home featured in every lifestyle magazine known to man. He was happy when all that was over. He and the guys spent most of their time down in the game room, at the pool, or in the field shooting skeet.

After Jo's concert last night, they'd stayed up late drinking whiskey and playing poker. J. D. and Rob faced off in a round of Guitar Hero and Rob won. They rewatched the episode of *The Band* where J. D. was a guest judge in the semifinals. The look of awe on those young guys' faces when he announced their name gave J. D. a rush. The band reminded J. D. of a younger version of the Empty Shells. That wasn't why he'd chosen them, no matter what anybody on Twitter said. They were talented and they were dedicated. They deserved that recognition. He didn't expect the show to launch their careers—if anything, he hoped it wouldn't do any damage to them. Reality television could follow people around like bad body odor.

All his bandmates had spent the night and now the game room looked like a demolition site. J. D. reached the top of the stairs and opened the door to the kitchen, where Rob stood at the island cooking bacon on an electric griddle. Rob's long hair looked stringy. They all looked like hell, probably. Rob flipped the thick strips with a fork; they were far tastier than the thin bacon they used to eat when they were just starting out and living in a basement apartment together in East Nashville. The smell of bacon had infused everything around them back then. The furniture. The paint on the walls. Jo's beautiful black hair. That shitty bacon was all they could afford then. The bacon Rob fried now came from a small organic farm here in Williamson County.

J. D. stood beside Rob and said, "A BLT is the finest of sandwiches, a truly brilliant construction. A suitable meal hours before the biggest career announcement of our lives. The BLT says, 'Yes, these boys have made it. They've really made it. No one can stop them. They're at the top.'"

Rob smiled but wouldn't look up. "Soaks up the liquor, man." Bacon grease popped and Rob shouted, "Hot damn." He used a kitchen towel to wipe his arm. Then he handed J. D. a head of iceberg lettuce. J. D. pulled off the lettuce leaves, ripping them in half and pressing them between two paper towels. Rob turned off the griddle and switched to slicing tomatoes.

J. D. moved toward a large basket wrapped in cellophane that had been placed on the side of the island. He opened the note on top of it all—thanks for coming on *The Late Show*. He peered through the clear wrap. High-fidelity portable speakers; cologne; fine chocolates; bottles of rare scotch, which J. D. never drank; and gift cards, along with some other stuff buried in there. He'd open it up later and let the guys pick out what they wanted. Donate the rest.

"My head hurts." J. D. pressed his fingers into his eyes to relieve the pressure.

"Mine too." Rob arranged the tomato slices on a platter and seasoned them with salt and pepper. "Country Music Hall of Fame. Two o'clock."

His housekeeper, Lydia, rolled a vacuum into the kitchen. "Grass everywhere," she said. "No more grass. Downstairs a mess too. You are blessed. Be neat."

"I know," J. D. said. "I'm sorry."

Lydia had emigrated from Poland after the Cold War, and she told J. D. horrible stories of the poverty she'd suffered, especially whenever she observed messy rooms or ungratefulness—J. D. had fifteen toilets; she'd had a pot. J. D. knew Lydia went door-to-door in Nashville on her days off handing out pamphlets and sharing the good news of Jesus Christ. Sometimes she left her damnation literature around the house, especially after hard nights of drinking, and the guys always complained. J. D. had asked her to stop and she hadn't done that in a long time, but J. D. appreciated that she had values. That she stood for something. Lydia often reminded him how lucky he was to have good friends, excellent health, and lots of money to give away if he chose, and she always encouraged him to donate to good causes. Lydia took every opportunity she could to remind him of why he was doing all this in the first place. His career was alive and well. His fans loved him. As long as he wasn't hurting anybody, he was happy enough.

Lydia switched on the vacuum and sucked up the trail of grass J. D. had tracked in on the bottom of his jeans.

"Don't let Chase B eat all that bacon," J. D. shouted. "Save me a sandwich."

"Will do," Rob shouted back.

J. D. used the elevator to ride up to his floor and take a shower. He passed the second floor, where his bandmate Aster stayed and where the other guys crashed after whiskey-drinking nights—Rob owned a house in Green Hills and Chase B and Danny lived in a condo overlooking the Cumberland River downtown, yet they all ended up at J. D.'s place more nights than not when they were taking a break from the road. When anyone questioned Aster about when he planned to move out of J. D.'s place, he'd say, "Why would I spend my hard-earned money on a house when everybody ends up staying out here anyway?" J. D. didn't argue. He was happy to have Aster as a roommate and he enjoyed when the guys stayed over. Otherwise the transitions from the tour bus to this empty house would be too hard on him. It was hard anyway without adding all that silence to it. The third floor of the house remained for guests, a recording studio, a music room full of the antique Dobros and fiddles he'd collected over the years, and a memorabilia room for his Grammys and his Oscar. The fourth floor belonged to him. J. D. showered and spent thirty minutes in the steamer. Shaved. Returned to his bedroom and tapped the room control panel to turn the south-facing windows from tinted to transparent glass, flooding his bedroom with sunlight. A lone hawk circled in the distance.

J. D. walked into his closet, selected his finest blue plaid shirt with pearl buttons, and put it on like an armor plate. Over this he buttoned a black leather vest. Then he chose his limited-edition dark-washed Wrangler jeans and black Ariat cowboy boots. He felt gratitude that he could wear jeans instead of the full-body rhinestone costumes Porter Wagoner wore in the seventies. Those suits had been steam-cleaned and were now on display at the Country Music Hall of Fame. J. D. slicked back his hair with pomade and put on his white Stetson hat. He was the face of the Stetson brand, so he could wear a different Stetson hat every single day of his life if he wanted to. Maybe someday this Stetson hat would be encased in glass at the Hall of Fame too. J. D. checked himself in the mirror. Flattened his collar. Shifted his hat forward. Folded his cuffs. This was who the boy had become. He wondered sometimes, though, if the boy would recognize the man.

The limo couldn't arrive soon enough to usher the band to the press conference. J. D. was done singing the same songs about regretting the past, loving his truck, and drinking beer on the weekends. J. D.'s next blockbuster album would surprise his fans, show them he was capable of writing his own music again. Prove that he hadn't just taken the easy way to easy money—or maybe he had, but he wouldn't any longer. Prove Floyd Masters wrong. The history of country music was full of fast-rising stars who burned out at the top. Couldn't sustain it, just like Floyd Masters. J. D. refused to be another one of those stories. Asphalt had done right by Jo Lover's music. They'd supported her vision and helped her stay close to her roots while growing her career. Asphalt could do right by the Empty Shells too. Maybe then Jo would respect him again.

J. D. picked up his phone to slip it in his pocket. But he paused. Told himself not to. He did it anyway. TMZ had already started calling them JoaNick. He clicked on images. Tabloid photos, mostly. The ring. Her left hand resting on Nick's chest. Perfect placement for the paparazzi. Her olive skin shone like copper; her inky-black hair looked as thick and soft as he remembered it. She still wore those busted-up red boots that she got the money for by stealing her daddy's moonshine and selling it to old man Garrick at the general store. J. D. wondered if Nick knew that story, wondered what she'd chosen to share with him about Gatesville. Jo had it hard back there, harder than anybody ever deserved. His red-winged blackbird. Best skeet shooter he knew and best whiskey drinker too. No singer could harmonize with him the way she could, and he doubted any singer ever would.

Jo had looked happy and settled when he saw her backstage at the Ryman last night. J. D. wished her every happiness possible, but he couldn't shake the feeling that when he hugged her, whatever had always been between them was still there. Only, she'd moved on from it and had learned, somehow, to love another man enough to share the rest of her life with him. J. D. dated but nothing ever lasted. He wished he could forget the connection between them, wished he could let go of his love for her for good, but he still hadn't figured out how to do that.

CHAPTER 10

Back in Time

A T THE EDGE of downtown Nashville, the murky Cumberland
River glided along, as if it knew it would flow forever and had no
need to rush. From the rooftop of the Asphalt building, Jo watched as
people strolled on the pedestrian bridge above the river, some alone,
some coupled, all very small from this vantage point. Jo had the strange
sensation of feeling like nothing and everything all at once, of being the
seer and the unseen. What conversations engaged them, what thoughts
repeated in their minds? What could it possibly matter if she could
never know? And what chance did she have to know, separated as she
was way up here, and waiting?

The afternoon sun gave off ambient light in its noon position in a
cloudless sky. The fully exposed sun made her grateful for the shade
of the canopy she stood beneath. Marie, who had been late to work
for the first time this morning, would be back any minute with the
journalist from *Vanity Fair*. Down in the lobby, swarms of reporters in-

terviewed Mr. Sullivan about his upcoming announcement at the Hall of Fame, thanks to Floyd Masters, who'd broken the story on his show this morning.

How would she be able to concentrate in this interview? Jo hoped they'd stick to the same old topics about her skin-care routine, her mountain-girl style, her music, and her struggles with dieting and staying in kick-ass shape in her thirties. With *Cosmo* and *Redbook* it was always about body image and the possibility of kids. *Ms.* focused on her songwriting, her journey, and being a strong role model for young women. *Playboy* and *GQ* asked questions about her sassy attitude and dating life.

Jo ate blueberries and drank coconut water. It had been Mr. Sullivan's idea to switch the interview to the rooftop garden, where it was hot as Hades, even under the shade cover. The breeze whipped strands of hair to the front of her face. They stuck to her red lip gloss. She should've made a few adjustments to her makeup before coming up here. She'd chosen to wear a pair of dark blue jeans with holes in the knees, her white COUNTRY MUSIC FOREVER tank top, and her red boots. The style consultant had disliked all of Jo's selections for today and gave up on her after an hour, too tired to keep fighting with her about the tank top. She wore a silver cuff on each wrist, onyx rings, her engagement ring, and a silver tree pendant necklace, all made by jewelers from Virginia, except the engagement ring, of course, which was an heirloom piece from Nick's family. It was a platinum ring with a seven-carat, Asscher-cut diamond surrounded by one hundred and fifty round, brilliant cut diamonds and sapphire accents. It was prettier than any ring she'd ever seen before. Jo could hardly believe it belonged to her, like the ring was on loan and would be due back at the store any day now.

Jo turned to the sound of the metal rooftop door banging against the brick wall. She was certain her manager, Evelyn, had told her a woman's name. But maybe she'd heard wrong. A wisp of a guy with a thick black beard and black rectangular glasses walked toward her. He wore jeans too, and a Grand Ole Opry T-shirt. Jo stood up from the teak love seat and extended a hand to him.

He wiped his palm on his jeans before he shook it. "Bryan Lein," he said. "Sorry for the last-minute change. Big fan of country music though, all the same."

"Love your T-shirt. Looks like we match."

Bryan stared at her through his thick lenses, which had a peculiar effect of shrinking his eyes.

With a folder of Jo's life clutched to her chest, Marie said, "May I bring you an iced coffee or water?"

"No thanks," Bryan said.

Jo sat back down on the love seat and watched Marie walk away. Jo called, "Hey, Marie. Please check and see if that tuning peg's fixed on the Gibson."

"No problem," Marie said before she closed the door to the rooftop.

Bryan sat in the bright green Adirondack chair across from her and placed his legal pad in the empty space on the table before him. At the top of the pad he wrote: *Interview with Joanne Lover, Asphalt Records, May 15.* He pulled out a digital recorder from his jeans pocket. "I'll ask questions here. We'll take photos later."

"Sounds good." Jo pushed her palms onto her knees to keep her legs from bouncing. Reporters made her nervous—you never knew what they were thinking until they published the story. Not once had it turned out exactly the way Jo thought it would. Bryan would shape her with his words, and readers would believe whatever version of her he printed. She had to be cautious not to reveal too much about herself in interviews, or else risk the tabloid magazines' publishing unflattering pictures of her face accompanied by a quote taken way out of context. Some truths about a person's life should remain secret, for the sake of others.

He clicked on the recorder. "First of all, congratulations on your engagement."

"Thank you."

"Can we expect a little Sullivan running around soon?"

"Doubtful," Jo said, and she knew it sounded sharp.

Bryan put his palms up like he needed to protect himself. "Had to ask."

Jo wiped her forehead with the back of her hand.

"So I had the chance to interview Nick Sullivan for an article a few years ago, right after he won his third Grammy. The guy's a visionary and a very busy producer in this business. Can you tell me a little about how you two met and how he agreed to work with you on your debut album?"

Bryan was skipping the nice-and-easy warm-up part and jumping right to the personal stuff. She'd expected some style questions about her favorite eyeliner and lipstick. Maybe he'd make all that up when he sat down to write the piece. Jo needed to settle in for this interview, appear as casual as possible: "So, Nick and I met years ago at the Thirsty Baboon, a great music venue and dive bar here in Nashville. I didn't know who he was, if you can believe that."

"That is hard to believe."

"He came to see some of my shows around town. Eventually he asked me to come by his studio to see what we might come up with together."

Bryan smiled like she was insinuating more than she intended. He wrote something down on his legal pad.

"Critics have praised you for the richness of your music with such minimal equipment. You don't use a band on every track. Was this Nick's idea, or yours, or a combination?"

Jo almost asked him why he would credit Nick first. Instead, she said, "I've always been interested in how big a sound I could make. I grew up around a very large family. My aunt and uncle lived next door with nine kids, and they were always at my house for dinner and then again at breakfast, and I was the oldest, so I was always changing a diaper or holding somebody. Plus I had my brother and little sister to look after. I had lots of responsibilities and wasn't allowed to make much noise. This is my childhood play, I guess."

Bryan nodded his head like it all made sense. She liked that. He looked up at her, adjusted himself in the chair, and leaned forward. "With Nick's production company supporting you, you could've signed with any label you wanted. You had offers from Solar and Universal. Why'd you choose his father's company? Were you two dating at the time?"

Jo tilted her head to the side. An odd question: no one had posed it to her in this way before. Most people considered choosing an independent label over a corporate label an inherent good, but he seemed to be suggesting she'd used her relationship to advance her career. "Asphalt offered me the best deal, for what I needed at that time in my life."

Jo's shoulders were aching. Journalists were supposed to be kind to their subjects. Or polite, at the very least. Why did this exchange feel so contentious? He might have been a fan of country music, but she had the feeling he wasn't a fan of hers. Jo eyed the door to the rooftop and wished Marie would return so she could have a witness.

"The Nashville sound has been dominated lately by a lot of male artists. Critics claim you've captured the attention of thirty- and forty-something female listeners. Do you think your recent campaign against male songwriters and performers has anything to do with that?"

She'd been responding to this question a lot lately, so she was prepared. "First," Jo said, and scooted to the edge of her couch, "I think women just like the music. Teenagers attend my shows too, for whatever that's worth. With that said, they probably listen to male country groups too, like J. D. Gunn and the Empty Shells. As for a campaign, I don't think that's what I'm up to. A campaign is intentional." Before he could respond, she continued. "Women respond to my music. They're way beyond the first heartbreak of high school or wanting to be seen as an object of lust in a country song. I speak to them where they are."

"Could speaking out backfire?"

"I don't see how."

"Does it make you feel pressure to live up to an ideal of who a woman's supposed to be?" Bryan held his hand over the legal pad, ready to catch whatever she did or didn't say.

Jo laughed. "Who is a woman supposed to be?" Jo was trying to maintain her composure and good manners, but it was growing harder by the minute.

"You tell me," he said. "Who is Jo Lover?"

A crow, bigger than any she'd ever seen before, its feathers iridescent, alighted on the tall circular table behind Bryan's chair and turned in profile. Jo stared above Bryan's head and into the one beady eye staring back at her. Every spring season of her childhood, she'd seen crows snatch baby birds from their nests and fly away from the bushes to have those little birds for dinner. Their bony bodies fit neatly inside the predator's talons. Each time she saw it happen she felt like she was witnessing an injustice, yet it was business as usual in the natural world. The mama bird might fuss but beyond that there could be no recourse. Jo had learned, eventually, to stop looking for it. The crow turned its head so both eyes faced her, as if prompting her to speak.

"What you see is what you get. But it's not about me. It's about the industry at large. It's about big radio and DJs thinking that most of the songs they play must be sung by male performers if they want to make any money. It's about how women are portrayed as one-dimensional in country music songs. Short skirts, bodies like Coke bottles, sitting in a truck cab like a pet and not a person. Always in need of saving by a burly man in a white T-shirt and a Stetson hat. There's always been plenty of hardworking women in country music. Gillian Welch is a poet. As are Alison Krauss, Reba McEntire, Emmylou Harris, Dolly Parton, Patsy Cline, Tammy Wynette, Loretta Lynn, and Kitty Wells, just to name a few."

"But you're speaking out in a way they didn't."

"I don't know about that. Loretta spoke out. What people did with what they heard is a whole different issue."

Bryan leaned back in his chair. The crow lifted off the table and a gentle wind from its wings reached Jo. Bryan turned and looked behind him, but the bird was already gone.

"One thing your fans love most are your red boots. They feel like those boots define who you are and your music. What's the story behind them?"

Jo ran her nails through her hair, tossed it to the side before she said, "My mama and daddy bought them for my sweet sixteenth birthday."

"That was a good present."

"It was."

"In other interviews you've avoided talking in-depth about your childhood in Gatesville."

Jo said, "Now, Bryan, you know that's flat-out not true. I've talked about my childhood many times in other interviews."

"Would you be willing to go into more detail for *Vanity Fair*?"

Why on earth had this guy been assigned to her? She stared at the sky, blue as a robin's egg. She had an answer rehearsed, which was the answer he'd probably read before, the answer he didn't want now, but it was the most she was willing to give him.

"There's not too much to tell. I guess that's why I don't talk about it at length. Pretty normal childhood. Gatesville Baptist Church on Sunday and Wednesday. That's where I got into singing. A good mama and daddy. Hardworking. Never enough money, but we made do. Lots of kids running around. Lots of mountain music played on porches. You knew your neighbor'd be baling up hay in the summer and another neighbor'd have fresh eggs if your chickens went on strike. Mailbox posts were fashioned from welded chains that rusted up real good in a year. The temperature could drop suddenly, especially in the spring. And the heavy wind was like a musical instrument. I always had chapped cheeks from the wind. Lots of waterfalls and creeks to play in. I spent as much of my time outside as I could. With so many people in a tiny house, it was the only space I had to myself. I was a happy kid all in all."

Bryan wrote down more notes. "Anything else you wish to add?"

"I mean, there were bad things too—" Jo paused to consider whether she should reveal this next bit. He was pressing for something new about her, and she figured this part couldn't haunt her in any way. "My older brother, Martin, was born mentally challenged. He was hit by a train and killed after I left home for Nashville."

"I'm sorry to hear that."

She'd never shared this truth before. Martin was just a couple years older than Jo but as innocent as a three-year-old. He'd gotten stuck during his delivery and didn't have enough oxygen. That was the story her mama told, anyway. But Jo always suspected it had something to do with her drinking too. Her breast milk was too toxic for Martin. He was her first, and it took her making his life what it was for her to figure it out. Her mama gave up moonshine for good and found the Lord before she became pregnant again. Jo often felt guilty that Martin had to suffer the consequences of her mama's bad decisions. Jo took the best care of him, never let anyone make fun of him in her presence or get in a fight with him, if she could help it.

Jo drank her coconut water, and the heat was almost too much to take. She said, "You know, there were hard times. Of course there were. We were poor as pickup sticks. But mountain people know how to rally. Mostly it was boring. I was given my first fiddle by a church member, and my parents let me play it outside where I couldn't bother everybody."

While Bryan was distracted with transcribing her words, she sent Marie a text and asked her to come.

"You were in a band with J. D. Gunn when he was discovered?"

Jo nodded. "The Sojourners. Awful band name and we knew it."

"You two were dating."

"He came out to Nashville first, and then me and his bandmate Rob joined him later. We all grew up together."

"But I'm correct about you all living together and being in a band together when he was discovered?"

"Yep."

"Were you surprised by his sudden success?"

"Not at all." She hoped her shortened answers would give him the hint to move on from this subject.

"Why didn't you stay with the band?"

"He went out to LA by himself for a while. I tried a solo thing here. The rest of the guys went out to join him eventually, but I didn't want to move to LA. How could anyone leave Nashville?"

"But you and J. D. Gunn were in a relationship at that time, correct?"

"Way back when."

"Some people have speculated that quite a few songs on your albums are about him, but you've never given a direct answer. Care to clarify?"

"No," Jo said. "I don't think I do."

"So, as you've probably heard by now, J. D. Gunn and the Empty Shells are set to join your label. Any chance of a band reunion in the future?"

"That's all a rumor still, Bryan."

"Pretty confirmed."

Jo smiled but refused to comment any further.

Bryan lifted a page on his notepad and reviewed what he'd written. "You donate a tremendous about of time and money to the Battered Women's Shelter of Nashville, headquartered here in Nashville. Can you tell me a little about why you've chosen that charity to support?"

Jo drank her water and then said, "I've met women there who've been hurt their entire lives. Physically and sexually abused by the people closest to them in this world, but they manage to keep on living. To keep being positive. That's real courage. I'm fortunate enough that nothing half as bad has ever happened to me."

Bryan's hand hovered over his notepad like a helicopter.

"Need me to repeat that?"

"No, I have it." He looked up finally. "Last question."

"Sure."

"Any secrets you wish to reveal about your workout routine? What keeps Jo Lover in such great shape?"

"Watch what I eat and do whatever my personal trainer says to do. He's the only person in this world who can boss me around. He's given me the week off, actually. I guess learning to take a break is important too."

Bryan smiled, and then he clicked off his tape recorder and gathered his stuff. "I think I have all I need. My photographer will take a few shots."

"Of course," Jo said. She stood up, as did he.

He stared at her for a moment, as if weighing a possibility, and then said, "May I ask you a question, completely off the record?"

"I don't know about that."

"You don't have to answer but it might interest you."

"Okay." Jo scratched her cheek with her nails and then crossed her arms.

"It's based on a couple testimonies from people in your hometown."

Jo forced herself to remain poised and unaffected. "Gatesville?"

Bryan adjusted the strap of his leather satchel on his shoulder. He shielded the sun from his eyes with his notebook. "They say you left behind a child in Gatesville to come to Nashville and pursue a singing career."

Jo opened her coconut water, looked Bryan in the eyes, and drank the bottle in full while he stared at her. She screwed the top back on and said, "You know, I consider *Vanity Fair* to be one of the better magazines, as far as the quality of the reporting goes. I never figured they'd waste time with small-town rumors."

"Like I said, it's off the record." He tucked his notebook into his satchel.

"Not only is that not true," Jo said, "it's malicious. And where exactly did I leave this supposed child? In a ditch?"

Without hesitating, Bryan said, "With your mother."

Jo breathed in slowly, and then she said, "Have you ever been to a real small Southern town, Bryan?"

He nodded.

"Ever lived in one?"

Bryan put on his silver aviator sunglasses. "I have not."

"Well that's it then. You just don't know that there's a long story about each and every person who lives in a small town like Gatesville. And there are bigger stories about anybody who manages to make it out."

"I understand," Bryan said.

Marie pushed open the door to the rooftop, and as Jo waited for her to walk over, she said, "I do appreciate you mentioning that to me though, Bryan. It's good to know what's circulating out there."

"No problem," he said.

Marie smiled at Bryan and then offered them both a coconut water. "No thanks," Bryan said.

Jo opened a new one and drank it down immediately.

"Jo has a lunch meeting scheduled for today, Mr. Lein."

"Do we have time for a few pictures?" he said.

"Of course," Marie said. "We can do it up here, if you'd like."

"I'll text my guy and see what he thinks." Bryan reached out to shake hands with Jo.

"So nice to meet you," Jo said.

"Good luck with your next album. I'll let you know when the article's finished." Bryan let go of her hand and left to go fetch the photographer. Jo wiped the sweat from his palm on her jeans.

Marie said, "The car's ready to take you over to Jack's once you're done. How'd it go?"

Jo sat back down on the love seat and stared straight ahead. "Please go down there and tell him there's no time for pictures. Then call my manager and cancel the article completely."

Marie sat down beside Jo. "What happened?"

"It's just something about him."

"Okay," Marie said, but Jo could hear the confusion in her voice. "I'll take care of it."

"Thank you." Jo waited for Marie to walk away before she let out a deep breath. Jo needed a few minutes alone before going to lunch with Nick and Mr. Sullivan. No reporter had ever pushed her so hard about her childhood and J. D., and she disliked feeling mistreated. He'd wasted her time too. She owed him nothing. And a spread in *Vanity Fair* wasn't worth the PR headache that would come if he wrote a story he couldn't confirm just to sell a magazine. Jo sent Nick a text to let him know she'd be on her way to lunch in the next hour or so. She glanced up at the sky once more, at the gray cumulus clouds gathering on the horizon. Jo tapped on the search bar in the browser on her phone and typed in her name, "abandoned child," "left behind," and "Gatesville." Pages and pages of links about her engagement announcement to Nick and her induction into the Opry. Jo made it to page thirty-six before the links switched to No Child Left Behind education policies. She gave up. Nothing of what Bryan suggested was out there. Absolutely nothing.

CHAPTER 11

Bar-B-Que

AT JACK'S BAR-B-QUE on Broadway, seated in a booth across from Mr. Sullivan, Jo watched as he bit into a brisket sandwich, the red sauce dripping down his fingers toward his starched cuffs. He caught it with a napkin before it could sully his shirt. He'd already taken off his yellow silk tie, placed it on the vinyl seat beside him, and unbuttoned his collar. He said, "Good God almighty, I didn't think I'd make it out of that lobby today. Rabid reporters, I tell you. Rabid. I'm amazed they didn't invite themselves to lunch. My driver took a very long route here."

Mr. Sullivan scooped up a forkful of baked beans and chewed what seemed like an endless number of times. Jo began to count but then made herself stop. The jaw joint pushed outward from underneath his skin as he worked on the meat next. Jo looked over Mr. Sullivan's shoulder to see if Nick had made it any further in the line to order their food. He had not.

Mr. Sullivan paused before filling his fork again. "You're awful quiet."

Jo sipped her sweet iced tea too hard. Lemon pulp stopped up the straw.

"Guess what?"

She raised her eyebrows.

"Got you an interview with *Rolling Stone.*"

Jo put her cup down and pushed it away from her. She wasn't ready to think about another interview. "Thank you," she said.

"I thought you'd be more excited." Mr. Sullivan leaned back in the booth and stretched his long arms out beside him. He smiled at her with a knowing pride. He and Nick had that same way about them. "You're on a roll. Forgive the pun." Then he leaned forward again and took a bite of coleslaw. White drops of dressing missed his mouth and landed on the table next to his plate.

Jo looked past Mr. Sullivan to see Nick standing in the cafeteria-style line at the glass partition, waiting to order their usual plates of pulled pork and three sides.

Mr. Sullivan wiped his mouth with his napkin. "How was *Vanity Fair?*"

"Fine," she said. Jo wound the paper from her straw around her pinky finger until the skin turned red as a raspberry. "Didn't ask me anything about my next album."

He nodded, scooped baked beans into his mouth, and waved his hand in the air like he was conducting an orchestra. "Reporter will follow you all day for this one though. I'll have him out to the estate with you and Nick."

"Why not my house?"

"Let's bring them out to the wedding site. Talk about the upcoming nuptials. Maybe they can take pictures of you shooting skeet or some-thing. Let your fans know you're not going soft just because you're getting married. You and Nick can talk about the collaboration process for the different albums. They'll eat it up. Talk about the next album too. With all the press you're getting right now, people are waiting for it. There's no way it won't be huge, not with Nick producing it."

Mr. Sullivan had made this insinuation about her music multi-ple times before, as if any solo artist who had teamed up with Nick would've done just as well. Sometimes, though, she feared what he sug-gested was true, that the reason her albums had had any success at all was due to Nick's talent more than her own.

"How does that sound?" Mr. Sullivan said.

"Makes sense, I guess."

"That's my girl," he said, and patted her hand. Mr. Sullivan wiped away the barbecue sauce from the corner of his mouth with a napkin.

Nick approached their booth. He carried two plates of their usual order: baked beans, slaw, and pulled pork smothered with Jack's special sauce. He placed the plates on the table and squeezed into the booth next to Jo.

"It's always so much food," Jo said.

"They're generous." Mr. Sullivan finished the rest of his sandwich.

Nick poured sauce on his beans and stirred them around. "What'd I miss?"

"*Rolling Stone* wants to interview your girl here." Mr. Sullivan wiped his fingers with a napkin.

"That's excellent," Nick said. He put his arm around Jo, brought her in close, and kissed her temple.

After Jo topped her pulled pork with slaw, she smashed the sand-wich bun down until she'd nearly flattened it.

"Be nice to it," Nick said.

Jo took a big bite.

"I have another surprise for you." Mr. Sullivan ripped open the Wet-Nap packet and cleaned his hands one finger at a time. "Loretta Lynn and Jack White canceled their spot for the MusiCares fund-raiser."

"Oh, no," Jo said. "Why?"

"She's got laryngitis."

"Poor Loretta."

"Big concert to cancel," Mr. Sullivan said.

That much was true. The annual MusiCares concert was a major industry-wide event where the best of the best in music entertainment—pop, rap, country, indie, rock—came together to celebrate musicians and their collective art form. It was a red-carpet, invite-only event like the Grammys, except more music legends, like Bob Dylan, attended since the show was for a good cause. Nick had a schedule conflict this year so they'd decided not to go. More than anything, she wanted to play that concert. She wanted to be introduced to the entire music world as a big player. She could hear the announcer saying, "Please welcome Joanne Lover to the stage."

"Are we planning to go now or something?" Jo said, and looked at Nick to see if he'd changed his plans, but he looked just as unsure of what his father was saying.

Mr. Sullivan clapped his hands together. "So that's the surprise, my dear. It's your turn."

Jo let out a shout. "You're serious?"

Mr. Sullivan nodded. Jo felt like this was an act of reconciliation, an olive branch for the way the J. D. Gunn deal was handled. She laughed and said, "I owe you so big. It's tomorrow night?" Jo pushed away her plate of food. She was too excited now to eat.

"Jo's the country music headliner?" Nick said. He seemed the least excited of them all.

Mr. Sullivan tempered his smile. "J. D. Gunn and the Empty Shells will be there too."

"That's what I thought," Nick said.

Jo eased back in the booth, holding her red plastic cup in one hand, swirling the tea around like a tornado. She tried to control her tone, but she had very little willpower now. She'd been pushed too much today, and now this? She said, "I won't open for him. It'll be an endorsement."

Nick said, "Jo deserves to headline that show."

Mr. Sullivan folded his hands together and bowed his head a moment before he said, "I want to showcase my two best artists on that stage. I don't know how else to say this, so I'll say it bluntly, out of respect for you: both of you know J. D. Gunn and the Empty Shells can't open for you, Jo. Maybe one or two more albums in the future, and they will. But that's not where we are in your career right now. So if you want to take part in this concert, which won't be an endorsement of any kind but will certainly expand your audience reach, then I'll announce it at the press conference. If not I'm happy to invite the Wayward Sisters, a choice I imagine you'd support, though it does seem like a huge opportunity for you to pass up."

Nick crossed his arms and leveled his stare at his father like a shotgun. "She won't do it."

"I'm certain you have her best career interests in mind, son, but why don't we let her decide?" Mr. Sullivan said.

As much as she wanted to deny it and accuse Mr. Sullivan of being a coercive sack of Music Row business shit, she knew what he said was true: MusiCares was too big to say no to.

"Jo?" Nick said, and now they were both staring at her.

"I'll do it."

Nick turned to her and gave her the most disappointed look she'd ever seen.

"Wise choice, I think," Mr. Sullivan said. "Will you come, Nick?"

"I fly to New York this afternoon."

Jo said, "Can you reschedule?"

"I can't." Nick removed his arm from around her shoulders. "This band's too promising."

"You'll see her play next time. And maybe in a venue you approve of. If it's worth anything at all, Jo, I think you made the right decision." Mr. Sullivan slipped his tie back on and buttoned up his collar slowly. He picked up his phone. "I'll have a car scoop you up tomorrow at one thirty PM to bring you to the airport."

Jo nodded.

Nick said, "You invited us to talk about the wedding."

"Right. I know." He put his phone away and raised his hands up like he was innocent. "Still Water Estate, then, for the big hoorah? You agree?"

"We did," Nick said.

"This wedding planner's breathing down my neck hard. Thinking about asking her out."

"Dad—"

"Yes, I know. You hate that kind of talk."

"Just focus."

"Nothing to focus on. Jo agreed so I'll send the plans through. You two don't worry about a thing. I'm happy to be the liaison."

Jo had been around them long enough to know it was best to stay quiet when they interacted like this.

"Did you agree to a date yet?"

Jo said, "Any time after the summer tour. October. November."

"October," Nick said.

"Good," Mr. Sullivan said. "The sooner, the better. You know the ditty: first comes love, then comes marriage, then comes Nicholas Sullivan the Fifth in the baby carriage."

Jo breathed in slowly. Nick massaged his forehead with his hand.

Mr. Sullivan said, "What? No applause?"

Jo had plenty going on in her life and career at the moment, and birthing an heir was the last concern on her list. If only she could tell him this. Nick too, though to his credit, he'd finally backed off from the future-progeny discussions. Not yet—that was her one and only response.

Mr. Sullivan checked his watch and then said, "The wedding planner would like to meet with you, Jo."

"Tell her as soon as I have a free afternoon we'll meet."

"You know I'm happy to help in any way I can. You're family now." He stood up from the table, put on his dark blue blazer, and adjusted the sleeves before he fixed the lapels. "I've got to meet the company lawyers in twenty. No time for banana pudding, I'm afraid. Eat a portion for me."

Jo never ate dessert. Less time she'd have to suffer with her trainer.

Mr. Sullivan said, "You think you'll start calling me by my first name before you start calling me Dad?"

"Probably not," Jo said.

"Good to see you, son. Have fun in New York."

Nick nodded. Mr. Sullivan waved at the countermen before exiting onto Broadway, the bell on the door signaling his departure. A clip of a song from the bar next door entered through the open door but then disappeared once the door closed.

Nick said, "He wears me out."

Jo used her straw to chisel through the clump of ice in her cup.

"Are you finished?"

"I am," she said, though she'd only taken one bite.

Nick balled up a napkin and dropped it in the center of his plate. "If J. D. hits on you tomorrow, tell him to go fuck himself."

Jo paused. His change in tone alarmed her. "You're not really worried about that?"

Nick stood up, offering his hand. "I saw the way he was looking at you at the Ryman."

"Don't be ridiculous." She let him help her up from the booth. Nick pushed the metal bar on the glass door and led them out of Jack's. Together they stepped out into the sweltering midday heat of Broadway, the Asphalt rooftop looming in the distance. In every direction she looked, tourists moved up and down the sidewalks, past the cowboy hat and boot shops, past the souvenir shops peddling whiskey shot glasses, past the bar signs, past the sounds of cover bands singing "Wagon Wheel" to people drinking tequila in the middle of the day. Jo detected the ever-present scent of urine from last night's shenanigans.

Nick stopped her and pulled her into an embrace. "You know I love you."

She held him tighter. "You don't need to worry about J. D., okay? All that's in the past, and I know he feels the same way." Jo's town car pulled to the curb.

"Will you call me after the show?"

She nodded. "Wish you'd change your mind and come." Jo wanted him to tell her that he might not agree with her choice but he understood as well as she did that going to LA tomorrow was the right decision to make for her career.

Nick opened the car door for her and kissed her on the cheek before she entered the backseat. Nick said hello to her driver while she buckled her seat belt, and then he shut her door. Nick waited on the curb until her car started moving. She waved good-bye to him, and then he turned from her and disappeared into the throng of tourists headed toward Fifth Avenue. Jo hated feeling like he was mad or disappointed with her. And since Nick avoided confrontation at all costs, she figured he'd never tell her how he felt either way, leaving her to stew in it.

CHAPTER 12

Back at the Baboon

DENVER HAD SPENT most of his morning at the Country Music Hall of Fame thinking about Marie, wondering where she was and who she was with, and organizing the early recordings of the Grand Ole Opry in chronological order for the audio lab. Once Mr. Sullivan from Asphalt Records and J. D. Gunn and the Empty Shells showed up, his work shut down. Reporters filled the atrium like locusts. Everybody in that building wanted to hear what they had to say, and, in fact, all the rumors had turned out to be true: that they were dropping Solar for Asphalt, that they were getting thirty million dollars over the next three years. Only the biggest band in country music had the power to make that move. Denver couldn't believe that the same day Floyd Masters had endorsed the Flyby Boys, he'd also broken the news about the J. D. Gunn deal. Denver decided to take that as a very good sign indeed.

During the press conference, Denver stood in the back of the lobby so he wouldn't be shoulder to shoulder with eager reporters. Platinum and gold records lined the wall above the fountain next to where they'd set up the podium. J. D. Gunn and his bandmates stood together next to Asphalt's CEO. The boys were wearing their finest country gear, Denver could tell. J. D. Gunn looked groomed by the biggest western-wear brands from the top down—bright white Stetson hat, probably pulled out of the box that morning; Wrangler jeans; black cowboy boots finer than any Denver had ever seen before. Denver dreamed of being signed to a label like Asphalt, with a big announcement made in the foyer of the museum. That's why he'd come to Nashville after college, for something like that to happen to him and Alan.

J. D. Gunn put an arm around Mr. Sullivan as he said, "Me and the boys are ready to start a new chapter in our career. We're grateful for everything Solar did for us as a young band, but now we're ready to see what kind of new music we can make with Asphalt."

Reporters' arms flew into the air after he spoke, all of them wanting to know what kind of response they could expect from Solar, but Mr. Sullivan promised everything about the deal and the contract resolution was sound.

Denver had heard all he wanted to hear, and he drove away from downtown wondering what it must be like to have that kind of exposure. Denver passed the towering AT&T building, dubbed the Batman Building, with its two sharp spindles rising toward the clouds. It was the most defining aspect of Nashville's skyline—the very first thing he noticed when he came to town from Knoxville. Now it loomed there for him. His life looked the same as it had two years ago; he was still working during the day for little to nothing and playing gigs at house parties and small bars like Santa's Pub, the 5 Spot, and the Thirsty Baboon.

He crossed the Cumberland River and entered the Five Points neighborhood. He parked in the gravel lot of the Thirsty Baboon. The pimiento-cheese-colored building looked much different in the daylight, more run-down, more beat up. It stood alone in a neighborhood of newly constructed condo units and trendy pour-over coffeehouses with brewing techniques that sounded like a Ford engine—V60, anyone? Where Denver came from people made pots of coffee from Mr. Coffee himself. It cost a dollar at a diner, not six at a shop. More and more it seemed like the Thirsty Baboon was the last shithole dive in this entire neighborhood, the last place where great music still mattered.

Buster, an ex–running back for the Tennessee Titans and the younger of the two brothers who owned the place, wiped down the bar top with a rag tinged gray by too many years of laundering. He waved at Denver. Reruns of *Hee Haw* played on the cube television mounted in the corner above the bar. The whole place was an homage to *Hee Haw*. Framed autographed pictures of the storied talent who'd played at the Baboon filled the walls. He'd just seen J. D. Gunn in the flesh at the Country Music Hall of Fame, and now his black and white headshot looked back at Denver, his autograph scribbled with a Sharpie. Maybe Denver and Alan would have their faces on the wall someday too.

"You forget something last night?" Buster tossed the rag at the red bleach bucket but missed and bent down to put it where it belonged.

"No."

He stood back up. "Good show, by the way."

"Thanks," Denver said. "And hey, did you notice that girl that came in with the Wayward Sisters last night? She was short, had blond hair. Pixie cut. Any chance you know who she is?"

Buster looked bewildered. "Pixie cut?"

"You know, really short hair. Really short."

Buster stared at him like he still had no idea. He popped open a Lone Star can and handed it to Denver. "Can't say I remember."

He knew it was a long shot, but Denver had thought it was worth coming over here and trying anyway. Denver held on to the back of the leather arm of the stool in front of him.

"Sit down and stay awhile," Buster said.

"Just this one."

"That's what he said." Buster pointed to one corner of the bar and there sat Floyd Masters. Denver hadn't noticed him sitting in the shadows when he walked in. He'd been too occupied with finding Marie. Floyd wore a blue denim shirt embroidered with red roses but no cowboy hat. He slouched over his Schlitz can like it needed protection, ate pretzel sticks, and stared at *Hee Haw*.

Buster said, "Slickest voice you've never heard on country radio."

Denver expected Floyd to yell at Buster, but he remained still.

"You hear me, you deaf sack of shit?"

Floyd tossed a pretzel stick over his shoulder.

"Don't go wasting the snacks now. I'll cut you off."

Without looking Floyd threw another pretzel right at Buster and this time hit him on the forehead.

Denver stared at this country music legend at the end of the bar—Floyd Masters had been an outlaw writing songs at Tootsie's Orchid Lounge on Broadway in the sixties well before Waylon and Willie exchanged their gray-flannel-suit shtick for outlaw jeans and vests in the seventies, well before Johnny was known as the Man in Black. Rumor had it that Floyd Masters was a mean drunk. He'd been into lots of bad stuff in his day. Coke, heroin, speed, downers, everything. Lost his entire empire. He was spread too thin, had too many salaries on the payroll. Moved into recording and production. Sent all his profits up his nose. Couldn't recover the way Waylon did. Couldn't start over. But he was a legend in some circles. He was a legend to Denver. Mostly his work was already forgotten, rarely got any radio play on the classic stations here. Supposedly, he was bigger than Willie and Waylon in Central and South America, but for all Denver knew, Floyd might've started that rumor himself. This small, white-haired old guy at the end of the bar wasn't living up to any bit of that reputation.

Denver waited for Floyd to move or say something more, but he seemed transfixed by the women in pigtails singing in front of fake cornstalks. Denver leaned over to Buster and whispered, "Does he always come here?"

"Yep."

"How come I've never seen him?"

Buster took a shot of whiskey and then tossed the empty bottle in the trash can. "When are you ever here when the sun's out, Denver?" Buster lifted the bar top to his right to let himself out and passed behind Denver's bar stool. "You need another beer, help yourself."

Denver said, "Think I could talk to him?"

"At your own risk, kid."

Denver watched Buster walk to the back of the bar, past the scuffed-up pool tables that tilted to the left. Couldn't get a fair game here. Maybe nowhere in Nashville. Buster opened the closet where a Kenny Rogers poster hung. Denver swiveled his chair around and crossed the black and white checkered floor marred by boot marks. He placed his free hand on the top of the neon orange jukebox. Everyone could agree on Hank Williams. He picked "I'll Be a Bachelor 'Til I Die" to start it off and then returned to his seat at the bar.

He wanted to thank Floyd for mentioning his band on his show.

Thousands of devoted country and Americana fans listened to him. If Alan were here, he'd go right up to him and just thank him. If Alan had been at the Country Music Hall of Fame earlier and had been that close to the CEO of Asphalt Records, he would've told him that he should listen to their LP, that they would be a great addition to the label. As he considered all the possible things he could say to Floyd Masters, Denver lost his nerve to say anything.

Floyd picked out a pretzel stick from the bowl and examined it, only to toss it back in. "Sorry damn time to try to make it in music, kid."

Denver paused midsip. Then he put his beer down on the wooden bar. "My buddy and I played here last night. You mentioned us. The Flyby Boys, I mean. You mentioned the Flyby Boys on your show this morning. We're really—"

Floyd waved his hand at Denver like he'd heard enough talk and turned back to *Hee Haw*. A shadowy figure blocked the doorway. Denver looked over to see Buster's older brother charging into the place. Sean came right up to him. "Is Buster in the shitter?"

"He's in the back." Denver pointed to the Kenny Rogers closet, right when Buster was heading back to the front with cases of PBR and Jack Daniel's stacked ten high.

"We need to talk," Sean said.

"I can go," Denver said.

Sean said, "No, you stay. Floyd, you listen too."

"I don't care about any of it," Floyd said.

"Damn it, yes you do," Sean said. "This affects everybody."

Floyd continued to watch *Hee Haw*.

Sean said, "The landlord's right outside."

"Speaking of that asshole," Buster muttered.

A lanky middle-aged guy in bright cream khaki pants, penny loafers, and a baby-blue button-up walked through the door. He carried a leather satchel in one hand and his iPhone in the other. He finished looking at the screen and slipped his phone into his pocket.

Sean went behind the bar to help Buster stock it. "We've got people coming in soon. Whatever you need to say you better say it."

"In front of your customers?"

"Damn right. This matters to them too."

The guy glanced around the room as if nothing in a place like this could possibly matter to a normal person. He removed a manila folder from his satchel and offered it to Buster, who didn't accept it and instead stocked bottles against the mirrored wall. The landlord dropped it on the bar top next to Denver's beer can. Denver read the white label on the front of the folder: "Phased Plan for Vacating Current Tenant."

"You can take that right home with you and wipe your ass with it. We ain't going anywhere," Buster said.

"You knew this could happen. The neighborhood's outpricing you and I'm selling. That's the end of it."

"We're gonna buy it from you."

The landlord laughed uncomfortably, and then he rolled up his sleeves. "I'm worried about you guys if you're still thinking like this. I'm willing to be flexible, to a point."

"Yeah you are," Buster said. "Look at how easy you bend over."

"Fuck you, Buster."

"Fuck you, you sellout. Just so they can put another ugly condo building here? That's what the city of Nashville needs. More shiny new condos. Fuck the bars and shops where the best songwriters and musicians got their start, where they bought their first guitars and hats. Screw all that history."

"One more month to figure out your plans," the landlord said. He'd gone red in the face. "That's it."

Sean threw a beer can across the room. It knocked off a framed Carter Family broadside from the wall. Floyd tossed a ten-dollar bill next to the bowl of pretzels. "That's how this world operates. Thought you boys knew that by now."

Denver and Alan couldn't afford to lose the Thirsty Baboon. This was the one place that consistently supported their music and made them feel like they had a real shot at success if they kept playing gigs and kept working hard. This place had launched so many great careers. Sure, they could change location, but it was something about the building, the neighborhood, the dirt it stood on that made this bar special. None of the musicians he knew could afford to lose this venue. Denver stood up and dropped a few dollars down. He couldn't think of anything to say to the brothers.

Sean shook his head. "It's on the house."

Buster sliced limes so hard Denver could hear each contact the knife made with the wooden cutting board.

CHAPTER 13

Taking the Bottle to Bed

T HEIR TOUR BUS, named Dolly, a million-dollar beaut of modern machinery, burned miles of highway beneath them. J. D. and the guys had taken off immediately after the press conference ended. He felt like a fugitive and wondered now if it had been a dishonorable choice to keep the move a secret from Solar. Mr. Sullivan assured him it was the only way, otherwise the deal might take much longer to go through. He'd been bombarded with calls from Solar all day long.

J. D. stared at the white ceiling of the tour bus. One endless note of white, like every choice he'd ever made converged into total nothingness. More and more he wondered if he'd ever make music as good as his early albums that won him the Grammy, Oscar, CMA Song of the Year, Entertainer of the Year. J. D. Gunn's blockbuster years. J. D. remembered picking up a magazine backstage at the Grand Ole Opry a long time ago and reading an interview with Conway Twitty. He said something about performers in country music who stopped having hits, that those singers were the ones who were led into something that wasn't them. That had stuck with J. D. ever since. He needed the right direction for their sound like he needed one more breath, just one more to keep his life moving forward. J. D.'s deepest fear was being invited on *Dancing with the Stars* and agreeing to it because he needed the money.

He was grateful for everything Solar had done to launch his career, but it was time for the Empty Shells to move on. Mr. Sullivan promised him growth and artistic freedom, and he'd already secured them the headliner spot at the MusiCares concert tomorrow night with Jo Lover as the opener. He wasn't sure what had convinced her to do it, but J. D. was beyond happy when Mr. Sullivan told him about Jo's decision. He wondered what she'd do if he asked her to join him onstage for just one song. She'd never agree, he was sure. J. D. propped himself up on the overstuffed plaid pillows his housekeeper had put in this room, along with the matching sheets.

The first time J. D. had shown Lydia the inside of the bus was the last time his room looked like it used to, with old sheets and ratty pillows. Stuff from the other buses they'd had over the years. What the room lacked in style, it made up for in comfort. J. D. nursed his whiskey, stared at a black smudge on the white ceiling, wondered what the hell it was but knew he wasn't going to stand up to find out. The bus hit a pothole and shook the honey-brown liquor in his hand, but then it settled down again, riding smooth once more. J. D. swiped his phone awake and tapped on Jo's name. He'd charmed Mr. Sullivan's assistant into giving him the number, said he needed to touch base with Jo about a few things before the concert. He'd been challenging himself to call her. What he wanted to tell her, he still didn't know. He figured she wouldn't answer an unknown number anyway. He took another slug of whiskey and tapped the green call button.

After five long rings she picked up. "Hello?" she said, her voice smooth as his whiskey.

J. D. had a million things to say to her all at once: he wanted to ask her about her day, what she'd been up to, what she'd eaten for dinner, what the last song was that she'd listened to. What did she think about his joining Asphalt? About the concert? Did she hate him? Would she ever forgive him?

"Hello? Is someone there? Who is this?" Jo said.

He wanted her to stay on the phone longer but he knew she wouldn't. He just needed to hear her voice.

"Okay, I'm hanging up," she said, and did, right then.

J. D. dropped the phone by his side. He was tempted to call her again, to reveal himself. To apologize. He took another pull from the bottle. And then his phone started to vibrate against his leg. He lifted the phone into the air. Somebody from New York. Was she calling back from a different line? Was that even possible? But it could also be somebody from Solar. J. D. stared at the string of white numbers on his screen. He could always hang up if it wasn't her.

"Jo?" he said. "Hello?"

A man's voice said, "J. D. Gunn?"

"Who's—"

"J. D., my name's Bryan Lein. I'm a reporter for *Vanity Fair* magazine and I'm writing an article about Jo Lover. I've been trying to get in touch with you through your label. I hope you don't mind that I accessed this number."

"I mind," he said, and switched his phone to the opposite ear. "Does she know you're calling me?"

"Look, I just need five minutes of your time to ask some questions about your shared past, about growing up together in Gatesville."

What right did this guy have to call J. D. on his private line, trying to pry into Jo's personal life? J. D. said, "That would take a whole lot longer than five minutes, Mr. Lein."

Someone started banging on his door. J. D. hung up on the reporter, and then he turned off his phone completely. He stood up from the bed and opened the door. Rob's ashy brown ponytail was tied back with a red ribbon. It was his new thing and he called it his founding fathers style. Solar had tried to get him to cut it or at least keep it long but not tied back. He'd refused. Their fans imitated it, which Solar would've known if they had checked Instagram.

Rob said, "Come play blackjack."

"Not in the mood."

"Can I come in?"

J. D. moved to the side to let Rob squeeze through the narrow pass. Rob had a habit of checking over his shoulder like an assassin might take him out at any second. It was a bassist's tick. J. D. had seen drummers do the same thing. If any instrument was replaceable in a band, it was one of those two. J. D. folded his bed into a couch and Rob sat down beside him, lit a cigarette. He offered J. D. one and he accepted it.

Rob ran his hand over his ponytail and adjusted it. J. D. picked up his Gibson guitar and ran through the chords he would use for the introduction to tomorrow night's opening song. He adjusted the capo to the fourth fret, raising the pitch to where he liked it, while Rob smoked and sat beside J. D., shoulder to shoulder. Through multiple rounds of interviews and write-ups in *Pitchfork, Rolling Stone, Billboard,* and *Vanity Fair,* the story about their band had spun into one where Rob acted as the levelheaded glue for the group. J. D., despite his "über-masculine height and voice," had been cast as the sensitive one.

J. D. said, "Some reporter from *Vanity Fair* just called my phone. Wants to know about me and Jo growing up. Says he needs five minutes. Did he reach out to you?"

"No," Rob said.

J. D. dropped his cigarette in one of the many empty Lone Star cans strewn all over the floor. Rob was the only person on the planet he talked to about Jo. It had always been that way and it was going to stay that way.

Rob said, "You good with her being there tonight?"

J. D. held the guitar against his chest. "It's her label."

"I tried texting her about it."

"What'd she say?"

"Ignored it."

"Think she's coming with Nick?"

"Probably." Rob gave him an accusing, sidelong stare like a cat.

"What?" J. D. said.

"She's engaged."

J. D. pulled on his cigarette hard. "Everybody knows that."

"He's good for her."

J. D. rubbed the smooth face of his guitar, which he'd nicknamed Deuce, after the burnt-orange tabby cat he grew up with. J. D. didn't have any brothers or sisters. Deuce was his one companion and the only living soul around during the countless hours J. D. had devoted to learning to play his guitar in his room. A farmhand had run over Deuce with his truck.

J. D. rested his chest against his guitar. "You think she'd play a song with us?"

"That's what I'm talking about."

"What?"

"Don't do that." Rob tried to take the Dickel bottle from J. D.'s hand, but J. D. pulled back.

"Let me have some," Rob said.

J. D. gave it to him and stood up from the couch. He had a hard time staying seated, dreaded the long rides for this reason. He pushed away the curtains from the one window in his room and looked out at the endless road, black and flat, the flash of the white reflectors the only light he could see. J. D. opened the closet to put his hat away. Rob snuffed out his cigarette on the sole of his boot.

"Use the can," J. D. said. "Your mama raised you better."

Rob dropped the burned-out butt in the empty Lone Star can. "Need a Xanax?"

"No." J. D. hated the way those pills made him feel, like he was once removed from his emotions. "Is your girl coming to the show?"

"You might as well start using her name."

"Think Tammy will stick around?"

Rob said, "Already told her she'd have my wolf pack."

"And she didn't leave you. What's wrong with her?"

Rob pretended to right-hook J. D. in the jaw. "Come out and play cards."

"Think I'll try to sleep."

"You sleep?" Rob said.

"Didn't used to."

"J. D. Gunn's getting old." Rob smacked J. D. hard in the center of his back. "Today was good. Don't think about anything else."

"I'll think about Tammy."

"Fuck you, you will not."

"See you in the morning," J. D. said, and opened the door to let Rob out.

CHAPTER 14

Memory Keeping Him Company

J. D. REMEMBERED HIS father coming home one afternoon while he was in the barn repairing a hole started by a determined woodpecker. The bird had been at it for years. His father didn't make a noise, but J. D. could always tell when he entered a room. He felt his father like chills on his arm. J. D. stood on the ladder and looked over his shoulder. The fading sun on his father's back made him look hunched over in a way J. D. hadn't noticed before. His father was only forty but looked much older. Years of hard work had a way of accelerating age for mountain people. J. D. had the same coming to him, either working his way up at the dusty rock quarry like his father or hauling out lumber from the forests surrounding Clinch Mountain.

His father said, "Son, I found you a fiddle player, just arrived in town. Gave over your set list to Jo's daddy. Y'all shouldn't need any rehearsing."

"Yes, sir. Thank you, sir," J. D. said.

The Brunswick Stew fall festival was only a few days away. J. D. climbed down the ladder with his hammer in hand. He had a million questions about Jo. His father walked out and fired up the riding lawn mower. The conversation was done, that he knew. He wasn't sure what Jo looked like or how his father found him. How old was Jo? Was he any damn good at the fiddle? Was he in the fifth grade too? J. D. wouldn't bring it up though. His father didn't appreciate his goodwill being questioned.

So on the first weekend of November, J. D. hauled his equipment down the front porch steps of the farmhouse. His father had bought the house after he became manager of the second quarry. By that time they had more money than most of their neighbors in the county, but that wasn't saying much since everybody in the town of Gatesville was so poor. J. D. traveled much lighter then, with one acoustic guitar and a portable amp on wheels—a cheap piece of equipment that he'd bought with money saved from painting his neighbors' fences and barns. His father waited for him with his Ford truck bed open and with the engine running. His daddy launched a rock out from under his tire with his steel-toed boot, adjusted his cowboy hat, and tucked in his black shirt with country rose embroidery to make sure it was as tight as it could go. It was one of his daddy's nice shirts. J. D. had the same cowboy hat and he wore his shirts just the same way.

"Where's your mama?"

"Said she'd come over later. Isn't feeling good right now." J. D. had checked on her right before he went outside. She was curled up in a ball and wrapped in the blue quilt she'd made for him when he was a baby. Her bedroom light was off. Said she had a migraine.

His father looked up at the second story of their white house like he could see her resting on the bed. He looked worried. J. D. should've asked why his mother always had a migraine, why she didn't get out of bed for days, but he didn't know how to ask his father these questions. He didn't have the language yet to define her depression. Instead, they worked on the farm together and didn't talk about it. Maybe if they had they could've done something for her. Maybe they could've saved her.

"Let's get going," his father said. J. D. lifted up the amp from the ground and put it in the back of the truck, along with his guitar case, and then he slammed the gate. He climbed into the cab next to his father, who turned on Buck Owens for the thirty-minute ride to town.

"You ready, John David?" he said.

"I am, sir."

Everyone else called him J. D., but not his father. If it wasn't "son," it was "junior," but mostly John David. His father was John David. He never got used to people calling him by his full name. His father lit a rolled cigarette and then offered one to J. D. He took it and smoked it slow as they rode down Route 11. The leaves on the trees had turned red, orange, and bright yellow. Smoke rose from the chimneys of small cabins where bridges over small creeks connected the yards to the road. Clouds covered the Clinch Mountain ridge, but J. D. knew where the mountains were even if he couldn't see them. They'd loomed there his entire childhood. Sometimes the mountains looked like a gateway to elsewhere, but other times they looked like a barrier.

J. D. and his daddy rode through Main Street and to the other side to reach Mr. Jenkins's farm, where the festival took place. Orange tape sectioned off the lot and they parked near the Port-a-Johns. J. D. stepped out of the truck and smelled a mix of wood smoke, hay, and rich beef stew.

His father opened the truck bed and pointed at the amp. "Want me to carry that?"

"No, sir," he said. "I got it." He picked up his guitar case and lifted the amp. He could've extended the handle to roll it, but he wanted to feel the weight of it.

A group of pickers and a fiddler who played at the Baptist church sat by the ticket booth and played for people walking through the gate. Because his father had donated money for the festival and volunteered his time building the stage, he didn't have to pay, and because J. D. was a performer, he didn't either. He liked that kind of access.

Mr. Jenkins looked like a skeleton, he was so skinny. J. D. hated shaking his hand and feeling the bones like he was one day away from the grave, but he put his amp on the ground and took his offered hand.

"Playing for us today, I hear. Better be good, boy."

His father laughed. "It better."

Mr. Jenkins squeezed J. D.'s hand harder and squeezed his shoulder with his other hand.

His father said, "I got to talk to Mr. Jenkins about feed prices. I'll be back at the stage to watch you and Jo."

"Yes, sir."

J. D. lifted his equipment and traveled on. He'd been coming to the festival since he was a baby. Nobody in town missed it. All around him there was activity. Children walked past with caramel apples in hand, and mothers balanced plates of barbecued chicken like waitresses. Adults and kids ran the potato sack races. The adults were the ones who fell down the most. J. D. had won once or twice before, but he didn't have time for all that anymore.

A kickball tournament was under way near the back of the farm. The Carter and Jones families were big rivals in kickball. They always had so many children they could make up entire teams. Other people were racing pigs and losing bets. Little girls in smocked dresses sold cupcakes with their mothers to fund-raise for Gatesville's elementary school. A storyteller gathered a group of children around her chair and told the same "Jack Tales" J. D. had listened to when he was small. Pastor John from Gatesville Baptist, where J. D. was baptized, shouted out his love for the glory land and his hope for all the sinners among him to reach God's celestial shore. J. D. waved at Pastor John as he passed, who paused only for a moment to breathe and say, "There's a cross for Jesus, yes there is, and a cross for me and you. Get ready, always be ready, to return home someday soon."

J. D. kept his head down and continued walking to the music tent, where an old string band had a square dance going strong. He sat on the bleachers and looked around for Jo. He searched for a boy his age with a fiddle case but didn't see anyone. Rob was supposed to meet J. D. here too. J. D. tuned his guitar while he waited and read over his set list just to make sure he would remember it. He tried to think of funny things to say to get the crowd interested, like "Holy hound dog, what a good-looking crowd this afternoon." Things he'd heard older pickers say that sounded good, but when he'd tried saying them aloud in his bedroom, they sounded awkward and false. The more he pushed himself for things to say, the more nervous and tripped up he became. He decided to wing it. Hope for something funny in the moment.

After a final two-step, Mr. Price came on the stage and said, "Let's hear it for the Ricky Crook Boys, everybody. That sounded real good. You can hear them again at the Pickers Festival in Galax coming up." He turned around to the band. "When is that?"

The bald-headed guy standing with the upright bass shouted, "Weekend after next."

The crowd clapped. Mr. Price said, "Thank you, boys, you did good.

Don't y'all go too far now. We've got a tip jar right up front, and if you liked these fellas, make sure you let them know it."

Money mattered. J. D. didn't mention this to his father, who'd already made it clear he thought J. D. was a fool for thinking he could make a living playing music. That's not what music was for. Music was for community and neighbors, for forgetting pain. A release from the day's troubles. Not for fame. Each day before supper, his father played Cajun songs on the front porch. He wound down from his hard work that way, but he always complained about how much his shoulders and back hurt. On the weekends he'd ice his lower back for hours. J. D. needed to believe he could make money doing this thing he loved so he wouldn't spend the rest of his life with a broken-down body.

"Coming up," Mr. Price said, "we've got the results from the raffle. Just thirty more minutes and we'll know who's taking home this John Deere beauty. In the meantime, go get yourself some stew. It's ready. There's barbecued chicken and plenty of sweet things. But hurry back to hear some old-fashioned string music from our local kids J. D. and Jo."

Hearing his name announced like that lifted him right off the bleachers, equipment in hand, and sent him straight to the stage. He tried to climb up before the other band stepped down, but the banjo player said, "Hold on there. We're old and slow. You'll be that way too someday, God willing. Give us some room now."

J. D. apologized and hopped back down. Mr. Price came over and shook his hand. "Where's Jo?"

"On his way." J. D. was going to play for this crowd, even if he had to go it alone. He figured once he was up there and getting started, Mr. Price wouldn't yank him off just because Jo failed to show up.

Mr. Price nodded his head. As the other band stepped down the metal stairs to come off the stage, Mr. Price grabbed J. D.'s shoulder. "You get a good look at this boy J. D. Gunn here. He'll be the next big thing to come out of Gatesville."

J. D. wanted that to be true more than anything else in the world, but the other pickers passed by like they'd heard it a million times before.

"Good luck," the banjo player said. And that was it. The stage was empty, minus a microphone. The stage stood just a foot above the ground, but standing up there made him feel like he was standing on the top of Clinch Mountain, towering over the valley that was his audience. Many years later he'd discover that an arena stage was more like climbing to the top of Mount Everest. J. D. plugged in his amp. The dance floor remained empty while he warmed up and waited for Jo. He was ready to start playing. Fifteen minutes later Mr. Price gave him the get-this-thing-going motion with his hands. He placed his mouth too close to the microphone and puffed loud as he tried to say, "Hello, everybody, I'm J. D. Gunn."

It looked like he'd hurt a few people's ears. He pulled back and repeated himself. His father was nowhere he could see and neither was his mother. He'd keep going on without them. A toddler girl clapped her hands and danced on the bleachers. Rob climbed up on the bleachers, skinny as a twig and with his big bifocals and a shaved head. His mama hated long hair on boys. Rob took a seat beside the girl and her mother. J. D. tipped his hat at them.

He deepened his voice to say, "Thanks so much for having me onstage today. I've got a fiddle player who might show up, but in the meantime I'm what you've got."

The crowd clapped.

"Hope that's enough." He adjusted a tuning peg and then opened with Hank Williams Sr.'s "I Saw the Light." It wasn't on the set list, but he'd been practicing it. He didn't have a fiddle player to worry about so he could chuck the set list if he wanted. He figured this song would be a good crowd pleaser too. Two couples came on the floor to dance to that first one. After the song, the little girl and her mother put five dollars in the empty Mason jar at the front of the stage.

"Thank you so much," J. D. said to them as they walked back off the stage. He added, "And watch out for that little one. She'll be flatfooting in no time." The mother smiled. More people gathered under the tent.

J. D. strummed his strings real low. "Thanks to Mr. Price for putting this all together and to Mr. Jenkins for hosting our annual festival. I hope y'all have a good time today. I'd like to play a Carter Family classic for you now called 'Will the Circle Be Unbroken.'"

He began the intro. Just as he was about to start the first verse, a girl carrying a fiddle climbed onto the stage beside him. Not a case, but an actual fiddle, out and ready to play. He stared at her. She looked to be about his age. He repeated the intro to the song twice over. J. D. didn't know what to do with her.

Jo.

Short for something he didn't know. Jo hopped to the front of the stage like she was right on time. She wore a long, navy blue dress over a white turtleneck and a pair of well-worn white cowgirl boots. She had the longest, straightest black hair he'd ever seen, set in two high French braids, and her eyes were as dark as molasses. The skin on her cheeks was as smooth as his guitar's face. She was thin—all legs and arms under those clothes, like a young Emmylou Harris. Out of respect for his mother, J. D. didn't keep posters of women he was attracted to on his bedroom walls. He did have a poster of Emmylou's *Roses in the Snow* album cover. Jo looked almost exactly like her, except Jo had full lips.

He noticed that immediately. And he noticed her breasts, because she actually had some, unlike most of the other girls his age, who were flat as washboards. J. D. thought she was the most stunning person he'd ever seen in real life. How had he missed this girl in town?

He continued to repeat the intro and looked back out to the crowd. His father stood by the bleachers with another man, who, as J. D. found out later, was Jo's daddy. He worked for J. D.'s father at the quarry. They smoked cigarettes together.

J. D. told the crowd, "I guess my fiddle player just showed up."

She laughed, and it was like nothing he'd heard before. She laughed without hesitation, without boundaries. It made him lean closer to her. Her laugh was a magnet. She stepped right in front of him and spoke into the microphone. "Hi there. So sorry I'm late. Got snagged in a potato sack."

The crowd laughed too and clapped. They were drawn to her, that much was clear. More people took a seat in the bleachers. Jo's hair smelled like a summer ripe cucumber cut straight from the vine. Copperheads and rattlesnakes smelled that way too—it's how you knew they were near. Jo was so beautiful that looking at her felt like poison.

"Ready?" she said to J. D.

To the crowd he said, "Let's try this one more time."

Jo began tapping her boot and watched him for the start.

J. D. was certain he loved her the moment she made that fiddle cry.

*O*nce again here's Floyd Masters coming to you from Vanderbilt's WHYW 87.3 FM, your morning broadcast playing the best country music known to man. That's right, good listeners of Nashville, it's time to wake up, put on a pot of coffee, scratch that belly, and turn up the slickest voice in country radio. Breaking news this morning, folks: Jack White and Loretta Lynn won't be headlining this year's MusiCares concert out in LA. Big shame, too. I never miss a chance to see those two perform together. Ms. Loretta's got the laryngitis. Happens to the best. Floyd Masters wishes you a swift recovery, little darling. Loretta and I go way back. Toured together when we were younger. She's nothing but goodness. The real deal. A coal miner's daughter with a heart of gold. Anyway, Jo Lover and J. D. Gunn and the Empty Shells have taken their spot. Should be a good show. No Jack and Loretta, but a good show nonetheless.

And you knew I had to say it, folks: I told you so about Asphalt Records signing J. D. Gunn and his band in that hush-hush deal. Asphalt's CEO is moving fast to get his new talent out there and on the road. Rumor has it that Solar Inc. is suing the daylights out of Asphalt. Who knows how far that'll go. Mr. Sullivan has a high-class team of lawyers on his payroll. I hear the cha-ching on the cash register from many miles away. With J. D. Gunn on the roster, that Clear Channel streaming deal will most certainly go through for Asphalt. CEO Mr. Sullivan is the titan of tune town now. No doubt about it.

You'd think a bomb had fallen from the sky on Music Row with all the press this deal's been getting. I think I've seen enough pictures of J. D. Gunn's mug shot on the cover of the tabloids to last my lifetime, thank you very much. And *what really gets my undies in a twist is that one day Jo Lover's speaking out about all the bad machismo country songs in the industry, and the next minute she's opening for one of the worst offenders in the business, in my opinion at least. I know she hasn't been willing to call out J. D.'s band specifically, but I will. He was a talented young musician who turned into a corporate sellout. Of all the singers I didn't want to see go down this path, it was Jo Lover. There hasn't been a singer like her in a good long time. I didn't want it to happen to J. D. Gunn either, but he's a lost cause at this point. Not Jo Lover, though. Not Jo.*

All these CEOs think the same way. They're always looking for a line at the bottom. Has the CEO of Asphalt found his new king and queen of country music? His new Will McCoy and Lucy Heart? If so, you can kiss Jo Lover's solo career good-bye. Soon all you'll see in the grocery store checkout line will be pictures of J. D. Gunn and Jo Lover with clipped gossip typed out above their heads. They'll be regulars on reality TV shows and people will speculate if they're dating, if Jo's engagement is off again, on again. Everybody will be focused on everything except what matters: the music.

That'll swallow Jo Lover whole—I tell you, she's not made for that kind of stuff. The best ones aren't. Loretta wasn't, Dolly wasn't, Tammy wasn't, Patsy wasn't. Some of them did a pretty good job of keeping their private lives private, but who knows what would've happened if they'd been trying to maintain an image in this climate. Any fool with a cell phone is the paparazzi now. Those ladies focused on making great music. Didn't have the whole world digging into their lives. Sure, they gave interviews. Sure, they had gaffes. But now everything goes viral. It's a sickness. It really is.

All right, now I'm in a low-down kind of mood. I need a caller to cheer me up. Let's see. We have Brick from Nashville on the line. Is that right? Your name's Brick? Yes, hello, Floyd. It's Brick. *Hello, Brick.* I just want to say that I don't agree with you at all about it being a problem that J. D. Gunn's a sellout or that Jo Lover's in danger of being one too. It's just one concert, Floyd. The sky isn't falling. Jo Lover's still a strong singer and songwriter. She hasn't sold out to a publishing company here or in Sweden to produce pop hits for her. And so what if J. D. Gunn doesn't write his own songs anymore? He's famous for a reason, Floyd. He's the most played artist on country radio for a reason. His songs are awesome. I wish I was J. D. Gunn. Better than being some has-been radio disc jockey. I just wanted to call in and tell you that I think you're wrong. There's nothing bad with what either of them are doing with their music.

Well, thanks for calling, Brick. You're entitled to an opinion, even if it's stupid. Brick must be a little deaf too, folks. Doesn't know good music when he hears it. And he didn't hear me asking for a cheerful caller. I won't be taking another call until later in the show. Maybe then somebody will have something worthwhile to share.

At times like these the only thing that gives me hope for the future is up-and-coming talent. You've got to hear the Flyby Boys. Both those boys are vir-tuosos on their instruments. Don't miss your chance to see them before they get too big. And keep supporting the small venues where real talent gets nurtured, like the Thirsty Baboon. Now it's time for some honest stuff. Here's a Loretta Lynn and Ernest Tubb duet to turn your day around.

CHAPTER 15

Silver Wings

LYNN, THEIR PERSONAL stewardess, reviewed all the safety features, showed them how to shift their leather seats into a full recline once they were at cruising altitude, offered them blankets and cucumber eye masks, and then asked for their drink orders. The air-conditioning was turned on high, a welcome relief from the blazing tarmac outside. "Make yourselves comfortable," Mr. Sullivan said, and then he sat behind them in his own office suite.

Jo wanted to have a drink and rest while envisioning herself onstage singing to the audience tonight. "Whiskey, please," Jo said.

"Nothing for me," Marie said in a solemn tone.

Marie hadn't quite been herself these past two days. Just yesterday, thirty minutes before the *Vanity Fair* reporter was set to arrive, Marie had run into Asphalt's lobby full of apologies. Jo had never seen her so disheveled before. Her bright blond hair lay flat around her head and she wore no eye makeup or lipstick. Jo had never seen Marie without black eyeliner. Jo had said, "Did you get mugged last night or something?"

Marie's mouth had dropped open. "That's how I look? It's that bad?"

"Pretty bad."

Marie had turned on her phone and reversed the camera to check her hair. She groaned and then said, "I met somebody."

Jo often wondered about Marie's personal life. They were friends, but Marie was an employee and younger than Jo by a decade. A boundary had to be maintained. Jo hoped showing up late for work wouldn't turn into a habit for her. She'd hate to ever be in the position to fire Marie—how many people her age came with a letter of recommendation from Willie Nelson, who, apparently, had known Marie since she was a child? Not to mention the stellar degree in PR and the overall lovely disposition that Marie possessed, which Jo had assessed the moment she walked into the room at Asphalt for her interview. As a little test for all the applicants, Jo asked for Conway Twitty's real name, which no one had answered correctly. "Harold Jenkins," Marie had said, without the slightest hesitation or impulse to consult her iPhone. Marie proceeded to tell Jo the story of how Harold changed his name to Conway Twitty to make his move from a successful career in rock 'n' roll to a career in country music. That had made the hire easy for Jo, and she couldn't imagine losing Marie now. But love shifted people, revealed parts of themselves they didn't even know. Marie could be the world's best assistant one day, MIA the next, and wake up wondering how she'd ever fallen so far.

Marie crisscrossed her legs lotus-style on the airplane seat. She stared down at her phone.

"Plan to see that guy you met?" Jo said as she reclined her seat.

"I forgot to give him my number."

"What's his name?"

"Denver." Marie smiled like his name was rock candy on her tongue. "I think Gaylene got his bandmate's number."

"Gaylene too? Y'all must've had fun."

"Too much. It won't happen again, I swear."

"It's okay," Jo said. "You're entitled to a personal life, Marie."

Marie rolled her shoulders back and fixed her posture. "I wish I could get him out of my head. You think I could ask Gaylene to give him my number? Or is that too desperate?"

"You think he'd want you to?"

Marie put her thumbnail in between her teeth and then said, "I think so."

"Then do it."

Marie pulled out her phone and rested it on her legs. She smiled as she composed her message.

Jo felt a pull of nostalgia in her chest thinking about all her late nights at Marie's age, about all the times she and the boys played at the Thirsty Baboon when they were just starting out doing gigs around town and calling themselves the Gatesville Fugitives or the Clinch Mountain Trio—it took them a long time to get their band name right, especially once Chase B joined the band; he wasn't even from the South. They settled on the Sojourners, but even that never felt wholly right. Probably an early sign it wasn't meant to be, but they had so many good nights trying to figure out their sound. They'd stay up until four AM, writing songs, drinking PBR, grilling food, and playing cards and Trivial Pursuit during their breaks. Jo hardly ever remembered sleeping. And then they had those summers where they played music festivals all over the country, moving from one state to another and camping out every night in the areas designated for musicians. Jo loved those outdoor venues, where a jump in a cold lake counted for a bath, where people danced with glowing hula hoops and painted their bodies with henna. Summer music festivals reminded Jo of the Brunswick Stew festival she, J. D., and Rob attended as kids. Nobody was smoking pot there, of course, and there was only one little stage for traditional bluegrass music and square dancing, but the spirit felt similar.

Jo and the guys figured out quickly enough that they were too country for the hippies and a little too hippie for country. Their gigs on the summer festival circuit only lasted a couple years before J. D. was discovered. But those were some of her favorite memories—passing flasks of whiskey around the fire with many talented, creative people whom Jo never saw again, all of them united by a life on the road where the next adventure was only one highway exit away. Mostly she missed being in a band where if you failed, you failed together, and if you succeeded, you succeeded together.

A chime rang out and then the pilot's voice came through the speakers. "Howdy-do to all of you in Mr. Sullivan's company here today. We want to wish you a safe, comfortable flight. We will land at LAX in four hours and fifteen minutes. The weather is clear from here to the West Coast. I'm told we have a special guest on the flight today. Happy to have you with us, Ms. Lover, along with your assistant, Marie. We have a special tune just for you."

"I hope it's not one of my songs," she whispered. Marie looked up suddenly, but then shook her head like that was impossible. A familiar lead-in. A soft opening, just a guitar. Merle Haggard's voice singing "Silver Wings" came trembling over the speakers.

Lynn returned with Jo's whiskey in a tumbler as the lyrics faded into Merle's guitar and the song came to a close. Jo said, "Please tell the pilot I said nice choice."

"Right away."

Mr. Sullivan called out from behind Jo's seat: "Nick said you'd like that one."

That Nick had selected the song for her should've occurred to her the moment it came on. She loved Merle's music and often played his records on vinyl while she and Nick made dinner together, but Merle would always make her think of J. D. Songs like that one were a sense of something you once had but lost. Every woman Jo knew had a song like that locked away in her heart.

"It's time for takeoff," the pilot said. His voice disappeared, and the wheels started moving.

Jo closed her eyes for a while. Once they were safely in the air and cruising, she hesitated to wake Marie up. Her mouth was open and her head rested against the closed window. The throes of new love had knocked her out. Jo remembered how those days made you feel invincible and how deeply you believed that nothing could lessen the intensity or interrupt it altogether.

Jo tapped Marie's knee, but she didn't stir. Jo shook it a little. Marie opened her eyes wide and sat up quickly.

"Did you bring the bag?"

Marie searched her purse and pulled out the small toiletry bag she carried for her. Jo unbuckled and walked down the narrow aisle of the plane. She passed Mr. Sullivan's seat. He was reading on his tablet, but before she passed all the way, he said, "Come sit with me on your way back."

Lines started coming to her right there: *I didn't ask for escorts / Or high heels or short skirts / But I'm sailing on silver wings / Beyond what the past did bring.*

"You got a pen and paper?" Jo said.

Mr. Sullivan patted himself down like he was giving himself a TSA frisk and eventually pulled a pen from the front of his shirt. Jo grabbed a clean napkin from his table, wrote down the lines on the headrest of an empty seat, and slipped the lyrics in her pocket. Maybe a refrain, possibly the chorus. She'd figure it out later. Songwriting was like fly-fishing. It gave her a high the rare times when she caught a big one.

After Jo used the bathroom and fixed her makeup, she returned to the cabin and sat in the leather seat across from Mr. Sullivan. He lifted the shield on his window: an expanse of blue extended to a never-ending horizon.

"Beautiful day to fly," she said.

"It is."

Mr. Sullivan called on Lynn to refresh his scotch. Before she walked away, Jo said, "Got any Throat Coat tea?"

"Want it with whiskey, like a hot toddy?"

"Reading my mind."

Mr. Sullivan shifted in his seat and adjusted his khaki pants. "The governor of California will be there tonight. A big supporter of the MusiCares foundation. Played guitar when he was younger. My assistant just sent me the lineup too." Mr. Sullivan scrolled on his tablet. "Looks like hip-hop goes first, then country, then pop. You'll go on right before the Empty Shells. Twenty-minute set. They'll get all those details straight when we get there."

"Should be fine."

The plane hit a bump. The pilot's voice came over the speaker. "We're entering an area with turbulence. Buckle your seat belts, please, and we'll be through it shortly."

The plane shook so hard it made Jo's whole body vibrate. They hit another small bump, and then a larger one. Jo gripped the leather armrest. Turbulence gave her motion sickness. She closed her eyes and hoped it would be over soon.

The plane settled down, and shortly after, Lynn returned with Jo's hot toddy and Mr. Sullivan's scotch. She served him first. "Thank you," Jo said.

Lynn handed her a napkin. "Even clear skies have turbulence."

"Sounds like a song," Jo said.

"Maybe so," she said.

"A song about heartbreak," Mr. Sullivan added.

"Aren't most songs about heartbreak?" Jo said.

The plane skipped from another wicked bump, and Jo's toddy splashed out of the mug and landed on her hand.

Mr. Sullivan handed her a napkin. Jo wiped the tea off her hand, but it still stung. Mr. Sullivan leaned back in his seat and stretched his neck one way, then the other. In a casual voice he said, "You love my son, don't you?"

Jo balled up the wet napkin and returned her focus to Mr. Sullivan. "What kind of question is that? Of course I do."

Mr. Sullivan sipped from his tumbler, and then he turned off his tablet and placed it in the empty seat beside him. He rested his drink on his stomach and again leaned back in his seat before he said, "The last one really got me. I had an assistant bring her to the rooftop of the Asphalt building. I had a light team ready to go in the bank building right next door. She walked out at midnight. The lights came on and spelled out the proposal. Not the usual 'will you marry me' line either. 'Be my wife.' Simple. I was proud of that one. The Sullivan men are romantics, Jo. We might not get it right the first time, or the fourth time. For me, anyway. But Nick's not like me. He's a better man. He knows how to commit."

Jo eyed Mr. Sullivan in a cautious way. Where was this coming from? "I care about your son a great deal, sir."

"I can see that," he said. "But he loves you. Without hesitation. You can't love two people at once, Jo. Not equally. Trust me, I know. Double love doesn't work out well in the end."

She had to curl her toes to stay in control. She tried for a nonchalant tone: "I don't love J. D. Gunn, if that's what you're asking me, Mr. Sullivan. And if that's what you're asking me, just come on out and say it."

"Where there's anger there's love still."

Jo tried to maintain her tone, but it was slipping: "I won't keep defending my love for Nick."

"I'm sorry I upset you, Jo. You and Nick, that's a good team. In marriage. In the studio. A golden ticket. I just don't want you to make a mistake. I care about you like a daughter, and I don't want you to do something you can't undo."

Some people had so much to say and believed so deeply in their right to say it. She'd met men like Mr. Sullivan all her life, grown up surrounded by them, though mountain people had a much better sense of when to zip it.

"Might I know where all this is coming from? You'll understand, I'm sure, that I wasn't expecting to have this conversation with you today."

"I know," he said, "and I'm sorry for being so forward here. I know you and J. D. shared something in the past. I don't know what exactly or how serious. All before he left for LA, I assume. Had to be. No breakup news in the tabloids or anything. It'd be different now, of course, for either of you to split with somebody. Nick is very angry with me right now about signing J. D. to the label and organizing the MusiCares spot for the two of you. He said some very awful things to me on the phone before he flew to New York yesterday. Awful things. And I couldn't help but wonder if it all stemmed from some kind of insecurity."

"He didn't mention any of that to me."

"No," Mr. Sullivan said, and smoothed out his tie. "He wouldn't. He's too proud."

That she had caused strife between Mr. Sullivan and Nick made her feel ashamed immediately, and then she remembered what Nick had said to her about J. D. after their lunch at Jack's Bar-B-Que and how insecure he had seemed in that moment. But she assumed he was being playful and sarcastic or just expressing a small worry that was sure to pass. Jo drank her tea and forced herself to appear as casual as possible before she said, "If he didn't want me to know, then why're you telling me?"

Mr. Sullivan nodded like he'd expected this response. Finally, he said, "Asphalt has the best lineup in country music now with the Empty Shells on board. The money Asphalt could earn from streaming outweighs any potential cost of litigation from Solar. I plan to close the Clear Channel streaming deal next week."

None of this seemed like reason enough for making her so uncomfortable about J. D. Jo unbuckled her seat belt, but Mr. Sullivan reached forward and placed his hand on her knee. His face shifted from a look of casual inquiry to one of serious intent. He said, "I don't want any drama between my artists to derail Asphalt's future. I hope that's understood."

"That won't happen."

"I've seen it happen before."

Jo scraped the heel of her boot on the carpet. "I'd like to go back to my seat now."

"I'm thinking of your best interest, Jo. It's just business. Please don't be mad. Nick wouldn't forgive me."

"I don't plan to tell him about this."

"That's probably best." Mr. Sullivan put his reading glasses on and picked up his tablet. "Tell me, have you heard anything about Ring-DingDong?"

Jo was confused by this change in conversation, and she wasn't sure if he was trying to keep her seated longer to interrogate her further or if he was trying to end their conversation in a positive manner.

Before Jo could respond, he said, "Supposedly it's a system that can snatch a portion of a song, any song, and upload it as a ringtone to your phone. Indie, country, pop. Big market concerns. Huge fucking concerns. Money comes from ringtones. Plain and simple. The dark days of Napster. We can't go through that again. In a post-Napster culture no one thinks they should pay for music anymore. And this ringtone thing is just another wave. You can't starve a thing to death and still expect it to move. The industry's as lean as it can go. We have to shut down that start-up. Keeps me up at night." His neck was red. The sweat on his brow glistened. He looked ill. He wasn't talking to Jo anymore, not really. He was talking to a boardroom. "Anyway," he said, "I've got an early meeting about it in LA tomorrow before we fly back. Let your assistant know."

Jo nodded and stood up. "I'd like to rest before we land."

"Me too." Mr. Sullivan pressed his fingertips against his eyelids like he was trying to press away a migraine. "Glad we had a chance to talk."

CHAPTER 16

Intruder

J. D.'S MAMA HUNG herself with a rope. He found her on the screened-in porch, but his daddy wasn't home so he had to cut her down himself. Later he told Jo that he heard his mama's knees crack to pieces when she fell onto the wooden floor. J. D. dropped out of high school soon after and took a bus straight to Nashville, left Jo and Rob and their little bluegrass band behind. Jo often imagined him nearly starving to death or begging for food or shacking up with strange women for shelter, but the postcards he mailed to her and Rob were positive and described Nashville as a safe place for people like them, where pickers were on every street corner and every potluck was accompanied by impromptu shows. He always ended by saying he missed playing music with them, especially missed the sound of Jo's voice.

Rob and Jo agreed that as soon as they graduated from high school, they were leaving Gatesville too. Jo's only hesitation was leaving behind Martin, who held down a job stocking shelves at a Walmart ten miles away, and tiny Isabell, who was only six years old by then.

Right before Rob picked her up for the trip, Jo sat outside her house with all the neighborhood kids who wanted to see her off. Most of them played kickball, except Martin and Isabell. He sat beside her and Isabell braided her hair, which Jo had taught her to do. "You scared, sissy?" she asked.

"Scared's for chickens," Jo said. She loved to feel Izzie's small hands resting on her shoulders.

"Who'll cook me breakfast?"

Jo pulled Izzie down from behind her and cradled her in her lap. "Don't you worry about anything. I'll be back before you know it. And as soon as I can, I'll have both of you come be with me in the city where all the cowboys live."

"Cowboys?" she said, her voice playful and sweet.

"Singing cowboys."

"Pinky promise?"

Jo linked her pinky with Izzie's and shook it. Martin reached out for her other hand and took that pinky. "Please don't go," he said.

Jo hated guilt more than anything else in the world. She smoothed down the cowlick near Martin's forehead. "Y'all go play some kickball. Have fun." Martin stood up and took Izzie's hand, and together they walked off. But then Izzie broke away from him and came running back for one last hug, her wild blond hair flashing in the sunlight.

Jo kissed Izzie on the cheek and said, "Go on, now." She did as she was told. Jo massaged her right shoulder and then hugged her knees to her chest. Jo rested her cheek against her forearm, wishing Rob would hurry up and arrive because she wasn't sure she'd have the nerve to go if he took much longer.

Then she heard the screen door open and she turned around to find her mama. She held out a small cloth pouch to Jo.

"What's this?" she said.

"Just open it," her mama said. She squinted in the sunlight.

Jo loosened the threads and pulled out a wad of cash.

"There's about three hundred."

"Thank you, Mama. How'd you—?"

"Never mind that."

All Jo had to her name was about thirty dollars from selling some of her clothes and stuffed animals at the church bazaar. Between school and her family, she had no time for a job. Her job was at home. Her mama must've stolen some of her daddy's moonshine money but she wouldn't accuse her.

"Don't you spend it on anything foolish."

"I'll pay you back, I swear."

Her mama walked up to Jo and embraced her, which was a rare occurrence. Softly, she said, "If you get big in Nashville, or if you don't, either way, you won't come back, you hear? You leave now, you don't come back," and then her mama released her from the hug. Jo secured the money underneath the red velvet lining in her fiddle case. She might lose her suitcase or her purse, but there was no way she'd lose her fiddle. Rob showed up a few minutes later, honking the horn of the Toyota Tercel he'd bought with the money he earned working at the quarry every day after school his senior year. He hopped out. "One-way ticket to Music City, USA."

Jo ran down the front porch steps into Rob's embrace. All of Jo's cousins rushed from the field and crowded around Rob's car. "How you going to fit any of Jo's things with that bass taking up so much room?"

"We'll make it work," Jo said, and pushed her one suitcase and her fiddle into the floorboard of the backseat. Rob threw his weight against the door to make it close. She started hugging her cousins good-bye. Izzie attached herself to Jo's leg and started screaming and wouldn't let go. Her mama came over and pulled Izzie off Jo's leg and held her tight on her hip. Jo wanted to kiss her good-bye but decided not to, in case it upset her again. Jo looked around for Martin, but he was alone in the field with the kickball. She called out to him and told him she loved him, but he never turned around.

Rob and Jo drove the four-and-a-half-hour trip to Nashville straight through. Jo thought about Martin and Izzie, worried about who would watch after them. Her mama was always so busy with church stuff and with all the cousins and neighborhood kids around. But she had to let it go. Rob played Conway Twitty and Dolly Parton albums, and in between they talked about J. D. and wondered what their lives would be like as each hour drifted behind them on I-40. They entered Nashville and took a wrong exit, which sent them straight into downtown and over the Cumberland River. Jo'd never seen a cityscape before in person, and she fell in love at first sight with those tall buildings and all their implied importance. They used a map to navigate East Nashville to where J. D. lived. The Five Points neighborhood was filled with run-down bungalows and gardens and spray-painted fences and overpasses. To another eye it might've looked like a dump, but to Jo, it looked full of promise.

J. D. was waiting for them on the front porch stoop, and he launched from the steps and opened Jo's door. He pulled her out of the car and wrapped her in a hug. "I almost didn't think you were coming."

"Here we are," Jo said. "This house is so nice, J. D. What a nice flower garden."

"It is," he said. "The basement's nice too. That's where we're stay-ing." She felt him studying her face to see if she might be disappointed.

"It's all perfect," she said.

"Get your stuff," J. D. said. "Need any help?"

"Just carry my bass," Rob said. Together the three of them walked down the concrete stairwell on the side of the bungalow, and J. D. opened the metal screen door. "*Mi casa es tu casa.*"

Jo walked in. There was a small kitchenette, but at least it had a stove, and there was a slightly larger living space with a sliding glass door that led to a fenced in backyard. There were two rooms on the other wall with a bathroom in between.

"Haven't shown you the best part," he said. J. D. came right to her and took her by the hand and led her to the closed door on the left. He opened it to reveal a bedroom with a double bed all to herself. Her own dresser. Yellow buttercups, the kind he always picked for her and left in her locker at school, were in a glass vase on the nightstand next to a reading light. He'd even placed all his old issues of *Guitar* on her nightstand, along with bath towels and washcloths. Lavender soap too.

"This means so much," she said in a soft voice.

"You're happy?" he said, and Jo nodded.

After growing up in a one-bedroom cabin Jo had assumed she'd make up a pallet on the floor in the living room and be done with it. She didn't know any other way of living. J. D.'s room had two twin beds. He told Rob he had a job lined up for him doing heavy lifting after concerts at the Bridgestone Arena, but Jo was on her own for work. J. D. had a few contacts at restaurants where he sometimes played gigs, so she might be able to get a job waiting tables. At the moment she didn't care too much about the finer details. She was so happy right where she was, so far away from Gatesville, in a new place where they all had possibilities.

But everything new has a honeymoon period, and Jo's only lasted three months before her daddy called. J. D. and Rob were building a small deck for rehearsals out in back of their basement apartment with scrap wood they'd found on the side of the road. Jo was watching them work when the phone rang. "Joanne?" her daddy had said, his voice higher than usual.

"Hey, Daddy."

"Is someone there with you?"

"Yes, sir. Why?"

"Hold on to something for me, will you?"

She leaned against the white refrigerator that grew mold no matter what cleaning solutions she used to prevent it. "You're scaring me. Is it Mama?"

"No, it's Martin. He didn't make it home from work today." Her father's voice trailed off.

Jo's blood pooled in her hands as she held the phone. "Call the police then, Daddy. Don't call me. I can't do anything from here. You think someone picked him up?"

Jo heard her mother in the background, and her cousins, all crying at different volumes. "What happened, Daddy? Talk to me!" Jo was shouting at that point. Rob and J. D. came inside, sweat soaked, hammers in hand.

"He was struck by a train walking home. He's dead, honey. Martin's dead."

"That's not possible," Jo said in a professional voice. "He knew not to walk the tracks. He'd always known not to do that. I told him all the time. I taught him not to do that. There must be some kind of mistake."

"We're sure it's him," he said in a tone that was tender in a way she couldn't recall him sounding before. "Come home."

She hung up the phone and couldn't cry. She told J. D. and Rob what had happened as if she were reporting on the weather. She returned to Gatesville for the funeral, took the red-eye Greyhound back to Nashville that evening, and swore to herself that it was the last time she'd visit her childhood home. It took her months after the funeral to cry about Martin, to let herself grieve for leaving him behind in Gatesville, where danger awaited him. Jo was washing dishes one rainy day when she nearly sobbed herself to death; that's how it felt anyway, like all the water she had in her body left her eyes and filled the sink below her.

After she returned to Nashville, her life resumed as if Martin had never died, as if he'd never existed at all. Navigating the city, working her two part-time jobs as a waitress at a beer garden and at a restaurant on Broadway, living with two guys, having no other friends: all of it began to wear on Jo. Trying to write songs and practicing with J. D. and Rob at night gave her the only relief she remembered from that time. All alone at night, she stared up at the popcorn ceiling, wishing she knew some way to make it smooth.

J. D. had a regular job playing second guitar in a rock band called Damaged Octopi. The band sucked, but it didn't stop girls from going to the shows. She saw how they watched J. D. One or two always hung around late, and she figured he'd have a girlfriend soon enough and Jo would have to suffer in silence when she came over and spent the night. Jo kept waiting for it to happen, but night after night, J. D. came home with Jo and Rob to the little basement apartment they rented. Walking home from the 5 Spot one night, Jo said, "Y'all can use my room, you know, if you ever need to bring somebody home. I can sleep on the couch."

Rob and J. D. remained silent, kept walking.

"Just putting it out there," she added.

"Thanks," Rob said. "I think."

Rob looked at J. D., who was smoking a cigarette.

"What?" Jo stopped walking.

"I mean, I don't know about J. D.," Rob said, "but that's like screwing in my parents' bed."

"Come on. You're serious?" She looked at J. D. He nodded in agreement.

"It's not like I fold your damn laundry. I'm not your mama." Almost immediately she felt bad for saying that in front of J. D.

"Doesn't matter," Rob said. "I couldn't do it."

"If you can't be yourselves, then I shouldn't be living here."

Jo started walking as fast as she could. Rob and J. D. started walking even faster than her just to make her mad. She'd been drinking tequila and she was always more sensitive when she did. Back at the apartment, Jo refused to play music with them and went into her room and kept the door closed for the rest of the night. She couldn't fall asleep. Midnight came and went. She didn't have enough money to live by herself yet, but she figured she could probably afford to rent a room somewhere.

In the middle of the night she heard someone turn on the faucet in the kitchenette. She rolled over to her other side and squeezed a pillow. A little later she thought she heard someone trying to open the door to her bedroom. Her heart began to beat fast. She was sure an intruder had broken into the apartment, probably snuck in through the backyard. They didn't always remember to lock the sliding glass doors. She sat up in the bed and imagined a huge man breaking in through the half window in her room, or the back door, or the front door, or coming down the stairwell from the house above. Would J. D. and Rob hear her if she screamed for help? Jo kept a Buck knife in her nightstand, and she pulled it out before she said, "Who's there?"

"It's me." J. D.'s deep voice was unmistakable.

"Hang on." Jo put on her underwear and a T-shirt, and then she opened the door a little ways. J. D. wore a pair of gym shorts and nothing else. His long torso was bare and smooth, and the muscles in his abs and biceps were defined from playing guitar and moving heavy equipment at his job. His skin was shiny, almost golden, in the soft light from her room. His black hair fell over his eyes. He shifted it to one side. Jo searched his blue eyes for a reason why he was standing at her door half-naked.

"I just need to clear something up," J. D. said, trying to whisper but growing louder like he always did when he was feeling righteous. "From earlier."

"It can't wait until tomorrow?"

J. D. shook his head. "I can't sleep." He braced one arm on the frame and looked down at her as he said, "There's no girl I want to sleep with in that bed except you."

Jo opened her mouth to speak but nothing came out.

"I can't tell you I haven't been with other girls since I left Gatesville. I have."

"I know. I never expected anything from—"

"Just listen," he said. "I can promise you that no matter where I was I was always thinking about you. And waiting for you every single day to come be with me. So see, you can't move out, because I finally have you in my life again. It's all I've wanted since I left home."

Jo moved behind the door, like she needed some kind of protection.

"Can I come in, Joanne?"

She remained behind the door and her heart beat just as hard as when she thought there was an intruder.

"Jo?"

She wanted him. She'd always wanted J. D. From the first time they met on that little stage at the Brunswick Stew fall festival, she knew she wanted to be in his presence every chance she could. She'd never thought about another boy her entire life.

"All right then," he said. "Good night."

"Don't go." Jo opened the door wider.

He didn't say a word, only walked into the room, picked her up, and buried his face in her hair. With his hand interlaced with hers, Jo led him to her bed and pulled back the covers on his side. He entered the bed first, and then he opened his arms to her. Side by side they stared at each other for a long time, saying nothing. He ran his hand through her hair and traced all the features on her face with fingertips callused from playing guitar. With his hand underneath her chin, he leaned down and kissed her better than any music they'd ever made together. They always had good rhythm. Jo removed her T-shirt and underwear and invited him on top of her. The weight of his body on top of hers calmed all the flutters in her chest. His rough fingers roamed her face and her breasts. They made love multiple times that night and spent the entire next day in bed together as a couple. They were in a place where they could finally be together, officially. After that night, J. D. moved all his stuff into Jo's room.

CHAPTER 17

Sound Check

WITHOUT FAIL, EACH time J. D. stepped off the tour bus he felt ten times taller. His cowboy boots hit the gravel outside the loading station for the theater and he lifted his arms up above his head, readjusting his Stetson and then scratching some strange bite on his stomach. Two blackbirds washed themselves in a large pothole next to J. D. Rob jumped off the bus behind him. J. D. only needed to hear it to know. Rob always jumped. Said it made his blood move.

"What time is it?" J. D. asked.

Rob dropped his brown satchel to the ground and shuffled through it. He pulled out his pocket watch, the one J. D. had found at the vintage store in Austin. Or was it Portland? Maybe Raleigh? Brooklyn? London? Kyoto? Berlin? Madrid? He couldn't keep up with the places he'd been. J. D. had bought that watch for himself, but he figured Rob would like it more. He'd slipped it in Rob's flannel shirt pocket while he was sitting up at the table on the bus, fast asleep and drooling. Then J. D.

and Aster put silver coins on Rob's eyes like he was dead. J. D. posted it to his Instagram and thousands of people liked it. The next day Rob put ice cubes in J. D.'s favorite boots. They'd melted and soaked right through the soles by the time J. D. needed to perform. Where were they then? Philly? No. Madison? J. D. gave up. He'd grown used to migrating like a confused bird with no direction home.

"It's one thirty," Rob finally said.

J. D. pulled out his cigarettes and lit one. "I'm starving."

"Should be catered."

Their bus driver, Guy, shouted, "Off the bus, fellas."

"Fuck you, Guy," Aster shouted back. Aster stepped down and dropped his book bag on the ground. He put his silver aviator sunglasses on and took a deep breath. "That's right, boys. Smell that? It's LA. Salt water and pussy. Home sweet home."

"Let's go," Rob shouted into the bus.

Chase B came off the bus next, stepping down the stairs sideways like he always had to do.

"Danny, stop messing with those dreads," Chase B called behind him before he made the final step down.

They all stood in a circle, adjusting to the sunlight. Traveling on the road as much as they did made them like a singular organism. An amoeba. They shared DNA at this point. Danny hopped off the bus just like Rob, but Danny was still a new member—a great studio drummer who had been brought on to work on their fourth album after their other drummer quit. Maybe Danny would stop hopping after another year or so on the road. They'd had this conversation already. Danny disagreed. He said, "Black dudes don't get down about the same kind of stuff as white dudes."

Aster had said, "What about Rob, then?"

Danny said, "Rob's an honorary black dude." They all called Rob the honorary black dude for a long time after that.

"So this is where they host the Oscars, huh?" Danny said.

Aster said, "Looks like a dump."

"It's the back of the building," Rob said.

"Where's the equipment?" Chase B lifted his trucker hat off his head and wiped the sweat from his forehead.

J. D. finished his cigarette and flicked it to the side. The loading lot was situated across the street from the Holly-View apartments, a two-story, whitewashed concrete building flanked by palm trees and a flat yard. Too much flatness for J.D.

Rob hit the buzzer and then banged on the metal door at the top of the loading dock. "J. D. Gunn and the Empty Shells."

A loud click came from the other side of the door, and a small guy wearing all black and a headset pushed open the door with his back. He looked like a twelve-year-old. "Expected you around noon."

"Got a late start," Rob said.

"We have to go straight to sound check."

J. D. ran up next to the kid. He stood a few feet taller than him. "Any chance I could eat before sound check?"

"Lunch was at noon."

J. D. said, "You're serious?"

"I can order from the Hard Rock Café. Have it here in thirty minutes."

J. D. smacked him on the back, accidentally shoving him forward a step. "Order anything, my man. For yourself too. What's your name?"

"Layton."

"Nice to meet you, Layton. And thank you."

They followed the kid—right turns, left turns, more left turns—until he stopped at a door with their band name posted at the top. The room was filled with tan leather couches and chaise longues, multiple bathrooms, and vanity mirrors with a large makeup station. There was a well-stocked bar. Tequila, whiskey, and bourbon: his three angels. Mr. Sullivan had taken care of that, J. D. was certain. Chase B, Danny, and Aster sprawled themselves out on the couches, one for each of them, but Layton said, "We have to go."

"Right now?" Aster said.

Layton nodded.

Aster cussed under his breath and stood up from the couch. Layton led them down the crowded hall to the stage door entrance. Performers, assistants, sound guys, tech folks—so many people moved up and down the hallway. Layton guided them to the stage. "Your food should be here soon," he said.

The auditorium seats were empty. A cleaning crew moved through the aisles, around where the sound station was set up for checks. J. D. stood in the middle with his guitar strap over his shoulder and the microphone right in front of his face. This is where he felt at home most of the time, right onstage. He loved this auditorium too. Second to the Ryman. He'd walked down that plush purple carpet and up these very steps to accept his Oscar for best soundtrack four years ago.

They all tuned their instruments. He turned and asked Danny if he was ready. "One minute," he said, and adjusted his cymbal. Rob nodded that he was ready, and then Chase B and Aster signaled the same. "Danny, you ready?" J. D. said again. He nodded. From the start, none of it sounded like it should. J. D. put his hand on the microphone and said, "More vocals. Less drums. Up the pedal steel and back down on Rob's bass."

They started in on the song once more but it sounded like they hadn't adjusted it at all. J. D. stopped playing. "Same thing. A lot less bass. I'm not asking you to rope the moon here."

The sound guys stood behind a fortress of technology in the center of the auditorium. They occupied that spot precisely to hear what J. D. could hear. It was off. But they couldn't hear it.

"Go again," one of them said.

He looked back at his guys. "One more time." They began. J. D. stopped. "It's off," J. D. repeated in the microphone.

He missed his count. "Sorry," he said. "All right, I'm ready." They started the intro to the first song they'd play: "Pretty Girl in a Monster Truck."

It was wrong, all of it. J. D. dropped his hands from his guitar before the first verse. The band stopped too—the sound of Chase B's pedal steel went zinging through the auditorium and then faded away.

J. D. gripped the microphone. "Now his pedal steel's too loud. What's wrong down there?"

Everything sounded off. The words he animated with his breath sounded hollow. How could J. D. stand up here and sing this song with Jo Lover listening somewhere in the wings? This was the exact kind of song she spoke out against, the exact kind of country song she despised. J. D. turned around, looked at his bandmates, and wondered if it embarrassed them to hear him sing these songs. They'd been together for years. Rob had to try to remember what it was like to sing music they cared about. As the paychecks had grown larger, the quality of their music had shrunk. He knew it. They knew it. How come they never talked about it in a serious way? Did they think J. D. was satisfied? That the money was enough? Or if they talked about it everything would disappear?

Aster sidled up next to J. D. He had his electric guitar hanging down the side of his body like a cowboy's holster. He moved J. D. away from the microphone. "Calm down, man. We'll get it straight. It's a big space."

"It sounds off."

"It's a little off," Aster said.

"It's all off."

Aster said, "But they're doing their job. So just chill out."

"I need food."

Aster took J. D.'s microphone. "You guys know when that lunch is coming? J. D. might turn to cannibalism."

The taller man in the pit said, "It's coming. Let's finish this."

J. D. glanced at Rob, who looked tired and annoyed as he leaned against his upright bass. He shook his head at J. D. Just as J. D. was about to lead into the song again, a door opened at the back of the auditorium and J. D. raised his head to the light, but he couldn't see in all that darkness. He heard the door close. How was he supposed to concentrate? No food. Tired music. Jo Lover somewhere in this building, ready to open for him tonight. She'd be standing right here soon and all he could think about was hugging her after her Opry induction and how he hoped he'd have the chance to hug her again. He'd settle for having a beer and just hanging out and talking, but there was something about what he'd felt when he wrapped her in his arms, how she stiffened at first but then let go. He'd felt her let go, he knew he had. J. D. couldn't stand the idea of her marrying another man if there was even a small chance she still had feelings for him. He felt like the only way to know was to sing a song with her tonight. He'd ask her onstage and he wouldn't tell Rob or the other guys beforehand. Jo couldn't hide her emotions when she was singing. It was his only way of knowing her heart.

Danny twirled a drumstick in one hand. "Come on, J. D. Let's do this."

J. D. placed his fingers on the guitar strings once more. "Just bring down the pedal steel some. That should do it."

CHAPTER 18

Prima Donna

J O STOOD BY the side exit door of the auditorium and watched J. D.'s difficult sound check. He couldn't see her, she was sure of it. J. D. wrapped his long fingers around the microphone and drew it close to his mouth the way he used to guide her chin close for a kiss. Instagram couldn't capture him like this, with his black hair falling forward in a loose curl, a little like Elvis's. A soft pearly light radiated from him, like it always had, and Jo wondered if she was the only person in the world who could see it. If only the song he was singing wasn't so terrible. She knew he could do better. He had to know it too. Jo backed out of the doorway of the auditorium before J. D.'s song ended and found Marie leaning against a white wall in the hallway, consumed by her phone and furiously texting away. Without looking up Marie said, "How's it in there?"

"Flooded."

Marie's head jerked up. "What?"

"Kidding," Jo said, and started walking down the hallway. "How's Denver?"

Marie smiled in that immediate, goofy, unself-conscious way that tells the world you're in love. "How'd you know?" Marie said.

Jo arched her eyebrow at her.

"I'll stop texting him, if you think it's distracting."

"I know it feels like you can be in love and fully focused on your career all at the same time, but most people have to prioritize." Jo almost said that most people have to choose, except it felt too harsh.

Marie put her phone in her pocket and showed Jo her free hands. "I'm one hundred percent focused on work. I swear. And I'm not in love, for the record."

Jo checked her phone to see if she had any missed calls. Two from Nick, and a long text message from him too. He said he missed her, loved her, and wished her good luck—no hint of the anger that Mr. Sullivan had told her about on the plane. Perhaps Mr. Sullivan had made it all up as an excuse to start that conversation with her. Jo put her phone away and said, "Can you work on getting us a flight out of here early tomorrow morning? Mr. Sullivan has a meeting and I'd rather not wait."

Marie went to her phone immediately and made a note. She waved her phone in the air and said, "Got it." They walked down the hall and turned a corner. "That's your room, right down there. I'm going to see about hair and makeup."

"Thanks," Jo said. She watched Marie power-walk down the hallway, and Jo unlocked the door to her dressing room, which was filled with white leather upholstery and chrome detailing on the furniture. Her vanity mirror took up the length of an entire wall, where a gift basket of fruit, whiskey, and long-stemmed white roses awaited her.

Nick always sent white roses. She put down her purse and lifted the note. *Don't be nervous. Love, Nick.*

She looked in the mirror and caught herself smiling. Jo removed a single rose from the vase and inhaled its tender, sweet scent. When she tried hard she could remember how intoxicating it felt to be with Nick in the early days. She remembered the first night she met him, after a show at the Thirsty Baboon. He was just some handsome gentleman with dirty-blond hair and blue eyes who looked rich and sat down at the bar next to her. Nobody wore a collared shirt and loafers to the Baboon. She felt a little surly from drinking tequila and leaned over to him. "Miss the turn for the country club?"

He smiled, drank his scotch, but didn't say anything.

"Guess so," she said. He wore a large copper-colored watch on his wrist. He looked like he'd stepped right off a yacht and into this dive bar.

"How's J. D. doing?"

She remembered studying his face for a long moment. Had she met this guy before? "If you know him, ask him yourself."

The guy flagged the bartender and requested his check.

Jo knew she'd never seen this guy at the Baboon before, but she'd seen him somewhere else. She just couldn't place him. "Who are you?"

"Nick Sullivan," he said. "It's nice to meet you."

Jo knew him, his name anyway—a prodigy producer who'd started working for RCA at seventeen, and his father owned Asphalt Records, a label they all dreamed of signing with someday. Jo knew him because J. D. had read a profile about Nick in *Guitar* magazine and ranted about his being a spoiled son who knew the right people to get exactly where he was. He didn't earn it. Didn't deserve it. She remembered accusing J. D. of being jealous of the guy, which he didn't deny.

"You know J. D.'s in LA?"

"I do," Nick said. The bartender told him how much he owed and he put down a fifty.

She drank one more shot of tequila.

"I like the way you play fiddle." Nick slid his leather wallet into his back pocket. "But I like the sound of your voice even more. Ever thought of making your own album?"

"Sometimes."

"Do you write?" Nick was facing her now, with one elbow resting on the bar. She refused to look at him directly.

"Sometimes," she said.

"Can I buy you a drink?"

"I thought you were just leaving."

Nick looked down and adjusted his watch, like he was nervous. "You know, I've been here a few times, but you haven't noticed me."

"Impossible. You stick out like a horse's dick."

"That's not very nice."

"No, it's not, I guess." Jo finally looked him in the eyes. "I should probably switch to water."

"We could take a walk."

"That sounds good, actually." Jo stood up from the bar stool, and they walked toward the exit.

Chase B cut in front of them before they left. He shook hands with Nick, and they passed compliments to each other, then, in a brotherly tone, Chase B said, "Jo, we have to get going."

"We're going for a walk."

Nick handed Jo a business card. "You should go with them. But I'll be back next Friday. Maybe we can talk more then." Nick shook hands with Chase B and said, "Take it easy." Nick strolled out of the bar like a breeze.

"You know who that is?" Jo asked.

"Everybody knows who that is," Chase B said.

As a ritual, Jo discarded the phone numbers men handed her on bar napkins, but on this night Nick was the only guy to hand her anything. Walking out the back door behind Chase B and Rob, with her fiddle case in hand, Jo stopped at the Dumpster. She hesitated to drop it in. Something told her to hold on to it.

Nick showed up the next Friday and asked her out to dinner to discuss the possibility of working together. She agreed and they went to a farm-to-table restaurant in Five Points, where she let Nick order everything they ate because she assumed his taste was finer than hers. She loved the goat-cheese-stuffed dates wrapped in prosciutto and drizzled with local honey. Later they went dancing at Robert's Western World on Broadway, and Nick could lead her on the dance floor in a way no other man could, not even J. D. And though it was true she did not feel the same magnetic pull toward Nick that she did for J. D., there was much to be said for feeling like she could trust his lead.

In the town car on the way home Nick said, "I'll pick you up tomorrow morning and let's see if we can make those stuffed dates together."

"For breakfast?" she said.

"Why not?"

And he arrived right on time, eight AM sharp, just like he said he would. Jo appreciated his punctuality, appreciated that she could count on him to do exactly what he promised. But the dish ended up tasting a lot less flavorful than it had at the restaurant. She remembered the disappointment she felt after the first bite—the perfect concept of a dish so rarely turned out the way you wanted, and relationships were a lot like that, at least in Jo's experience.

Marie entered the dressing room, along with another girl who looked to be the same age as Marie. Both had soft, flawless skin and spunky haircuts, but the other girl's hair was neon pink. She carried a suitcase-sized makeup box with her.

"This is Bekha."

Jo sat down at her vanity mirror. "What magic can you work?"

"Lots," Bekha said with a distinct LA accent. She hooked up her curling iron and unloaded hair products, styling tools, round brushes, teasing combs.

"Your Mary Poppins bag," Jo said.

"I know, right?" Bekha circled the makeup brush in the powder and then covered Jo's face to mask her flushed skin. She rubbed bronzer and blush on the apples of Jo's cheeks. "You have gorgeous skin," Bekha said. "Great bone structure."

Bekha applied smoky eye shadow and heavy black eyeliner that fanned out at the edge of Jo's eyelids and made her look like a cat. Three layers of mascara and an application of burgundy lipstick and Jo was ready for the stage. Bekha organized Jo's hair with clips, coated each section with hair spray, and then curled and curled and curled until she had volume and bounce. She brushed out Jo's hair so the curls wouldn't be so tight. And boom. Just like that, she was Jo Lover, country music star. She'd had none of this glamour when she met Nick Sullivan at the Thirsty Baboon. Not even a touch. She washed her hair twice a week back then and wore it straight or in a ponytail. Beneath all this shine she still felt like the same person she was when Nick sat down beside her.

"And with two minutes to spare," Jo said. "Nicely done. Please move in with me and make me look like this every day."

Bekha smiled. "No rent? I might take you up on that." Bekha put her hands on Jo's shoulders. "Seriously, you look beautiful, and all my friends, we love you. We don't even like country music."

Jo stood up and gave Bekha a hug.

"You need your boots," Marie said. "Hang on." She went into the adjacent room to retrieve the boots, and Jo turned to the mirror and adjusted her cleavage in the gold-sequined dress, a selection her stylist and Jo could finally agree on. A piece of fringe was trapped underneath the hem. Jo freed it and said, "How do I look?"

"Killer," Bekha said.

Jo paused. She swiped her teeth with her tongue to remove a smear of red lipstick.

"Oh, no way," Bekha said. "The red boots. Can I hold them?"

"Sure."

Bekha held them close to her chest. "Is this weird? I hope it's not weird."

"Take a selfie with them," Marie said.

"Can I?"

"Sure," Jo said.

Bekha posed with her hand held out straight and took a succession of pictures with her mouth puckered, not puckered, in a smile, agape, in an O. She handed Jo her boots and then scrolled through the pictures she'd just taken. She showed her favorite one to Jo. "I love it," Jo said.

"Will you pick me to dance?"

"You should be easy to spot with that pink hair." Jo put on her boots.

"I'm counting on it then," Bekha said as she wheeled her suitcase out the door, where a handler was waiting to escort Jo to the stage for her performance.

CHAPTER 19

Glass Hearts

S TAY ON THE right," the technician shouted as if they were inside a busy suburban shopping mall.

Just a few more feet and J. D. would see all of his guitars lined up in a metal stand near his microphone like books on a shelf. He needed to see his equipment to calm his nerves. That feeling he had as a boy before he climbed onstage and played at the fall festival hadn't left him, and he hoped it never would or it would be a sure sign he'd lost his will. The technician stopped and turned around with his hand held in front of him like a crossing guard, and he pressed the headset to his ear before waving them forward.

J. D. noticed Aster talking to some girl, probably an agent or publicist of one of the pop singers, even though Aster had sworn off starlets years ago. He had women waiting for him in every city around the world and was very proud of that. On the Internet he was rumored to be the hot "man whore" of the group, like an updated James Dean in a black fedora, cigarette hanging from his lip. Girls had nicknamed him "the Trouble" and he'd accepted it as the highest compliment. Aster wore a black T-shirt with TROUBLE LOVES ME stenciled in white letters on the front. Rob shouted for Aster to catch up with them and he hustled to rejoin their line.

J. D. rounded the corner, hoping to see Jo, but she was off the stage already. There stood the microphone all alone in the center of the stage, a large red rug behind it with the band's equipment set up and ready to go. She'd sung into that microphone just moments ago, warmed it with her breath and filled the entire theater with her trembling, lilting, Southern-accented voice, unlike any he'd ever heard before. The lights above the stage were off so that a short documentary about the history of the MusiCares foundation could play on the large screen. The tech guy signaled for the band to come out.

"Let's do this right," J. D. said, and they all followed him onto the stage. J. D. secured his Fender Stratocaster over his shoulder, right where it needed to be, and Rob picked up his electric bass first to check the tuning pegs. Danny adjusted the height of his cymbal. Multiple stagehands came out and checked their equipment once more like a race car pit crew. Then the documentary ended and Danny started a steady beat on the kick drum to arouse the crowd before J. D.'s lead-in. A cone of white spotlight landed on J. D., and then another one shone on Aster as he riffed on his electric guitar until it sounded like a scream, which was what he was famous for when he hooked up with J. D. out here in LA. Chase B joined in now on the pedal steel and made it ring, and Rob followed in on the bass. Danny kept them all in line with the drumbeat. The crowd cheered.

J. D. led them straight into their most requested song and sang: "*Your truth is your truth | My truth is mine | And we're damned as we're living, damned as we try."*

The band followed his lead. Aster nailed a long guitar solo, and toward the end of the song most of the crowd was standing. To finish, J. D. turned to his guys, lifted his guitar, and they landed it on the downbeat together. The song disappeared quick, like a trout breaking water. J. D. wiped off the heavy sweat from his brow with the lucky handkerchief Jo had given him back in Gatesville. He tucked it away in his back pocket once more and looked to the side of the stage, hoping to see her standing there. Mr. Sullivan stood in the wings with his arms crossed and talked to another man who stood beside him. J. D. looked to the other side of the stage, but she wasn't there either. He almost lost the will to ask her onstage with him, but he knew she was in the building, could feel her close by, and J. D. refused to let this night pass without seeing her.

He pulled the microphone close to his mouth. "Thanks, everybody, for being here tonight. I know you were hoping for Jack White and Miss Loretta Lynn. Incomparable, I know. We'll do our best to entertain you. Hope Miss Loretta gets better soon. I want to give a big shout-out to the reason we're all here tonight. We love the MusiCares foundation. Everybody gets down on their luck sometimes, so it's good to have this safety net for artists in our industry. Be generous, folks, and enjoy the show."

According to the set list, J. D. should've moved straight into a more recent song written by a songwriter in a cubicle with a guitar and a piano in downtown Nashville. Most of their new songs came from that wellspring, but he didn't feel like singing that song tonight. J. D. switched out his electric guitar for the trusty acoustic Gibson that he'd had since he first moved to Nashville. He returned to the microphone. He said, "Jo Lover sure put on a good show, didn't she?" The crowd cheered. "I know it. She always does. Who'd like to see her one more time? Get her out here to sing a song with me?"

The crowd moved from a basic response to a loud, rolling wave of approval.

J. D. turned around to the side to see if she had appeared in the wings, but he caught a glance from Rob, who mouthed "no."

"She's bound to be around here still. Has Jo left the building? Joanne Lover, come on out here, let's do a song together. Like old times. Y'all knew we were friends, longtime friends, didn't you? Grew up together."

A few claps scattered throughout the auditorium.

"I guess you didn't know. She's been giving me a hard time since I was a boy. Joanne Lover, where are you? Let's do one of those old songs we used to love so much."

The crowd clapped and chanted Jo's name over and over again. They wanted to see her, J. D. wanted to sing with her, so that meant everybody won. Rob hurried up to J. D., gripping the neck of his electric bass with one hand and pulling J. D. away from the microphone with the other. "Don't do this, man."

"It's my decision," J. D. said, and pulled out of Rob's hold. Rob backed away ten feet and stood there staring at him. J. D. remembered that look of Rob's too well. The first time they'd ever met as boys started with a fight. Rob had just moved to Gatesville and J. D.'s mama forced him to show Rob the walk to school even though J. D. didn't want to. Rob's mama dropped him off at J. D.'s house and J. D.'s mama made a big fuss over J. D., hugged him a bunch and licked her thumb to smooth down his hair. His mama was always like that, one day smothering him in love to the point where he thought he couldn't breathe, the next day

unresponsive and unable even to sit up in bed from the sorrows, which
is what she called that consuming feeling. Rob witnessed one of her
good days. The entire time they walked to school Rob taunted J. D.
for having such a pretty mama and about her loving him so much she'd
licked him. J. D. tried to control his temper for the whole walk—he
remembered trying really hard—but right before they reached Gatesville Elementary he swung at Rob and missed, left himself open for
Rob to punch him in the nose, which he did, and then J. D. punched
him in the stomach. They backed away from each other and stood ten
feet apart in a stalemate until J. D. forced himself to keep walking to
school, with Rob lagging behind him. Funny thing was, J. D. couldn't
remember how any of this was resolved, only that not too long after
that, they became friends. But J. D. would never forget facing off with
Rob, just like he was doing now, and that familiar feeling of anger in
his chest.

Rob walked over to Aster and leaned in to tell him something. J. D.
looked at Chase B and Danny for some support. Chase B sat at his
pedal steel looking off into the wing, but then Danny added a drumbeat to the audience's enthusiastic cheers, like a good friend should.
Chase B followed Danny, and even Aster joined. But Rob stood with
his arms slack by his sides. J. D. went back to the microphone and said,
"Joanne Lover, are you in the building?"

People laughed. J. D. pumped his arm in the air to encourage the
crowd to keep clapping for her. He turned back to look at the right
wing of the stage, and Jo stood next to Mr. Sullivan. Her arms were
crossed, but then she uncrossed them and started gesturing with her
hands in a very aggressive way. She was angry, J. D. had no doubt. He
wasn't sure how to take any of this back now. How could he say, "Never
mind, Jo Lover, I'd rather you stay away," when the audience sounded

so eager? Mr. Sullivan leaned over and she leaned down to listen to him while he repeatedly used his arm to motion out toward the stage. Jo shook her head again and again, but then she wrapped her arms around her waist and her shoulders dropped down a little. Jo pulled away from Mr. Sullivan and smoothed down her dress. A tech guy handed her a fiddle.

"I think we found her," J. D. said. "Here she comes." The entire audience exploded with cheers.

Jo walked out with a huge smile on her face—for the audience, not for him; that much was clear. She waved at the crowd and people waved back. J. D. moved to the side so she could share the microphone, but she didn't look him in the eyes. She kept her gaze locked forward on the audience. "Thank y'all so much for inviting me back out. It's always a pleasure to play for such a good crowd."

The crowd whooped.

Jo smiled. "So, J. D., I don't know if this crowd wants to hear us singing an old tune."

J. D. moved toward her to speak into the microphone and she took one step back from him. He wanted her to look him in the eye, but she wouldn't. He had to settle for her profile. "Which one of my songs would you like to sing then?" J. D. said, and Jo immediately turned her face to him with her eyebrows furrowed. He continued: "Or maybe this crowd would enjoy an old tune."

The crowd made their consent known with extended applause.

"All right then," Jo said. "Let's do an old one."

J. D. leaned down into the microphone, so close to Jo now that he could smell the perfume of her hair. He said, "When we were kids and just starting out, me and Jo liked to play from the old Southern songbook. Hymns and whatnot, like 'I'll Fly Away' and 'Will the Circle Be Unbroken.'"

"That's a good one," Jo said, and the crowd applauded in response. "Let's do that one, J. D."

J. D. put his hand on her bare shoulder, but she stiffened at his touch. "We moved on to writing our own songs, remember?"

Jo narrowed her eyes at him and hesitated before she said, "I do."

"You remember cowriting 'Glass Hearts' with me?"

"You mean those breakable things?"

"That's the one."

J. D. backed up from the microphone and went to his guys. "Just me and Jo on this one. Nobody else."

He returned to the microphone, where he and Jo shared a single spotlight. J. D. entered the song with the acoustic guitar and then Jo joined him with her fiddle. Her voice met J. D.'s right on time and in perfect harmony, and right then he felt their connection glowing like a bonfire flame ignited once again from coals left over from the night before. She had to feel it too. Had to. How could she not? J. D. let her take the first verse, and she remembered the lyrics of the song they wrote together all those years ago. She remembered every single word. He might've broken her trust. God knows, he'd made terrible mistakes and would do it all differently if he had the chance. But she hadn't forgotten their songs. That gave him hope she might forgive him someday.

The heat of her breath warmed his chin as he came in on the chorus with her. J. D. closed his eyes. Together, they kept on singing.

CHAPTER 20

Gone Viral

S TANDING IN LINE at the Barista Shack in LA at nine o'clock at night—the place was packed with people—Marie checked her phone in case she'd missed a call from Jo in the ten minutes she'd been waiting in line. Nothing. Jo wanted good coffee, so Jo was going to get good coffee even though Marie couldn't really remember a time when Jo had requested coffee. She'd seen Jo drink one or two cups ever in all the time they'd known each other.

Marie looked up to see if she'd moved any further toward the table where cashiers with oiled mustaches and black aprons waved their hands as they discussed the flavor of each particular coffee bean. With deep enthusiasm the tattooed baristas preached about where the bean was grown, at what altitude, how it was roasted, how very deeply committed the farmer was to organic practices; meanwhile, the line continued to snake behind Marie. She was now in the middle. All she wanted was to buy this coffee and return to the Dolby Theatre.

The pour-over magic this place peddled might make Jo feel better. Marie had never seen her face as pale as it was after her performance with J. D., which was incredible, not that she'd ever tell Jo that. Marie had expected Jo to request a really stiff drink after that experience, not coffee. A good coffee. Just one cup of really good coffee. With sugar, no cream. Marie stepped forward, drummed her fingers on her phone. She crossed her arms, uncrossed them, leaned to the side to see how much further she had to go. An audible protest escaped her lips. The people in front of her turned around and sneered like she'd just lit a cigarette.

Marie checked her phone finally to see if Denver had texted back. This was the one place where she felt like she could text without Jo's disapproval. The Flyby Boys had a show tonight so she didn't expect to hear from him until tomorrow. She checked her work email account again. And finally. Finally. Finally. She'd reached out to her connection at the Bluebird to land Alan and Denver a showcase—she asked for favors so rarely—and her contact had sent her an email and said yes.

Denver had been calling her Marie the Magnificent in his texts today, said he was blown away by who she was, who she worked for, how successful she was for someone their age. Denver had no idea what she could do, and this filled her with an addictive kind of pleasure. She wanted to help him and Alan any way she could because she really believed in their music, the way she believed in Jo's. The line moved forward all at once. Suddenly Marie was much closer to the iPad register than she'd thought possible two minutes before. An email from Jo's manager popped up. She opened it and read: *Hey, Marie. Have you seen this yet?!?!?!?! People can't stop tweeting about it. Follow this link.*

Marie tapped on the link to find J. D. Gunn and Joanne Lover standing side by side onstage, frozen in time. Just an hour ago, she had been standing there on the side of the stage, watching all of this happen. She had felt the power of the two of them singing as one, a moment cast now as motionless. She pulled out her headphones from her purse, plugged them into her phone, and hit "play" to hear them singing again. Jo and J. D. became animated on her small screen, deep in song, in total harmony. She couldn't quite tell where one voice began and the other one ended. This could not compare to hearing it live for the first time, but it came close.

Marie scrolled down her phone to find the number of views, and had she been drinking coffee, she might've spit it out. The video, posted over an hour ago, had four and a half million views already, and counting. Millions. Not thousands. Millions? "Holy shit," Marie said, and the young couple in front of her turned around and gave her a strange look. She pulled out both headphones from her ears. She immediately called Jo, but no one answered. It was Marie's turn to order. Her barista had a bright ruddy beard with the name Holiday written on his name tag.

"Two black coffees to go, please."

"Which roast would you like?"

"The strongest."

"We have a variety of growers from Peru—"

"Anything," Marie said. "Just the fastest, please."

The smile left his face and he turned his attention to preparing her order. Nashville had coffee shops just like these and normally Marie would have humored their passion for the beans. But not right now. She stepped to the side of the register to wait and tried calling Jo again but still received her voice mail. She considered calling Nick, but something felt wrong about that. Marie called Mr. Sullivan instead, who picked up right away. "Yes, hello?"

"Hi, Mr. Sullivan. This is Marie, Jo's assistant. I'm so sorry to bother you and I wouldn't normally, but I was calling to see if you'd heard about the YouTube video going viral." Marie watched the barista pour hot water slowly over the coffee grounds.

"I just did," he said, and sounded as gleeful as she'd ever heard him. "I tried knocking on Jo's door."

"She's resting."

"Tell her it's great news. In fact, don't. I'd like to tell her myself. Could I see her in twenty minutes?"

"Yes, sir," Marie said, and felt a twinge of panic. She tried texting Jo this time. Holiday brought over the coffees in a brown recyclable tray and Marie hustled out of the Barista Parlor and back to the car waiting for her. She asked the driver to speed back to the Dolby Theatre, which he did with great enthusiasm. The coffees spilled on the tray and on her pants. He dropped her off at the backstage entrance, where Marie quickly moved through clearance and passed J. D. Gunn and the Empty Shells coming down the opposite side of the hallway.

J. D. crossed the hallway and Marie slowed down. He was so tall and Marie so short that she felt like she was viewing some kind of cathedral when she looked up at him.

"You're Jo's assistant, right?"

She held the coffee tray against her chest and reached out a hand for him, which he took. "I'm Marie."

"Good to meet you." He let go of her hand. "We've been trying to call Jo. Does she know about the video?"

"I'm about to tell her," Marie said.

"Y'all are welcome to come celebrate on the bus, if she's up for it."

Marie detected a hint of concern in his voice. "I'll ask her," Marie said, and lifted the tray. "Coffee's getting cold." And she felt very acutely like J. D.'s lead guitarist, Aster, was leering at her. Marie smiled at them all in an apologetic way and moved past them, continuing on to Jo's suite a few doors down. Marie steadied the tray in her hand like a waitress and put her hand on the doorknob, turned it, but it was still locked. She turned it again and again and then stepped back from the door. She knocked softly. "Jo?"

Nothing.

Marie glanced down at the guys, who were talking to Mr. Sullivan now. They were all looking down the hall at her. She leaned against the wall beside the door, and then she eased herself to the floor and placed the tray of coffees next to her. She had no idea why Jo had shut her out. Marie refreshed her phone: almost five million views and climbing.

CHAPTER 21

Locked Door

THE EMPTY SHELLS finished a second set, and afterward the crowd kept calling for Jo to come back onstage with them, kept chanting "J. D." and "Jo," "J. D., Jo, J. D., Jo," until it sounded like one long name—JDJo, like one identity, like oneness, until she almost couldn't stay away from the crowd any longer. She locked herself in the dressing room to keep herself from going down the hall and walking right up there with J. D., fiddle in hand, for the encore the audience desired. Jo hadn't felt that much happiness onstage in a very long time, and the surge she felt now was as close to flying as any she'd ever experienced.

Her own set tonight had gone well too—not a single mistake—yet the Jo and J. D. duet would replace her solo performance in the audience's memory. And Jo understood why. She felt the power between them as artists. That song they'd written all those years ago was good then, and it was now. Great songs don't lose their power with age. Jo had sent Marie out for a pour-over coffee because she knew that errand would take a long time to complete, but all Jo really wanted was a Mason jar mountain mule—moonshine, ginger beer, and a squeeze of lime. She wanted to clink glasses with J. D. and tell him just how incredible it was to sing that song with him.

Marie called her, texted her, and had now returned and was standing right outside her door, jiggling the handle and knocking to come in, but Jo wasn't ready to see anybody. Not yet. And as she sat at her makeup table and watched herself in the mirror, she felt the first wave of euphoria receding and a tide of wandering melancholy taking its place. It could've always been this way if they hadn't sacrificed each other for their individual careers. It could've always been just like this.

With a makeup-removal wipe, Jo massaged her face until her cheeks turned pink like the skin of a newborn baby. Off came her smoky eye shadow and her thick mascara in trails of muted black traveling down her face, dripping from her jawline and onto her exposed neck. Next she brushed her hair until the curls returned to straight black hair, just like she'd worn it for most of her life. Plain fingernails, that's what she wanted. When was the last time she had just plain fingernails? No bright polish to match whatever new outfit she'd been told to wear onstage. She wiped her nails with cotton balls soaked in polish remover, but the color wouldn't come off completely. She exposed the stained red nails underneath the shine.

Marie knocked again.

Jo threw the wipe away in the trash can and then stared at her hands pressed on the vanity table amid a spattering of tools to make her beautiful. Her hands had so many wrinkles. So many tiny Xs patterned up and down her fingers, and on the corners of her eyes too. How much she'd aged since she and J. D. last sang together like that.

"Jo," Marie said, and jiggled the door handle some more.

Singing up there with J. D., all smiles and joy—joy she couldn't control because she loved singing so much—had made her feel like she was living a lie. She'd lived lies almost her entire life. Jo stared at the plain-faced woman in the mirror staring right back at her, a person Jo recognized so little because she so rarely saw her.

"Please let me in. I don't want to say this through a door," Marie called from the other side. "Listen, everybody's tweeting about your duet. It has like five and a half million views on YouTube already. You should see all the crazy-good comments people posted. Listen to this music critic: *J. D. Gunn and Jo Lover are better together than I've ever seen them apart. They have to have to have to have to sing together again. Is there an album in their future?* And what about this one: *There was Porter and Dolly, Loretta and Conway, George and Tammy, Emmylou and Gram, and now Joanne and J. D. Instant classic.*"

Jo turned her face to the door as if an alarm had gone off in the building. Marie said millions, she was certain she'd heard that right. Jo felt a panic gripping her chest like a vise. Jo couldn't hide when they harmonized together, couldn't play the sassy, red-boots-wearing, unattached Joanne Lover the audience expected her to be, not when she sang with J. D. The audience could feel that thing between them. Whatever it was, she believed they could feel it. How else to explain those numbers Marie had just said? Did Nick know? It was well past midnight in New York. He might not find out until the morning.

She heard Mr. Sullivan's voice outside her door, and then a knock. "Joanne, stop prettying yourself in there. Let me in for a minute."

All Jo wanted was to be alone and people just kept coming at her. She forced herself to take deep breaths, counting to ten and then back down to one as she exhaled. Jo quickly slicked her hair back in a high ponytail, covered her face with a foundation powder, and then opened the door.

Marie entered with the tray of coffees held out like an offering bowl, and Mr. Sullivan followed in behind her. He opened his arms out wide. "Well done, my dear. Well done. This is the most money ever raised for MusiCares. And you know why? Not those other acts, I promise you. It was country music's win tonight." He hugged her hard, like a father might, and then Mr. Sullivan released Jo from his embrace. Marie offered Jo one of the coffees, which she accepted and held between her hands, the paper cup warming her palms. Marie said, "The Empty Shells invited us to their bus."

"You should go celebrate. Their fridge will be stocked with the finest champagne soon. Would you like to go?" Jo asked Marie.

"If you do."

Jo walked over to her vanity and began applying concealer under her eyes and a new application of eye shadow and mascara, knowing, of course, that she could never match the skill of her makeup artist, and then she debated whether or not she could go on J. D.'s tour bus without her face and hair set the way it was for the concert. Immediately she concluded that if she couldn't go to his bus without covering her face with paint, then there was no way she could still be in love with him. If she loved him, she wouldn't hesitate to go just as she was.

Marie walked up behind Jo and met her eyes in the mirror. "Want me to curl your hair?"

"Would you?"

Marie gestured for Jo to sit down, and Marie went to her bag, fetched one of Jo's travel curling irons, and plugged it into the outlet next to the table.

"No scotch?"

"Never did develop a taste for that." Jo smiled.

"I didn't know that." Mr. Sullivan poured himself a whiskey, stood next to Jo's vanity, and raised up his tumbler to toast with the air.

Marie ran her thin fingers through Jo's hair and brushed it with a round brush. She wrapped a wide section of hair in the curling iron and wound it up until Jo could feel the heat on her scalp. "Have you heard from Nick?"

"Not since yesterday." Mr. Sullivan sipped his drink. "He's still mad at me, I presume."

"Will he be madder now?"

"If I know my son, then I'll be the only one to blame for this little duet."

"That's not true," Jo said.

Mr. Sullivan picked up her eyelash curler and examined it as if it were an artifact at an excavation site. "If you know someone as a child, you know the fundamentals. Nick always held on to a grudge for much too long. Luckily for us, he's never been quick to anger."

The last part was the Nick she knew best, the part she knew was true, without any doubt. Nick and Jo never fought. He maintained a calm and gentle disposition, especially in the studio, which made him such a great producer. Theirs was the least dramatic relationship of any she knew, but she worried sometimes that all of this calm and quiet masked a truer self underneath. Nothing seemed to bother Nick like the presence of J. D. Gunn, but Nick was a reasonable man. He'd understand that this was none of Jo's doing.

Marie worked her way around Jo's head with the curling iron, and slowly Jo's hair was returning to all its voluminous glory. Mr. Sullivan seated himself on Jo's couch behind her, where she could still see him in the mirror.

He said, "You know I was right, don't you?"

Marie yanked Jo's hair by accident and quickly said, "Sorry."

"Right about what?" Jo said.

"You and J. D. make an excellent collaboration."

Jo opened her mouth to deflect, but Mr. Sullivan continued quickly: "The fans have spoken and they want a J. D. Gunn and Jo Lover collaboration. If a song you two wrote a decade ago was this well received, imagine what you could do together now. Just imagine it. Not just one or two songs. An entire album, Jo. And I promise you, and you have to know it's true in your gut, that it's destined to be your biggest album yet. A blockbuster album. I already spoke to J. D. He agrees. He knows it."

Marie avoided Jo's stare as Mr. Sullivan spoke, but she slowed down on the curling iron work, and then put it down and brushed Jo's hair very lightly like it might catch fire if she brushed it out too fast.

"Could I at least have some time to consider this?" Jo said. "To discuss it with Nick?"

"I want to tell you sure, you know I do, for my son's sake too, but in this case it seems so very inevitable, Jo. You witnessed the response from that crowd. It was magical."

She stood up from her chair and poured herself a whiskey neat.

"You two go celebrate. I'll be offended if you don't help yourself to some of that champagne."

"We'll be flying back separately in the morning," Jo said. "Just so you know."

Mr. Sullivan looked at Marie and she nodded in confirmation. She said, "Jo has a thing. A radio thing."

"I will see you when we return to Nashville," Mr. Sullivan said, and then he finished the rest of his scotch and left the empty tumbler on the coffee table next to a stack of *Vanity Fair* magazines.

CHAPTER 22

Tour Bus Hayride

C HASE B PUT Merle Haggard's vinyl album *Okie from Muskogee* on the record player in the side enclave of the tour bus and said, "It's time for smoking." Aster sat on the leather couch lining the tour bus and restrung his Stratocaster. Rob stood up front and talked to their driver. Before Merle finished singing "We don't smoke marijuana in Muskogee," Chase B had his glass bong out, ready to pack. Danny and Chase B sat at the kitchenette table and smoked together, and Aster put away his guitar and joined them. Rob returned and dropped down on the couch beside his girlfriend, Tammy, and whispered in her ear.

J. D. couldn't read Tammy's body language. She pinned her hands between her knees and looked stiff but J. D. could also see a big smile on her face as she leaned into Rob's arm. Other people's love had always confounded J. D. He could try to guess about the dynamics between two people, but he was usually wrong. He'd figured out a long time ago that you can never really know another person, no matter how much intimate time you share together. People were always capable of surprise—a lover one day, a total stranger the next. Danny offered the glass bong to J. D. and he took a huge hit.

"Sit down, J. D.," Danny said, and moved over closer to Chase B so that J. D. could have a seat at the table.

"Blackjack," Aster said, and shuffled the deck of cards in his dexterous hands, then he started to deal. "J. D., how about you bet the house, your boots, the Range Rovers, the boat, the Porsche, the Montana camp, your beloved Dobros and dulcimers collection—the entire damn estate on this one hand." Aster dealt J. D. in with one card facedown and a king of diamonds face up. He pointed at J. D.'s mystery card. "Could be an ace."

J. D. lit a cigarette and drank his whiskey. He left the cards untouched. "And if I lose, who'd inherit all my stuff?"

"The band," Chase B said, and blew out smoke in J. D.'s direction.

J. D. lifted the edge of his card to find a five of hearts.

Aster offered the deck to J. D. and asked if he'd take a hit. J. D. nodded and Aster smacked the card down. "There's the ace," Aster said.

Now J. D. had sixteen, not enough to win, probably, yet close enough to bust.

"Will you bet it all?" Aster said.

"What's mine is yours already."

"That's true," Aster said. He picked up the bong, inhaled, and on the exhale said, "For now. But you wait. This viral video is just the start. Next thing you know it'll be a Gunn and Lover tour, and since Jo's the woman and women always get what they want in these matters, it'll be her band onstage with you and not us."

"Damn," Chase B said. "You think that could happen?"

"It can happen," Aster said.

Rob stood up from the couch and surveyed the blackjack table.

Aster said, "So bet your estate. That way we'll get something out of that choice you made to ask her onstage tonight."

"Yeah, man," Danny said.

J. D. looked to Rob and said, "Tell them that won't happen."

"Can't."

"Why not?"

Rob shrugged.

"Why can't you tell them?" J. D. pushed.

"You left us behind before."

Now the joke was starting to wear off, and J. D. felt his temper rising from the deep. He knew Jo might not ever forgive him fully, but he thought Rob had. J. D. said, "That was a long time ago."

Quietly, Chase B said, "You shouldn't have brought it up like that, Rob."

Rob sat back down with Tammy.

At least Chase B was willing to speak up for J. D. "I bet the estate, then. The whole fucking thing. Rob's chicken coop too."

Aster smiled. "One more hit?"

"I'll stay," J. D. said.

He offered the deck to Chase B and Danny, but they declined. "Show me your cards, boys."

Chase B and Danny both overturned their cards without any enthusiasm. They both busted. J. D. revealed his combined score of sixteen and waited for Aster to reveal the dealer's hand. He leveled his stare at J. D. "You love that fishing pond, man. You're willing to lose it?"

"I am."

Aster flipped his cards over to show a king, a queen, and a three. "Busted, J. D. wins," Danny shouted, and punched Aster in the arm, who started laughing, then swept the table clean and gathered all the cards back into the deck. J. D. stood up from the table and turned his back on all the guys. He opened up the cabinet, pulled out the cherry moonshine, and drank it straight from the Mason jar. He felt the rage dissipate from the center of his chest.

Chase B shouted, "Jooooaaaaanne Lover's in the house. Yes, she is." J. D. turned his attention to the front of the bus to find Jo and her assistant, Marie, standing there. Rob swung Jo around in the small space at the front of the bus. Chase B stood up and hugged her too. Jo let out a huge laugh that sank right into J. D.'s body. She still wore that gold-sequined dress she'd had on when they sang together earlier, her hair was still curled and done up for the stage, but she had bare lips and wore much less eye makeup. J. D. liked being able to see her, really see her, with nothing covering up her face. Jo smiled wide and looked right at him—that look always did him in like the full moon rising over the mountaintop. J. D. stood opposite her and watched her face in the haze of the cabin.

Rob pulled out a small-batch Dickel from the cabinet above the sink. He opened the top with his teeth and held out the bottle to her. "Ladies first." Jo accepted the bottle, but then she offered it to Marie, who took the first sip, then Jo tipped it back.

Danny said, "Now Jo's here, we can hit up the good stuff." Danny opened the refrigerator. J. D. stood behind him and saw bottles of gold-foiled Cristal stacked one on top of the other like a glistening pyramid. Danny handed a bottle to Jo. He said, "You two should do the honors. Six million hits in a few hours? You're bigger than Brooklyn." He put two fingers in his mouth and whistled.

Chase B stood up, clapping. "Pop that cherry soda." He took a bong hit with one hand and continued to slap his thigh with the other.

J. D. pulled out his pocketknife and sliced off the foil. His thumbs were on the cork. Then Jo said, "Hold up." Her hand was on his hand for the first time in so long that he felt his body go cold. He wanted to grab it and hold her. Forget the bottle, take her to the back room, away from everyone else. Share this drink and talk. But the bottle was all she wanted. She shook the bottle hard while the boys growled, "Yeah," and Tammy howled, "Get her, girl."

"There," she said, and handed it back to him. "Now open it."

He made sure champagne rained on her first. Everybody huddled around J. D. as he raised the bottle high and waved it all around to baptize them all with this wasted money. They pulled out one bottle after another until everyone was good and wet. Bottles of whiskey, scotch, tequila, and champagne moved like freight out of the kitchen. Bottles on tables, bottles on couches, bottles up front with Guy in the driver's seat. George Jones's number one hit "White Lightning" spun on the record player. The electric guitar hit high notes and the chords rolled. Danny pretended to brush the drums as the girls started a breakdown. Everyone sang, "*Ssshhheeeew, white lightning.*"

Jo and Marie took shots of tequila and danced. Jo's black hair stuck to her cheeks like tattooed lines, her mascara ran down the corners of her eyes, and one thin strap of her gold dress hung off her shoulder. To J. D. she looked like a Rorschach test. And she skipped high off the ground, her knees up, her feet bare. He danced with her, in rhythm. She closed in, steely-eyed and locked on him, and took his vest in her hands, pulled him closer, and then gave him a drink of tequila straight from the bottle. She did the same for Rob, who danced right next to them.

Rob shouted: "I can't believe you're here, Jo."

She hugged him, her smile generous and radiant. Then she moved

on to Chase B and Marie and then back to J. D. They all danced together like the old days when they'd come home from a show, build a
bonfire, and start a dance party with whoever showed up. They were
dancing so much now that the tour bus started shaking.

As the sweeping tempo slowed and the song came to a close, Chase
B said, "Crack open that lemon moonshine, J. D."

J. D. pulled out the quart-sized Mason jar from the cabinet above
the sink. Bright yellow lemons rested at the bottom of the tinted liq-
uid. He passed around the jar and Jo came over to him, George Jones's
voice louder than her own, louder than everybody's. She leaned in
close. "Got any clothes I could borrow?"

He wanted to tell her no—the thought of Jo wearing his T-shirt and
gym shorts pained him somewhere deep—but what kind of man would
he be if he said no? J. D. drank his moonshine and nodded. While Jo
used the bathroom, he laid out his clothes for her on the bed, and when
she entered the room, J. D. started to leave. But she grabbed his arm
and said, "Hang on. I need help unhooking this damned dress."

J. D. put down his lemon moonshine and walked over to her, her
back turned to him, her lovely shoulders exposed. J. D. wanted to trail
his fingers along her spine like he was tracing a string of pearls. Jo
lifted her hair up, revealing a tattoo of a thin black circle at the base of
her long neck. He'd almost forgotten it was there.

"May it be unbroken," she'd said after she surprised him with it in
New Orleans on a two-day break between gigs. He knew what she
meant. May we be unbroken. Us. Jo and J. D. Beignets and café au lait
when they woke up in the afternoon, gigs at night, followed by chicken
and sausage gumbo for lunch and hurricanes to drink away the hang-
overs. Touring all over the country in a shitty shuttle van together.

That tattoo reminded him of a wedding ring, permanent but hidden unless you knew where to look. J. D. wanted to place his hand on the side of her neck and gently pull her into him, feel her warm back rest against his chest and smother his face in her hair.

Jo reached back and tried to grab the hook. "Can you get it or what?"

He couldn't touch her. "Maybe I should go get Marie."

"Just try one more time." Jo kept her back to him. "She's pretty drunk."

"I'm sorry," J. D. said.

"It's just a hook."

"That's not what I mean."

She faced him, her dark eyes narrowed, her face so close to his he could see the small lines around her eyes. He said, "I'm so damn sorry for everything, Jo. All these years have passed. I know it doesn't mean much now, I know. I still need you to hear it."

Her cheeks became red and she quickly turned back around. In a casual voice she said, "That was so long ago, J. D. Really, I've let that all go."

J. D. placed his hand on her shoulder, and after a moment, he felt her breathe in deeply.

Jo said, "Maybe you should go ask Marie to come," as she reached back for the hook and unsnapped it herself, the dress falling fast from the weight of the fabric. With her forearm, she caught the dress on her cleavage, but just barely. She peered over her shoulder. Her voice went soft when she said, "I'll be out in just a minute."

J. D. closed the door behind him and returned to the common area, where Chase B stood on top of the table, bent over like a stripper and waving his ass in the air. His jeans fell down to his knees. He would've tumbled headfirst if Danny hadn't caught him. Dollar bills fluttered out of his pants like green confetti as J. D. poured himself another bit of moonshine. The sun had set in Los Angeles.

"So what're we doing?" Aster said. "We staying or going?"

Rob stood next to J. D. and said, "*Vanity Fair* after-party or we go straight over to the Marquis party. That's where our rooms are booked."

They were all looking at J. D. for the final say. "Marquis."

J. D.'s bedroom door opened and Jo walked out in his COUNTRY MU-SIC FOREVER white T-shirt and a pair of his mesh workout shorts. J. D. stared at her, and everyone became quiet.

"What's all the fuss?" she said, and leaned against the cabinet. She placed one slender foot on top of the other, something she'd always done when she was nervous. Her toenails were painted red. Jo held her boots and dress in one hand.

"This train's a-moving," Chase B said. "You coming?"

Aster said, "Let's get you a car to take you back to your hotel, so you can get your clothes, and then you can ride back to the Marquis. Marie can come with us."

Marie swayed a little, raised her hand in the air like a Southern preacher, and said, "Absolutely. I go where my people go."

Jo lowered Marie's arm. "We just wanted to have a drink," Jo said. "And we had fun, so thank you, but I think we should be getting back now. Early flight tomorrow."

Jo and Marie moved toward the front of the bus, where Jo helped Marie sit down on the couch. Marie dropped her head in her hands. J. D. brought a trash can to the front of the bus.

Jo rubbed Marie's back and accepted the trash can. "I've never seen her so drunk before."

"I'm not drunk," Marie shouted.

J. D. said, "Let me help you take her back."

"That's okay," Jo said. "It's not far."

"I'm not drunk," Marie screamed again, and jerked away from Jo.

"Well," Jo said.

Guy was in the driver's seat reading a *Playboy* article about their band. J. D. said, "Call us a car, will you?"

Guy closed his magazine and pulled out his cell phone.

J. D. nodded, and then he sat down behind Guy's seat and reached for his father's Gibson, which was resting in a case beneath the couch. He opened up the case and lifted the guitar out. He strummed. The guys went back to drinking and telling stories. J. D. fingered the chords to Merle's "Always Wanting You." He said, "You feel like playing while we wait?"

"Sure."

J. D. slid out the fiddle case from underneath the couch, opened it, and handed the instrument to Jo. She moved to the edge of the seat and picked up the fiddle. She ran the bow over the strings a couple times before she said, "Let's play 'I Walk the Line.'"

J. D. tapped his foot to count them off. Danny turned off the record player and joined in with a hand drum. And then everybody joined in and their voices filled up the bus as they repeated the song three times over. Jo sang the lead, but J. D. kept up with rhythm guitar. Her eyes were closed, her thick eyelashes cast down. This kind of serenity was how J. D. remembered her best.

Guy tapped J. D. on the shoulder. "Car's about to be here."

J. D. continued strumming until Jo's fiddle slowed down and came to a close, and then J. D. said, "It's time to go."

Guy opened the doors for them and right outside a town car awaited. Jo went down the steps first. Rob came over and said, "Hang on a minute—let me say bye." He hugged Jo and helped Marie walk down the bus steps. Jo said, "Have fun at the Marquis."

J. D. moved to enter the car when Rob said, "You're leaving too?"

"I'm helping with Marie. I'll meet up with you at the Marquis."

Before Rob could tell him not to go, J. D. slid into the car next to Marie and shut the door. Marie dropped her head on J. D.'s shoulder.

"Where to?" the driver said with a thick Jersey accent.

"East," J. D. said. "Back to Nashville."

"Say again?"

"He's joking," Jo said.

"Better yet, carry us back to old Virginny."

"Where?" the driver said again.

"The Four Seasons," Jo said, but this time she laughed, which was the best sound in the world and all J. D. wanted to hear.

CHAPTER 23

Shades Pulled Down

JO REMEMBERED A late-summer night when she, Rob, and J. D. had finished practicing their little bluegrass ensemble in J. D.'s barn, and his mama invited them to stay for dinner. J. D.'s mama used fine ingredients in the foods she cooked—Jo had never seen balsamic vinegar before and wasn't too sure she should eat something black on her fresh garden greens, but she refused to ask what it was, afraid of sounding poor and ignorant. She felt a little bit out of sorts around J. D.'s family. Jo's home was only half the size of the barn J. D. had for practicing music.

After dinner J. D.'s parents put a Ray Price record on their phonograph and moved the antique sitting room furniture to the side so they could dance together. Mrs. Gunn closed her eyes and rested her head on Mr. Gunn's shoulder. J. D. looked like his mother, with his dark curly hair and blue eyes, and that dreamy way he looked out of them. Jo couldn't remember her own parents ever caressing each other, but they had so many of Jo's cousins running around all the time it was hard to even remember her parents in the same room together.

J. D.'s nose and cheeks turned a muted red as he watched his parents moving together in slow time. When the song ended, Mrs. Gunn came over to J. D. and petted his face. "My handsome boy." Then she turned to Rob and Jo and said, "I've always known he was special, knew it when he was growing in my body. I'd talk to him and he'd kick right back. We were talking together even then."

She kissed him on the forehead and with her face close to his, she said, "Don't you ever forget that, okay? Don't ever forget how special you are."

Mr. Gunn came over and took her by the arm. "You spoil him."

She tousled his hair. "Can't help it."

Mr. and Mrs. Gunn retired for the night and left them all a little uncomfortable from that sudden affection. But Jo never doubted that J. D. was special or that he would become famous, if that's what he wanted. It was what he'd wanted, no matter what he thought of his life now. The city of Los Angeles moved past her window in a blur of palm trees and neon lights until the driver finally pulled in to her hotel and dropped them off at the entrance. People stared at J. D., Jo, and Marie as they entered the open-air lobby, where a concrete fountain filled with live pink flamingos greeted them all. Jo overheard a passerby ask her friend if it was really them. The hotel staff at the reception desk waved as they walked by. Marie stumbled along between them.

More people approached J. D. and Jo in the lobby. A teenage girl said, "I just saw you guys on YouTube. That was awesome. Will you do another song like that?"

"Maybe so," Jo said, and then raised her eyebrows at J. D. Jo knew that millions of people had watched that video already, but to have someone tell her in person made it feel real for the first time.

Jo rubbed Marie's back and looked to J. D. as a crowd surrounded them like they were a nucleus inside a busy atom. Marie took J. D.'s arm and they all walked to the elevators and Jo pushed the button to go up. The crowd followed them still. Jo's chest felt tight.

Marie stumbled but J. D. held her up. "Are people videoing this?"

"No," Jo lied.

"Are you his girlfriend?" another woman shouted from behind them, the sound of disappointment clear in her voice. The doors opened and the elevator operator insisted no one else could ride. They ascended until the elevator released them onto their private floor, where J. D. carried Marie to her suite. Marie managed to find her swipe card and opened the door. She flung herself halfway on the bed, and J. D. lifted her up further. Jo took off her shoes and covered Marie in a blanket, but she threw it off. "Hate being hot."

J. D. picked it up off the floor and put it on the bed next to her. "Just in case."

They turned off the lights and left Marie's room. J. D. followed Jo into her room next door and took off his hat. "May I?" he said.

"Sure," Jo said, and J. D. poured himself a whiskey neat in a glass tumbler. "Want one?"

"I'm okay." Jo sorted through a closet full of clothes that her stylist had sent along. She wanted to return J. D.'s clothes before he left. She selected a breezy wrap dress. "I'm going to change real quick. And thank you for helping me. She was super drunk."

"No problem." J. D. slapped his stomach. "She lacks our Appalachian tolerance."

Jo laughed. "Her liver will thank her later."

J. D. opened the doors to her balcony and a warm breeze settled in the room. He stretched one arm above him and gripped the top of the door frame. "Let's go swimming. You have a suit?"

Jo stopped on her way to the bathroom. "I do."

"I'll ask them to close it down for us. Just me and you."

His hand curved around the phone on her table, the muscle in his forearm contracting just like it did when he chopped wood as a boy. He ran his other hand through his hair and shook it out some. One drink by the pool. That was her limit. One and done. Jo found her bikini in her suitcase and went to change in the bathroom while J. D. talked to the front-desk employee. When she returned from the bathroom in her robe, he said, "Taken care of."

The elevator operator descended them to the pool entrance floor. J. D. changed into the workout shorts he'd let Jo borrow and immediately cannonballed into the pool. Jo sat down at the edge of the pool, her legs dangling in the warm water. He was still under there, his flesh bright and shining like a dropped coin. J. D. had a magician's talent for holding his breath; he could last for three minutes, sometimes longer, and the first time he demonstrated this ability, Jo, Rob, and J. D. were at the rock quarry swimming hole for the second or third time ever. After band practice, they rode on J. D.'s four-wheelers to the quarry, where J. D. was willing to dive headfirst off the seventy-foot cliffs into the green water below. They all swam until the sun set behind the wall of blasted mountainside. J. D. had brought a basket of snacks his mom made up, mostly some fresh goat's cheese, sourdough bread, and blueberries she grew in the front of the house.

Rob rolled American Spirit tobacco in Zig-Zags. They lay out on the rocks, all on the same handmade quilt. J. D. owned a portable CD player, and they listened to Led Zeppelin, Nirvana, the Steve Miller

Band, Rush, Elvis, the Beatles, and the Rolling Stones. From the interviews J. D. gave, people might have thought he'd grown up listening to nothing but hillbilly music, like Jimmie Rodgers and Doc Watson, or Howlin' Wolf blues. But they fed their ears on rock music too.

Jo didn't own a bathing suit during those quarry swimming days. Her T-shirt and jean shorts stuck to her legs like papier-mâché as they climbed up the cliff behind J. D. to watch him jump. His daddy and mama had warned them about the jagged rocks down at the bottom. "Mind your jumping," Mrs. Gunn always told them before they went. "Make sure you get a good five feet out." Rob and Jo refused to jump, but J. D. seemed to thrive on pushing himself beyond where other people were willing to go. One time he cannonballed off but didn't surface immediately from the dark green water below. Thirty seconds passed, then a minute.

Rob said, "He's dead. Holy fucking shit, he hit his head and he's dead. He's dead. J. D.'s dead. What do we do, Jo? Go in?"

"He'd float up, right? If he hit his head?" She wasn't sure if this was scientifically accurate, but she didn't trust J. D. either. Who could fully trust a guy who'd jump without hesitation?

Another minute passed. They both ran down the hill to the water's edge. Thirty seconds passed. "I'm going in for him," Rob said, and launched into the water.

And as soon as he did, J. D.'s pale body surfaced like a sperm whale and tackled Rob from behind. They started wrestling right there in the water. J. D. was playing at first, but then Rob punched him in the stomach and J. D. punched Rob in the jaw. Jo screamed for them to stop. She jumped on them in the water. When J. D. stood up, she socked him right in the nose, the bright red blood mixing with the murky water. He grabbed his face and his eyes welled up.

Jo took Rob by the arm. They all walked out of the water and rode home together in silence. They missed band practice for two weeks. Jo's hand hurt too much to hold her bow, but finally, J. D. found Rob and Jo fishing at Pike's Creek one afternoon. He said, "I swear that's the last time I'll ever do that." And he never pulled a stunt like that again. The idea of his dying made Jo so angry that she couldn't forgive him for months—and that's exactly how she knew she loved him.

Jo kicked her legs in the pool water and drank from J. D.'s tumbler of whiskey. He'd been down there a solid three minutes, maybe four. She placed his drink on the pool's edge, slipped into the water, and then swam to the bottom of the deep end. He flipped over on his back, his dark hair floating above his head like they were in outer space. He waved at her and said something she couldn't make out, not with all those big bubbles escaping from his mouth. She laughed, letting all her air out, and immediately had to surface.

J. D. surfaced too and spit out water. "Let's do a diving contest."

Jo treaded water. "How old are we again?"

J. D. smiled just like she remembered from those rock quarry days, so carefree and easy. Maybe that boy she knew was still in there somewhere.

"Come on," he said, and splashed her.

Jo laughed and splashed him back. "How about I watch you dive?"

"Rate it?"

"Sure." She swam freestyle to the edge of the pool, climbed up the ladder, and sat on the side. He lifted himself up from the pool's edge, his back muscles contracting as he did. J. D. climbed the small diving board. He paused, lifted his arms high, and began stretching, first his hamstrings, then his shoulders.

"Anytime's good," Jo said.

"It's going to be amazing." He ran to the end of the board, bending it like a professional, and then with one knee up his massive body sailed over to her, rocking waves into the pool and soaking her. She wiped the water from her face, and then she felt his hands on her ankles. She pushed off the edge before he could pull her in.

"How was that?" he said.

"Nine point two," she said as she swam to the side.

"What?"

"Your form wasn't quite right."

"My form?"

She nodded.

He flexed his bicep. "I think my form's pretty good."

Jo climbed up the ladder and toweled off before wrapping herself in her robe. Side by side, they rested in the lounge chairs and stared at the motionless pool, which was so still it was as if Jo and J. D. had never been there. J. D. placed his Stetson hat on his head, just over his eyes so she couldn't see his face anymore. Bare chest and arms, calves and feet: that's all she could see. She leaned toward his chair and looked closer at his arm, where a tattoo of Jo's eyes used to be. "When'd you cover that up?"

Unmoving, like he was at the spa having a facial, J. D. said, "A while ago."

"What is it now? A garden snake?"

He laughed and lifted his hat. He stared at his arm like he was second-guessing it. "I thought it looked like the road."

"Why didn't you just get it removed?"

"I like knowing they're under there." And then he shielded his eyes once more with his hat and rested his head back.

After J. D., Jo, and Rob had won the Stanley Brothers amateur contest when they were ten years old, they spent the summer touring venues in Southwest Virginia. That summer, while their peers were tanning by the lake and working on farms, Rob's mama drove them around the circuit in her van. They felt big-time. At a small music festival in Floyd County, right before they went onstage, J. D. held Jo backstage by her arm and told her he loved her for the first time.

Jo remembered feeling stunned and saying, "What?"

He said, "I had to tell you or I couldn't sing."

Jo didn't respond, but she could think of nothing else the entire time she played. She repeated what he'd said to her each night while trying to fall asleep. Even now she wished she'd told him she loved him too. She sometimes feared she would never love anyone again the way she'd once loved J. D. Gunn. Not even Nick. But there were different kinds of love in this world. The kind of love Jo needed in her life right now was different from what she needed back then.

J. D. took off his hat and placed it on the circular drink table beside him. He drank his whiskey and lit a cigarette before saying, "A reporter called me wanting to ask questions about us and Gatesville—you know about that?"

"When?"

"Yesterday."

"From *Vanity Fair*? Did you talk to him?"

"No."

"I canceled it. He shouldn't be calling anymore."

"I get it."

Jo stretched her arms above her head and held on to the metal bar at the top of the lounge chair. "I heard your daddy married the librarian."

"You remember her?"

"I think so. Miss Pratt. Red hair? Short?"

J. D. smoked and nodded. "She was my mama's friend."

Jo wasn't sure what she should say to this, so she just kept quiet.

"What about your parents?"

"Daddy's gone deaf. He was always half-deaf. Too much whiskey for his fevers as a baby."

J. D. nodded. "I think my daddy's always been deaf." He scratched his face. "You keep up with the rest of your family?"

"A little."

"Isabell?"

"Mama sends me updates, I guess. I send them money."

J. D. put out his cigarette and offered Jo his whiskey. Jo took it and said, "Can we talk about something happy?"

J. D. stayed quiet for a minute, readjusted his towel, and then said, "You remember that first time you jumped onstage with me?"

"At the fall festival?"

"That's the one," he said.

"Yeah, I remember."

"I expected you to be a boy."

Jo laughed out loud. "You never told me that."

"My daddy didn't tell me your full name. Just called you Jo."

"Remember Rob coming up to us afterward with that tip jar full of money and asking if he could join the band?"

J. D. nodded. "Remember his buzzed head? How pale it was, like a cue ball? He wore those thick glasses."

Jo couldn't recall the glasses. "It's nice having someone remember the little things you forget." Sometimes she felt like her heart was encased in cement, but when J. D. smiled like he did now, the dimples in his cheeks so near, she felt her heart change form, felt it turning fluid. "Those were good times," she said.

J. D. nodded. "Too bad we don't play music like that anymore."

Jo feigned a gasp. "J. D. Gunn not plugged in?"

"Stop," he said. "I love playing all that stripped-down music just like you do."

"Who could tell?"

"Yeah, well. I do."

"Doesn't bring in the big cash, I guess."

"I know."

Jo placed her feet on the ground. "I bet Rob's wondering where you are."

"Probably so."

"I think we should go," Jo said. J. D. nodded, but he seemed reluctant to leave his lounge chair.

They rode the elevator back to her floor so J. D. could change back into his clothes and pick up his phone and wallet. Jo tightened her robe and sat on the edge of the bed, legs crossed, and waited for him to change before she did. J. D. returned from the bathroom in his white T-shirt, jeans, and heavy silver belt buckle, the one with his band name on the front. He adjusted the buckle. "Sure you won't come to the Marquis? Last chance."

"Not my scene," Jo said, and stood up to hug him good-bye.

J. D. held her tight around her waist. When she began to pull away from the embrace, he let her go some, but then he pulled her in again. Jo felt his breath on her skin, right beneath her ear. Softly, he said, "Nothing ever felt right like this."

She'd almost forgotten this feeling. J. D. used to be her best friend, the person she'd always been able to share her life with, all the joys and the sorrows too. Letting J. D. go all those years ago felt like a cavity inside her chest stuffed with a thousand pounds of wet sand. J. D. moved her hair off her shoulder and placed a palm on her cheek. Being here together, holding on to each other like this, seemed normal to her, and she felt the impulse to drop her robe, let J. D. remove her bikini top and expose her breasts, take one nipple in his mouth, moan from the warmth of his tongue, rub her bikini bottom against his hand, softly at first, then harder, seal herself against his body and caress his smooth back with her nails, and be together like they once had been—but just as quickly as this impulse came, Jo shut it down.

She sat on the bed and cinched her robe's tie. "It was really good to hang out. Like old times."

J. D. looked as if he was about to speak, but then he touched the bottom of her chin lightly with his thumb before securing his hat on his head and smiling at her like he was watching the sun rise. He was so beautiful to her in that moment, so much the mountain boy she'd once loved, his blue eyes lit up with innocent joy like two paper lanterns.

J. D. picked up his cowboy boots from the floor, and in a quiet voice he said, "See you back in Nashville."

Jo nodded and hugged herself tightly as he closed the hotel door behind him.

CHAPTER 24

Contract

THAT ROWDY NIGHT at the Thirsty Baboon, Jo had been drinking lots of tequila shots with lime and salt like she did during those days, like they all did. J. D. remembered the place being more crowded than usual and Jo couldn't find room to dance on the floor in front of the stage. She put down her fiddle and jumped onto the bar instead, and everyone turned to watch her flatfoot from one end to the other, her feet like two birds soaring over the beer cans and shot glasses. The bartenders hustled to remove any object in her way.

Men whistled at her so much J. D. almost quit playing, just put his guitar on the stand and shut the whole thing down. And then after the show, he watched two men approach Jo at the bar, men he'd never seen before at the Thirsty Baboon. The tall one wore a fine-looking suit with tan leather brogues, but the short guy had on jeans and a T-shirt, nothing special. J. D. didn't feel like fighting with either of them. Jo had brought that attention on herself, so she could fend for herself; that's what he'd decided. J. D. left her there and joined Chase B and Rob on the back patio, along with their opening band, and together they passed a joint.

Jo came outside with those two guys following after her. She wore a big smile on her face, almost an anxious smile, as she hurried over to the picnic tables where J. D. sat with the guys. J. D. stood up. "What're you doing?"

"Bringing these guys out here to meet you."

J. D. shook their hands. "Nice to meet you, gentlemen. Now fuck off."

Jo's eyes grew big as silver dollars and the men looked at Jo, then at each other. The taller, well-groomed man leaned down and said something to his short friend.

"You got something to say?" J. D. said. "Say it to me." J. D. shoved the taller guy and he stumbled backward into a group of people smoking cigarettes and drinking beers.

Chase B and Rob stood up. Rob put his hand on J. D.'s shoulder and said, "Don't start this shit, man."

The shorter guy stood right in front of J. D., so close J. D. could see the thin hair on the crown of his head. "My name's Mark Kern. This is Monty, he's my producer. We're out here from LA scouting for a movie. We were told if we want a singing cowboy, then we should come watch you. You seemed busy after the show. We were talking with Jo, who thought you'd be interested in making a soundtrack for the film, maybe appearing in a small part too."

J. D. wiped his palms on his shirt, prepared to shake hands, but the taller man said, "I can't work with assholes."

Jo's eyes burrowed a hot stare into J. D.'s face.

Mark looked over at the producer. "Yes we can, Monty. We do that all the time."

"Sir," J. D. said, scrambling for some way to come back, "I'm just drunk. Had too many shots of tequila from the crowd. I'm sorry. I'm very interested in talking with you."

"You free for lunch tomorrow?"

"Sure we are," Jo said, smiling.

"Just J. D. for now," Mark said. "Let's keep it small."

"Oh, okay." Jo's smile faded. "I understand."

That was the first time J. D. ever witnessed Jo refuse to push back, saying she understood something she didn't agree with at all. A few days later the director flew J. D. out to LA for an initial meeting, and then they flew him out a second time alone for a trial period in the studio. They promised if they liked what they heard, they'd offer him a contract. They found an agent to handle it for him, and a manager too. News of his movie and album deal struck Gatesville like a snakebite. Jo's mama mailed her the *Clinch Mountain Herald* article, which, Rob told him, Jo burned in the bonfire that evening.

His daddy called. "When you coming home, son? You've been gone so long I'd hardly recognize you. I'm getting older and I want to see you."

J. D. said, "I don't know. Can't seem to get back to Nashville, even."

Then his daddy's tone changed: "You haven't forgotten everybody here, have you? Forgotten where you come from? Don't be foolish with all that money."

Each time he called, the conversation was some sorry version of this one. J. D. usually hung up without saying good-bye and soon he stopped picking up the phone if he knew it was his daddy calling. With Jo and the guys, the conversations were different. Early on Rob was supportive. He'd ask, "Should we move out there with you or wait or what?"

"I'm coming back to Nashville when all this is done. What's the point of everybody moving out here, only to go back in six months, if that?"

"Are they still planning on us being in the studio with you?"

J. D. had no real answer to offer Rob, only the answer he hoped was true. Eventually, Rob stopped asking him about it, about much of anything. One time he accused J. D. of throwing over their band for a solo career. He and Rob didn't speak for almost two months after that. Jo wanted to keep the band together in Nashville, and they were still booking steady gigs, playing all around the region. Jo was singing his lead, and no matter how many times J. D. told them he missed the band, no one seemed to believe him. When his loneliness started to feel like his only companion, J. D. changed his mind and implored Jo to come join him, just for a few months.

"We're playing shows here, J. D. This way when you come home, the band can pick up where we left off," she said. "Plus, I'd miss Nash-ville. Don't you?"

"I do." He stopped asking her to come to LA, and the longer they went without seeing each other, the more they fought on the phone. Chase B called sometimes. Those were his only easy talks.

Everything back east felt like it was receding from him. LA became his present. He was writing well. People appreciated him out there, told him how talented he was. J. D. felt certain that this movie, this soundtrack, would give his band the exposure they needed to move beyond the dive-bar circuit and break into a major label with radio airtime too. Jo and the guys might not have understood yet that he was doing this for them, but in time he was certain they would all realize it. The movie studio promised J. D. he could bring his band out to play a few songs on the album too, but first they wanted to introduce him to a guitar player named Aster, recently graduated from rehab and ready for a new start. He'd been playing with the best rock bands in LA for the past fifteen years.

J. D. and Aster went to the beach and ate avocados. They took surfing lessons. Mark Kern, his director, took J. D. and Aster to fancy dinners and to parties in Malibu. He started to feel like he'd never see Jo again. Aster often said, "Forget her, man. This is LA." By that point J. D. had written a third of the soundtrack with the studio band. J. D. didn't think of himself as an actor or a costar, even if that's what his manager, his agent, his director, Aster, and everybody else called him. He'd never been in front of a camera before, never been on a set. His director promised to walk him through it. Plus he only had a few lines, no big deal, and he'd already reviewed the script. Seemed simple enough. He'd just be himself. All he had to do was step out of the race car, remove his helmet, shake out his hair, say a few lines, and be done with it. He would start shooting his part in the movie in a few more weeks and soon after that the movie would wrap. He wanted Jo to visit, just once, before he returned to Nashville. After he'd already arranged the flight and bought the tickets for her, J. D. called Jo from the break room at the recording studio to surprise her. It was the first time in his life he had the money to do something like that for her.

But her tone sounded more distant each time they spoke. She said, "Me and the guys got a show at the Baboon on Friday, the Five Spot on Saturday, the Basement on Sunday. Plus I've got work in the afternoon. I can't just take off because it finally suits your schedule, J. D."

"You're serious?"

She didn't respond.

"Jo, it's almost done, all of it."

"When?" she said.

"Soon."

"When, J. D.?"

"I'm not sure but soon."

She went silent once more.

"Are we trying to make this work or what?"

"I don't know."

"Don't say that, Jo."

There was a long pause on her end of the line. Finally, she said, "I don't know how to live apart from you like this. And who knows what your life's going to be like going forward."

Aster walked into the break room and pointed at his wrist to tell him it was time to go back in the studio. J. D. nodded. He waited for Aster to leave the room. Quietly, he said, "It's lonely out here, and I miss you."

"I miss you too," was all she said.

On a recent call, J. D. had asked Chase B about Jo and pressed him about whether any guys were lurking around after shows. Chase B mentioned something about a guy wanting to take a walk with her the week before but promised J. D. it ended at that. But it made J. D. restless; he couldn't sleep at night. He finally had the nerve to ask her what had been on his mind since that conversation: "Have you met somebody?"

In a defensive tone, she said, "No."

"Jo?"

She sighed. "I haven't met anybody like that, J. D. I mean, Nick Sullivan was at the Baboon the other night. He wanted to take a walk. But it was just friendly. I didn't go."

J. D.'s chest swelled, like his entire body had expanded a foot. Chase B had failed to mention the guy's name. "Nick Sullivan, the producer? As in Asphalt Records?"

"Yes."

"Stay the hell away from that guy."

"It's really no big deal. Since you asked, I just felt like I should tell you."

"So I'll be pissed and far away where I can't do anything about it?"

"There's nothing to do. Nothing happened. He was just, I don't know, nice. Like a friend."

"Rob's a friend. That guy—Nick Sullivan is not a friend."

"You know what I mean."

"I don't, Jo. I really don't." From the hallway outside the break room, Aster whistled for J. D. "I have to go. This is the worst fucking call."

"I'm sorry."

"Call me later," he said. "I love you."

Jo hung up first. She hadn't cheated on him, J. D. knew that in a rational way, but that didn't stop him from feeling like she had. It was something about her voice. She sounded charmed or smitten in a way she hadn't sounded on the phone since J. D. left for LA.

Aster entered the room without knocking. "Everything all right?"

J. D. put the phone in its cradle.

"Want a sip of coke?" Aster offered him a mirror and a rolled-up bill.

J. D. passed.

Aster snorted a line. "There's a cast party tonight at Julia Fox's place. Mark wants you there. We're going, right?"

"Yeah," J. D. said, and tried not to sound heartbroken. "We'll be there."

J. D. tried to call Jo back after his session but no one picked up. That night, Aster drove them down Highway 1 with his Jeep's top down, which made smoking a joint difficult. Aster drove with one hand, re-lighting the joint with the other, and as he handed the joint to J. D., he said, "You shouldn't have a girlfriend while you're out here."

J. D. smoked. With his free arm outside the window, he let the warm Pacific Ocean wind push back his palm. J. D. tried to fight it and keep his hand steady, but Aster was driving too fast. He pulled his hand back inside the Jeep and passed the joint back to Aster. "You ever loved a woman before?"

"Nope." Aster said it like he was proud. He sucked the joint down to the nub, flicked it out of the Jeep, and sent it sailing down the highway. The Pacific Ocean was a solid mass of blue glass in the distance and looked like it couldn't be pierced.

J. D. pulled out another joint from the glove box. "She's met some rich fucking producer. Nick Sullivan."

"Douche."

"Heard of him?"

Aster sucked on the joint and looked at J. D. like that was the dumbest question he'd ever asked. As he tried to keep the smoke trapped in his lungs, Aster said, "That's what you need then. Some rich fucking actress." And then he exhaled and the wind ushered away the smoke.

J. D. accepted the joint.

Aster said, "Julia Fox is single. I saw her scoping you."

"Whatever." J. D. moved the hair away from his eyes. He gripped the headrest behind him.

"No, for real."

"I'm not interested."

"Bullshit. Everybody's interested in Julia Fox."

J. D. stared out at the ocean and watched the white shorebirds fly in the empty expanse—suspended there between the cliff and the sky. He knew it was pointless to argue with Aster, so he let Aster talk the rest of the way there about all the benefits of a hookup with Julia Fox, until they arrived at her house and Aster finally stopped talking. Every party J. D. attended in LA was the same, just in a different locale. Everything was free, and everything was luxury. Julia Fox's house had an infinity pool, floor-to-ceiling windows that made J. D. feel exposed and uncomfortable, waiters in bow ties, platters of gourmet foods, house music, multiple bars on multiple levels, white long-stemmed roses in crystal vases, and strangers passing by, brushing arms and shoulders.

J. D. pulled one waitress to the side. She had freckles and cute, rounded cheeks. Seemed nice. He asked her to keep the whiskey coming to him steady. He handed her two hundred dollars. "Anything you need," she said, and she wasn't joking. She never forgot him the entire night. With each drink he emptied, J. D. thought less about Jo and Nick.

Aster swam naked in the pool with a bunch of fake blondes he'd met as soon as they walked in. That's what Aster did, he gathered women like it was his sole ambition in this life. J. D. went outside and rested in a lounge chair, wishing he had his hat so he could cover his face and block out the party. Nobody wore cowboy hats out here, unless they were on set. People had stared at him funny when he first arrived so he'd stopped wearing it outside the apartment. He kept on his cowboy boots though. He refused to get rid of everything about himself that was real.

Aster started a game of naked Marco Polo in the pool. He said, "If I catch you, I squeeze."

The girls laughed. J. D. sipped his whiskey, and from behind his chair, he heard, "Having any fun?"

J. D. sat up and turned around to see Julia Fox, who seated herself on the lounge chair next to J. D.'s.

"Great time."

"I can tell." She pulled her blond wavy hair over one shoulder and smiled. She wore a large circular hat on the top of her head, which framed her hair around her face, and she wore a long crystal necklace. She reminded J. D. of a folksinger from the sixties. Julia drank her martini and crossed her legs. The short white dress she wore grew shorter. She had legs for days. Julia had come to the recording studio once before, and J. D. had seen her on the set when Mark gave him the tour. They'd said hello in passing and she had smiled at him, but that was all. He'd thought nothing more about it.

Aster whistled from the pool. "Hey, J. D."

J. D. looked over and Aster did a backflip in the pool, showing his ass to everybody. J. D. said, "He's insane."

Julie raised her eyebrows and half-smiled. "I knew him before he went to rehab. He's tame now."

"I'll take your word for it."

She moved the hair away from her face, and J. D. noticed that her nails were very long, like talons, and painted red like burgundy wine. She said, "I just wanted to stop over here and tell you how much I like the music you're making for the movie."

"I appreciate that." J. D. drank his whiskey.

"I think that story about how Mark and Monty found you is hilarious."

"He told you?"

"He's told everybody." She licked her lips and then sipped her drink. "I mean, it must be weird going from a dive bar in Nashville like you did. Mark put you on a catapult."

"How's that?"

"You're serious?" She scooted to the edge of her lounge chair. Her knees almost touched J. D.'s. "You're going to be famous after we make this movie. Probably really famous. You haven't thought about that yet?"

"I guess I haven't."

"My experience was much more gradual. Plays to commercials. A better agent, small roles to bigger ones. I just think it's fascinating what you're doing. And you seem so calm about everything. So handsome and mysterious, like you're already super famous."

J. D. had been in love with Jo for many years and he'd been faithful, but all that monogamy hadn't made him stupid. He knew when a woman was hitting on him. "This is just how I am."

"I like how you are." She smiled at him again.

Aster climbed out of the pool and shouted for everyone to watch him do a cannonball. He splashed a few fashionably dressed people standing by the edge of the pool, and they didn't seem too happy about it as they walked away and went inside.

Julia said, "I know Aster's your only friend out here. So if you ever want to, we could go out for drinks. You like margaritas?"

"I like the idea of them."

She laughed. "You've never had one?"

Anybody could see that Julia was gorgeous, like she'd stepped out of a fashion magazine and sat right down next to him. All his life he'd expected women like her to treat other people as nobodies, but she seemed genuine and kind.

"Just let me know." She stood up and waved at someone across the pool. "Aster has my number. And try to have some fun tonight, okay?"

That night J. D. tried calling Jo again but Rob answered and told J. D. she didn't feel like talking. He couldn't sleep and took a walk on the beach alone. He decided he'd play a pickup game of volleyball the next day and that margaritas sounded good. He asked Aster for Julia's number so he'd have someone other than Aster to talk to.

When J. D. told Aster about his talk with Julia, Aster said, "You should hit that, dude."

"A drink. That's it."

He called Julia that afternoon, and she was free and she loved playing volleyball too. They spent the day in their swimsuits, ate carne asada tacos and chimichurri sauce from a food truck, drank margaritas at a seaside bar, and built a bonfire on the beach that night. J. D. played the guitar for her as she sat wrapped in a blanket. Aster met up with them, along with strangers from the beach. Nothing happened between Julia and J. D. that night, but the next day blurry images of them having drinks, laughing together, and leaning in close at a seaside bar were published in all the tabloids. There were red circles around J. D. and questions about Julia Fox's mystery man. They made sure to guess who he was, and they guessed right.

After that, the paparazzi followed him everywhere, even without Julia around. Jo refused to answer his calls. He called anyway, on the hour, every hour, then every ten minutes, until she finally asked Rob to tell him that she never wanted to speak to him again so to stop calling. J. D. spent every day with Julia to forget about her. Slept with her, and it was satisfying enough but nothing like being with Jo. The movie wrapped a month into his relationship with Julia. J. D. had the chance to return to Nashville, but he couldn't imagine going back there and not being with Jo. Not until he had to. J. D. chose to stay in LA until the movie came out and convinced Rob and the guys to join him— they had music studios and connections at their disposal now to finally work on an album together. Jo jumped into production with Nick Sullivan. Never looked back.

It's your master here, that's right, Floyd Masters coming to you from 87.3 FM. And we're warming up, Nashville. Stretching pretty good. There's a breeze out there today. Better be grateful for that. Don't expect it to last. No way. Not this summer, where every day's going to be hot, hot, hot. No relief. But enjoy today. Today should be upper eighties. Clear skies. Sunshine. Love. Lots of love out there today. I bet you folks are thinking, why would old Floyd Masters be talking about sunshine and love at five in the morning? Well, I'll tell you what. I wouldn't normally. I should be telling you about the traffic that's backing up on the belt. Like it does every single damn day.

But today I want to talk about lovers. Joanne Lover specifically, and that duet with superstar J. D. Gunn that went viral over two weeks ago. Y'all know my feelings about that boy, going off to Hollywood and becoming the poster boy for all things Southern, all things country music, like Gene Autry and Buck Owens did so well back in the good days. Those boys were the real McCoy. The real singing cowboys. Those boys held strong to the music's roots. That boy J. D. never did seem to figure out whether he wanted to be a rock singer or a country star or a pretty boy on a silver screen acting as country as country can be.

Now, I know everybody loves him. You listeners might too. He's a handsome devil, I'll give him that. Looks like Elvis. Sings like Waylon. Can write a good damn song when he tries. Though, not recently. Not in years. But now he's hooked up with Joanne Lover and that little lady can write a song. Their duet video's all over the Internet, still out there and spreading like the flu.

God bless us all, because you know what's happening now. Joanne Lover and J. D. Gunn are gonna make music together. I have it on good authority that Mr. Sullivan will announce the new album in the next day or two. J. D.'s returned from his West Coast tour. He and Jo are set to do a publicity blitz on radio and TV.

I know what you're thinking. You're thinking a J. D. Gunn and Joanne Lover album will be incredible. You'll buy it. I bet so. Asphalt's CEO is betting on that too. Lots and lots of people want it. Young people who rot their ears on pop music love that video. They don't even listen to country music. Just that Auto-Tuned repetitive pop crap out of LA and New York. But they love J. D. and Jo. Asphalt's gonna push this collaboration between them, but it won't work out. It just won't. I've known those two since they were playing gigs together at the Thirsty Baboon. They've got a past. The past doesn't cooperate so well with the present. Hard to let things go. Hard to compromise. And listen up, you tell them Floyd Masters saw it first, folks. You heard it here first.

And don't forget that Clear Channel country music streaming deal either. I mentioned it before and I'll keep on mentioning it. That streaming deal is everything for Asphalt's future. Only one label gets to land it, and if Asphalt's CEO scores that contract, he'll guarantee Clear Channel and Asphalt big profits. The artists will get screwed out of royalties even more than they already are. God help radio when it happens. Everybody'll be streaming the same damn country music hits made by Will McCoy or Lucy Heart twenty years ago and all the hits since then. They'll binge on it. That's all they'll know. And they want to call it vintage country music. What's the world coming to? Twenty years is vintage?

You know, I'm not so worried about J. D. Gunn. He already turned into something he shouldn't be. But Jo Lover. I'm worried about her sound. She's held true to the roots this whole time. She knows that great country music has always been about the human condition. What will happen now that she's set to work with J. D. Gunn? Will all that promise disappear? All right, callers, it's time for you to weigh in. Let's hear it, Jenny from the university area, what's on your mind?

Hi, Floyd. *Hi, Jenny.* So, Floyd, I loved that duet. Loved it. And I'm a fan of both of theirs. I want to see what they can do together. I think you're too negative. Your outlook is not sunny and full of love like you say. And it should be. This is good for country music. Two big artists teaming up together is good for the business. It's all good. You seem worried about the future instead of seeing this as the way to a better future. *You done, Jenny?* I am, Floyd. *Well, thank you very much for calling. But I think you're wrong. She'll get swallowed up. Who'll be left making something real? Tell me that. Next caller, please. Denny from down in Franklin County. Howdy, Denny.* Yes, hello? Yes, Floyd, I think you're right. Nashville wants to be LA, wants everything to sound like rock and pop music. That's the future. There's rappers singing country and country singers rapping in their music. I don't know what's happening but it's just not good. I think J. D. and Jo are better off staying separate. That's all I'll say.

Wise thoughts from a wise caller. You know, I'd normally take more callers, but I think you're good and ready for some music now, listeners. This one's for all my fans down in Honduras. That's right. People in Latin America love listening to Floyd Masters, which is more than I can say about my fellow countrymen. Those folks down there are some deeply dedicated country music fans. And they love the outlaws. So I've got some Willie and Waylon for you now. Enjoy these rounds of songs. This is real country.

CHAPTER 25

Rolling Hills

NICK AND JO were spending the weekend at his father's estate in Williamson County—an expansive brick mansion on a hill with more rooms than Jo could keep track of. She risked getting lost inside the house if she wandered around too much. Her favorite thing in the world was driving by Bear Creek Farm to see where Hank Williams Sr. once lived. That place was owned by Will McCoy and Lucy Heart now. Nick had attended parties there as a boy, which made Jo slightly jealous.

He woke her up with a surprise brunch of homemade buttermilk biscuits, sausage gravy, mimosas, and coffee. They ate together in bed. Jo reached out for his hand, held it, and let her thumb lightly caress the top of his skin just the way he liked it. She knew all his favorite spots and could find them in an instant. Jo loosened her robe at the waist, and Nick glanced down at her breasts and then kissed her while he moved the robe off her shoulders completely. He kissed her from the earlobe down the side of her neck, pausing to make time for her collarbone before moving down to her belly button, and then below. His tongue made small warm circles on her clitoris. Jo brought his face back up to where she could see him because that's exactly what he liked. The tenderness turned him on. They kissed like this for a while before Jo slid under the covers and took him in her mouth. He came quickly. Jo removed the covers and rested by his side. He kissed her temple and squeezed her inner thigh, stroking it gently while they rested in silence. Since returning from LA, all Jo wanted was sex. She propositioned Nick in the shower, in the car, at his studio, at the kitchen table—he always obliged.

They showered together and then Jo and Nick drove four-wheelers down to the stables. They'd called a truce about the viral video a few days ago, promised not to argue about the song or the album anymore, though Jo could feel a tension in Nick's presence whenever his father or anyone brought it up. Even her mama was unsupportive when Jo had called to check in with her. First thing she'd said was, "I heard about some video of you and J. D. Saw his daddy at the general store the other day. He told me. People talk about it. You know how I feel about that boy. Remember Matthew chapter seven, verse six, Jo. 'Do not give dogs what is sacred; do not throw your pearls to pigs. If you do, they may trample them under their feet, and then turn and tear you to pieces.'" Jo promised her mama it was nothing like that and that she didn't need to worry about her.

Jo sped through the fields, crushing the tall grass and leaving winding paths in her wake. She created an artificial breeze the more she pressed on the gas. Jo loved this kind of riding—speed she knew how to control. The sun hung like a polished yellow sapphire just above the undulating hills in the distance. Max ran after them, barking as he tried to keep up, stopping at times to locate a scent. Jo kept looking behind her to keep track of him, but Max had the entire estate mapped out with his nose. Jo often found him begging for scraps down at the smokehouse.

They crested the hill, Nick's four-wheeler picking up speed, hers dragging a little. She twisted the rubber handle to feel a kick from the engine. The stables came into view and Nick beat her there. Jo parked next to him. Nick moved off the machine and shook hands with Mario, the groundskeeper.

"Ms. Lover," Mario said, and came to her with both arms extended and wrapped her in a hug. He smelled like hay and Old Spice. He had a tan, weathered face and a strong jawbone. "Soon Mrs. Sullivan."

"Ms. Lover," she said. "Always."

Mario looked a little confused, and then Nick explained in Spanish that she planned to keep her last name. Mario nodded in an exaggerated way and said, "*Mujer moderna.*"

Nick said, "Is Mary ready?"

Mario pointed back at the stables. "Yes, sir, Nicholas."

Jo wanted to say, "Yes, sir, Nicholas Sullivan the Fourth," but she quelled the impulse. He hated hearing his full name spoken aloud. Nick disappeared into the stables, and Jo dug a hole in the ground with the heel of her boot. Soon a shadow came over the ground and Nick approached on a sleek black horse whose coat was shinier and darker than Jo's hair, and behind him followed the horse Jo would ride to tour the grounds and map out the wedding ceremony and reception. Her horse's flesh reminded Jo of melted milk chocolate and she had long white hair at her ankles like leg warmers. Big eyelashes. A sweet girl, no doubt. Both horses, who clearly trusted Nick, stopped at his command.

"My knight in shining armor," Jo said.

Nick climbed down and came to Jo with a pair of new leather riding gloves with country roses etched along the wrists. Jo slipped on the right-hand glove first and then the left-hand one. Her engagement ring snagged on the leather—it surpassed in beauty any ring she'd ever seen before and she loved that it had been in Nick's family for generations, but it wasn't practical.

Nick said, "The pond will shine like gold at the reception."

Jo petted Mary behind her ear. All of Nashville's finest would be in attendance at their wedding, and Jo was a little worried about riding around on a horse, just waiting for it to jump up, legs kicking, and drop Jo flat on her back for everyone to see. Irrational, maybe, but she didn't grow up with horses, wasn't sure how to anticipate them.

Jo put her hands on Nick's waist and looked him in the eyes. "Swear this one's nice."

He touched her cheek with his gloved hand. "Mary's the very best. I've had her since I was a boy." Nick adjusted Mary's light brown saddle. Jo walked over to Mary, looked into her bulging black eyes, and sent a telepathic message for her to be calm. No sudden movements. No kicking. Mary seemed to understand. Jo latched on to the saddle and placed her foot in the stirrup.

"Up you go," Nick said from behind as he hoisted her up. And just like that, Jo was perched above everyone, her legs spread wide with a massive, breathing creature between them.

"If we go to Tahiti for the honeymoon, we can ride horses all around the island."

"Sounds amazing," Jo said. She'd leave the honeymoon decision up to Nick. Without his spontaneous vacations to London, Paris, Tokyo, or whatever whim he had next, she'd probably never have left her house in Nashville except to go on tour. Nick mounted his horse, and with a small kick of his left leg, he made his horse move forward and so did Mary. It felt like riding on a slow-moving train.

"I think you'll come to like it," he said. "Our kids are going to ride. We'll all ride together as a family."

Jo's laughter echoed in the valley, echoed all the way to Nashville and into deep space. One thing at a time. And maybe not even then. This would hurt his feelings. It had, before, when she'd said it, and she knew he'd respond like he always did with the guarantee that she'd change her mind about having children—once her career calmed down, after another smash album. After, after, after. And all she wanted to say was no.

Nick said, "I'm surprised nobody in your family rides. Maybe we can ride together when we go visit."

Jo folded the reins into layers to make it shorter and gripped the mass in her left hand. The closest Nick would ever come to visiting Gatesville was through her songwriting. He would have to settle for meeting her family here in Nashville at the wedding for the first time. It would probably only be her mama who would come. There was so much of her past that she couldn't share with him, and Nick didn't want to see where she grew up—even if he thought he did, it was better this way.

Jo glanced far afield, beyond the mansion on the hill and the guesthouses in the distance, and the smokehouse, and the pool house, all of them so small now from this vantage point. Somewhere beyond these rolling hills, down the road just a little ways, J. D. Gunn's house existed. The feelings that had arisen while she spent time with him in LA were glimmers of the past trying to push forward, and Jo told herself that they were fleeting. She'd been telling herself that every single day since she returned. J. D. slipped into her mind when she wasn't paying attention, and wishing him away never worked. Jo's body rocked in motion with her horse's steps, and the rhythm calmed her like meditation. Jo reminded herself to stay in the present. She said, "Marie invited us to the Bluebird to see her boyfriend's band the Flyby Boys. She says they're incredible."

"I've been hearing that name around."

"Show's in two days, I think."

"I should be free."

"Hey, Nick."

"Hey, Jo."

"After this, can we shoot some skeet?"

"So you can show me how it's done?"

"That's right."

"Sounds fun."

Jo appreciated that Nick was in such good spirits and that this little getaway had repaired any tension between them. Nick called Mary's name and she began to trot faster. Jo wished she could command her horse to run.

CHAPTER 26

Honky-Tonk Night Time Man

T ELL IT AGAIN, Marie."

"Seriously?"

"One more time." Gaylene looked around the table at Alan and Denver, and then back at Marie. "It's funny, right?"

"I don't think it's funny," Alan said.

Denver added, "I agree with Alan."

Gaylene adjusted in her seat and crossed one of her legs over the other, the rip in her jeans spreading wide at the knee.

Marie drank her beer. Her stomach felt sour. "I shouldn't have told that story."

"No one here will repeat it," Alan said.

Denver grabbed Marie's hand and squeezed it. She looked over at Gaylene, who was reapplying her scarlet-red lip gloss, which she did obsessively when she was well on her way to drunkenness.

"I don't think he saw me," Marie said. "He walked the other way down the hall."

Gaylene said, "I don't blame her. He's a good-looking hunk of man meat."

"Hey," Alan said with a voice that sounded slighted. Then he smiled.

"Not as good-looking as you." Gaylene cupped her hand on Alan's chin and shook it a little. Alan drank his beer.

"Leaving her room in the middle of the night?" Denver said. "That's definitely the walk of shame."

Alan nodded. "It's a hard business for love. Always on the road, always meeting interesting people."

Denver started peeling away the label on his PBR bottle. Marie had always promised herself she'd never fall in love with a musician for those same reasons Alan had listed—unfortunately, she broke promises to herself all the time: to stop biting her nails, to stop eating cookie-dough ice cream at three AM, to exercise more, to dye her hair less, and to never, ever date a musician. "Swear you won't tell anybody, Gaylene." Marie pinned Gaylene's hands down on the table. "Swear."

With a sassy voice she said, "I don't care who she gets dick from."

Marie massaged her temple. She shouldn't have said it at all. She didn't mean to. Work was overwhelming her. Paparazzi. Interview requests. Jo's social media explosion. It felt like Jo and J. D. had a million appearances coming up and Marie felt exhausted by it all. Plus, this was the first time she'd seen Gaylene since returning from LA. Marie started talking about the new album; the video going viral, which everybody already knew about; and the tour bus party, her experience with extreme drunkenness, waking up in the middle of the night and not knowing where she was and going to Jo's room only to find J. D. leaving with his boots in hand. She hadn't even told Denver that part. If she could retrieve the story from their heads and burn it, she would.

"I'm drunk," Gaylene said.

Alan nodded his head in an exaggerated way.

"Drop me at home, will you?"

Alan finished his beer and crushed the can. Marie sensed that Alan was no longer interested in Gaylene, or maybe he never had been—so hard to tell with boys. Once Gaylene started drinking, she couldn't slow down, and that impulse strained everybody's patience.

"You coming back?" Denver said.

"Probably not," Alan said. "But I did want to buy Marie one more drink, as a thank-you."

"Hearing a great show tomorrow night will be thanks enough," she said.

"No pressure," Denver said.

Alan helped Gaylene put on her purple cardigan. She couldn't seem to find the second sleeve. "The amazing Marie," Alan said.

Denver held Marie's hand.

Gaylene pointed at the vast array of bras slung on the bull's horns above the Thirsty Baboon's entrance. She said, "Those look like mistletoe. I want to hang mine up there."

"Another night." Alan waved good-bye to them and guided Gaylene out of the bar.

Denver leaned over to Marie, kissing her softly on her neck. "Want another one?"

Marie nodded and Denver stood up to wave his hand at Buster so he could see Denver over all the other people waiting for drinks. Friday-night shows at the Thirsty Baboon were packed when the Flyby Boys played. Everybody flocked to the bar for a drink before the late-night band started. The neon-orange jukebox filled the place with music in the meantime, and though it was hard to hear above all the commotion, the one song Marie had punched in finally floated over the crowd. Dolly Parton's voice rose above all the noise as she sang, "*Jolene, Jolene, Jolene, Jolene / I'm begging of you please don't take my man.*"

Denver brought back two beers and pushed his chair closer to Marie's to free up space for the growing line to the girls' bathroom. He leaned back in his chair and put his long arm around Marie, which always felt good to her. Denver felt good. She liked that he was so tall she had to lift up on her tiptoes just to kiss his cheek. She craved his company all the time and had spent every free moment with him since returning from LA. Any time she witnessed something funny or confusing, she immediately imagined narrating it to Denver. He was the one and only person she wanted to share her life with, and he swore he felt the same way about her.

Denver leaned close to her ear. "So how come you didn't tell me?"

Marie drank her beer slow before she said, "Wanted to pretend I didn't see it, I guess."

"Why's she marrying Nick then?"

She shrugged. "I think she loves him."

"That's confusing."

Marie took Denver's hand and almost asked him if he thought a battered heart was the only outcome of loving another person, but she remained quiet—she didn't want Denver to wonder if she was having doubts about their new relationship.

Denver said, "Is that possible, to love two people at once?"

"I don't know." Marie squeezed Denver's hand. How could she know? Marie had only been in love with one person and that was Denver. Marie thought she knew Jo pretty well, very well even, since she was the person who spent the most time with Jo, but now she was a totally different person. And Jo's life seemed so perfect to Marie: the beautiful house and pool, the beautiful closet full of beautiful clothes and beautiful jewelry, the luxury cars, the perfect dog with beautiful blue eyes, the devoted fans, the most talented and best-looking fiancé a girl could ask for, fame, money, beauty—Marie couldn't understand why Jo would betray Nick and risk losing all his love and devotion. What could she possibly be missing that J. D. could give her? In fact, all this time, Marie had thought Jo despised J. D. and his awful music. By all accounts of what she said out loud, any person would think so. Marie was certain Nick had no idea about J. D., since he was at Jo's house last night.

Marie peeled off the sticker on the empty glass bottle Gaylene had left at the table. She said, "You know that feeling after being on the road and sleeping in different beds and then you come home to your own bed? And it's familiar in a way you don't even notice or think about?"

"Yeah."

"I think her love for J. D. is like that."

Denver rolled the bottle between his palms. Marie pulled at Denver's collar and brought him down for a kiss, and he took her face in his hands and kissed her deeply, tenderly. Somebody nearby shouted: "Get a room."

They both started laughing midkiss. "Maybe that's good advice," Denver said.

"Yes it is," she said, and kissed him once more before they both stood up, left their half-empty bottles on the table, and walked out of the bar together. Dolly Parton's yearning voice called out over the outdoor speakers, pleading still for Jolene not to take her man just because she could. They walked to Denver's car, hand in hand, and the gravel shifted with each step Marie took.

CHAPTER 27

Country Music Television

A KNOCK. MR. SULLIVAN answered the door. J. D. heard her voice before he could see her: he craved hearing her voice the way he craved playing music if he'd taken too many days off. Mr. Sullivan widened the door and J. D. hoped she was here without Nick Sullivan. After the night they'd spent together in LA, swimming and laughing, he could think of no one but her. J. D. wanted to be around her all the time, tell her jokes and swap stories about growing up. The thought of Jo sharing her time and laughter with Nick made his body feel pummeled by jealousy.

Jo stepped in, refusing to look anywhere except at Mr. Sullivan. She wore dark eye shadow, scarlet-red lips and nails, a solid black tank top, and jeans so tight it was hard for J. D. to look at her directly. Jo wore her hair in two long braids down her back and smiled at everybody. Marie followed in behind her.

J. D. stood up and said to Marie, "I hope that moonshine didn't hurt you too bad."

Marie looked over at Jo in a skittish way and J. D. wondered if he shouldn't have reminded her of that night or, perhaps, the traumatic hangover that awaited her the next morning. Marie immediately turned her attention to her phone.

Mr. Sullivan shut the door behind Jo and stood in a wide stance with his arms crossed.

Jo seemed like she was looking at everyone and no one at the same time, like she could see an angel hovering above them all. "How was the West Coast tour?" she said.

J. D. sat down on the leather couch next to Rob. "Fine," he said. A piece of lettuce fell off Rob's fork and landed between them.

"Whatever," Aster said, and sat down in the recliner with a plate piled high with double-decker sandwiches. J. D. knew what Aster was about to say. He'd been saying it every day since they'd left LA and played shows from there to Texas. Aster took a large bite of his sandwich, and with his mouth full of food he said, "Nobody else wants to talk about it. But I do. The crowd wanted you and J. D. Everywhere we went they were screaming for J. D. and Jo. Didn't give a shit about the Empty Shells."

Mr. Sullivan smiled wide. "That's a good thing, son."

"Bullshit," Aster said.

"For now, it's good." Mr. Sullivan pulled a chair from the table, turned it around, and straddled it. "I'm this close to securing the Clear Channel deal." Mr. Sullivan held his fingers in a pinched position before adding, "Hell, I walked in and they practically begged me to sign the contract after that video went viral. It's good for everybody. Asphalt will be the most profitable label in Nashville by year's end and that profit will come back to you."

"Fuck streaming," Aster said as he continued to chew.

Mr. Sullivan stared at Aster like he was a creature from the deep. "You won't be saying that by Christmas, Aster."

Marie brought Jo a bottle of water from the catering table. Jo opened the cap. "Just one more interview today after this, right?"

Mr. Sullivan nodded.

Aster said, "You two should sing. That's all anybody gives a damn about. They don't want to hear you talk."

Jo slid her thumb into her jeans pocket and exposed her hip. She stared at Aster with a withering look.

"What about the Nashville Music Festival?" Aster said. "We're still playing that show with J. D.?"

"Yes, son," Mr. Sullivan said in a weary voice. "You sound paranoid."

Aster sank his body back into the recliner and lifted one empty hand in the air. "With all due respect, sir, I've been in the music business longer than anybody in this room except you, and I've seen plenty of shady shit go down."

Mr. Sullivan adjusted his suit jacket and turned his attention back to Jo. "You two have a radio interview after this, then I'll announce the new album at a press conference. You'll make it official at the Nashville Music Festival next week. Sound good?"

J. D. said, "I'm good with that."

She looked at Mr. Sullivan and nodded.

Mr. Sullivan looked at J. D. "You two have an interview together in five minutes. You'll talk to each other directly out there, correct?"

"Of course," she said.

Mr. Sullivan said, "Whatever's going on here, fix it. Or fake it. But don't take it out there."

Chase B and Danny stood behind the couch, and J. D. heard Danny whisper, "What's going on?"

"Nothing's going on," Jo said in the most reassuring voice J. D. had ever heard. J. D. thought that she might be excited to see him after their hanging out together in LA, but now she seemed so distant, like the small speck of Venus in the night sky.

"Good," Mr. Sullivan said. "Also, J. D., *Vanity Fair* wants an interview with you. You should expect a call about that soon."

"Wait," Jo said. "An interview with J. D. Just about J. D., right? Not about me and J. D.?"

"That's what I understand. The same old thing he's done a million times. Why?"

"No reason."

"I have studio time reserved for you starting tomorrow."

"Will we be with them?" Aster said.

"Not immediately."

Aster lifted up both his arms like he was praising the heavens. He looked at Rob and said, "Told you so."

Mr. Sullivan checked his watch. Another knock came from the door, which Mr. Sullivan opened, and a voice said: "They're ready."

J. D. stood up from the couch, as did Jo, who let her eyes meet his just long enough for him to smile before she turned away once more. They'd go out on set in front of all of those cameras and tell the interviewer about their childhoods and about their early days playing music, and avoid talking about being in a relationship back when they were both starting out. Focus on their bond as kids. Their friendship. The publicist had a plan. They both knew the plan. Wear this mask.

Tell that story. But J. D.'s impulse was to take Jo's hand in his and walk out there united and tell the whole truth of how he felt about her in that single gesture. How could she seal herself off from him forever? J. D. was convinced, 100 percent certain, that Jo was still in love with him. J. D. couldn't let her marry Nick Sullivan—that would be the biggest mistake of both their lives.

Jo walked side by side with Mr. Sullivan down the hallway, and J. D. followed with his bandmates as they all made their way to the studio, where a blond interviewer in tight bedazzled jeans and a low-cut white blouse awaited them. J. D. had been interviewed on CMT many times in the past, but he hadn't met this woman before. She introduced herself as Brandi and shook hands with each of them as they were being fitted with tiny microphones. She said, "I'm such a huge fan. You two are amazing together."

Jo smiled but kept her attention on the technician as he clipped the microphone to the strap of her tank top.

"Just take a seat there. I'll sit here and then we'll get started."

Jo sat on the black leather stool and crossed her legs, her red boots in full view of the camera. J. D. sat on the stool beside her. He kept one leg on the ground, his other leg propped up on the metal ring at the base of the stool.

Brandi adjusted her hair. She said, "Check one, two," into her microphone and gazed into the dark row of cameras. "We're ready."

A short man wearing a headset came out of the darkness behind the cameras. "Here we go, in three, two, one."

The lights on the cameras turned from red to green. Heat from the white lights above made J. D.'s face start to sweat.

To the camera, Brandi said, "Welcome to CMT News! Today I'm joined by Jo Lover and J. D. Gunn. We're so lucky to have them in the studio today. Ever since their duet went viral at the MusiCares concert a couple weeks ago, they've been the hot talk of country music." Now Brandi turned her attention away from the cameras. "So what's it been like to have your duet go viral?"

With a large smile and big, enthusiastic eyes, Jo said, "Amazing, for me. J. D. is used to being the face of country music, of course, so maybe it's less intense for him."

J. D. said, "It's all been a big surprise. In a good way."

Brandi clasped her hands on one knee. "Country music has a long history of duet couples. Johnny and June and Dolly and Porter come to mind. Will McCoy and Lucy Heart in the nineties. People think you two are the next big duet in country music."

"That's a huge compliment." J. D. crossed his arms.

"Jo?" Brandi said.

"Agreed."

Brandi stared at Jo, maybe expecting her to elaborate, but Jo stared right back with a permanent half smile on her face. Brandi readjusted in her seat and said, "You two seem like such a natural fit onstage. You grew up together, so do you think your longtime friendship is what makes this collaboration so successful?"

"Absolutely," Jo said. "Knowing someone for so long, you can anticipate and trust the other person's moves. I think that's important when you share a microphone."

"Makes sense," Brandi said. "So what's your favorite memory of Jo?"

"Oh no," Jo said, and laughed. "Careful now."

J. D. laughed too. "Man, there's so many stories."

"Just one," Brandi said.

J. D. dropped his arms, then crossed them again. "I guess, you know, the first time I ever met her. We were set to play together at the Brunswick Stew fall festival in our hometown of Gatesville. My daddy set up our gig and all he told me was that I'd be playing with a kid named Jo. I thought she was a boy."

He looked over at Jo, who was staring down at the floor with a real smile on her face that she was trying to hide as she shook her head.

Brandi said, "When'd you figure it out?"

"When she jumped onstage with her fiddle out and ready to play. She wore white boots back then."

Both Jo and Brandi laughed. "That's too cute," Brandi said. "How old were you?"

"Young things," Jo said. "Just ten years old." She turned her face to J. D. after she said this and her fine, dark eyes flashed at him just like they had when she hopped on that stage and took over his microphone.

"So here's the question everybody's asking. When will you sing together again? And can we expect an album in the future?"

"We're so glad people want to hear us sing," Jo said.

"That's right," J. D. said.

Brandi said, "Is that a yes, then?"

Jo tugged at the top of her red boot. "I'll be joining J. D. and the Empty Shells for a couple songs at the Nashville Music Festival."

Brandi clasped her hands together like this was the greatest news reported all day.

J. D. added, "Album's in the works."

Brandi said, "I know all of you out there will agree with me that this is very good news for country music. Thanks to both of you for taking time to come on the show today. I can't wait to hear the album. And just one last question, Jo, about your upcoming wedding."

Jo sat up straight on her stool like she'd been called on to answer a difficult question in class.

Brandi said, "Has a date been set? Or is it still a secret?"

"No, not a secret," Jo said, her cheeks flushed suddenly. "It's October twenty-second."

"You heard it here first, CMT viewers. Congratulations, Jo."

"Thank you," she said, and smiled for the camera.

Out of mercy, J. D. wished Jo would look him in the eye after what she'd just said to the entire world. Was he alone in feeling connected to her again after the time they spent together in LA? He refused to believe she couldn't feel their love. He knew she did. Saw it in her smile and her eyes during the interview. That's why she couldn't look at him face-to-face, because she was denying herself—the girl J. D. grew up with, the girl he gave his whole heart to, was drowning inside this glamorous woman seated beside him.

Someone shouted, "And cut!" from the darkness. Brandi stood up and unclipped the microphone from her shirt, as did J. D., grateful to be done with the acting.

Jo said, "Thanks again" to Brandi, and without saying a word to J. D., she walked away.

"Jo," he called after her, but she kept moving like she couldn't hear him.

Brandi said, "I just love her," as she took out a business card from her back pocket and handed it to J. D. "If you ever want to grab a drink, there's my number."

J. D. held the card in his hand, unable to focus on it. He stared down the dark hallway where Jo had disappeared. J. D. handed Brandi his microphone.

She said, "A drink, J. D.?"

"Yeah," he said, and tucked the business card into his back pocket. "Sure, I'll call."

J. D. had to prepare himself to go to the radio station now and deliver the same stock interview and listen again as Jo announced to the world that she would marry Nick Sullivan on October 22, that she was ready to move on and leave J. D. behind for good. And he'd sit there with his headphones on and pretend he was so very happy for her, as happy as the whole damn world seemed to be that she was marrying the wrong man.

CHAPTER 28

The Bluebird

TELL US WHO'S in the room. Or maybe don't. Don't tell us. Don't is better." Denver drank down his water. He couldn't get enough. The more the tables filled up at the Bluebird, the more his thirst increased. In an hour he'd be sitting at the drum kit in the middle of their first set, needing to pee and regretting he'd drunk water to begin with.

"I want to know," Alan said. He wore his finest classic country gear tonight. Big black Stetson hat, embroidered cowboy boots. The rhinestone pattern of country roses on his suit jacket matched the pattern on his pants. They wore matching silver bolo ties. Denver stared at him with a singe of panic searing his stomach. The bolo ties were a bad, bad idea. Too cliché. A bolo tie would kill their career before it ever had a chance to start. Alan looked over at Denver like he was reading his thoughts and placed a heavy hand on Denver's shoulder. Alan said, "Denver's freaking. Don't tell him, Marie."

"No, go ahead and tell me. Who's here? Is Asphalt here?"

Marie drank water from a metal canister but she drank it slowly. She screwed the top back on and said, "I'm siding with Alan on this one."

Alan put his arm around Marie. "Did Denver ever tell you how he thought he'd never see you again? After that first Baboon show?"

"Whatever, Alan," Denver said. He caught Marie smiling at him and he had to smile back.

"Bugging. Heartbroken," Alan said. "You walked out that morning and he looked like an orphaned puppy or something."

"You can stop repeating that story right about now," Denver said.

Marie wrapped her arms around Denver's waist. "But I like hearing it so much." She kissed him on the cheek.

Denver had no idea how he'd been struck lucky in love but he finally had. He and Marie had texted back and forth while she was out in LA with Jo Lover and they'd agreed to meet at the Baboon again when she returned. He'd never forget that it was La Cabeza Roja night at the Baboon; Denver's favorite Mexican polka band had filled the bar with the sounds of brass instruments, and everybody was dancing, in pairs or alone, except Denver, who leaned against the bar and waited for Marie to show up. Finally, a girl came straight up to him and said, "Remember me?" She'd dyed her hair cherry red. Blond to red is a big transition. He could tell it hurt her feelings, the way he reacted, seemingly unable to tell the difference between her and the other girls who'd come up and asked him to dance before she arrived. He quickly made up for it by insisting they get out of there and go someplace decent for food. They ended up at Hattie B's for plates of hot chicken. Here they were weeks later. Denver was actually happy. He wasn't sure he'd ever felt genuine happiness before. No girl Denver had met so far in Nashville had her life put together like Marie, and he wanted to tell her all of this, and more. It choked him, this need to tell her, and the bedroom seemed to be the only place where he could communicate these feelings.

Marie held her phone and checked it every two seconds, in between scanning the room. Occasionally, she stopped to smile at Denver before going back to whatever she was doing. Marie made Denver feel like a slacker, like he had to prove to her that he was going places, that he was ambitious too. Maybe tonight would be the jump start their band needed to finally land a record deal—plenty of great artists had been signed right here at the Bluebird. Denver was so desperate for something miraculous to happen. His hands were clenched from tension, so much that he feared he wouldn't be able to play his drums. What if tonight was the night? What if tonight they'd finally get their break? What would happen to Denver and Marie if he had to go on the road immediately? Would he be able to focus on Marie and his music equally? Was it possible to love them both?

"I better go take a piss before we start," Alan said, and moved behind Denver, patting him on the shoulder a couple times as he passed.

"You okay, Denver?" Marie said.

All the square tables in the Bluebird were pushed close together and near the front of the stage for their solo performance. As the tables filled, there was less space to maneuver. Denver couldn't believe he was inside this building looking out at an audience ordering wine and food, ready to hear them play. Denver tried to recognize industry faces in the soft light of the restaurant, but he couldn't. There was a long line of people standing outside and waiting for a canceled reservation to open up a table. A group of older women stared at him through the glass, the neon-blue sign illuminating their faces.

He knew, from what Marie had told him, that a mix of people was here. Fans of good writing. Floyd Masters listeners. Maybe Floyd Masters himself, but Denver hadn't seen him arrive yet. Industry people were definitely coming, she promised. Marie had invited Jo Lover and Nick Sullivan. Plus Mr. Sullivan of Asphalt Records had told Marie he'd be coming out to listen with one of his A & R guys. She'd told Denver to expect suits from other labels to show up too, which meant they were probably in the room staring at him right now. People were definitely staring at him.

"Denver." Marie tugged on his arm and leaned close to him. Softly, she said, "You look a little spooked. Maybe you should go warm up or something."

Marie started to walk away but Denver grabbed her hand before she moved too far away from him, and he brought her in close and kissed her on her cheek gently. "You're amazing, Marie. I don't want a day to go by without me saying that to you."

She squeezed his hand. "You're going to be just fine. Trust me."

Alan returned from the bathroom, and Marie walked over to the small hostess's desk by the front door.

"She tell you who's here?" Alan said.

"No."

"Better that way," Alan said, and stepped onto the low stage. Denver followed behind him, taking his place at the drum kit, where he fitted the metal harmonica holder over his neck. Alan draped his guitar strap over his shoulder like it was a knight's red sash. As Alan strummed and tuned the pegs, the audience quieted down and turned their collective attention toward the stage. Denver's heartbeat slowed down finally as he stared out at the crowd staring back at them with so much anticipation present on their faces, at Alan's back as it leaned over the guitar, at his cymbal shining in the low lights of the Bluebird—this was it, he told himself with his foot resting on the kick-drum pedal, ready to call the place to order. This was definitely, definitely it.

CHAPTER 29

The Highlands

Nick parked his Range Rover at the greasy-spoon diner across the street from the Bluebird, which was lit up with soft light and ready to host the Flyby Boys' performance. He and Jo crossed the street together and Nick reached out for her hand to hold. Jo accepted it even though she felt a film of shame all over her body—a barrier of tiny atoms strung together to hold in the truth of her distraction. She thought about J. D. constantly. Wondered where he was and who he was with, if he was thinking about Jo, if he was drinking whiskey and sharing his bed with another woman, if he and Rob were telling stories about Gatesville without her.

A few times the past few days, Jo had almost told Nick all this because she had no one else to share these feelings with and because the feelings confused her—it would only hurt Nick unnecessarily to know she'd spent time with J. D. in LA after their duet went viral. Nick was bothered enough just knowing their fans on Twitter discussed whether or not J. D. and Jo were in love and if her marriage with Nick would still go through. Jo hoped her recent announcements about the wedding date would help to ease all of those rumors, and yet she felt a pang in her chest that she didn't quite understand each time she entered a room with J. D. Tomorrow they had to be in the studio together, and she was dreading it. Her only wish was to stop thinking about him, but each time she saw him, her thoughts picked up speed.

Nick and Jo walked across the small parking lot to the front door of the Bluebird. From the outdoor speakers in front of the restaurant Jo could hear a band warming up inside. A long line of people were still waiting to secure seats. At least it wasn't raining. People would queue up like this in the snow if there was somebody inside they absolutely had to see.

Someone behind her said, "Oh my God, is that Jo Lover?" Another person said, "I think it is. Hey, Jo. Jo Lover, is that you?" And another voice: "She's coming to see the Flyby Boys too. That's huge."

Jo turned around and smiled. She couldn't tell exactly who was shouting at her. "Hey, everybody," she said, and waved. People held up their phones and took pictures of her, their flashes going off, like paparazzi, which had been happening more since the video with J. D. went viral. She couldn't go to the store or the gas station without some version of this happening to her. She saw Marie standing by the door and waved at her. Marie opened the door so Jo and Nick could slip by the long line. Inside, the warmth of a close crowd of listeners, all that love and respect for the players, welcomed her. The soft yellow lighting illuminated the memorabilia on the walls. Jo was on the wall. So was J. D. Separately. Their images would be plastered on the wall long after Jo and J.D. were gone. Sometimes coming to the Bluebird felt like stepping inside a mausoleum.

Marie said, "Thanks for coming."

"Excited to see these guys finally," Nick said. "I've been hearing their name all around town."

"I reserved us the best table." To the hostess, Marie said, "I'll take them."

Jo and Nick followed Marie to a table for three at center stage, front row. Nick leaned down from behind Jo. "I see my father. Hold my seat."

Jo put her purse on Nick's chair as Nick made his way to the back of the room near the bar, stopping and shaking hands with people before standing next to his father, who was dressed down in khakis and a collared shirt. No blazer. The other two guys with him wore print T-shirts and roughed-up jeans. There was no way for the musicians onstage to know who was watching for business and who for pleasure. Nick gestured toward their table and Mr. Sullivan waved at her.

A young waitress with dark hair piled in a messy bun secured by a pencil came over to take their order. "Whiskey neat, please," Jo said.

"And you, miss?"

Marie said, "A water's fine."

"Be wild," Jo said.

Marie forced a smile. Jo wanted to ask her what was wrong with her, but she knew Marie would fake an answer. She'd been acting differently since they got drunk together on the tour bus in LA. At first Jo had blamed it on Marie's wretched hangover, then wondered if she was mad at Jo for letting her lose control. That didn't seem right either. Jo considered it might be a problem with her new boyfriend, but things in that department seemed like they were going well for Marie and Denver. Jo wasn't sure what to think. Something personal was her only guess.

Marie turned her attention away from the band. "I really do appreciate you and Nick coming."

"Happy to support your boyfriend's band," she said.

Marie scratched the blue laminated tablecloth. The white cotton edges were still frayed, just as they'd always been. The waitress brought back their drinks and just as quickly was off to another table. The kick drum sent out a rapid beat and a hush fell over the crowd. Nick returned to his seat, leaned over to Jo, and kissed her on her temple. He wore a big smile on his face. This was how he always acted about new bands. Nick lived on the possibility of discovering the next big thing and his giddiness was contagious.

"You order me something?" he said.

Jo sipped her whiskey but stopped with the glass at her lips. "I wasn't sure what you'd want."

"I always drink scotch." He stared at her for a moment like he was seeing her for the first time.

"I'll grab the waitress when she comes back around."

"That's all right. I'll catch her." To Marie, he said, "The guys in the back are charged up about this band."

"Oh, good," Marie said. "They should be."

"You really believe in these guys," Jo said.

"I do."

The lead guitarist brought his mouth to the microphone and said, "Welcome, everybody, to the Bluebird Café."

The audience clapped and a few people in the back whistled.

"We want to thank everybody for coming out for our debut here at the most important establishment in Music City, USA. Denver and I, we love this town, love Nashville and all it's offered us so far. We're just super humbled to be here. Thanks to Dan for organizing all this and to Marie for hooking us up with Dan. She bribed you, didn't she, Dan?"

"Oh yeah," Dan called out from the sound station in the back.

"Thought so," Alan said. Denver nodded and crashed the cymbal. Everyone laughed.

Nick looked over at Jo and smiled. These two had charisma; she could tell that's what he was thinking too. The front man especially. It hadn't occurred to her until this moment that this was an up-and-coming country band with a black man out front on lead guitar and vocals. She tried to remember any black country musicians who'd started from the bottom and made it to the top since Charley Pride, but she couldn't think of anybody. Not a single person came to mind.

Jo leaned over and said, "What's his name?"

"Alan," Marie said. "He's incredible."

Jo had to hear them play to know if they were the real thing, but if so, being here at the Bluebird could change their lives forever. Jo had launched her solo career here and she hadn't had anyone up onstage with her to take the heat of all those staring eyes. She really missed being with J. D., Rob, and Chase B on that night, but she'd made it through all on her own. The stakes were so high in a place this intimate. Couldn't fudge a single emotion the way you could at an arena, where the massive stage, lighting, huge TV screens, and graphics separated you from the audience. You couldn't hide at the Bluebird.

Mr. Sullivan had come out to hear her debut at the Bluebird too way back when, at Nick's insistence. Nick had set her up here the way Marie had arranged this gig for the Flyby Boys. Anyone would've been flattered to have the head of Asphalt at her show. After Jo finished her second set, Mr. Sullivan hung back and waited for the room to clear, waited for the other labels to talk her up. Then he took her aside and said, "I believe in my artists, Jo. Believe in their ability to direct the market and not have the market direct them. If you sign with Asphalt, you will help continue to grow this label and you will have artistic freedom. Can't say the same for the corporate labels in town. If you take a risk on me, Jo, I promise you won't be disappointed."

He was so passionate and so was she. She signed with Asphalt, no questions asked. Mr. Sullivan offered a stellar contract too. Another solo artist who signed with her at the same time ended up being dropped after her first album sold poorly. She refused to let that happen to her. Nick nurtured her vision, encouraged her to experiment with chords, helped her restructure her songs, while being super gentle in his feedback. She and Nick worked really well together and had for years now with multiple albums behind them. Their relationship was built from this mutual respect.

The drums quickened their rhythm to the sound of Alan's guitar picking. But then the music stopped and Jo took Nick's hand under the table and held it tight. Alan removed his acoustic guitar and handed it behind him to Denver, who stood up to play. Alan strapped on his banjo, tuned a string, and then said, "The banjo descended from African instruments; probably most of you know that already, and you probably know that African-American string bands used to feature the banjo in their songs until the 1830s, when white musicians started painting their faces black, speaking with a black dialect, and playing their own style of black string music on the banjo. Well, black folks gave up this instrument for a long time after that and picked up the guitar instead. But string music just doesn't sound right without a banjo. So to remind us all what an incredible instrument this is, I'd like to open with a Flatt and Scruggs standard titled 'Blue Ridge Cabin Home.'"

Alan began the downward stroke on his banjo, and then his searching, lonesome voice filled the Bluebird. Jo closed her eyes as Alan sang about loving the Blue Ridge Mountains of Virginia and yearning for home. She opened her eyes after Alan finished the final chorus. His eyes remained closed as he finished the song, and he let the hollow twang of the banjo finish what words could not. Jo knew this song by heart but she knew the feeling better. Jo and Alan were born from the same soil and it was real for him still. It was in the timbre of his voice as he sang; he reminded Jo of the pickers who used to gather outside the general store in Gatesville for the Friday Night Jamboree. Denver returned Alan's guitar before sitting down at the drums, and then Alan strapped on his electric guitar and led into the next song, which had a Springsteen rock influence.

Denver bore down hard on the drums. Jo glanced at Nick and he was totally absorbed by the music. How to describe their style— Americana musicians with country at their core, maybe? These two guys played music that was some kind of special. Jo believed the Flyby Boys would take off soon. Perhaps tonight, even. Jo hoped so, hoped musicians this good could still make it in Nashville.

Jo was deep inside the cave of the Flyby Boys' music and felt a creative rush of emotion flowing from the stage to the audience. Could she and J. D. make real music together again like this? Was J. D. capable of doing that anymore? Was Jo capable of doing that without Nick? Jo wasn't sure, and she feared that with J. D.'s producer in the studio with them tomorrow instead of Nick, their chances of creating anything meaningful were slim at best. Nick had helped shape Jo's music for so long that she didn't know what kind of artist she would be without him anymore, and if the album failed, if they couldn't write together, would that be it for her and J. D.? Sometimes Jo thought that would be best for both of them, but most of the time the thought of never again playing music or singing with J. D. filled her with a deep and abiding sorrow.

CHAPTER 30

Off in the Studio

J O WOKE UP early; ran five miles with her dog, Max, on the winding paths at Centennial Park; rested at the base of the Parthenon building; and stretched on the grass. The sun rose over downtown Nashville, filling the sky with soft pinks and oranges against a baby-blue backdrop. She and Max walked home, and she was surprised to find Nick's Range Rover in her driveway still—normally he'd be up before her and at his studio before sunrise. Jo wiped off Max's wet paws and fed him a small bit of bacon, told him he was the best dog that ever lived, and let him run loose ahead of her. The sound of his wild paws chasing after his plush toy signaled to the entire house that they were home.

The smell of coffee greeted her like a maid before she rounded the corner to her airy kitchen, where Nick stood at the butcher-block island cooking breakfast. The French doors leading to her patio and fountain were wide open, and a small breeze lifted the corners of her white lace table runner. The ceiling fan circled without being on. Jo had trained her devil's ivy vines to climb the frame of the French door and up the fishing line she'd attached to the ceiling. One of the vines had fallen off its trail. Later, Jo would help the plant find its way again. Nick looked over at the doorway and said, "How was your run?"

"Hard." She wrapped her arms around Nick from behind. He pulled her to his side with his free arm and held her close. As Nick scrambled eggs with the spatula, Jo washed her hands and then returned to his side to eat a bit of grated Gruyère cheese. Nick poured the egg mixture in her cast-iron griddle.

"A man in the kitchen is the sexiest thing in the world."

"I cook just to hear you say that."

Jo opened the refrigerator and retrieved a bowl of oranges. She sliced each one in half and then pressed the pulp in the juicer. She heard the scrape of the stainless steel spatula against the pan; her mama used to wake up everybody in the house with that sound. She prepared enough food to feed a small village, that's how it seemed, and every single day she scrambled eggs from their chickens if they were laying and made a side of oatmeal. And if any food was left over, they had that for lunch as well. Jo had sworn off oatmeal a long, long time ago. She still enjoyed scrambled eggs, but only the way Nick made them, with fancy cheeses, exotic salts, and cracked pepper. Jo poured a glass of fresh juice for each of them.

"Thank you for breakfast." She offered him the juice glass, which he accepted. "Another long day." Jo drank her juice. "Wish you were going with me."

Nick moved the egg mixture gently from one side of the pan to the other until it started to become firm. "You don't need me, Jo."

"It's not about need," Jo said, even though she wasn't quite convinced of that herself. "It's about desire. I love being in the studio with you."

She placed her palm on his smooth forearm and Nick smiled but didn't respond. He hadn't seemed surprised when she returned from the studio yesterday frustrated because she and J. D. couldn't write. They'd spent most of the day talking to J. D.'s producer. Nick disliked the collaboration—he'd told her multiple times he thought it was a terrible move for her career, but she implored him to be supportive. She'd already agreed to make the new album, and he knew just as well as she did that his father wouldn't accept any other answer. Being in the studio required so much energy and emotional investment that when she returned to the house at the end of the day, she needed to feel confident that Nick would be free of any resentment. But after yesterday's nonstarter in the studio, Jo wondered if Nick was right about their musical visions being incompatible.

She ate blueberries out of the open plastic carton on the countertop. "Heard anything about the Flyby Boys? Weren't they something? So much energy."

"They're crazy talented." Nick lifted the griddle and let the scrambled eggs fall to the plate. "I'm sure they'll be snapped up quick."

"I'm going to shower," she said.

"I'll leave your breakfast in the warming drawer."

"You won't eat with me?"

Nick washed his hands at the island sink and dried them on a terry-cloth kitchen towel. "Meeting my first band in fifteen minutes." He kissed her on the center of her forehead, and she could smell his clean, pine-scented cologne. "I'll cook dinner too."

Max ran into the kitchen and Nick knelt down to try to wrestle his red and white rope out of his mouth while Max playfully growled. Max would turn out the victor, as always. Nick patted Max hard on his side, making a hollow sound, and then he stood up and kissed Jo good-bye once more. After Nick left, Jo had just enough time to eat, shower, blow out her hair, put on a light coat of makeup, and drive over to the recording studio at Asphalt, a place she'd never actually entered despite releasing multiple albums with the label. She recorded at Nick's studio across town, and already she missed being at Nick's place with its worn Persian rugs, midcentury furniture, and Snoopy phone by the front door. This place looked splattered in neutrals. Oatmeal walls, brown leather furniture, chrome fixtures—all of it brand-new and lifeless.

Jo knocked on the door of the sound control room and immediately heard J. D.'s voice. She knocked again and Benny, J. D.'s producer, opened the door. He was a burly man with a large red beard. Benny moved to the side and revealed J. D. sitting at the sound station, his black cowboy boots propped up on the table. He wore a black vest over a T-shirt and dark jeans, and he looked so handsome and confident. J. D. said, "You ready?"

"Ready as ever." She looked through the glass at the recording room, where all of their instruments, multiple microphones, and earphones were set up.

J. D. stretched his arm toward the door. "After you."

Jo entered the room and J. D. shut them inside. Jo sat on a stool, put on her headphones, and picked up her acoustic guitar. She strummed while she waited for J. D. to settle into his space. "I've got something I want you to hear," he said, excited like they were about to go to the circus.

"You wrote something already?"

"Last night."

J. D. strapped on his acoustic guitar and dug deep into his jeans pocket before pulling out his pick. Jo let her arms rest on her guitar and she closed her eyes to listen as he played a terrible, empty song. The words said nothing; they were just words, words, words. No real emotion, no real narrative either. When he finished she gave him a small smile and he immediately removed his guitar. "You didn't like it."

"I like some of the chord changes."

"But you don't like the words."

Jo scratched the back of her neck. "Why don't we just pick around and try writing something together?"

"Benny liked it."

"Okay," Jo said.

"But you don't."

She gripped the yellow legal pad on her lap. "Want me to share something of mine?"

J. D. crossed his arms and his knee bounced up and down. "Go ahead."

This tension had never existed between them when they were writing music together in the past, and she felt like they were both trying to prove something to each other now as they offered up their work. Jo sang him the song she'd started writing on the plane ride out to LA, but he stopped her halfway through.

"What?" she said.

"That's a female vocalist's song."

"It could work as a duet. You didn't even listen to the whole thing."

"I heard enough."

Jo felt a coldness take over the room like an invisible blizzard had just moved through the studio. She scratched out all the lyrics she'd brought with her. "I still think this song could go somewhere, J. D."

"Then finish it for a solo album," he said, and adjusted the capo on his guitar to the third fret.

"This isn't a solo album. We need to write together. Agree on something."

"Except you don't like my lyrics."

"You don't like mine either," Jo said with a raised voice. She glanced at the producer shielded behind the glass. Benny had his arms crossed and stared out at them with a look on his face that said, "This isn't what I signed up for." Benny scratched his large red beard, pulled on it hard, and then leaned forward, and his voice came over the speaker in the recording studio: "I'm happy to sit here and get paid to listen to you argue, but if you can't try and write something together, I'm not too sure how much I can help you."

Jo stood up from her stool and picked up her fiddle, plucked the strings like a guitar. "I knew this wouldn't work."

"It's not the lyrics or the producer or anything else. It's me and you, Jo. That's the issue."

Jo quickly looked over at the sound room, where Benny was listening to every single word J. D. said.

"Can we talk in private?" she said.

J. D. lifted off the seat and said, "Benny, could you give us a minute?"

Benny stood up in the other room. "I'll be back in ten."

Jo placed her fiddle on its stand and buried her hands deep inside her jeans pockets. Outside of this glass box, Jo was certain she and J. D. could write songs that mattered, something real, but nothing worked here between them. Nothing. She and J. D. weren't good trapped like this. J. D. sat back down on the round black stool, hunched over his guitar. Jo shook her foot like they were waiting to see the principal.

J. D. said, "Maybe we should release a couple covers of old songs, let them go viral. Free press for Asphalt. And then we can move on and work on separate albums."

"That's what you want?" It hurt her to think he could let it go so easily.

J. D. put his guitar in its stand. "I want to write real songs with you, Jo. That's what I want, but being here together like this, in this space, it doesn't work for me."

"Should we tell Mr. Sullivan we've changed our minds? Creative differences?"

J. D.'s pensive stare was fixed on the ground, and then he pushed the overhead microphone away from his face. "Let's go home."

"No way I'm going to your place."

"No," J. D. said. "Like home, home."

"Gatesville? You're serious?"

"Let's rent a house. Look, I knew it before we walked in here today. This place just doesn't work for us. And if we want a chance, want to complete this album together, we have to try something different."

What would she tell Nick? She was going out of town for a spontaneous spa weekend with no cell phone service? Those existed, surely, but it was another lie. Layers and layers of lies. She felt like she was six feet below and looking up at Nick, dirt pouring down on her face. He would never approve of her going home with J. D., not in a million years, even if she swore it was only a work trip, even if the mountains were exactly what they needed: fishing, hiking, swimming, shooting skeet together—anything to find common ground.

"You need to decide, Jo. We stay here and quit or we go."

"I own a farmhouse near Clinch Mountain."

J. D. stared at her for a long time, and the longer he looked at her the warmer her cheeks became. He said, "Let's go there then," and picked up his guitar to place it in the case. "I'll drive."

"You can't drive a Tesla to Gatesville."

"We'll rent something. Like a Buick."

"Or a Ford."

J. D. packed up his equipment quickly. Jo wasn't sure if she needed to say this but something inside forced her to tell him, if only to feel better about what they were about to do: "J. D., you know when we go there, it's just for work. Nothing can happen between us."

He latched his last guitar case slowly without looking up at her, and then he rested his hand on his bent knee. "You planning to pack your stuff or what?"

If she pressed him, he'd only grow more defensive. That was the way he'd always been—deflect the subject whenever the conversation veered too close to the heart.

CHAPTER 31

Homeward Bound

I N A RENTED Ford Escape, J. D. drove them the whole way home to Virginia. At truck stops, they bought roasted peanuts, jars of local honey, hoodies with the names of small towns on the front. They asked each other trivia questions they made up on the spot. What's the name of a baboon's red ass? What would music sound like on Mars? They drank Coke. Jo was in charge of the stereo and they harmonized right along with Emmylou and Gram.

"When's the last time you took a road trip outside a tour bus?" Jo said.

"No idea. Sure is fun though."

"I think I've forgotten." Her phone started ringing and she picked up. She said, "Hey, I won't be able to make it for dinner tonight, and Marie's coming to the house to take care of Max. I had a really long day and I'm headed to a resort for the weekend, just to relax some after all that."

J. D. gripped the steering wheel as he listened to her lying to Nick Sullivan. Why would she have to lie if they really trusted each other? If they really loved each other?

"I know," she said, and then she made a low humming noise J. D. remembered really well from their long-distance phone calls. "Right," she said. "It went well. Okay. Yeah, I'll be home Monday. It's just the weekend. Okay. Love you too." She tossed her phone in her purse like she was sailing it into the pit of a volcano. Jo propped up her arm on the passenger-side door and rested her head against it.

"Mind if I smoke?" J. D. said.

"I do mind, actually. But we can stop if you need to."

"I can wait," he said, and turned up the volume of the Bill Monroe playlist. Jo closed her eyes and napped while J. D. drove. She woke up once he slowed down on the curving mountain roads and passed the sign for Gatesville: WHERE MOUNTAINS AND MUSIC MAKE MEMORIES. "Was that sign always there?" he asked her as they neared town.

"Think so."

The low rolling mountains surrounding Gatesville and the tall meadow grass like velvet in the sunlight made J. D. feel grounded suddenly. Large herds of black cows chewed grass near the wooden fences. Wild Queen Anne's lace, red columbines, and tiny daisies flowered on the sides of the roads, and horses walked through fields of buttercups so yellow it looked like the sun had melted all over the land. Jo stuck her bare feet out of the window, let the wind blow through her long hair. She said, "Sometimes I forget how beautiful it is here."

J. D. drove them past their old swimming hole at the rock quarry, which was shut down now, for how many years he didn't know. They drove by the Gatesville elementary school and middle school and the high school that J. D. had dropped out of. All of this happened without music in the background. Old brick buildings moved past their windows, same as they were before. J. D. was surprised by how easily he navigated around Gatesville. He had no trouble finding Route 58 to drive by his daddy's house. He could see his mother standing there, right above the kitchen sink, her brown hair matted down from soapy dishwater. She always wiped away loose strands with the back of a soapy hand. She was always there, whenever he was coming home. Dead now how many years? She was dead. J. D. thought of her only as he remembered her alive. Never well, but never dead. Dressed to perfection in the morning with makeup applied flawlessly and hiding everything she was feeling from the world, except on the days when she was too sad to leave her room. On those days nothing felt tidy in the house. J. D. could see her still. There she was at the kitchen sink— washing away the leftovers from the plates, her hair curled, her dress ironed so that not a single wrinkle showed.

"House looks nice," Jo said as J. D. drove by slowly. "At least your daddy's maintaining the place."

J. D. picked up speed and said, "Where to? Your old house?"

Jo's red painted toenails curled over on the dashboard and she held her hands together in her lap. She looked over at him with a sly smile.

"What?" he said. He swerved some to stay in his lane as he drove around a bend, the Appalachian Mountains a verdant outline against the sky.

"I have a crazy idea."

"I'm listening."

"I desperately want some sherbet from the general store."

"Sunrise sherbet?"

"Whatever kind," she said.

"You think they sell that still?"

Jo shrugged. "Can't hurt to try."

J. D. hesitated. "What if we see somebody?"

Jo gathered her hair into a ponytail. She seemed to be considering the possibility. There were plenty of people neither one of them wanted to bump into on Main Street.

She said, "Everybody's at work, don't you think?"

"Probably."

"We'll pretend to be someone else. People tell us all the time how much we look like those famous singers. No, we're just driving through on our way out west."

J. D. laughed at her and looked over for a moment while he was driving. She bit her lower lip as she smiled at him. "So, we'll do it?"

"Posthaste." Being with Jo in the car like this made him want to lean over and kiss her despite that diamond on her finger. He knew he couldn't do that. He knew they were here to write together and work, but he suspected this might be the very last time they ever had a chance to drive around with nowhere to go and laugh at nothing and sing old songs and just be friends. And as much as J. D. wished like hell that she wouldn't marry Nick Sullivan in October, he wouldn't ruin this time by telling her. He'd savor every minute they had alone.

J. D. parked the Ford Escape on the side of Main Street where the spots were free and most were available. An elderly couple walked hand in hand down the sidewalk and said, "Hi there," as they passed by J. D. and Jo. Everything felt like it was moving in slow time. The barbershop was empty and the drugstore next to it had an American flag moving gently in the mountain breeze. The wig shop across the street had a CLOSED sign in the window.

"Shall we?" Jo said.

J. D. and Jo walked down the street where he and his daddy had walked every Sunday, and sometimes during the week, to go to the hardware store up the way and talk to Gus about feed prices for the farm. The general store still had the red and white striped light mounted on the brick wall outside the front doors. Nothing seemed to change here—the mountain range remained fixed in the distance, the white lettering on the windows refused to fade, and the smell of fresh kettle corn greeted J. D. immediately when Jo opened the door and the brass bell chimed above them. The big oak barrels were filled to the top still with every kind of hard candy a kid could want.

"Good afternoon, folks," someone called from the back of the store. Appalachian string music played over the speakers.

"Oh my God," Jo said, and grabbed ahold of J. D.'s arm and tugged him to the side of the store where the white freezer stood. Sure enough, they sold the sunrise sherbet with stripes of blue raspberry, orange, and watermelon.

An old man with thick white hair and a blue apron walked up from the back of the store and met them at the freezer. "How you doing, you two?"

"We're better now," Jo said.

"You aren't from around here, are you?" He spoke in that unhurried and gracious way that J. D. associated with the people here. Knowing the mountains were so old and would be there long after you died had a way of humbling people.

"Just passing through, sir," J. D. said.

"Ah," he said, and nodded his head. "We're the gateway to the western frontier. That's what Gatesville was known for back when the settlers were headed that way for something better. Bet you didn't know that."

"No, sir," Jo said with the sweetest highland accent. "I didn't know."

But J. D. knew she did. A person who grew up in Gatesville knew all that. Any old-timer with ten minutes would fill you in on the town's history after church, at the fall festival, at the Friday Night Jamboree.

"What can I get you?"

"Two scoops of sunrise sherbet, please." Jo looked up at J. D. "That all right?"

"Perfect."

The old man leaned deep into the freezer and placed one large curled scoop of sherbet apiece in paper cups. He stuck a small wooden flat spoon in each one and handed it to them over the glass. "You two sure you're not from around here?"

"We're sure," Jo said.

"Familiar faces, I guess."

Jo smiled at J. D. "This one's on me," she said.

Jo went to the counter to pay while J. D. stood in the center of the general store and looked at a freestanding shelf of books all focused on the history of Scott County, Gatesville, the Appalachian Mountains, and bluegrass and country music. J. D. walked to the opposite side of the shelf and the wooden floorboards creaked beneath him. They sold CDs right there at the top, and he found his albums for sale and Jo's too. J. D. studied his most recent album cover. Just his face and a cowboy hat. That's all he was in Nashville, he guessed, but being here and far enough away, he knew the man on the cover wasn't the man standing here with a cold cup of sherbet in his hand.

Jo nearly skipped back to J. D. She looked disappointed. "You haven't had a bite yet?"

"I was waiting for you."

"Really?"

J. D. nodded.

"That was nice." She filled her spoon with all three colors and J. D. followed her lead. They both took a bite at the same time. The cold sweetness coated his tongue like he was tasting his entire childhood in a single bite. Jo covered her mouth as she said, "Holy cow, that's so good. Let's buy another scoop."

So they did, and then they walked out of the general store together and down Main Street side by side while they finished their sherbet. They tossed their cups in the trash can near their car, and Jo said, "What should we do now?"

"You don't want to go play music?"

"Not really," she said. "I'm having fun."

J. D. wished he was wearing his hat to block out the sun bearing down on the top of his head. "You think that patch of wine berries is still there?"

Jo's eyes widened and lit up in an instant. "Off the Devil's Bathtub trail?"

"Yeah."

"I bet you anything they are." Jo moved straight for the car.

"You remember how to get there?"

"Think so."

He handed over the keys, and then J. D. climbed into the passenger seat. Jo drove them away from Main Street, down Mountainbrook Hollow, then made a left turn on Moles and another left on Shining Creek, which turned into a gravel drive before Jo made an ascent to the trailhead. As they moved deeper into the mountains, the temperature dropped and they rolled the windows down to smell the spring earth with so much new life growing upward. Jo drove slowly on a rickety wooden bridge over a wide creek with various shades of rust-colored stones visible in the clear water, and soon after, she parked the car in a small gravel lot. They entered the trailhead, which quickly turned into a shaded rhododendron forest. Flaming orange azaleas were in bloom, so J. D. knew the wine berries had to be ripe. Jo hiked on the narrow trail ahead of him. "It's close to the swimming hole, if I remember right."

A little while later Jo stopped abruptly. "I think they're in the woods over there," she said, and she pointed up ahead, way off the trail. They stepped into the overgrowth of the forest, and Jo moved through slowly at first but then started picking up speed until she disappeared down a small hill. J. D. followed after her, but he heard her shout, "They're here," before he caught up with her at the patch of green bushes that he remembered so well, the branches weighed down by the soft red fruit.

"You're brilliant, Jo," he said, and picked a delicate berry and popped it in his mouth, the juice exploding almost immediately as he bit into it. Jo made a small basket with her T-shirt and started gathering fruit. He helped her pick, and then she carried the fruit back to the trail. The sun filtered through the tree canopy above as J. D. and Jo climbed the mossy limestone rocks at the swimming hole. Jo sat down and placed the fruit in a small indentation on the rock. The creek water emptied into the sun-filtered pool.

Jo had a smirk on her face when she said, "I dare you."

J. D. stripped down to his underwear and jumped into the frigid pool. The shock of the cold nearly stole his breath. He treaded water while Jo took off her boots and dropped her feet in the water. She immediately withdrew her feet. "You're crazy. It's like ice," she said, and placed a berry in her mouth.

J. D. couldn't withstand the temperature any longer and pulled himself up onto a sunny spot on the rocks and lay out there to warm his body.

"Open up," Jo said, and tossed a wine berry at J. D., which he caught in his mouth. She laughed.

"I always loved it here." J. D. placed his arm behind his head and squinted his eyes to see Jo, who was stroking the moss on the rock beside her.

"You seem like your old self here," she said.

He sat up and wiped the dirt from his palms. "So do you."

Jo stopped eating the wine berries in her hand and the smile faded from her face. "I haven't changed."

J. D. stood up and put his clothes back on, his underwear wet and soaking through the back of his jeans. "I guess that's what you've been thinking all these years," he said as he latched his belt buckle into place. "That I've sold out and you've stayed true. I'm not saying I haven't changed, but you can't sit on that rock and act like you haven't changed too. You have. More than you know. The girl I grew up with, the girl I loved, wouldn't let her label push her around and tell her to do this and do that, wouldn't let other people make decisions for her. The girl I knew would say the hell with all that if she didn't want it. You've sold out too. Maybe not in your music like I did, Jo, but in your spirit. I always thought your heart was honest but now you're somebody different depending on who's around. You're one person around me, another person with Nick, another person with his father, somebody else onstage. You act like somebody you aren't and you've been acting like that a long time."

Jo stood up fast, like there were red ants underneath her. She was taking quick, shallow breaths—he could see her chest rising and falling like a blackbird's wing. Her face was alert and he was waiting for her to yell at him, to say terrible things. The hurt look on her face made him regret what he'd said, even though that's what he believed.

Jo threw away the berries into the pool of water and wiped the red juice from her palms onto her jeans. "It's time to go," she said, and hiked up the rocks without another word.

CHAPTER 32

In the Veil of Clinch Mountain

J O STAYED UP the entire night, until the earliest birds woke up and started singing in the darkness. A soft rain followed, and Jo listened to the drops on the red tin roof of her farmhouse and wondered if J. D. had been able to sleep on the floor below or if he was restless too— those things he'd said at the Devil's Bathtub repeated on a loop in her head. They'd hiked away from the swimming hole in silence, and Jo had driven down the curved roads toward her house and didn't say a word. She showed him to his room on the second floor and told him to help himself to anything in the kitchen. Even though it was light out- side still, she wished him good night before coming upstairs and col- lapsing onto the four-poster bed. The grandfather clock chimed from one hour to the next. As night approached, Jo clutched a pillow and ar- gued with J. D. in her head. She told J. D. he was wrong about her, that her heart was honest. She imagined marching down the wide wooden staircase to his floor, banging on the door with her fist, and saying this to his face, but the hours continued to pass until the darkness gave way to the soft rays of morning light entering through the large windows in her bedroom.

Jo heard the sound of an axe splitting wood and wondered if her groundskeeper had come to check on the land. She opened her closet, wrapped herself in a silk robe, and walked over to the window across from her bed. Jo pushed the sheer white curtains to the side and looked out to see the top of a bright orange sun rising over the hazy Clinch Mountain ridge. Coral-pink clouds filled the sky and the sun's pearly rays fanned upward. Jo moved to the east-facing window, where the fishing pond and woodpile were in clear view. J. D. stood tall and straight as the trees in the woodpile once had been. He wore the same jeans he'd arrived in yesterday, but his torso was bare, the axe in his hand remained slack at his side, and he had one boot propped up on the stump. His head was lifted upward as if a heavenly host stretched across the sky. She placed her palm on the windowpane and wished he would turn around and see her and know the pain he'd caused her with those words—only J. D. could speak the truth to her that way. He was the only person in her life who ever could. The sun lifted between the peaks of the ridge until the color faded from deep orange to canary yellow.

Jo closed the curtains and held the fabric in both of her hands. He was right that Jo hadn't been living honest. She'd been living lies ever since Travis Goode interrupted her life—an eighth-grade boy who should've been in high school, a boy who always wanted Jo's attention at lunch or after school, was always making jokes about her poor-looking shoes, a boy she ignored because his eyes had a vivid meanness in them. He and a group of boys followed after her and her brother, Martin, as they were walking home from Gatesville Middle School and kept after them, saying, "You dumb rock. Why can't you get things right in Miss Dunlap's class? You stupid or what? Something's wrong with you. What's wrong with him, Joanne? You can't talk neither? Is the whole Lover family a bunch of retards?"

Jo said, "Who's the retard, Travis? Shouldn't you be in tenth grade by now?"

The other boys let out a long "ooooh" sound and hit Travis on his arm. "She told you."

Jo wished J. D. and Rob had walked home with them. They'd gone fishing right after school, when Jo was expected to help her mama fry catfish and wild ramps for dinner. Jo held Martin's hand and told him it'd be all right, even though her heart was being whacked in her chest like a rug on the line. Martin made clicking noises with his teeth. They kept walking, didn't turn around, but then a large rock, bigger than her fist, hit Martin on the back of his head and knocked him down. He tucked himself into a ball on that dirt road and started crying and screaming.

Jo picked the rock back up and sailed it at Travis Goode and hit him in the face. She shouted for them to go away and leave her and Martin alone. Travis and two other boys ambushed Martin while he was on the ground, and each of them gave him swift kicks in the stomach, in the back, in the neck, in the face, calling out, "You retard crybaby." Jo lunged at Travis, punched him right in the jaw, and then a sudden blow knocked her to the ground. Travis kicked away at her back and her stomach. She felt like she was going to vomit the entire time, but she refused to close her eyes. She watched her brother try to protect his head. Travis stopped beating on her for a moment and she removed her hands from her face to see his dark buzzed hair, his thin lips, his stocky torso towering above her, the sun like a halo on his back. He turned to look at the other boys.

"Make them stop, please," she shouted at him, the iron taste of blood in her mouth. "He can't help himself," she begged until he kicked her in the chest, stole her breath, dragged her into the ditch on the side of the road. Travis pinned Jo down with his heavy body, spit in her face, rubbed his spit all over her, and it smelled like the cough syrup everybody knew he drank before school. Travis pushed her underwear to the side and forced himself inside her and it burned worse than a skinned knee, burned like nothing she'd ever known before. She clawed at his face, his back. Broke all her nails trying to get him off her.

He punched her until her eyes were so swollen she couldn't see him anymore. In her ear he said, "You ever tell anybody, I'll kill your retard brother. Kill you too. You're nothing but a broke whore."

She could feel the weight of him on her still—suddenly Travis's body seemed to hover above her like a swan, wings beating down hard. Her arms extended for miles beyond her body, a shifting in the distance between her and the world. Travis lifted her head and slammed the back of her skull into the ground, and she heard a sustained ringing in her ears, smelled burned hair all around her. He jumped out of the ditch and left her there, where she wept and listened to Martin moan.

The boys ran away, calling them both freaks. Jo refused to let Martin see her crying since that would've scared him worse than his beating. She crawled out of the ditch and held Martin's purple face in her lap as he whimpered and bled, swollen as an eggplant. "It's okay, they're gone now," she told him. "They're a bunch of no-good fucking cowards, Martin. They're afraid of you because you're different, that's all." He cried some more. She told him she loved him. Sang the hymn "Shall We Gather at the River." Eventually she was able to help him stand up and they limped to the creek in the woods, where they washed off.

Jo shielded herself behind a large poplar tree, lifted her dress, and found bright red blood in her urine-soaked underwear. Jo lightly touched her fingers on her stinging skin to find the tear. She took off her underwear, wiped away the mess with it, and buried the evidence in a hole beneath the roots. At home inside their tiny kitchen, her tall, skinny mama stood with two of Jo's little cousins at her feet. She had flour for dredging the catfish all over her hands and shirt. Her mama fussed over Martin and cleaned him up. She placed frozen packages of venison sausage on Jo's black eyes. "Good girls don't get in fights with boys. They don't do things like that. What's wrong with you?"

"It wasn't my fault," Jo said softly.

Her mama didn't ask Jo who had done it or how it happened. Instead, she told her, "Be perfect, Joanne, as your heavenly father is perfect." And then her mama made her finish frying the catfish for supper. Twelve years old and Jo knew what kind of meanness was in this world. Jo could still smell the NyQuil on Travis's breath. She would smell NyQuil forever, in her sleep, in line at the grocery store, right before stepping offstage, randomly while she was singing.

A few months later her mama would accuse her of being impure and shamefully persuaded by the lowly flesh, an unclean sinner at the age of twelve. She remembered her mama reminding her again and again that Jo was the salt of the earth. But if the salt loses its saltiness, how can it be made salty again? It is no longer good for anything, except to be thrown out and trampled by men. That year they went to her grandmother's cabin in Kentucky, where her mother forced her to study the Bible to the point where she believed God hated her. She felt his wrath especially close on the nights she prayed the baby would die inside her, quick and painless. An abortion was out of the question; her mama had made that clear from the moment she started to show. The rounder Jo's belly became, the further she made her way from the gospels of Jesus to Revelation. During her labor, during the worst contractions, her mama told her that she loved her, that she'd always wanted another child after Jo but that God had cursed her for what happened to Martin, and that God had now chosen Jo's womb to deliver a baby to her. She thanked Jo for this gift. A gift for Jo too. Isabell would be her little sister. Finally—a sister. Her mama never let Jo hold Isabell when she was a baby. Told her it was for the best.

Jo was too afraid to expose Travis Goode. Only J. D. knew the truth about it all, and he nearly beat Travis to death at school. He waited for Jo and her mama to return from Kentucky with the new baby before he did it so she could watch the blood seep from his mouth. Got himself suspended. After that her daddy forbade her to go to the Gunn house and there were plenty of rumors going around Gatesville about who Isabell belonged to—some said it was J. D.'s, others said it was Jo's cousin's; almost nobody believed it was her mama's but that's the story her mama told without fail.

Their little bluegrass ensemble had gotten pretty successful by then, but it couldn't survive without Jo's fiddle, and J. D. refused to replace her. They played together on the weekends at Rob's house, and she snuck out to go swimming with them at the quarry. Otherwise, Jo stayed alone outside and played music. Country music was for people who hurt. Singing country songs allowed her to tell a story, and she could escape and be somebody else for a little while through a song.

She loved murder ballads, the ones where women were doing the killing, not the other way around. Country music was her healing.

Jo dressed herself in her jeans, a white blouse, and her red boots so she could go downstairs and ask J. D. to take a ride with her. The past would always be an impasse between them, between her and the whole world, if she didn't try to set this one thing right.

CHAPTER 33

Split Wood

J. D.'S PALMS PULSED with blood and were blistering from splitting so much wood—he couldn't sleep all night, not after everything he'd said to Jo and knowing she was in a bedroom right above him. He wanted to go upstairs and apologize, but she would've refused to answer or turned him away. He would've started chopping wood at three AM if he didn't think it would disturb her. As soon as the sparrows had begun singing, J. D. had put his jeans on and rummaged through Jo's basement to find a decent axe. He'd settled up with most of the wood down here until the sun had risen and cast a beautiful tapestry of color on the sky. He'd been missing a Virginia sunrise and didn't even know it. Sweat poured down from his forehead even as he was resting now against the willow tree with its long green branches reaching into the pond water below. His chest and arms were aching from all that work, but all the worry that had consumed his sleeping hours had abated.

J. D. heard the screen door smack against the frame of the front door. He pushed his foot off the willow tree's trunk and through the curtain of branches he could see Jo standing on the wraparound porch and looking in his direction. The three-story white farmhouse with its red tin roof and large antique windows had to have been built in the 1800s, J. D. guessed. It reminded him of the house he grew up in with his mama and daddy, though his house wasn't nearly this big and had nowhere near the amount of acreage. Jo's body looked so small against the brightness of that large house and all that forest extending far beyond the two of them. Here she had a wall of natural protection from the world. No wonder she'd kept the house a secret all this time.

J. D. parted the willow tree's thin branches and walked out so Jo could find him. She stared at him for a moment before making her way down the long staircase in those red boots. He'd been rehearsing what he'd say to her when he saw her this morning: he was sorry for everything he said; he felt hurt by the way she thought of him; he wanted her to like him again, to respect his character; he loved her with every pulse inside his body; and she couldn't marry Nick Sullivan, not when the two of them had so much left unfinished. If she was marrying anybody, it should be J. D. He was ready to tell her all of this. Jo walked across the high grass filled with dandelion weeds, the white heads ready to lift off with the wind and disperse seeds. J. D. wiped away the sweat from his face and his chest before putting on his white T-shirt.

"Morning," she said as she came closer, but she stopped a few feet away from him. "You've been busy."

He nodded, and then he swung the axe downward into the stump and left it suspended in that position. How to say to her all that he'd practiced in his mind? What words could formulate his feelings in the right way with her standing right in front of him? His chest swelled with the desire to say it all at once, but his mind felt empty.

"That needed to get done," she said. "So thanks."

"Ready to play music?"

"No," Jo said, and bent down to pick a tall piece of meadow grass. She wound it around his wrist like a bracelet. "What you said really hurt my feelings, J. D."

He tried to speak but she shook her head and said, "Please just listen. It hurt but you were right."

"I shouldn't have said it like that."

"Will you ride with me to my mama's house?"

J. D. wiped his lips. "You know I'm the last person on the planet your mama wants to see."

"Which is why I need to go."

"You're sure about this?"

"I am."

J. D. picked up his hat from the ground to signal to her that he would go with her if that's what she needed. They walked together up the hill, away from the pond, and toward the gravel driveway. J. D. reached out and took Jo's soft hand in his. "It'll be all right."

Jo let him hold her hand all the way to the car and she only let it go when he opened the car door for her, and as he shut her inside, he felt unsure if he was ready to witness Jo tell her mama the truth about what happened all those years ago, which was a pain J. D. had barely comprehended then. He experienced it only as a constant rage that a thing like that had happened to the person he loved. If he could've killed Travis Goode, he would have. He almost did when he beat him so bad J. D. got kicked out of school for weeks. J. D. had dreamed about murdering him almost every night while Jo was away in Kentucky, hidden away for being pregnant.

When Jo returned to school the next year, he slipped notes into her locker and left bouquets of buttercups on her desk. Her mama and daddy slighted him every single time they saw him out in town or at church. J. D. knew they never confronted him because of who his daddy was at the quarry, but that didn't stop them from believing that J. D. was Isabell's real father, that J. D. had brought their oldest daughter into the ways of sinning by sleeping with her. She refused to tell her parents about what Travis had done and she refused to claim that Isabell was anything more than a little sister. There were always rumors that he might be the daddy, but J. D. was strong enough to hold that secret for Jo. The only time it hurt was when his own mama came into his room crying and saying, "Tell me that's a lie, J. D. Please tell me." He swore on his life that he wasn't, and it was the only time he denied being the father.

CHAPTER 34

What Was Lost

J O DROVE SLOWLY up the long gravel driveway leading to her mama and daddy's new home, a much nicer place than the cabin she grew up in. The hills rose alongside them and a single white pony with brown spots galloped in the distance. Her parents had a nice view of the mountain range now, plenty of acres to farm and lumber to sell if they chose to. Jo parked the car right in front of the porch, where a group of pygmy goats chased each other at the bottom of the steps.

"Want me to wait here?" J. D. said.

"I'd like you to come too."

They both stepped out of the car and walked toward the house, where her mama's white peonies were in bloom in the flower beds. Confederate jasmine grew thick on the latticework against the foundation of the house. The sweet scent of white and gold honeysuckle flowers vining on the fences filled the air all around them. Jo made her way up the brick steps, but J. D. paused behind her. "I'll hang here."

But before Jo could even make it to the top, her mama opened the screen door and walked outside in a pink muumuu nightgown with her thin hair in tiny red curlers. She looked like she'd just come up from the baptismal waters and was seeing the world anew. "Joanne?" she said in a confused voice. "Is that you?" She stepped all the way out on the porch before Jo could even respond. "What're you doing here?"

"I have a place over off Route 71."

"You do? You never told me that." Her brow furrowed and she placed a hand on the center of her chest. "And who is that? Oh my word. Is that J. D.? J. D., is that you?"

"Yes, ma'am."

Her mama narrowed her eyes and then gave Jo a cold stare. "Why'd you bring him here? Are you not marrying Nick?"

"May we come in?" Jo said.

"Not if he's coming in with you."

"Mama!" Jo shouted. After all these years, it surprised Jo that she'd still treat J. D. this way. "I'll stay on the porch then. Where's Isabell?"

"Working at the grocery."

"And Daddy?"

"Watching TV."

Jo heard her daddy shout, "Who's there, Nan?"

"It's the mail," her mama called back, which was fine by Jo. She didn't need him coming out here right now. Her daddy had always been like a shadow on the wall of her childhood, and he'd become even more disconnected after Martin died. Her mama kept one hand on the open screen door like she might turn around at any moment and go back inside. "Is this about the reporter calling?"

"From *Vanity Fair*, Mama? Name's Bryan Lein?"

"That's him."

"When?" Jo said.

"A week ago or so. Why's he calling me, Jo?"

She rested her back against the white column on the porch. "Just hang up if he calls again."

The wind chime on the other side of the porch filled the silence between them. Jo looked her mama in the face and saw so much of herself there—they had the same oval face and eye shape, the same eye color. She wondered if she saw herself in Jo, if that was normal for a mother and a daughter.

"Why'd you come here, Jo?"

"I don't know."

One of her mama's curlers fell a little and hung near her forehead. "Why don't you come back later on and visit when I'm dressed?"

Jo went down one step and almost walked away completely but then forced herself to say: "Do you remember when Martin and I came home from that fight back in middle school, when my eyes were beaten shut?"

Her mama shook her head even as she said, "I remember."

"I was raped, Mama."

Her mouth fell open. "No you were not."

"I was. Travis Goode." Jo pointed at J. D. and said, "He was the only one who ever knew the truth, Mama, the only one who ever did anything to defend me. He wasn't the one who did it. He wasn't Isabell's father. And he let people say all that about him and he never denied it. He did that for me."

"Joanne," her mama said in a breathy voice. "Travis had a bad bout after high school, Lord knows he did, but he works for your daddy at the quarry now. He goes to church."

"I know."

She placed her hand over her heart. "Why would you come all the way here to tell me such terrible lies?"

"Because it's true, Mama."

"Doesn't make any sense." Her mama eyed J. D., who stood behind Jo at the bottom of the steps. "Why would you wait all this time?"

"I knew you'd act just like you're acting now. But I'm not twelve anymore, Mama. I'm not scared."

"Makes no sense," she said, as if she didn't hear Jo at all. "Izzie says he's always so nice to her and talks to her for so long at her checkout line and always asks about what you're—" Her mama's voice lowered like she was taken over by a different thought and she lingered there awhile before looking directly at Jo. Her brown eyes softened and she let go of the door finally, letting it close behind her. She walked toward Jo slowly, like her legs were weak.

"It's true, Mama," Jo said. "He's the father."

"How could he?" she said with a shaky voice. "How could Travis do such a thing? He's the one who beat you?"

Jo bit the inside of her cheek and nodded. "I think you should tell Daddy and Izzie the truth."

Her mama shook her head. "I can't."

"Izzie deserves to know, Mama. I want her to know."

She stood there holding herself and shaking her head until the loose curler fell to the ground. Jo bent down and picked it up for her. As she handed it back, she said, "It wasn't J. D."

Her mama nodded a little and then looked past Jo to where J. D. was standing at the bottom of the steps. She said, "Forgive me, son." And then she started crying and Jo couldn't look at her anymore. "I didn't know."

Her mama opened her arms and Jo let her hold her. Her mama's hair smelled like coffee and maple syrup. "Y'all come inside, please. Have breakfast."

Jo let go and said, "We'll come back some other time."

Jo and J. D. both said their good-byes and waited until her mama went back inside before J. D. drove them away. Jo felt like a felled tree had been on her body since she was a girl and finally someone had come along and rolled the trunk away. She immediately took out her phone from her purse and sent Marie an urgent text message asking her to follow up about the *Vanity Fair* article. She clearly remembered asking Marie to cancel it. Marie had never let her down about anything before, but Marie had arrived to work late that day and she'd been very distracted. What if she forgot? Jo felt relief from telling her mama the truth but she didn't need the whole world to know.

"You okay?" J. D. said.

Jo reached out for his hand to hold. "I'm glad you were with me."

"Me too."

"I can't play music today." She pulled her hand back and tied her hair in a ponytail.

J. D. placed his hand on the steering wheel.

"Want to pick blueberries with me?" Jo said.

"Where?"

"My place."

"You've got bushes?"

"Hundreds," she said. "But the birds steal most of the fruit."

"They always do."

J. D. turned on a Johnny Cash playlist and drove them home, where Jo showed J. D. the way to the blueberry fields. A small creek cut a valley through the land, and Jo saw a mother deer and her fawn on the bank drinking water together. They hiked through the woods that abutted her house and soon they arrived at a clearing where her groundskeeper had well-maintained rows of green bushes, all flush with clusters of mostly ripe berries. Some were still pink. There were yellow plastic buckets on the picnic table next to the fire pit. Jo handed J. D. a basket. "Fill it up and I'll make blueberry pancakes for breakfast."

She entered a row of bushes and J. D. moved a couple rows down. She pulled the largest, roundest berries to eat right then and there, and she felt like she could taste the sun in the warm juices. Her fingertips were stained a deep purplish red as she ate more fruit than she was placing in her basket. Each time she looked up J. D. was looking at her. He ate a handful of berries and smiled. She continued to work her way down, one bush at a time. Cardinals flew in and out of the rows like they were dancing with the bushes. Jo made it all the way to the end of her row with her basket half-full and she met J. D. there.

He walked over to her. "Think this is enough?" He'd filled his basket to the brim and smiled wide at his achievement. No one had ever looked at Jo in such a genuine way, and it made her think of the Bible scripture she remembered from childhood about the eyes being the lamp of the body. J. D.'s blue eyes always burned bright with kindness.

"Did you eat some?" she said.

"A few."

The large poplar trees growing along the creek created a blanket of shade over them. Jo selected the biggest berry in her basket. "Here." She lifted the fruit to his lips and placed it on his tongue, but before she could pull her hand away, he took it in his and kissed her fingertips, then he secured her hand against his heart. J. D. said, "I love you so much, Jo. I never stopped."

Jo felt her cheeks begin to pulse. She'd expected him to thank her for the berry and admit how delicious it was. But not this.

"Say you won't marry Nick."

"J. D."

His face became shadowed with an earnestness she hadn't seen before. "You can't be this way with him, Joanne. You know you can't."

"I can't be this way with you—not in Nashville."

"Please don't marry him." He waited for her to respond, but she wasn't sure what to say. J. D. turned away from her and hiked back toward the house, blueberry basket in hand. A cardinal flew right in front of her and stole a berry from a bush, and then it darted away again until she lost sight of the small red body in the woods.

CHAPTER 35

The Whole Way Home

JO WAITED FOR the griddle to heat up on her stone countertop, and her entire body felt like a helium balloon weighted down by a sadness in her heart. Nashville was tomorrow, and today she had the privacy of this farmhouse, this chance to write real music again with J. D., these ripe blueberries, and J. D.'s love wrapped all around her. She'd given her whole heart away to him years ago and he'd never given it back, not fully. Jo blended baking powder, salt, and sugar into the flour and grated a cinnamon stick over it before putting it aside to whip the eggs, butter, vanilla, and soured milk. She hummed to herself as she added the flour to the wet mixture slowly until small lumps appeared, and then she dropped in two large handfuls of blueberries, stirred them around as the batter swirled and changed colors from khaki to light purple.

J. D. sat in the living room, which opened to the kitchen, and he strummed his guitar absentmindedly while he waited for breakfast, then looked up and caught her staring at him. He smiled. She smiled back. He put his guitar on the couch and entered the kitchen. "Can I help you?"

She tested a small dollop of batter on the oiled griddle and it started sizzling. "I like listening to you play. I'll be finished in a minute."

He returned to the living room and strapped his guitar back on. Jo poured silver-dollar pancakes onto the griddle and waited for the air bubbles to appear before she flipped them. J. D. started picking out a catchy riff beginning in the A chord before moving to the E. He sang:

> *Summers at the quarry with you smoking cigarettes.*
> *Diving to the bottom letting out a trail of breath*
> *The glory years are good until they're gone.*
> *Now I can't even get you on the phone.*

Jo stopped staring at the pancakes taking form on the griddle and dropped the metal spatula on the countertop. Her heart felt hooked on a fishing line and he was pulling. Now, that was a song. A good song. "Sing that again, J. D."

"You like that?"

"I really, really do." Jo left the kitchen, sat next to him on the couch, and picked up her guitar. She followed along with him as he figured out the chords and pacing. He sang the verse again, and while he did, Jo grabbed a pad of paper from the coffee table and sketched out another verse. J. D. repeated his part again and again while Jo wrote, and then Jo said, "Listen to this." On her guitar she demonstrated the chords—D before moving into A, then E, and then she sang:

> *Kissing in the cornfield, the moon was in a cloud.*
> *Love was just a whisper that we never spoke aloud.*

The footprints sink deep into the clay.
Now I can't believe a word you say.

J. D. smacked the face of his guitar. "Holy shit, Jo. How'd you come up with that so fast?"

"I don't know," she said, just as astonished as he was. "We need a chorus."

J. D. moved into C sharp, then B, then E:

And even though you don't owe me a thing
Just like a blackbird on the wing
You flew away and now the town feels lonesome, mean, and blue.
Now all of the gossip's about you.
And I know just how much of it is true.

"This is it," she said. "This is the first song of the album. Let's call this one 'Lonesome, Mean, and Blue.'"

J. D. took the pick out of his mouth. In a wistful tone, he said, "I thought I'd never write something like this."

"It doesn't sound like anything you've ever done before."

"Doesn't feel like it either." He played the chords again. "Think I got another idea." He started playing and then stopped to start writing on the notepad. He looked up and said, "What's the smell, Jo?"

"Oh no," she said, and jumped up from the couch and ran into the kitchen, where she found dried-up pancakes burning on the griddle. She scraped them onto a plate and then tossed them out in the trash. She returned to the living room with a bowl of blueberries. "I burned breakfast."

"That's okay. I'm not hungry anymore."

Jo placed the bowl on the coffee table and picked up her guitar again. "You need to write down that first verse you sang."

"I know, I know." J. D. worked out this new song with more patience than she'd thought him capable of—starting a line and stopping half-way, only to start again. Jo followed his chords on her guitar and tried shifting the pace. It felt like no other life existed outside of this one. No Nashville. No fans. No Nick.

J. D. adjusted himself on the couch. "Tell me the truth, now. I'll start with G, then C to D." He played the chords for her.

"I love it," Jo said. "Let's hear it."

Then he sang:

A cigarette burns beside the kitchen sink.
You said that you just needed time to think.
It doesn't matter who was wrong or right.
Yeah the past ain't going anywhere tonight.
The bourbon in the glass is getting low
And there's just static on the radio.
The truth is edging closer to the light.
No the past ain't going anywhere tonight.
Your yellow sundress billowed in the door.
Wish we could be like we were before.
Now all we have is the heartache and the lies
And the past ain't going anywhere tonight.

Jo covered her face with her hands, and then she separated her fingers and pretended to sneak a look at him. "Just like that?"

He smiled. He looked so deeply proud.

"This is going to be an amazing album, J. D. Amazing. Mr. Sullivan's going to be shocked. These songs will be incredible once we hunker down. I can hear them rounded out with bass, drums. I hear a steel guitar. Definitely a pedal steel. I want to put the fiddle to them. Let's call it *The Whole Way Home*." Jo reached out for his hand. "It doesn't feel forced anymore. There's hurt but they're honest. These songs feel so good, J. D. This is us."

Jo brought the bowl of blueberries to her lap and scooped some into her palm. J. D. took off his guitar and ate a handful of fruit. She offered him the bowl but he leaned over and kissed her on the lips, gently at first, and she could still taste the juice of the berry on his tongue. She almost pulled away but then his kiss turned urgent. She dropped the bowl on the couch, the fruit spilling to the floor, and she wrapped her arms around his neck. She kissed him with that rhythm they'd always had. Jo felt like they'd opened a paper heart that had been folded in half for far too long. They stopped kissing and J. D. hugged her tightly. "I love you, Jo."

"I love you too."

He studied her face, gently moved a lock of hair away from her forehead, and then held her chin in his hand. He kissed her jaw right below her ear and then kissed her neck. "Make love to me," she said to him softly, her fingers gripping his curly hair. J. D. lowered himself to his knees and lifted her T-shirt off and kissed her softly from one hip to the next, and then further below, where he lingered with his tongue. She pulled his face up a little and held his cheek against her bare stomach. She removed J. D.'s white shirt and ran her hands up and down his firm chest, pulled him on top of her and dug her nails into his shoulder blades. He unbuttoned her jeans and she removed them completely, along with her bra, and then she guided his face to her breasts, where he filled his mouth with one and massaged the other. He met her face again and sealed his mouth over hers. He entered her and moaned deeply as their bodies moved in sync with each other, like they were waltzing together in three-quarters time.

CHAPTER 36

The Long Run

S HE RANG THE doorbell, greeted them. Denver kept the door propped open with his leg. Alan danced in celebration behind the door but the thin girl with a severe stare couldn't see him. She said her name was Jena, that she was here on behalf of Mr. Sullivan and Asphalt Records. She handed Denver a thick manila envelope, turned around to go, but then stopped and walked back up the front stoop: "Don't sign it without talking to your manager."

"We don't have one."

"Well, somebody. A lawyer should look it over."

Denver felt a little unnerved by her insistence. He thanked her for delivering the contract and then shut the door. Alan stopped dancing long enough to take the envelope from Denver's hands, and then he started jumping up and down and shouting, "Here it is, man." Alan's eyes looked glossy, like blown glass—in all their years as friends in Knoxville and then here in Nashville, Denver had never seen Alan get so emotional. Only one other time came slightly close to this, and that was their senior year when the Tennessee Volunteers won the NCAA Outback Bowl.

Finally, all these years of hard work were going to pay out. That's what Denver told himself; that's what he and Alan believed as they sat down to read over the thick contract. They pored over it fast, excited just to have an offer. This contract was the only one to come in after their Bluebird show. Plenty of A & R guys from labels big and small had stayed after the show to pay compliments to their style, but so far only Asphalt had delivered. Denver stood and held his hand up for a high five. Alan lingered over the contract, mouthed words to himself.

"I'm up here," Denver said.

Alan looked up. All of the enthusiasm drained away from his face. "Did you see this?" His finger rested on a block of text. "About expanding."

Denver sat back down next to Alan. "Let me see." It took him a minute to read through the dense language. A new lead man—Alan on the side, second guitar, no lead vocals. "I understand bringing in other guitar players to back us up but not replacing you. That's got to be a mistake."

"They don't slip things in contracts by mistake."

Denver tossed the contract on the glass coffee table covered in empty beer cans and unwashed cereal bowls. "No way we're agreeing to that."

They stayed silent for a long time. Ten, fifteen minutes at least. Alan stared straight ahead, his chin cupped in his hand.

Denver and Alan stayed up drinking late into the night. Denver couldn't remember if it was his idea or Alan's to drive to Vanderbilt University's campus and seek out Floyd's advice, but here they were,

waiting outside his broadcast room, both of them hungover and exhausted. It was seven AM. Denver created black streaks on the linoleum
floor with the heel of his boot. Early-rising students with bulky back-
packs passed by them on their way to Music Appreciation 101 or some
other filler course. Floyd walked out with a pack of cigarettes in hand,
with his white hair sticking up all over the place and his head bowed
deep, his eyes on the floor. Alan and Denver stood up from the metal
folding chairs they'd found in the hallway. The sound of the chairs
lurching across the linoleum floor attracted Floyd's attention.

He studied them for a moment. "I need a smoke," was all he said.
Floyd waved for them to follow him out through the back door to where
they kept the massive Dumpster for the building. Flattened Styrofoam
from discarded to-go food littered the gray gravel. The heat cooked
the trash and the whole place smelled like rotten diapers. Denver covered his nose.

Floyd inhaled, the cherry on his Marlboro Light growing fast, then
fading. "I'd say I was surprised to see you two except I'm not. Your contract stinks," Floyd said. "And not just because it's a shitty three-sixty
contract. That stinks too."

Alan looked over at Denver, Denver back at Alan. Denver said,
"How'd you—"

"Stuff that stinky has a way of polluting the air in town. Like a paper
mill, if you know what I mean."

"Can I have one?" Alan said, and reached out to Floyd. Alan had
never smoked, not in all the years Denver had known him. He doubted
Alan even knew how to inhale, but Floyd gave him a cigarette promptly
and then he handed one to Denver.

"I know what the problem is, but nobody'll admit it," Alan said, and
took a deep drag of his cigarette. Denver waited for a cough that didn't

erupt. Alan kept his arms folded against his chest and only moved his forearm to bring the cigarette to his mouth.

"You mean that you're black as night? I'm not being racist, now. I think you're a damn fine country artist. Star material, Alan. Denver here's good, but you've got the songwriting too, and that twang in your voice, it's the real thing. I hear a lot of put-ons in this town, boys from Syracuse, New York, who come down here and get nicknamed Tex somehow. Hell, Taylor Swift faked a country accent all the way to billions. But your voice sounds like it came from the land of the cotton. You know that Iris DeMent song? I know you do. I don't mean anything racist about that either. Cotton's cotton. The whole damn country's responsible for that crop. The whole world's responsible for its legacy. Look, the truth is, you're more talented than anybody I've seen in a long, long time, but you're a black man. A very, very black man. A great country singer. In a perfect world, what would it matter? I don't own the labels. I'm just telling you what I think here—it's exactly what you're thinking too. It's why you came here. You want the truth. The truth is they won't find a more talented front man for the Flyby Boys."

Denver couldn't believe what he was hearing. Were they overreacting? Assuming? Misinformed? Or was this just the truth?

Alan nodded along with what Floyd was saying, and when he stopped talking, Alan whispered, "Goddamn it." He crouched low like he was about to field a ground ball. Denver and Floyd stared down at him, and when he screamed for all of Nashville to hear, Denver closed his eyes so as not to witness his friend in this troubled state surrounded by all this trash. The wind brought another whiff of rot and Denver remembered the burly dude coming up to Alan after their set at a house party their senior year. He was red in the face from drinking too much. His cheeks matched the color of his hair. He hit Alan on the shoulder, and in a drunken slur he said, "Hey, you—how did some black boy from 'Bama learn to play honky music?" And the guy had a big, surly smile on his face and asked the question with an accusatory tone instead of hate. Denver wanted to punch him. Or he wanted Alan to do it. But Alan kept his composure and told him in great detail about how growing up he'd spent a lot of time at his grandparents' house during the summer. His granddaddy practiced the fiddle with his all-black string band in his grandmother's beauty shop, where Alan sat in and drank a cold Orange Crush and played along on a small guitar, and he went on and on about each man who played in that band, his full name, occupation, life story—Bobby Jenkins, plumber, orphan, harmonica wizard, bingo master—all the stories for each and every man in his granddaddy's band, until the guy grew bored and walked away to do a keg stand. Denver had always respected Alan, but he remembered feeling especially proud to know him in that moment when somebody else, Denver included, would've ended up angry and in a fight.

"It's a damn shame." Floyd smoked his cigarette. As he exhaled he said, "Where's the Charley Pride since Charley Pride, my friends? I was on the wrong side of opinion way back when Charley was just starting out, but he expanded my whole mind. My whole mind. Hasn't been a Charley since, though. And that's not from a lack of black talent in country music. You know that. There's plenty of talent here in Nashville. Plenty. A great community here too. But the community is not in charge of finding new bands and getting them in front of the big audiences. Who's in charge? Who decides which bands get played on the radio? Look, I wish I thought Asphalt would be the only offer of this kind. But my fear is that no other offer will come in for you after this one. As a band, that is. You'd get signed quick as a songwriter, Alan. You could have a damn fine career in that direction. Denver here's a drummer. There's always some band in need of a drummer. You got to figure out if that's what you want, or if you believe in your band enough and what the two of you make together. Nobody'll figure that out for you."

Denver kicked the gravel away. Alan stood back up. They all smoked together, arms crossed, saying nothing.

Floyd dropped his cigarette to the ground and crushed it with the sole of his boot. "You boys know that Robert Earl Keen song 'Paint the Town Beige'?"

"I do," Alan said.

"You know the first refrain, about leaving the fast life for a country road? I don't know it by heart—"

Alan said, "About the mother lode?"

"Yeah," Floyd said, "that's it. That's right. I think that's what you got here, boys. You got to make a choice. Break up the band, go in different directions for the mother lode, and that's just a maybe. Or stick together, fuck the fast track, trade it for something pure. A respectable kind of fame. But it won't turn you into commercial superstars. Won't get you that kind of money if that's what you're after."

The morning sun made its ascent over the brick building.

"I'm heading down to Honduras tomorrow for a couple weeks to tour. They still love Floyd Masters down that way. You could go down there or try another city, like New York. Seoul loves country music too—even have a bar named after old Floyd Masters up there. They've got good taste in the classic stuff. I've got one more broadcast in the morning before I fly out. I'm afraid I've got to go now though, start getting things settled at the jailhouse. Better known as my girlfriend's house."

"Thank you for your time, sir." Alan extended his hand for Floyd to shake. Floyd took his hand, pulled him in close for a hug, and patted him hard on the back. He shook Denver's hand good-bye. "Don't make a dumb decision, you hear? Think about the long run."

"Yes, sir."

"Damn shame," Floyd said as he patted Alan on the shoulder one more time before moving past them and back into the broadcast building, leaving the smell of smoke in his place.

Alan buried his hands in his pockets. "You believe it now?"

"I'm sorry, man." Denver removed the rolled-up contract like a scroll from his back pocket and twisted it in his hands. "What should we do? You want to be a songwriter?"

"Only if you want to be somebody else's drummer."

"No way," Denver said. Who else knew about this shitty offer? Did Marie? And what would this mean for their relationship? If they had to leave Nashville to try to break in somewhere else, Denver would have to leave Marie behind. With a life lived on the road, he doubted a long-distance relationship could work.

"We came here to keep this thing together," Alan said. "They want our band to look a certain way, to conform to how they think a country band should sound and act. I'm not doing that, Denver. If they can't see that country music looks like this too, then I can't be part of it. I won't. I won't play the blues either. Or R & B. I just won't sell music. I'd rather never sell it than sell out to some corporate brand of what my music should be."

"I know," Denver said, and handed the contract to Alan, who gripped it in both hands before ripping it in half, then tossing the shreds on the ground with the rest of the rotting trash. Alan dug the scraps into the gravel with the sole of his cowboy boot until the water beneath the rocks soaked through and turned the contract translucent.

*N*ashville, this is Floyd Masters coming to you from Vanderbilt's
WHYW FM airways. All my loyal listeners out there, I know what
you're thinking this morning—what's with Floyd? Did he forget his coffee? Is
he constipated? Why does he sound so wistful this hot and dry June morning
in the greatest music city that ever was? If you're thinking along these lines,
friends, then you're on the hound's track. Good blood up ahead. Good blood. I'm
a little sad this morning. I couldn't say that to you if I was John Boy and Billy.
No, we'd be playing some damn quiz show that meant absolutely nothing to
your day. Nothing at all. Would it change your life to play Wordy Word? You'd
smile, you'd laugh. I can hear your thoughts, my good listeners. "A laugh, a
smile—that can change an entire day, Floyd." *I hear you, I hear you. I
really do. I'll try to make you laugh too, later, but right now, I'm feeling a little
low, so why can't I share that with you? We live in such a happy culture. It's
like a cult.*

*I'm just a little nostalgic this morning, and a little humphed too about the
state of things in this town. Nothing wrong with that. So look, most of you
know I'm heading down to Honduras for a while. Got a tour set up down there.
America, y'all might've forgotten old Floyd, but not the bright people of Honduras. They're not afraid of a little hurt. While I'm gone, reruns of my best shows
will play for those of you who need to hear my voice to start the day off right.
Bless you, the one soul this applies to.*

*Yeah, Floyd's got a case of the nostalgias today. They'll make you blue in
the face, by God, if you let them. Horse-kick you in the heart. I was thinking—*

that's all nostalgia starts from, just thinking—and I was remembering being a young lad in Nashville. Rode a Greyhound up here from Lubbock, Texas. Stepped off, breathed in that country music. It was in the air back then. I felt sure, so damn sure, I'd make it big. All I wanted was to hear my voice on the radio and knew I'd be on the Bluebird stage in no time. I was nineteen, bold, and stupid. Kept a Buck knife in my muddy boots, which I had to pull out once or twice. I still got those boots and that knife in the closet. Floyd holds on to things.

Nashville was a whole lot harder than I thought it'd be. Good thing too, 'cause if I'd known I might not have come. Where'd I be now? Dead. I'd surely be dead. I remember one time, I was working for a Port-a-John company here in Nashville, dumping waste from construction sites—I must've gagged thirty times a day. I remembered my daddy telling me I'd be slinging shit one day if I kept on with music. There I was, and my daddy was right. But then one day I finished up working early and got a call I'd been waiting on for ten long years in Nashville. Dolly Parton liked my song "Freewheeling Believer." She wanted to record it. All I wanted in this world was to hear my song on the radio.

I wanted to call my mama at the Lubbock beauty salon and tell her to turn on the radio and listen to her boy's words coming straight from the Madonna's mouth. Damn, I had a thing for Dolly. Who didn't? Who doesn't still? Anyway, even with a gal like Dolly liking your song, that was still no guarantee it'd be on the radio. So I wrote to the label. I wrote to them and told them how much it'd mean to me, and more importantly, I told them how much it'd mean to my mama and her beauty salon friends, to hear that song on the radio. Well, wouldn't you know it? Not a single response came to my letter. Not a single one. That's when I learned a very important lesson about the music industry— label executives don't have mamas. No they don't, folks. Orphans, the whole bunch of them.

And that's why you never heard "Freewheeling Believer" on the radio. It did happen for me. Eventually. I got my break. Squandered my good fortune too.

Made a bunch of friends along the way. Merle, Waylon, Kris, Willie. My best memories are writing at Tootsie's with some of those fellas. I don't often play my music on this station, but I'm leaving today so I want to play the song that changed my life. That can still happen. I need to believe that can still happen for all the young, hardworking, talented musicians trying to find a life here in Nashville.

Seems harder. Everything feels stuck. Maybe it's the South—or damn, that's not fair, now, is it? Always blaming everything backward on Sweet Dixie. The South is defined by its history, the same way America is defined by the South. You're stuck, America. You look so advanced with your tiny technology. You look so modern. But you're stuck. Slinging shit.

I won't be taking callers this morning. I'll catch you on the road again when I return from that far-off land. I've got a long set for you this morning. To kick it off, here's my first hit single, "Bitter Fever," performed by yours truly, as heard on the radio way back when.

CHAPTER 37

Shotguns

PULL!" J. D. SHOUTED to Rob. Two clay pigeons sailed into the air. J. D. flipped the safety lock off, aimed for the middle, and shot his Italian-made Perazzi SCO shotgun. Both pigeons exploded. Nobody congratulated him. He handed the gun to Danny. The other guys held their guns limply while they waited their turns. J. D. had all his best guns out today. Normally he'd insist they all shoot his low-level Beretta SO4s, but today he was letting them use his Perazzi. J. D. selected his Fabbri over-under to try next. "Pull," J. D. called, and then he hit every single target.

The thought of where Jo was and what she was doing, if she was with Nick and if he was making her smile, nearly killed him. Since he'd returned from Gatesville, he couldn't make it through the night without the aid of whiskey and melatonin. For so many years now he'd believed he wouldn't be with Jo ever again, but now a relationship with her felt close. J. D. believed someday she'd return to him, just show up one day, walk right through his door like no time had passed. He was more in love with Jo now than he'd ever been before and he felt like he was waiting for his second life to start. She wouldn't marry Nick Sullivan. J. D. was honoring her request for a few days of space back in Nashville to figure out how to tell Nick the truth and break off the engagement.

"Damn," Danny said. "I hate going after you, man."

"You know you're a better shot." J. D. rested his shotgun on his forearm. As always, Danny shot every single clay pigeon launched into the air. J. D. stared above them at the lone red-tailed hawk circling underneath a sunset sky. It was nearing dusk. The leaves on the trees showed their pale undersides—in the past hour there'd been a sudden break in the heat and humidity. Everything felt eerily still, like a thunderstorm was coming.

"You want to shoot again, Mr. Sullivan?" Danny said.

"Not really."

"Mind if I do?" Chase B said.

"Don't mind a bit." Mr. Sullivan handed off the gun to Chase B.

"Who taught you to shoot so good, Danny?" Mr. Sullivan said.

"My daddy hunted deer, quail, anything that moved."

"Why'd you ask it like that, Mr. Sullivan?" Aster reloaded shells in his double-barrel.

"I didn't ask it any certain way."

"Yes, you did," Aster said. "You didn't think black boys could shoot shotguns? Danny here knows how to swim too, you racist prick."

"There are plenty of guys who can play an electric guitar in this town, Aster. Plenty of guys who'd take your job in a second."

"Nobody half as good as me."

"Is he always this arrogant?" Mr. Sullivan said to Rob.

"Always."

"Danny," Mr. Sullivan said, "that's not what I was saying. Or how I was saying it. You know that, right?"

Before Danny could answer, Aster said, "Pull!"

Chase B launched the pigeons for him. Aster missed both. "I wish your daddy had taught me."

"You needed him," Danny said.

As he passed off the shotgun to Danny, Aster said, "So tell me again how many songs Jo's singing with us tonight."

"Two," Mr. Sullivan said. "Three at the most."

"Three too many," Aster said.

Chase B drank whiskey straight from the bottle of Dickel, and then he offered the handle to Mr. Sullivan, who put his hands up like he was about to be shot. "I'm a scotch man." Mr. Sullivan adjusted his stance in the grass. He spread his legs wide apart and kept his arms crossed.

"Pull," J. D. called, and Rob launched the pigeons. J. D. cleared the air.

Mr. Sullivan scratched his chin. "How's the album coming along?"

"It's coming," J. D. said.

"So this is why you've come all the way out here and honored us with your visit today," Aster said.

"Aster, I'm certain I couldn't be in a band with you, much less live with you. I don't know how you boys do it."

J. D. released the safety on his gun. Reloaded shells. "Pull," J. D. called again. Shot all five in a row. The hawk continued to circle above it all.

"Ever think you might hit that bird?" Mr. Sullivan said.

"Nope." J. D. rested his gun against his leg.

"So give me a gauge," Mr. Sullivan said. "Album's working out but slowly? Steady? Or rapid production?"

"Yeah, J. D. Tell us," Rob said.

J. D. refused to talk about it with the guys—all they wanted to know was when they'd be in the studio with him and he had no idea. He'd dodged all of Mr. Sullivan's calls too. "Have you asked Jo?"

Mr. Sullivan swatted a fly away from his face. "Why should I ask her and not you? Is it not going well?"

"It's good."

"I'm having lunch with her and my son today to discuss their wedding. Perhaps she'll be a little more forthcoming." Mr. Sullivan looked at his watch. "Speaking of which, I should get going."

J. D. handed off his shotgun to Chase B in exchange for the Dickel. He took a long swig and then wiped his lips with the back of his hand. "Wedding plans?"

Mr. Sullivan nodded. "Head back with me, will you?"

J. D. walked with Mr. Sullivan toward a bruised sky in the distance. J. D. heard the first call of thunder. Mr. Sullivan said, "It's a nice piece of land you have here." Mr. Sullivan pointed east. "My estate's that way. Hank Williams used to live down that way too." Mr. Sullivan stepped on a dandelion and the white spores lifted up and scattered around them. "Are you happy with Asphalt so far?"

"Yes, sir."

"I secured the band a suite for the upcoming Titans season."

"That'll make the guys happy."

"Anything more I can do?"

"Is the Solar dispute done?"

"The lawyers handled it. That's what I pay them for. I pay my artists to be brilliant. All I need from you is focus in the studio. The Clear Channel–Asphalt streaming deal will be announced very soon. Need to keep things smooth until then."

As they neared the house, J. D.'s landscaping crew came into clear view. They were hard at work removing debris around the swimming pool area. They trimmed dead leaves away from the rosebushes lining the black iron fences.

"Jo's ready for tonight?" J. D. said.

"As far as I know."

"You're having lunch with her and Nick. About the wedding?"

Mr. Sullivan stopped walking. He said, "Look, I don't know all that's between you and Jo."

"I was only asking."

"Come on, son. I understand these things."

J. D. shielded his eyes from the sun's last showing before the clouds blocked it out. "No, sir. I don't think you do."

"We need to avoid any drama on the label right now. I told Jo this before. Now I'm telling you."

J. D. stopped walking and squared his body to Mr. Sullivan. "I love her, sir."

Mr. Sullivan placed a hand on J. D.'s shoulder. "I like you, J. D. Beyond business and whatnot, I think you're a good man, but Jo's marrying my son and that's that. These intense feelings always fade with time. I'll forget what you told me. It's best for the label and best for Jo. Why risk driving one of you away from the label if things don't work out? You two will benefit hugely from this collaboration and the Clear Channel deal. The king and queen of country music. Nobody can touch you, so don't let your feelings interfere with all that. My son loves her, and he's good for her."

The rusted red weathervane on the top of the pool house shifted from one side to the other.

"Come on," Mr. Sullivan said, urging J. D. forward. "Let's keep walking."

"You go ahead," J. D. said.

"You sure?"

J. D. nodded. "I left something back there."

Mr. Sullivan shook J. D.'s hand, and J. D. remained in the middle of the low-cut grass and watched Mr. Sullivan walk to the house alone, his stature growing shorter and thinner with every step he took. Had Jo changed her mind? Was she refusing to return his calls because she planned to marry Nick still, despite what happened in Virginia? Why would she have lunch with his father and discuss their wedding if not? He removed his phone from his back pocket, even though he knew he couldn't text her, in case Nick looked at her phone. Jo and J. D., that relationship mattered the most now, yet it seemed secondary in her world still. He wanted her to cancel the lunch, to tell Nick the truth immediately. A bee landed on J. D.'s arm and he flicked it away; a streak of lightning carved through the brooding clouds like a white vein. His phone began to vibrate in his hand and a local number came up on the screen: "Hello?"

"Will you confirm whether or not you're Isabell's father?"

A fury rose to his tongue and sat there like a heavy sack of coins: "I'm not her fucking father," he yelled, and then immediately, he knew he had to find some way to take this back. "That's not what I meant. Hello?" The line was dead. J. D. tried calling back, but no one answered. The voice mail message repeated the phone number to him. Fat raindrops began to fall from the sky and J. D. saw his guys cresting the hill with all of their equipment. He tried calling Jo to tell her what he'd just done but she refused to pick up the phone.

CHAPTER 38

The Call

I T'S ALL MY daughters can talk about, I swear it is. J. D. Gunn and Jo Lover. They've made me watch that video so many times. And the interviews. Not that I don't love it. But they seem obsessed with 'Glass Hearts.' It's such a good story. Most anticipated country album of the summer, right?" The wedding planner, Missy, paused for a sip of chardonnay. She held one skinny finger in the air to indicate she'd start talking again as soon as she was finished. And Jo knew that much was true. They were having lunch at Mr. Sullivan's Still Water Estate to discuss the wedding, but Missy talked so much no one else could put in a word. Maybe wine did that to her. She was a tiny package of a woman. Short, extremely thin, with a black French bob. Her red lipstick distracted from all her other features. Mr. Sullivan seemed amused by her.

"So," Missy continued. "How old were you and J. D. when you wrote 'Glass Hearts'? Like ten years old?"

"More like twenty-two." Jo glanced over at Nick, who stiffened visibly.

"You and J. D. knew each other as kids, though, right? I read that somewhere," Missy said.

"We grew up together." Jo wished Missy would change the subject—each time Missy said J. D.'s name aloud, Jo feared the love she felt for J. D. would spill out on the table like wine, that all her desire to kiss him again would be as visible as the fresh-cut lilies in the center of the table. Since they'd returned from their trip to Virginia, she'd thought only of his body and those songs they wrote together, and it was deeply unfair to Nick. She needed time to handle her engagement with Nick and she wished J. D. would stop trying to call her. She had very little willpower to ignore him.

"I just think that's so cute," Missy said, and surveyed everyone. "Isn't it cute?"

Mr. Sullivan sat at the head of the long mahogany table. He filled Missy's white wine glass nearly full. Behind them all, beyond the French doors, the cloudless sky shimmered. Jo saw the stable hands riding the horses across the ridge for their afternoon exercise.

"You know what's cute?" Mr. Sullivan said.

"What's that?" Missy said, leaning toward him with a sly smile on her face.

"All the revenue those two best friends produce."

"Oh stop," Missy said. "You're so crass."

Nick tossed his white linen napkin on his half-eaten plate of lamb rib, pearl onion au gratin, and baby fennel salad. Jo couldn't eat her meal either.

"Son?"

"May I be excused?"

"We have dessert."

"Not hungry." Nick moved his chair and prepared to stand. Jo followed his lead.

"Now, hang on." Missy pulled out a small Moleskine notebook. "I have just a few more questions about the reception."

"The tea olive hedges will be blooming all over the estate just in time," Mr. Sullivan said. "Your wedding will have its own perfume."

"Isn't that lovely, Jo?" Missy said.

Nick looked over at her. She offered Missy the smile she was looking for.

Missy said, "We'll make sure we set up the stage and reception tents along those hedges. The dinner will be held down by the pond. Correct? And the hot-air balloon rides. Did you two discuss that? They'll all be white. So beautiful. And the horses will carry you from the ceremony here at the house to the dinner. Yes?"

Jo sipped her Manhattan. She felt too guilty to speak, and their silence seemed to make Missy uncomfortable, so she filled it with talk.

Missy wrote something down. "Let me see . . . oh, yes. We'll light candle boats on the pond at dusk. And your dress. You have your dress selected, right?"

Jo shook her head. All the leather-bound books of designer dresses Missy had sent over were still on Jo's kitchen table gathering dust.

Missy closed her notebook and placed it on the table. She laughed in an astonished way and then said, "Well, why not?"

"I don't know."

Missy leveled her gaze at Jo and made her feel like this was an unacceptable answer. "I sent you many, many books. You should've found one that you love by now."

Mr. Sullivan studied his son, and then he said, "Jo's a busy woman and perhaps she'd rather see dresses in person. How about hiring a personal shopper for her?"

"That might help." Missy opened her notebook once again and wrote something down. "I'll arrange that. Also, your guest list, Jo. I'll need that in three weeks, at the very latest."

In a single swallow Jo finished the rest of the Manhattan left in her crystal tumbler. All she wanted to do was finish the conversation she'd begun with Nick before they sat down to this damned lunch.

"Anything else?" Nick said.

"Be patient, son."

"I've been more than patient."

"So just a little more," Mr. Sullivan said.

Missy said, "And thank you for being so patient, Nick. I promise you I'll give you the most beautiful wedding you could dream of."

Nick rested his elbows on the table and folded his hands together.

"Forgive him," Mr. Sullivan said to Missy. "But his foul moods pass quickly."

Nick stood up.

"I understand you're busy," Missy said. "Just two reminders. I have selections available for the guest gifts at Cartier. Under Jo's name. When you have a chance, look those over. And please remember the bride's and groom's gifts."

Nick nodded. "Is that all?"

Missy checked her notebook. "I believe so. We'll schedule another lunch in three weeks, okay?"

"Sounds good," Mr. Sullivan said. "You're excused."

Nick pushed his chair out quickly.

Jo said, "Thank you for lunch," and followed Nick out of the dining room doors to the expansive terrace overlooking the estate. "Nick?" Jo said as she tried to keep up with him.

He said nothing but braced himself on the stone balcony wall. Water from the ivy-covered fountain spritzed Jo's face. "Nick, please turn around and talk to me."

Nick put his hands in his pockets. She sat down beside the fountain and gripped the smooth edge of the stone. Jo looked back toward the house, where Mr. Sullivan and Missy were still seated at the table and talking. Mr. Sullivan turned around completely to look at them on the balcony. "Let's go somewhere private to finish talking."

"Explain it to me," he said in a raised voice. "I want to know exactly what happened. I can't understand it. That lunch was unbearable, Jo. What have I done to make you change your mind so suddenly? Is it the album? We can postpone the wedding if that's what you need. But to call it off completely? Why, Jo? Why?"

"I'm so sorry, Nick." Jo stood up and walked toward him but he backed away from her like she was a threat. "This is the last place I wanted to tell you, but you've been in the studio nonstop."

"That's my life, Jo. You know that."

"I do. It's just, this was my first chance to talk to you and I didn't want to go through lunch without saying it first."

"But you won't give me a reason."

Her phone started vibrating in her jeans pocket. Jo pulled it out and saw a local area code.

"I'm going to the stables." Nick walked down the curving stone staircase where the four-wheelers waited below. Jo stood up from the fountain and walked to the other end of the balcony, and she waited for Nick to start the engine before she accepted the call: "Hello?"

"Jo, this is Bryan Lein, the reporter from *Vanity Fair.* I interviewed you about a month ago."

Jo closed her eyes and took a deep breath. "My assistant canceled that article, Bryan."

"It's finished, Jo," he said.

She heard static on the line as she walked back toward the fountain. "You didn't hear me right."

"My editor asked me to make this call as a courtesy. We followed up on the rumors that you did leave a child behind in Gatesville to come to Nashville. You gave birth to a girl named Isabell when you were twelve and she was raised as your younger sister. J. D. Gunn confirmed the story and stated for the record that he is not Isabell's father."

"J. D.?" she said, and closed a hand over her mouth to keep herself from screaming. How could he betray her trust, after everything they'd been through? He was the only person in the world who knew the truth and he gave it away freely to this reporter? Nick crested the hill on the four-wheeler, putting distance between himself and her.

"Jo? Are you there?"

She remained silent. Kept her hand on her mouth.

"Jo?"

She swallowed hard.

"Do you care to comment?"

"No."

"We will print the story as is. This is your chance to comment."

She grabbed her chest it hurt so much. She'd have to tell Mr. Sullivan. He'd put the PR team in overdrive and turn the story into a victim narrative for her fans.

Jo balled her hand into a fist. "How much to kill the story? The whole thing?"

Silence.

"Hello?" she said with deep anger. "You did not just hang up on me."

Finally, Bryan said, "This is your last chance to make an official comment, Jo."

She hung up on him. Jo stared down at her phone and hesitated before calling the last person on this earth she wanted to talk to right now.

After three rings, Jo heard shuffling, then a "Hello, this is Mrs. Lover. Who's this?"

In a shaky voice, she said, "Mama?"

Quietly, she said, "Joanne? You in trouble?"

Jo leaned her torso over the balcony and looked down at the far drop to the bright green grass below.

"Joanne?"

"Did you tell her?"

Her mama went silent on the other line.

"You haven't told her?"

"No."

Jo blurted: "That reporter knows, Mama."

"What?"

"He knows about Izzie."

"How's that?" Her voice sounded cold.

"He knows, Mama, and he's printing it. You need to tell Izzie before it comes out. Or I will."

"I'll have nothing to do with it. Isabell is my child, no matter where she came from. Bunch of sinner nonsense. This is the world you've chosen."

"Okay," Jo said. When her mama started talking like this, she knew there was no talking left to be done.

"Don't call about this again, Joanne." She heard the line go dead.

That old landline phone connected hard with its plastic cradle. The screen on Jo's phone turned black. She gripped the darkness in her hand, and then she smashed it on the stone railing, turned it to plastic bits and glass shards. Jo launched the motherboard as far away from her as it would go before rushing back into the dining room and interrupting Mr. Sullivan and Missy as they ate dessert. "Is everything all right, dear?" Missy said.

Jo wiped away her tears. "There's an emergency with my dog. Nick went to the stables while I took the call from the vet. Will you please let him know? Tell him I'll call later." And then Jo gathered her purse and cardigan and went out to her car. No one at Asphalt needed to know right now. She'd let it surprise everyone like a quarterback sack. That story Bryan thought he knew was about a different girl. Jo was not that girl. Nick wouldn't understand. Not in a million years. He and Mr. Sullivan would never understand. Even if they thought they could, she wouldn't want them or anyone else defining her as the girl a tragic thing like that happened to a long time ago. Now the whole world would know her truth. It'd be reprinted in every magazine known to man and she'd be forced to explain it, to reveal the rape to millions, and relive it again and again. She wasn't ready to give this story to the world. What would her fans think when they found out, once they knew she'd been lying about who she was all this time? What would happen to her career? How could he—Why would he hurt her so deeply again?

CHAPTER 39

Nashville Music Festival

MARIE RAN TO Jo with an extra-large bottle of water in her hand. "You sure you're feeling okay?"

"Just dehydrated." Jo felt dizzy, like she was on drugs or something. She hadn't been able to eat or drink anything since that reporter called her earlier in the day. It had taken everything in her personal arsenal of willpower to force herself out of bed for this appearance with J. D. and the band. She'd debated canceling altogether except she lacked the energy to field questions about why. And Nick had been calling her all afternoon to check on the dog and to find out when they could talk. She had nothing left to give anybody.

"Could you find me some crackers?"

"Five minutes tops." Marie broke into a near run through the dark throngs of people backstage at the Nashville Music Festival. J. D.'s voice sailed through the night air, flooding over a crowd of thousands, all of them decked out in hot-pink, neon-green, and cobalt-blue glow lights on their heads and arms. So much love flooded from the stage and around it, into the crowd and back from it.

Marie returned and handed Jo a small package of animal crackers. "It's all I could find."

Before Jo could say thank you, J. D.'s voice came clear over the microphone: "The Empty Shells want to invite a very special guest up onstage with us tonight. Some of you good people might've seen our duet a little while back." The crowd cheered, more than Jo had expected. He continued: "If you haven't seen it, you got to stop living under that rock called your parents' basement. Get out of there! Escape! The rest of y'all know the lovely Joanne Lover. Give her a big welcome."

No time for crackers. Jo handed her bottle of water to Marie and stretched a winning smile across her face as she climbed the illuminated metal staircase. As she crested the stage she saw J. D. turned right toward her. The entire band was dressed in suits and ties like the early Beatles. She'd never seen the Empty Shells looking so tailored. She'd chosen a crystal rhinestone dress, tight and short. J. D. stretched out his arm, beckoning her to join him as if he weren't the one who knew the truth about her life and then hand-delivered it to a reporter in search of clickbait.

Jo looked out at the dark sea of a crowd and then turned to J. D., who smiled at her like only a best friend could, like nothing bad had ever passed between them, like they shared nothing but good memories and sweetness. And he made the inside of her body feel like lava. Just the sight of him. Here stood the only man she'd ever be able to love, the only one, and she was walking to him as if that love were open, shared, and true for all the world to know.

Rob winked at her. Aster played the riff of "Foxy Lady" as she walked to the microphone. She made a big show of laughing at him and doing a little strut to where J. D. stood. A stagehand brought her Gibson acoustic guitar to her. J. D. stepped away from the microphone, leaned down, and tried to kiss her on the cheek but she pulled back and said, "Don't."

He lingered there and whispered, "I've been calling and calling you, Jo."

The heat of his breath warmed her ear, his facial hair against her cheek rough like a sugar scrub. She had the urge to hold him in her arms, but she also wanted to punch him in the nose. "How could you, J. D.? That was my truth to tell."

"It was an accident."

"They're publishing it, J. D."

He grasped her left hand and held on so hard her engagement ring dug near to the bone. She jerked her hand away.

"Please forgive me, Jo."

"Again, J. D.?"

"You have to forgive me. I love you so much," J. D. said. "I said it without thinking."

He stepped toward her like he might try to pull her body in close. She turned her back to the crowd completely. "You're too impulsive, J. D. That's always been the trouble." Jo didn't care if the crowd felt confused or noticed the conflict happening between them onstage.

"Don't say that, Jo."

"I love you. I think I'll love you until I die, but I don't trust you and I can't keep doing this with you anymore."

J. D. looked crestfallen, like Jo had shot a bullet into a mirror and fractured his face into a thousand pieces. Jo couldn't keep looking at him broken up like that—she stepped away from him and went to the microphone. "How y'all doing out there? Let's give a shout-out to this amazing music festival."

J. D. had to join her, and he stood so close to her, Jo wasn't sure if she'd be able to play her guitar well. She took a step to the side, but he followed her like a stalker. J. D. moved his mouth to the microphone, looked down at her, and then said, "We're about to play one of the songs that'll be on the album we're making together."

The crowd cheered so loudly and for so long it made Jo forget her troubles for a moment, but then a surge of guilt passed through her for lying to the fans like this. She almost took the microphone and admitted that there'd be no album, that they'd all been misled. They'd all know the truth about Jo soon enough.

"Let's hear it," someone screamed from the front of the crowd. Jo could see four rows of faces illuminated by the stage lights. J. D. leaned over to her once more. "I'm making a little change." J. D. turned to his band and put an arm up to quiet down the drums and bass. "We'll play 'Glass Hearts' for you folks right after we play a song that we grew up singing. How's that sound? Y'all want to hear an oldie?"

The crowd cheered. Somebody said, "Hell yes," and whistled like a rancher calling cattle.

J. D. said, "When me and Jo and Rob here on the bass were little kids, we liked to play this John Denver classic. I hope y'all don't mind if we change it up a bit. We like to replace 'West Virginia' with 'sweet Virginia' 'cause that's where we come from. That's home. Okay with you, Jo?"

"Can't go home again, J. D."

"Let's give it a try."

The crowd roared. The stagehands brought out Jo's fiddle and she placed it underneath her chin. Rob switched out to the upright bass and came to stand right beside them. Rob led them into the song, just like he used to. Jo always sang the first verse, but then J. D. joined her for the chorus. They sang together like they were back home again in J. D.'s barn, back when nothing bad had happened to any of them yet, back when the walls of that barn felt like a fortress—Rob with his thick glasses and his bad acne just starting to show and that first upright bass so much taller than he was; J. D. skinny like a bird's leg and holding up a guitar like he'd been born with it on; Jo learning what it meant to give herself over completely to the sound of a fiddle. The crowd swayed before them, quiet before the acoustic calm. She felt a wave of nostalgia rolling from the collective mass before her and into her body. Jo glanced over at Rob, all grown up but still the happy boy she remembered, and J. D. too, his eyes closed in song, his face tender and honest as he shared a song that defined their early days as musicians, a song that had taught them how to play their instruments better. Jo wanted to stay in this moment forever, to share all this love in a small protected pocket of space and time, but of course they couldn't. This would be the last time they all three played together. Their childhoods existed downstream, winding further and further away from them to a place where they would never exist again. Jo dropped the bow away from her fiddle, wiped away her tears, and walked offstage before the song came to a close.

She heard J. D. call her name and turned around to see that he had followed her almost all the way but stopped at the edge of the white lights beaming on the stage. A valley of darkness separated them. J. D.'s face was animated by a sorrowful yearning. He said, "Come back out, Jo. Please. Let's finish this."

"That was it," she said, and wrapped her arms around herself. "That was the last time."

J. D. bowed his head and held his guitar against his stomach like it was a beloved child, and then he turned from Jo and walked slowly back to his band and his microphone, right where the audience expected the King of Country to be.

CHAPTER 40

The Time Would Be Now

I T'S KIND OF cute seeing you at work, in your uniform and all." Marie had a bad habit of acting overly cheerful, so much that it rang false, in an attempt to make the people she cared about most smile when they seemed down. "Not sure why I haven't come here for coffee before." Denver failed to respond to all of her conversation starters. He stared beyond her too, at the throngs of tourists coming through the revolving glass door. Marie heard the rush of the fountain and the chatter filling up the massive atrium leading into the Country Music Hall of Fame.

"Maybe I'll just go then," Marie said. "Since you'd rather be having coffee alone." She had a bad habit of passive-aggressiveness too—she knew all of this but wasn't sure how to change it. Being in love with Denver forced her to see her imperfections and shortcomings in a way she never had before. Marie moved to stand up.

Denver reached for her hand. "Don't go."

"Will you tell me what's wrong, then?" Denver looked terrible, like he hadn't slept in days and had been drinking more beer than water. Had he even showered before coming to work?

"Alan's ready to leave."

"Why's he here?" She put down her paper cup of coffee, the holder slipping down to the table, and looked over her shoulder for Alan.

Denver let go of her hand and took a gulp of coffee. "I mean Nashville. He's ready to leave Nashville."

"Where would he go?"

"Chicago. New York. LA. Austin. Memphis. He even mentioned Richmond, Virginia. Something about a small label there who's eager to produce us."

"Us?" Marie said.

Splotches of crimson blossomed on Denver's cheeks. "Asphalt sent us a contract."

"That's incredible, Denver—wait. Shouldn't we celebrate this? Why would Alan want to leave now?"

"It's a terrible contract."

"Three-sixty contracts suck, I know, but they're the norm now."

"It's not that, Marie. Asphalt wants a new front man for the band. Wants Alan to step aside."

Marie placed her hands on her lap, hidden by the table. She chipped away at her black nail polish. "Mr. Sullivan said that to you? Maybe you misunderstood him."

"It's written in the contract."

"You're serious? Let me see it."

"I don't have it with me. You have to trust me that it's in there. And it seems really fucking racist."

Marie didn't know what to say. She'd never heard of anything like that written into a contract before. How could Asphalt not see what had been so clear to her from the beginning? Without Alan as the front man, there could be no Flyby Boys. "So wait for a better offer."

"We've been waiting." Denver leaned into the table and rubbed her bare leg with his sneaker. "I really don't want to leave Nashville. You've got to know that. Alan doesn't either. We both love this town. Breaks my heart we can't find a place for us. I want to believe we can find it somewhere else, but more than anything, I want to believe we can still find it right here, that something will open up for us someday."

"I'm sure it will, Denver. Leaving now seems so impatient."

He drank his coffee down and dropped the cup on the table. It made a hollow sound. "Alan's angry. I've never seen him so angry before. I don't know if he's ever been angry like this in his whole life, Marie. He has to get out of here, even if it's just for a year."

"And you'll go with him."

"We'll come back. That's what I'm hoping." Denver pushed himself forward, almost out of his seat. "I know this sounds crazy and you'll say no. I figure you will, but I have to ask because honestly I don't know how to leave this place behind and you in it. I don't know how to do that, Marie. I want you to come with us. I love you so much. Fell in love with you the moment you walked into the Thirsty Baboon. I can leave Nashville behind. It'll hurt but I can do it. I don't know how to leave you, Marie. I really don't."

Marie shook her head. That's all she could do. She had no words for what he was asking.

Denver grabbed her hands. People at other tables glanced over, perplexed. "Be our manager. Be whatever you want for the band. But God knows you have to be with me. I don't know what I'll do without you."

"Do you have any idea what a big ask that is, Denver? I can't just decide right here."

"You'll find a way to talk yourself out of it, Marie. Follow your gut. Come with me."

Marie had a great career, excellent job security, and good money. She had much more going for her in Nashville than Denver did. He wanted her to give all that up to follow him around with no promise of an income or a future?

"See, you're thinking. Do you love me, Marie?"

Did she? Did Marie love him this much?

"Do you, Marie?"

"I don't—I don't know," she stammered. "I think so. I think I do but that's not what this is all about. That's not enough."

"It's everything," he said. "I know I love you."

"You wouldn't ask me to give up everything if you loved me, Denver. You'd stay right here and let Alan go."

"You wouldn't love me if I was the kind of guy who would make a choice like that." Denver stood up, his body casting a long shadow over their table. "My break's up."

"So that's it then? We'll leave it like this?"

"You know where I am, for the next week."

"Jesus, Denver. That soon?"

"I can't give up on the Flyby Boys." He leaned down, kissed her on her cheek, and lingered there for a long minute. "I love you," he whispered in her ear. "You know that. No matter what you decide, I hope you do know that."

"I do," she said softly.

He pulled away from her, and something about it felt final, like it would be the last time she felt the warmth of his skin so close to hers. She watched Denver walk up the ramp to go back to work, and he disappeared into the belly of the Hall of Fame. Marie picked up her empty paper coffee cup and recycled it on her way out of the building, and as she moved through the revolving glass door, Marie thought about how young they both were, just twenty-two. Young enough to make choices, to have so many choices to make. Her mother had once told her that as she grew older her choices would become fewer but the consequences greater. If there was ever a time to take a risk and make a big mistake, now would be the time. Traveling around the country with no schedule to manage sounded so appealing, but could she leave behind this life and everything she knew? Could she leave behind Nashville? Her career? Jo? She wouldn't want Denver to leave Alan. She'd never ask that of him. It was too much to ask of anybody, even if you were in love. Especially if you were in love. You shouldn't ask someone you love to let go of so much.

CHAPTER 41

Visitor

J O COULDN'T FIND her off button. She followed the decluttering guru's advice to keep what brought her joy and toss everything else by category: pots and pans, cleaning supplies, clothes, shoes, purses, makeup, jewelry, hats, coats, books, CDs, DVDs, craft supplies—when was the last time she'd made a craft?—candles. Why did a girl need so many champagne-scented candles? By the looks of the various unwanted piles, it seemed like nothing brought her joy anymore.

Next stop, the overgrown flower beds in her big backyard. That was why she'd bought this place—for the sense of acreage, for the sense of home—but now all the weeds had to go. Jo's elderly neighbor glanced over the privacy fence. She'd lived here three years and still didn't know her neighbors on either side. Her dog, Max, sunned himself on the cobblestone sidewalk leading up to her big patio with a fireplace built into the back of the house, a big fire pit too. Even a brick pizza oven, which she'd used exactly once. Jo sank her gloved hands in the mulched dirt. Pokeweed and green vines with thorns had taken root.

The sound of the bronze handle on her wooden fence woke up Max. He barked and trotted toward the gate with his hackles up, his tall ears alert. Jo had forgotten to lock it.

"It's me," Marie hollered from the other side.

Jo tossed her trowel in the dirt and grabbed Max by the collar. She rubbed down his white fur to calm him, and then she opened the fence gate while holding Max back. He gave Marie the sniff-down before allowing her to enter. Marie clutched a black leather notebook to her chest.

Jo released Max and he went running around the yard, spraying all the trees. "What'd they say?"

"I'm so sorry, Jo." Marie handed Jo the leather notebook. "They faxed the article. It's in there. I really thought I'd handled it. I did call and I followed up."

"Did you read it?"

"Of course not."

"When does it come out?"

"Tomorrow."

Jo placed the notebook on her wrought iron patio table.

"Am I fired, Jo?"

"No," she said. "None of this is your fault." Jo walked back to the flower bed surrounding the fountain in the center of her yard. A large red metallic ball rotated at the top, water coating the smooth sides. Jo watched it turn and turn, always in motion but never leaving that one place.

Marie followed her.

"Sit with me by the fountain for a second."

"You're worrying me."

Jo removed her gardening gloves. "There will be some PR issues, I think. About my past."

Marie tilted her head to the side. "How so?"

"Some things about my childhood."

"Is it minor or major?" Marie had her phone out, ready to act on whatever Jo told her.

"Major."

"You won't tell me?"

A murder of crows hovered above in the maple trees, and then they swooped down to the grass, hundreds of them, looking for food, looking for something. Anything. How long would she be telling this damn story to people? She'd managed to tell no one except J. D. for well over twenty years and now she'd spend the rest of her life reckoning with it in public.

"Will you deny it? Whatever it is?"

"I haven't thought that far ahead," Jo said.

"Your fans would forgive you for anything, whatever it is. It's the people who don't listen to your music that worry me. All of a sudden they're going to have an opinion about you, people who couldn't sing one of your songs even if you helped them. Millions of people. Especially with the duet going viral. Should I arrange a meeting with Mr. Sullivan and the Asphalt PR team?"

"I don't want them knowing the reporter warned me."

"Okay," Marie said, but Jo could hear in her voice that she was unsure about this decision.

"How's Denver?"

"Just saw him," Marie said. "They got an offer from Asphalt."

"That's good news."

Marie tightened her lips together.

"Isn't it?"

"The contract, it's just, I don't know, it's not good. Mr. Sullivan wants them to find a new front man for the Flyby Boys. Move Alan to second guitar, songwriting. They won't sign it." Marie looked stricken.

Jo swatted a mosquito that landed on her arm. "Tell them to wait it out."

"Alan wants to leave town. The way things went, they don't think they can hang around here. Denver asked me to go with them, to manage them."

Jo should've anticipated this from the moment Marie met that boy. "Go where?"

"I don't know yet."

"You love him?"

"I do." Marie scratched at the leather notebook in her hands.

"Did you think this through?" Jo said. "You're so young and this relationship with Denver is so new."

"I'm not going with them. I don't see how."

Jo studied her face. The way Marie's eyes narrowed, Jo could tell she was saying less than she was feeling. Jo pointed to the flower bed. "Want to help me weed? It's good therapy."

Marie shook her head. "Just had a manicure."

"I've got gloves."

Marie looked at her nails. "Better not."

"If you change your mind, gloves are on the table." Jo leaned down and pulled out wild grass growing between the fountain stone and the gravel. She'd always admired the fortitude of grass to grow wherever people didn't want it to be.

"How was the spa?"

"What?" Jo said.

"Your spa weekend."

"Oh," Jo said. She threw the grass back onto the ground. She was so tired of lying. Tired of it. She felt like she'd run a marathon and was ready to collapse. "I didn't go to the spa."

"You said—"

"I went to Virginia. With J. D."

Marie's face pulled away suddenly and she scooted to the edge of the concrete.

"What's wrong?"

"I saw him leave your hotel room in LA."

Jo nodded her head slowly—this explained so much about the way Marie had been acting around her lately. "Nothing happened in LA."

"It didn't?"

"No."

"Why'd you go to Virginia?"

"To work on the album."

"Jo, I really need to apologize to you. I misjudged this entire situation."

"No you didn't. I love him, Marie. And we did sleep together in Virginia."

Marie remained silent for a while, but then she said, "What about Nick? Have you told him?"

"I told him I couldn't marry him."

Marie tucked the side of her bangs behind her ear. "I know this isn't my place or anything, Jo, but I think you should tell him the whole truth. I know you. You'll never feel right about it."

"I plan to."

"And J. D.?"

"What about him?"

"Will you be together now?"

Jo shook her head. "It never works between us."

Marie rested her phone in her lap. "I don't know what happened," Marie said. "But I'm sorry."

"Me too."

Max leapt up from where he rested by the fountain and bounded toward the locked gate to the backyard. He barked and then howled as if sirens were going off.

"What's wrong with him?" Marie said.

A girl's voice said, "Is this Joanne Lover's house?"

Jo stood up quickly, and Marie did the same. She said, "Think it's someone from the press?"

"Is it?" The girl's voice sounded desperate, like she was searching for water in the desert.

Marie pulled out her phone and shouted, "Go away. We're calling the cops."

"No!" the girl shouted. "No, please don't. I'm Isabell. Jo's sis—I mean—My name's Izzie. Please, is this her home? I just drove here straight from Gatesville."

"Isabell?" Jo shouted, and ran up the stone pathway to where Max stood on alert at the gate. She quickly unlocked it, and there she stood, tall and lanky and beautiful, all grown up at nineteen, her long blond hair swept over one shoulder and black Jackie O sunglasses hiding most of her oval face. She looked nothing like Travis, which relieved Jo—she just looked like herself, and she was far more glamorous than Jo remembered. How long had it been since she'd last seen her? Her sophomore year?

"Jo?" Izzie shouted, barreling into a hug. Her hair smelled like raspberries. "Oh my God, Jo."

Jo wrapped her arms around her. "You're so tall, Izzie. Does Mama know you're here?"

Izzie wouldn't let go of Jo. "I left a note, told her I was coming to find you. I always knew, Jo. I always did. No matter what you and Mama told me. I knew I was yours. And I always wanted to know the truth but I knew nobody would tell me. Mama finally did, last night. Sat me down before dinner. I was supposed to go out with friends but I couldn't."

"She told you everything?"

"Me and Daddy." Izzie released Jo from the hug and took off her glasses. She had big blue eyes, almost a gray color. She said, "An article's coming out about it. It's true, isn't it? All of it?"

Jo said, "I wish you'd found out some other way."

"Travis always talked to me so much when he came through my line at work. It felt weird sometimes. I know he's married and all, but I even wondered if he liked me. I mean, he never said much that was interesting. Just basic stuff. Town gossip and the like. It just seemed so strange how much attention he gave me. Except he knew. That's all. He knew." Izzie's cheeks flushed and she gripped her stomach. "Makes me feel like I could puke."

Hearing this enraged Jo. Jo knew Travis walked the streets of Gatesville and still had a life there with friends and a wife from some other county who had no idea. That had been enough to keep Jo away, but Travis talking to Izzie so casually made Jo wish he were dead. Dead and gone. He knew what he'd done, that much was clear.

Quietly, Izzie said, "He raped and beat you in front of Martin?"

Jo nodded. Marie gasped loudly behind her. Jo turned around and faced her. She'd almost forgotten Marie was there. "Izzie, this is Marie, my assistant."

Izzie nodded at her.

Marie crossed her arms. "Will the article expose all that, Jo?"

"Only about Izzie."

"But the other thing?"

"No."

Izzie started crying now. Her shoulders shook as she said, "I wish somebody would've told me a long time ago. Daddy said he'd kill Travis. He'd find a way to kill him at the quarry. He can't fire him because he's a good worker, but he'd put him in harm's way, that's what he said. I cried seeing him that angry, all red in the face and making us repeat everything so he could hear it right. I think he was wishing he'd heard it wrong. I've never seen him so angry."

"I hate that for Daddy."

A small breeze lifted Izzie's long blond hair over her face. She tucked the strands behind her ears and said, "Didn't you hate me, Jo?"

Jo wrapped Izzie in a hug once more. "I didn't hate you. I loved you. I always loved you, Izzie. Mama was just trying to protect me and you. I thought I was protecting you too by keeping all this a secret. And myself. But I should've told you. I've been living with these lies my whole life and I don't want to live like that anymore."

"I wish I wasn't here." Izzie wiped away her tears. She pulled the sunglasses off the top of her head and put them back on. "I thought about running away for good to California or somewhere. But I have no money so I came here."

"I'm glad you came here."

"I still think of Mama as Mama."

"I know."

"Think she was worried about that."

"Probably so." Jo dropped her gardening gloves on the leather note-book on the table. "Come on, let's go inside and call her. She'll worry herself to a heart attack."

"But can I stay with you, just a couple days?"

"Of course."

They began to walk up the flagstone steps to Jo's open patio doors, but then Izzie stopped. "I know this is stupid and there's nothing that can be done about it now, but I wish I hadn't been made that way, Jo. I wish I was Mama's and not yours."

Jo grabbed Izzie's hand. "You *are* Mama's. You always will be."

"What should I do, Jo?" Marie called from behind them.

Jo pointed at the notebook on the wrought iron table. "Read it and let me know how bad it is."

CHAPTER 42

Speaking of the Truth

NICK COULD'VE BUILT any studio he wanted, decked out with all the latest equipment for high-fidelity sound, or he could've chosen a different route and used his golden key to all the best studios in Nashville, LA, and NYC, if that was the kind of guy he was. He had his father's money and influence, but he'd never capitalized on it, choosing instead to work his way up in Nashville by his talent and reputation alone. He'd saved up his money from working in the studios around Nashville until he had enough to purchase this house, and he'd made it famously known as a place where artists could record and be comfortable. Jo would always appreciate this most about Nick.

Jo used the basement entrance of the remodeled ranch, and though no one was downstairs and no lights were on in the recording box, she heard movement upstairs. She passed by the regulation-size pool table and the nickel-plated bar stools, past the refreshment station, up the staircase, and she opened the wooden door to the sound of Nick's laughter fluttering through the house. As she stood in the hallway, she knew this was the last time she'd be welcomed in this space.

Other male voices rose and fell. Jo called out, "Hello?"

"Yeah?" Nick said.

"It's me," Jo said. She could hear a rolling chair moving across the floor. Nick glided into the hallway and looked disappointed at the sight of her.

"I'm sorry to drop in like this. I just wasn't sure when we'd have a chance to talk."

Nick rolled the chair back into the sound mixing room. She heard him say, "Can you guys give me ten minutes?"

And then a group of five bearded guys in tight jeans appeared from the sound mixing room and passed by Jo in the narrow hallway. They had their plaid shirts rolled up to expose their sleeves of tattoos. Jo waited until she heard the front door slam before she rounded the corner and found Nick at his mixing board. She sat down beside him the way she always did when they played back her songs and considered different tracks.

Nick opened the mini fridge underneath the mixing board and grabbed a bottle of water. He snapped off the cap and drank it down halfway. "Next band's coming in twenty minutes."

Suddenly Jo's body felt so hot from nerves that she could feel her skin's pores dilating. Nick braced his elbows on the edge of the mixing board. He said, "You wouldn't return my texts."

"I'm sorry."

Nick finished his water and threw the bottle in the trash can.

"I know you're mad at me. You have every right to be."

"I'm not."

"You sound like it."

"I'm hurt, Jo. Hurt and confused."

"That's why I came."

"Unless you've changed your mind, then I don't want to hear it."

"Nick."

"No."

"Nick, listen to me."

Nick turned the volume dial up and down between his fingers and rubbed his forehead with his free hand. "So you haven't changed your mind."

"No," she said softly. "I haven't."

"Is it the timing of the album? The stress? Because all of that I can understand, Jo. We can push the wedding to next spring or fall."

"It's not the album."

Nick leaned his body back into the black leather chair and sounded defeated when he said, "What is it then?"

"It's J. D."

Nick stood up suddenly and walked to the back wall, where he opened the liquor cabinet and poured himself a scotch. From behind he looked so much like Mr. Sullivan. It was easy to imagine that one day he would be CEO of Asphalt Records. He'd be married to some wonderful woman who deserved him so much more than Jo did. They'd have a family and he would be much happier than he ever would've been with Jo. Nick remained at the bar with his back to her as he emptied the tumbler and then poured himself another.

"Did you sleep with him?"

"Yes."

He turned around now. A weaker man would've thrown the tumbler against the wall just to hear the glass break, but not Nick. He kept his composure. "When?"

"A couple days ago. We went to my farmhouse in Virginia to work on the album—"

"Farmhouse?"

"I should've told you."

"So the spa trip was complete bullshit. How much more don't I know about you?"

She waited until he finished swallowing his scotch before she said, "Will you at least sit down with me?"

"That much more, huh?"

"Please, Nick."

"I'd rather stand."

Jo rotated the engagement ring on her swollen finger.

"Be straight with me."

She looked Nick in his eyes, which were usually so soft and untroubled but had now darkened with anger. What she had to say made her want to run all the way back to Gatesville, back into that little girl's body that knew nothing but bug bites and skinned knees and knots in her hair, a spanking here and there. But Nick deserved to know the truth before the rest of the world. "When I was twelve I was raped by a boy I had to go to school with every single day of my life. I had a baby but never told my parents the truth. *Vanity Fair* found out about all this and plans to publish an article tomorrow."

"Jesus." The red tint of his face quickly changed to a pallor. He ran his hand through his ashy blond hair and then smoothed his palm on his jeans. "You have a kid?"

"She's my little sister. That's how my mama raised her."

Nick left his scotch on the wet bar behind him and came forward to sit down beside her. He propped one foot up on his knee and picked at the thread on the side of his waxy brown loafers. Jo took his hand in hers and he let her hold it as he stared down at the floor, and right then she couldn't stop tears from starting. "I am so sorry for how unfair I've been."

"Do you love J. D.?"

"I wish I didn't."

He leaned over and gripped his knees like he might vomit. "You've been lying to me this entire relationship." His face turned red once again, his eyes glossy. "The worst thing is that I love you so much that I want you to be with whoever makes you happy, Jo. I always thought I was the one. Not J. D. He's broken your heart more than once."

Nick was right. J. D. had broken her heart over and over again. How to quit her love for him? If someone could have shown her, she'd gladly have followed.

"So what now?" Nick said. "You two will live happily ever after? Make albums? I loved that other woman I thought I knew. That woman had some integrity. This person though? I would've never fallen in love with her. You'll sacrifice your solo career and fold into his."

"Stop," Jo said. "Please."

"You know I can't work with you again."

With each word that left his mouth Jo felt a coldness enveloping her heart. Nick considered himself responsible for Jo's success. He'd always denied it, but clearly he felt like he defined her sound. Jo's breath caught in her chest, made her feel like she was choking, and she couldn't respond to him. Nick looked away from her. Then he stood up and poured himself another drink.

"Do you plan to tell my father? Or will I have to? Have you even considered what he might do?"

"Are you threatening me?"

"I'm being honest," Nick said. "I still love you, Jo. I'm deeply in love

with you. You dropped a bomb on us. I can't stop loving you just because I'm heartbroken."

"I haven't told him."

"Will you please go?" he said. "I need to be alone."

Jo slid the engagement ring off her finger and walked to him. She
tried to meet his eyes but he refused to look at her as he accepted the
ring in his palm.

CHAPTER 43

The Fallout

H ER FANS CALLED Jo and her mama redneck liars and unfit to parent. The comment threads on her Instagram and Facebook pages were either sympathy for her lost chance at motherhood or downright hatred for all her lies. Some people posted comments just to tell her she deserved what was happening to her now for being so dishonest. People commented on Jo's appearance for no good reason, saying she looked wrinkled and tired, that she should quit singing because she was too ugly to look at anymore. Horrible things. Even her biggest fans blasted her, saying she wasn't the strong, honest woman they thought she was.

Her manager and Marie fielded requests from every entertainment and news channel that mattered—Oprah wanted to chat, as did *The View,* along with every other female-centered radio and television talk show. They even tried to coordinate interviews with J. D. and Jo together, which was never going to happen. *Rolling Stone* magazine requested to bump up their interview sooner than they'd originally scheduled. Fans asked if she felt like a mother. On social media her fans debated whether she could feel like a mother after all this time. Reporters called Asphalt with the same questions. Did she feel like a mother? Was she angry that her chance to be a mother was stolen from her? Was she angry? People wanted her to be angry. No matter that she had been twelve and thought of Izzie as her sister and probably always would. People wanted tears and transformation and a sad, shameful story to follow in the headlines, only to forget about it the next week.

After the story had broken an hour ago, paparazzi had set up camp outside the front doors of Asphalt Records. But they showed up at her house first, like ants at a picnic—a photographer scaled her backyard's privacy fence, invited himself onto her back patio, and snapped a picture of Izzie washing her hands at the kitchen sink. Isabell screamed so loudly Jo spilled her coffee. Jo's phone wouldn't stop ringing. She only agreed to talk when Mr. Sullivan called Marie in a panic and insisted that they all come straight to the label.

Mr. Sullivan stormed into the office where Jo, Marie, and Isabell waited with multiple assistants; Jo's manager, Evelyn; and the head of PR. Jo sipped chamomile tea.

Mr. Sullivan said, "Everybody out, please. I need to speak to Jo alone."

Marie and Izzie looked at her for permission and she nodded. Within seconds, the room cleared and Jo was alone with Mr. Sullivan, who stood in a handsome slate-colored suit, his cell phone in hand, ready to wield it like a pistol. He stared out of the window and down to the street below. "Vultures," he said, and then he turned to Jo. "Is it true?"

"It is."

"That girl?"

"Her name's Isabell."

Mr. Sullivan poured himself a scotch over ice and then poured her a whiskey neat. He handed it to her.

"Thank you," she said, and poured her warm tea into the crystal tumbler.

Mr. Sullivan tightened his platinum cuff link. "I spoke with Nick this morning. I'm disappointed about the engagement falling through, Jo. But that's another issue altogether. Right now we need to focus on this problem. At least J. D. isn't the father, or we'd have a circus here. Look, I've talked this over with the PR team. We all agree that you should deny the validity of the story."

"I just told you it's true."

"Doesn't matter what's true. If we cast doubt on the article's reliability, that doubt will linger in the minds of your fans who love you. They're more likely to side with you, Jo. I think it's the best choice right now to protect your image. I've got a press conference assembled downstairs right now waiting for your statement."

Isabell had suffered the truth now—Jo couldn't stand in front of a row of cameras and deny that truth with Isabell in the same room with her. Mr. Sullivan had no right to ask her to keep on lying just to protect his label.

"They'll be more aggressive if we keep them waiting."

Jo drank down her hot toddy and placed the tumbler on his desk with a thwack. "Let's go, then."

Mr. Sullivan opened the door to the entire team waiting on the leather couches in the midcentury-inspired lobby outside Mr. Sullivan's office suite. Marie and Isabell stood up with their arms crossed, like they'd been waiting for the surgeon to come out of the operating room and provide an update. Marie walked straight to Jo and said, "What's happening?"

Mr. Sullivan said, "We're headed down to the lobby for Jo's official statement." He snapped at one of his assistants, who hustled over to Jo and handed her a typed script: *The* Vanity Fair *article published this morning is misleading and misinformed. My privacy has been unduly violated by the rumors unsubstantiated in this work.*

Jo read it twice over as Marie and Izzie looked over her shoulder. Izzie whispered, "That's what you'll say, Jo?" Jo folded the script in half and imagined cutting out a heart like the ones she used to make as a child for Valentine's Day at school, too poor to have real cards like the other children.

The elevator door chimed and Mr. Sullivan's assistant held it open as the PR team and the lawyers and the other assistants filed in. Mr. Sullivan waited to enter until Jo stepped inside. He hit the "L" button and the doors closed before the weightless feeling of the descent began. Jo felt like everyone in the mirror-paneled elevator was darting their eyes from Jo to Izzie and then to the ceiling, never letting their gaze lock on them for long. Jo felt like they were ashamed of her and about what she went through. Isabell stood arm to arm with Jo, and then she hooked arms with Jo and held her hand.

They reached the lobby and the elevator doors opened to a sea of journalist strangers followed by cameramen and assistants holding boom microphones. She heard an ambush of her name and Izzie's name, like a million arrows had been shot in the air and were on course to follow after them. A reporter thrust a microphone in Marie's face and asked if she was Isabell. Jo pulled Marie back in line as they made their way to the podium in Asphalt's slick white lobby with abstract art and platinum records lining the walls along with blown-up pictures of Asphalt's greatest talent. Jo's image was plastered up there behind the podium—big smile, glittery dress, red boots, and one arm holding a microphone raised high in the air. Jo stood beside Mr. Sullivan at the microphone while all the reporters closed in to hear what she had to say. She unfolded the script on the podium and smoothed out the crease. Mr. Sullivan rubbed her shoulder, and she had no idea if his affection was real or for the cameras.

Cameras flashed in all directions like large diamonds catching the light. She tried to look up but the amount of people before her and the nonstop flashes forced her to keep her face down, staring right at the page. Jo told herself that she still held the power to tell the whole of her story. She leaned in close and said, "I know you're all here because of the article published this morning in *Vanity Fair*. It's already gone viral, so I called this press conference this afternoon to say that what the reporter wrote is mostly true."

Mr. Sullivan dropped his hand from her shoulder but she couldn't look at him or she'd lose her nerve.

"I have never shared this truth with anyone out of shame for what happened to me when I was twelve years old. No matter what the article suggests, I wasn't a preteen mother who left my child behind to come to Nashville. I gave birth to Isabell, who was raised as my little sister, and that's how I always saw her."

Jo paused to breathe and glanced over at Isabell, who anxiously scanned the room of reporters. Hands flew in the air, the flashing lights increased, and a cacophony of noise filled the atrium. Lines of scripture she'd memorized as a girl in Sunday school struck her now with a clarity as clear as the key of C: *You are the light of the world. A city on a hill cannot be hidden. Neither do people light a lamp and put it under a bowl. Instead they put it on its stand, and it gives light to everyone in the house.*

Jo adjusted the microphone in front of her. "I was beaten and raped by a boy who lived in my town and went to school with me, and I got pregnant. I had to go to school with him every day for years after that."

She finally allowed herself to look at Mr. Sullivan, who stood a few feet away and stared at her with a detached expression. Jo continued: "I kept it silent out of fear and a need to protect myself and my family, but I realize now that I made a mistake letting Travis Goode get away with what he stole from me. Rape goes unreported all the time, and I want my fans to know that if anything like this has ever happened to you, I'm speaking out for you too. I'm with you. Music was the only thing that saved me. Going forward, I plan to spend as much time with my family as possible, and for that reason, I'm canceling my summer tour that's set to kick off in two days."

Mr. Sullivan launched forward like he was about to cover the microphone with his hand, except it was too late. What she'd said existed in the world and there was no way for him to extract it from the information byways.

"I won't be taking any questions at this time." Jo smiled and said, "Thank you all for your time and your sensitivity." And then Jo left the podium. Mr. Sullivan grabbed her arm, brought her close to his body, and leaned down so close that she could smell the faint acrid scent of scotch on his breath: "All of your upcoming concerts are sold out now."

Jo's stomach felt weighed down by stones—she knew why so many people suddenly wanted to see her in concert: to connect her face to this story.

"I won't agree to this."

She pulled away from him and looked him in the eyes: "You can't force me to tour."

He stood erect. "I'll have no choice but to fire you, Jo. I could hold you financially accountable for your next album and the cost of this tour. Do you understand that? Out of respect for my son and the relationship you shared, I won't. But no other label in town will work with you again after this. You'll be too costly."

"I understand the consequences, Mr. Sullivan."

He raised his eyebrows in astonishment: "That's what you want?"

"It is." Jo turned from him, and she could feel his stare on her back as she pushed her way through a group of reporters.

Marie and Isabell hurried over to her. Marie said, "I called a car to the back entrance."

Isabell hugged Jo, and in a deep highland accent she said, "I can't believe you just did that."

Jo held her and patted her back gently. She said, "Let's go home."

CHAPTER 44

Choose

A LL DAY J. D. hadn't felt right. He'd woken with a buzzing above him, like his neck had stretched three feet high and his head was a buoy. J. D. stood on the balcony of the Bridgestone Arena in downtown Nashville, where he could see his name and image on the large LED screen outside of the arena. J. D. was due onstage in twenty minutes. He stared out at the bright city skyline—the lights from the illuminated Korean War Veterans Memorial Bridge were reflected in the Cumberland River below, and the AT&T building was aglow. The two spindles on top of the building looked like goalposts in the hazy black sky. Or like two different ways to climb.

J. D. took a long drag of his cigarette and listened to the crowd roar for his opening act, the same group he'd singled out and supported on the reality TV show *The Band*. He and the guys had Madison Square Garden tomorrow, and then they wouldn't be back down south for a while after that. J. D. knew he should feel large and powerful standing at these heights and looking down at the teeming city like it was a miniaturized stage set, but tonight he felt small compared to all that life.

From behind, J. D. heard: "What the fuck, man? I was looking all over for you. Mr. Sullivan wants to see you."

J. D. offered him the pack of cigarettes and Rob slid one out. J. D. loved Rob and he loved his band. They were much more than brothers. When you created music together, each band member played all the family roles at once. It was the biggest, deepest bond he'd ever known, but he felt it most when he played music with Jo. He lifted his Stetson to smooth down his hair.

"That story's all over the place. I feel awful for her," Rob said, and then exhaled. He sent a trail of ash from his cigarette over the balcony. "I remember hearing my mama talk about it one time at a lunch after church with a bunch of the ladies who planned the bazaar with her. I guess I always thought it was true that she'd had a kid. I asked her once and she just kept on fishing, just didn't respond. I asked her if you were the daddy—I'd heard that too from those church ladies—and she told me she'd steal my tongue if I kept on talking about it. Made me swear never to mention it to you. I thought that maybe it was yours, but then I knew that wasn't true. Nobody ever said anything about her being raped though. I remember you beating the shit out of Travis and I didn't know why. Figured he was such a dick, it made sense. I guess she told you the truth, didn't she?"

J. D. couldn't bear to talk about what had happened to her. Not to anyone. All he wanted was to be in her presence, make her smile, hear her laugh, see her eyes crinkle, and protect her from all the hurt he'd caused. J. D. had driven to her house but she wasn't there, and he'd tried calling her every ten minutes for an hour but it kept going straight to voice mail. J. D. kicked a piece of gravel off the balcony, sent it sailing below. "I feel like there's a bullet hole in my chest."

Rob flicked his cigarette over the balcony and adjusted his ponytail. "You ever thought that it's just not meant to work out between you?"

J. D. remained silent. The last of Rob's smoke trailed downward.

"I love the two of you more than anybody I know. But something's always wrong. If it doesn't work, it just doesn't work. You know I wish like hell for you both that it would."

J. D. felt something whirring above his head again and it made him feel light-headed. "I don't think I can keep going, Rob."

"Here we go."

"I mean it."

Rob's voice turned hard: "It's not just you, J. D. It's not always about you. We're at Madison Square tomorrow. You can't just quit."

J. D. pushed himself back from the railing. "I'm telling you I can't do it. Every day without her is one day too many."

"You mean, *we* can't do it. *We*, J. D. Not just you. You've been hoping someday it'd all come together. You could have her and us and your fame and your music. All of it. I've been sitting by and watching you go at this for years. Jesus, since we were kids."

"I feel a hole inside me that just keeps getting bigger, Rob. Nothing fills it but being with her."

"I'm sorry, man. I know that hurts." Rob opened the door. "But right now we've got a show to play."

Rob went in first, turned right, and J. D. followed him toward the backstage entrance, where the rest of the band was waiting with Mr. Sullivan. As soon as Mr. Sullivan spotted J. D., he walked straight to him with his hand out, ready to shake. "There he is."

J. D. shook hands with Mr. Sullivan.

"Wanted to be here when you kicked off your summer tour. And to make sure you're feeling good about it."

"How is Jo?"

Mr. Sullivan guided J. D. a few feet away from his band. "She canceled her entire summer tour."

"I heard that."

"I suppose you knew she cut off her engagement with my son? What role you had to play in that I still don't know."

"I wasn't aware, sir." J. D.'s body no longer felt stretched and disconnected. If she'd called off the engagement with Nick, then there was a chance she loved him still.

"Threw away her whole damn career."

"She needed space."

"There's no space in this business. Look, I'm damn sorry for what happened to her. She probably doesn't think so, but I am. She's gone back to Virginia for who knows how long. Truthfully, the label doesn't need Jo like it needs you. I need to make sure you're not planning anything drastic and that you're still committed to making the album the two of you started. I'm looking for a new female vocalist to join you."

"To replace Jo?"

"What other choice did she leave me, son?"

"We wrote those songs together."

"You'll write more. And your band will be with you. Everybody wins."

J. D. turned around to see his band. Chase B shoved Aster in the arm and Danny leaned over, he was laughing so hard. He couldn't imagine the guys asking him to make the decision to replace Jo on their songs. J. D. understood that Mr. Sullivan was thinking like a businessman, but he wasn't sure how to get through to him that he was only thinking with his heart.

A backstage technician dressed in all black walked up to J. D. and said, "It's time."

Mr. Sullivan patted J. D.'s shoulder and then they shook hands again before Mr. Sullivan said, "Good luck, boys," and waved good-bye to the band. As Mr. Sullivan headed for the executive box, Rob said, "What the hell was that all about?"

"Nothing."

"You all right, man?" Chase B said.

"Aster, hold off at the start."

"Whatever you need."

Rob said, "You sure you're okay?"

"Everything's fine," J. D. said, and then he heard the announcer call out: ". . . who you've been waiting for. J. D. Gunn and the Empty Shells, everybody." The sound of twenty thousand fans screaming for him to take center stage in the arena made the floor vibrate beneath his boots. Cheers that loud always made him feel like a battery being recharged. J. D. adjusted his hat and tucked his white T-shirt tight into his jeans. "You ready, boys?"

"Let's go," Rob said.

His band led the way and J. D. followed them to his microphone as deafening applause greeted them. White lights and neon glow sticks dotted the vista of the risers all the way toward the sky, where J. D. could see no stars. The air was humid. A small breeze moved through the arena. J. D. strapped on his electric guitar and lifted one arm up high toward his fans, who shouted out to him, and to the executive boxes, where Mr. Sullivan sat with the best view of the stadium. "How y'all doing out there?"

The screams increased to a frenzied pitch.

"It's so good to be here in Nashville for the start of our summer tour.

Now, I know some of you might be expecting Jo Lover onstage with me tonight."

The applause softened. J. D. said, "She won't be here. Y'all may have heard her news today and that she's canceled her summer tour. She and I won't be making our album together any time soon."

J. D. heard a scattering of boos emit from the dark sea before him. "I'm asking y'all to have mercy on Jo and what she's going through right now." The arena grew more silent than he'd ever heard before. "I had to watch her go through all that when we were kids and she was braver than any person I've ever known. Now, my label, Asphalt Records, wants me to finish making that album we promised you. Thinks we can add another female voice to the songs and everything will be good and you'll want to buy it. But the one thing I knew way back when we were kids, and what I definitely know right now, and what you know too, is that Jo Lover can't be replaced on any song or on any album. She's the only woman I've ever loved and she's irreplaceable."

The applause picked up once more to a height greater than before.

"So you won't be hearing a collaboration any time soon, not unless it's Jo Lover's voice that's harmonizing with me."

J. D. lifted his electric guitar in the air and sent his fingers flying up the neck of his instrument, then slowly back down until the guitar started to sound like it was singing a lament. Aster joined him on a long solo riff—J. D. fell into the sinkhole of the music and played the guitar like it was just Aster and J. D. in a garage somewhere making it up as they went. The longer they played together, the more the crowd clapped and screamed in support. Rob came in on the bass before Chase B made the pedal steel fly, and then Danny crashed down on the drums to fill the arena with this improvisational sound that was much different from what they'd done before. The only real mistake J. D. had ever made was trying to succeed in this business without Jo. Sharing it with her was the only thing that had made it all worthwhile, and he hoped that wherever Jo was in the world right now, maybe, just maybe, she could hear this song calling out for her forgiveness.

CHAPTER 45

The Home Chord

JO WAS CLEANING dishes in the airy kitchen and the smell of fresh-baked apple pie filled the farmhouse with the cinnamon scent of a season yet to come. She lined a metal pan with paper cups for the blueberry muffins she planned to bake for their picnic by the creek. Baking was the only activity that kept her mind off J. D. Isabell walked into the kitchen wearing linen wading shorts, a red tank top, and a wide-brimmed hat. She examined the resting apple pie on the counter and said, "I can't wait much longer."

"It's got to cool down."

Izzie held her long blond hair back as she inhaled the scent rising from the crust. "The tackle box wasn't in the closet."

Jo placed the apple pie on the ledge of the open window. "Try the cellar."

Izzie looked exhausted at the prospect of continuing this search, but it was her idea to go fishing. They'd stayed up too late last night in

Jo's room talking about what Izzie wanted to do with her future. She'd said, "I think I want to counsel kids and families who've experienced trauma, like ours." Jo promised Izzie that she'd pay her college tuition and board in full as long as Izzie started filling out applications immediately. If it was too late for the fall, she could always begin in the spring. And then Izzie jumped up on the bed and said, "Let's go fishing tomorrow," which sounded like a fine idea.

Marie returned to the kitchen just as Izzie was leaving. "I found the fishing rods. Put them by the front door."

"Thank you. Where were they?"

"Way back in the closet," she said as she hopped onto the countertop. Marie placed the bowl of fresh-picked berries in her lap and ate them one by one. "Did you watch that J. D. clip I sent?"

Jo nodded. After Izzie had left her room last night, she'd watched the clip at least a hundred times until she passed out with the phone in her hand, but Jo wouldn't admit that to Marie.

"Think you'll ever talk to him again?" she said.

"I don't know." Jo had considered calling J. D. last night and then changed her mind to email him instead and tell him that the past was past, but she knew he was busy with the tour and her heart still felt raw. She wasn't even sure how'd she say exactly what she needed to tell him. All she knew was that she was consumed by thoughts of him all day and all night, and the one and only thing she wanted now was to feel his arms wrapped around her like nothing had ever gone wrong between them.

"I think you should call him," Marie said.

Jo folded the blueberries into the batter. "How's Denver doing?"

"They're in Brooklyn. Finally found an apartment."

Jo pulled open a drawer to find a measuring cup and then she started scooping the mixture into the cups.

Marie cradled the bowl of blueberries in her arms. "I miss him."

Jo wiped away the excess batter from the rim of the pan with a towel and then slid it into the oven and set the timer for eighteen minutes. "You should go see him."

"I wish."

"I'm serious, Marie. I can't ask you to wait around here on me. I think you should go visit him, see how it feels there. You can always come back. Isabell and I will be just fine."

Marie put the bowl to the side and wiped away a streak of purple juice from her chin. "You are being serious."

"I am."

The sunlight entering through the windows created square patches on the floor and the white lace curtains lifted upward with the breeze. Jo could tell Marie missed him very much. While Denver was on the road, they texted each other constantly, but it wasn't enough. Jo knew that feeling all too well. It would never be enough.

Marie hopped off the countertop and pulled out her phone. "I'll just text him and see."

Isabell returned to the kitchen. "No way I'm going back down there, Jo. There's these weird half-spider half-cricket bugs."

"I'll go in a minute," Jo said as she walked into the living room and sat down at her Steinway to play music while the muffins baked. Max rested on the floor beside the bench. Jo fingered the piano with a song she'd had in mind since she left Nashville, called "The Right Side," and so far she was stuck on the first verse and a small chorus:

> *I lost the boy in the worn-out boots,*
> *Then lost the men in the fine silk suits.*
> *I left the keys in the ignition.*

Mama called it a premonition.
Lonely river under the stars tonight.
Got to get back to the right side.

Izzie sat down on the couch behind her, picked up Jo's mandolin, and started plucking the strings as Jo worked on the song. Turned out Izzie had a pretty good ear for singing and playing music too. J. D. was the only person missing in this living room. She could hear his voice in harmony with hers as she sang aloud and she felt certain he'd have helped her push forward in the writing, helped her unlock the next step in the lyrics. Jo stopped playing the piano to write down the lyrics, and then she stood up from the bench and placed her notebook on the coffee table next to the day's paper.

The *Scott County Virginia Star* had published a front-page, full-length article about Jo's press conference and investigated the rumors about Travis. Her daddy had called last night to tell her that news reporters from all over the country had surrounded Travis's home like a swarm of locusts and that Travis had quit the quarry and left town with his wife. This was as close to a confession as Travis would ever give. At least Jo could be at peace knowing he would never be in Gatesville again. The past couple of days her mama had delivered tuna casseroles, macaroni salads, baskets of fruit, and cards from all the different churches in town, as if the entirety of Gatesville were apologizing to her family for what Travis had done.

Marie returned to the living room.

Jo said, "Did you reach Denver?"

She smiled. "He wants me to visit."

Max jumped up at the same time and started barking at her. "What is it?" Jo glanced out the windows that overlooked acres of pasture and her fishing pond. Max barked louder and then raced to the front door.

"You expecting somebody?" Marie said.

"He goes crazy for deer." Jo stared down the hallway where Max had disappeared, and he was silent. When she called him back he wouldn't come.

Marie said, "Want me to go check?"

"I'll let him out," Jo said, and went down the hallway where Max scratched at the door. He looked up to her with his sweet blue eyes, and she scratched behind his ears. "Calm down, buddy. We're going."

Max stood at attention, started barking again, right at Jo, then at the door. The hackles on his back went up and Max started jumping up and down and howling as loud as he could. Jo unlocked the front door and Max shot out as if he'd been called on a rescue mission. Jo followed after him onto the porch, where the ceiling fans turned in the breeze and English ivy scaled the handrail.

"Max," she called as he ran down her sloped gravel driveway and disappeared. The chartreuse-colored mountains in the distance curved gently against the blue sky, and the sun wasn't quite high enough for the fishing to be poor yet. She walked down the front steps to take the back route to the cellar, where she was sure she'd find the fishing-tackle box. As she made her way around the side of the house, Jo heard Max barking again down the road and he sounded near. She paused to see if he was coming back up the road. She heard the sound of footfalls on the gravel. Jo walked through the gentle branches of the willow tree next to the porch and out to the driveway, hoping more than anything to see that white Stetson hat cresting the hill. She moved forward and shielded her eyes from the sun, but only the mountains loomed in the distance. A pair of robins flew out from the willow tree.

Jo walked back inside and went straight to the kitchen.

"What was it?" Izzie said.

"Just a deer."

Jo put on her mitts and removed the lightly browned muffins from the oven. The blueberries had busted open; purple lines cascaded down the brown sugar streusel topping. Jo was just about to ask Marie and Izzie if they wanted a warm muffin with butter when the doorbell chimed.

Both Marie and Izzie stood up quickly.

Without a word, Jo hurried down the hallway toward the closed wooden door. She heard Max barking on the other side of it, and without hesitation, Jo opened the door to see J. D. standing right there like an apparition with Max at his side. J. D. held his white hat against his chest and smiled at her sweetly as he offered her a small bouquet of bright yellow buttercups. She accepted the flowers and for a moment she thought she was hallucinating that he was standing right there in front of her.

The screen door rested against J. D.'s back. "We were on the way to New York and I asked Guy to take a detour."

Jo's eyes widened. "You brought your bus here?"

He looked behind him and then back at her. "Well, not right here. Couldn't make it up the driveway."

Marie called, "Who's there— Oh."

Jo turned around to see Izzie and Marie smiling at each other. Izzie said, "We'll give you two a little privacy."

J. D. said, "May I come in?"

"I can't believe you made your band come all this way—"

"Because I love you, Jo. And I can't stand being away from you anymore. I want to be with you and nobody else." He gripped the door frame. "I want to finish the album we started. I don't want to give up on it."

Everything J. D. said was exactly what Jo had longed to hear, but unlike Jo, he was an Asphalt artist still. J. D. belonged to Nashville. Jo said, "You owe the label that album."

"Let Mr. Sullivan sue me then. Everything in the world I need is right here. I want to record our music and distribute it ourselves. Bring the guys in on it too. Bring what's best about Nashville. Start our own thing. Nothing else feels right anymore. We can do this together, Jo. I know we can. Maybe we can start a school. A school for traditional mountain music."

"Come inside," Jo insisted, tears heavy at the corners of her eyes.

"Not until you say yes. Not until you tell me that this is the life you want to share with me too. I love you so damn much, Jo. I need to know."

Her body was shaking. It was impossible to say anything at all. "Okay," she finally blurted out. "Okay, yes. Let's do all that. Everything. More even."

"And I'm never leaving you or doing anything to ever hurt you again. Do you hear me, Jo?"

He was tearing at her heart, like he was piercing it with swords. "I hear you."

"I need you to believe me."

"I do, J. D. And I love you too."

He raised her left hand to his mouth and kissed the center of her palm. "May I come inside?"

Jo nodded and stepped back to let him in.

*H*owdy, Nashville. Y'all are good and awake by now, I reckon. Good morning, sleepyheads. This is your old friend Floyd Masters, back from that glorious little place called Honduras. Remember me? Floyd doesn't feel so old anymore. Nope. Floyd feels like a young man after all that love I felt from the good people of Latin America. Bless them. Just two nights ago I came home and felt a renewed love for the best damn music city the world has ever known—that's right, New York, that's right, LA. Paris, London—y'all got nothing on this here town.

I go down to Honduras, come back home, and it's hotter than I remembered, hotter than it's ever been. Now nothing's the same. Nothing. Well, the barbecue's still good. Jack White and Loretta Lynn are well and back on tour. God bless that. But down on Music Row? It's a Nashville city breakdown, that's what it is. Seems like Nashville needs Floyd Masters to stay put. If I were a more arrogant man—the years are beating that out of me—but if I were a more arrogant man, I'd say this city needs me now more than ever to stay right where I am, broadcasting to you each morning, just to keep functioning. Floyd Masters can't stick around though, Nashville. My soul is young, but I've got old bones. Old, brittle bones. I can't be here forever to keep an eye on things.

And what have we lost? The Flyby Boys flew away, that's what I heard just as soon as I got back. Looks like some people in this town—the real music lovers—are taking it pretty hard, so I'll take that as a good sign. Maybe they'll fly back. Maybe Nashville will be ready to treat them right the next time. Flyby Boys, if you're listening, we want you back. Go see what's out there but come *home if elsewhere turns up empty. Give Nashville a second chance. And what about the Thirsty Baboon? Listeners, you think a little local place like that can survive in a condo climate like this one? They're set to close their doors next month, folks, but it looks like there's a resistance building. Maybe, just maybe, it'll save the Baboon. I've got hope for this town. Don't know why, but I do.*

What a mess, too, for Jo Lover. What a sorry mess with all the TMZs of the tabloid world and all the talking bobbleheads on TV discussing her past. Nobody deserves that. Jo Lover, if you're listening, which I know you're not, but if you are, just know old Floyd Masters wishes you the healing you deserve. Listeners, you've heard my thoughts about that sellout J. D. Gunn. You know my feelings. But you know what, he and I finally agree on something. Jo Lover can't be replaced in this business, my friends. So I sure do hope to hear that sweet modern voice of female country music again on the radio somewhere down the road. Breaking news, too. J. D. Gunn and the Empty Shells did not show up for their concert at Madison Square Garden last night. The only thing empty was that stage. The leading man was nowhere to be seen. Rumor has it, he won't be at his Brooklyn show tonight either. Rumor has it he's left town, gone to be with the woman he loves like a damn fine country song.

Sometimes you have to live it honest, folks.

Sometimes you have to live.

Acknowledgments

THIS NOVEL WOULD not exist without the brainstorming and unwavering support of my agent extraordinaire, Alexandra Machinist. She, along with my editor, Rachel Kahan, helped to midwife this novel into the world. I am deeply indebted to Alexandra and Rachel for their patience with my writing process, their guidance along the way, and faith that I would complete this book, even when I wasn't sure I could. Many thanks to the entire team at William Morrow for their support of my first and second novel. I'm grateful for the talents of my copy editor, Aja Pollock, as well.

I researched the history of country music and the country music industry extensively for this novel. I had the opportunity to study at the Frist Library and Archive at the Country Music Hall of Fame in Nashville, where I had access to the earliest recordings of the Grand Ole Opry. Many thanks to the associate librarian Becky Miley, who coordinated my visit and helped maximize my experience with the library's resources.

During my research period for this book, I met incredible musicians who allowed me to enter their lives and take a novelist's look around. The idea for this novel began one night while I sat on a bar stool and watched J. P. Harris play a small gig in the corner of the room. And I wondered what it would be like to live his life, to go from town to town, play his songs, and spend his life on the road. And though his band's too big for that bar gig now, I will always remember him there. And my deepest gratitude to Chance McCoy, guitar and fiddle player for Old Crow Medicine Show, who stayed up into the early hours of morning to talk with me about his path into the music industry. His sensitivity and charm inspired me. I wish him many blessings for his future. Thanks to Ameripolitan musician Dale Watson for allowing me to visit with him on his tour bus, and to Jack White, who walked into the Frist Library and Archives at the Country Music Hall of Fame while I was researching and whose unexpected presence halted my work. I met Jack White at the exact right moment in my writing process. I needed to imagine a bigger world for this book, and he triggered it.

The writing process might be lonely, but researching doesn't have to be. Thanks to my sister, Megan Ihlefeld, and my friends Emily Williamson, Leia Jones, and Rhiannon Leebrick for traveling with me to Nashville. One should never go dancing alone at Robert's Western World, but if you must, there's always somebody ready to two-step. Likewise, thanks to my friends and colleagues Jennifer Daniel and Helen Hull for many nights of dancing at the Thirsty Beaver Saloon in Charlotte. During my greatest struggles with this manuscript, Brian and Mark, co-owners of the Thirsty Beaver, intuited when I needed a whiskey neat on the house.

I relied on a small but mighty group of readers for this book. Many thanks to my mother, who enthusiastically reads everything that I write; and my sister, Rachel, who is always eager to read whatever I'm working on next. Thanks also to my colleague and friend Charles Israel for being a champion of my creative work, and to my friend and fellow novelist Kim Wright for putting her story doctor skills to work on my manuscript. Thanks many times over to my Victorian scholar friend Bonnie Shishko who spotted a phrase in my manuscript and encouraged me to consider it for the new title.

I'm grateful to my friends and colleagues Julie Funderburk, Mike Kobre, and Norris Frederick for checking in with me along the way to see how the novel was progressing. Many thanks to all of my colleagues in the English and Creative Writing Department and to Queens University of Charlotte for their continued support.

While writing this novel I often thought about my graduate school days at McNeese State University in Lake Charles, Louisiana, where after tough, long fiction workshops, all the writers gathered at Martini's (which sounds much fancier than it was) to drink beer and listen to songs on the jukebox loaded up with great country music. Thanks to my workshop mentor, Neil Connelly, for inviting me to study down in the bayou, and to Joshua Canipe and Christopher Lowe for always playing Hank Williams.

My deepest thanks to my daughters, Hattie and Mimi, for their unconditional love.

Lastly, how to thank my husband, Morri Creech? Tireless reader, daily supporter, brilliant songwriter. Morri and I wrote one song together at 3 AM, the lyrics of which are included in the chapter "The Whole Way Home," but after that night, Morri wrote an entire album, filling our house with music every day while I wrote. His creativity is endless.

We touched the depths with this one and surfaced together.

About the Author

Sarah Creech is the author of the novel *Season of the Dragonflies* published by William Morrow in 2014. The novel was a SIBA Okra pick for the summer of 2014. *Publishers Weekly* described the book as "charming and suspenseful . . . a memorable debut." Creech's short fiction and essays have appeared in various publications, including The Cortland Review, WritersDigest.com, *storySouth,* and *Literary Mama.* She lives in North Carolina with her husband and children and teaches at Queens University of Charlotte.